Echoes of Silence

Anne Malcom

ECHOES OF SILENCE
Unquiet Mind #1
By Anne Malcom
Copyright 2016 Anne Malcom

Edited by: Hot Tree Editing
Cover Design: Sarah at Okay Creations
Cover image Copyright 2016
Formatting by Max Effect

Dedication

To every unquiet mind.

May you find the beauty of silence.

Chapter 1

"**Light reading?**" **a deep voice asked, making me jump out** of the world that had replaced the garage around me.

Mom and I had stopped, or more accurately, been forced to stop on the way to the movies. Our car had decided to die right outside the aforementioned garage—luckily for us. I hated to think what would have happened had we been on a lonely stretch of road. Neither of us were exactly savvy with the workings of motor vehicles. Mom had ordered me to stay in the car, on account of who this particular establishment belonged to. The Sons of Templar. A motorcycle gang. Or club, as they called themselves. I had a feeling the distinction was important. I didn't know much about them since we were new in town, but we knew Zane, our neighbor, was a member.

I regained my wits remarkably quick, especially since the boy leaning against my mom's car could be considered as nothing less than smokin' hot. His midnight black hair fell like inky silk around his shoulders, and he was tall. Even though he was currently leaning, I could tell from the length of his limbs he was *tall*. Those limbs were seriously impressive, and sinewy forearms rested against the open window I was curled up against. With him only inches away from me, I could see the veins pulsing in them if I looked hard enough. His eyes were the most vivid blue I'd ever seen. They almost stopped me from exploring the rest of his face. Almost. It was perfectly proportioned, with a defined jaw that looked like it belonged to a man, not a boy, who I guessed would be about my age. So yeah, he was smoking hot. Literally *smoking*—a cigarette.

I put my book in my lap and narrowed my eyes at the offending death stick. Some kids, a lot of kids my age, smoked those things for various reasons; image, weight loss, or the pursuit of the elusive 'cool.' With his male model good looks, leather jacket, and general 'devil may care' attitude, this boy did not need something as trivial as a cigarette to make him cool.

"Those will kill you, you know," I pointed out, ignoring his question.

He smirked and shrugged. "So I've heard," he replied in a voice that sent strange shivers down my spine.

"So, either you don't think the nicotine, tar, and arsenic you are subjecting not only yourself, but *me* to, will affect you, or you just don't care?" I asked with sarcasm that was automatic to me. I had my mom to blame for that.

His small smirk turned into a full-on grin. "Freckles, it's just one cigarette. I won't be dropping dead right here and now, don't you worry"—his gaze turned blazing—"neither will you," he promised.

Freckles?

I swallowed.

"So," he moved the subject on, nodding his head to my lap, "*War and Peace*... English Lit?"

I glanced down at the book I had completely forgotten about—something I would have thought not five minutes ago was completely impossible. I didn't forget about books the same way I didn't forget about oxygen. They were necessary to my survival. That and music.

"No," I said finally, "just... reading." I didn't add it was for the second time, not wanting to look like a complete nerd. I would never be ashamed of my utter love of the written word, but I didn't think this hot boy would appreciate the extent of my addiction. Few did. Books were so much a part of my life, a part of me; I didn't know which parts were real, and which were constructed from the pages of a book.

He nodded in what looked like approval, taking a long drag of his smoke. He purposefully turned his head to exhale away from me. "Yeah, read that in ninth grade. I'm onto *Anna Karenina* right now, digging it," he said, shocking my proverbial socks right off. His eyes flickered back to mine. "You read it?"

I gaped at him then nodded slowly, not speaking or anything, just nodded like an idiot.

He grinned again, showing a beautiful array of white teeth. I stared at his mouth, transfixed with it. I idly wondered what his lips would taste like.

"What's your name, Freckles?" he asked, his eyes turning lazy.

"Lexie."

My mind was still on kissing him. I was lost in the thought, maybe because I'd never done that with a boy I'd just met. Scratch that, I'd never done that with a physical boy. Only in fantasies featuring long-dead musicians and action movie heroes.

"Lexie," he repeated.

I concluded my name had never sounded more awesome than when the hot guy in front of me said it in his husky voice.

"Killian," he continued.

"Of course," I said without even thinking.

He raised a brow. "Of course?"

Shoot.

"Um, well, of course, a boy like you would have a name like Killian. I wouldn't have been surprised if it was Heathcliff. No last name," I babbled, like an idiot. "Scottish?" I guessed, my mind unwillingly picturing him astride a horse wearing the absolute crap out of a kilt and whisking me away to his castle.

3

I had to physically shake my head to get my mind back to the present and out of my daydream. I lived half my life in dream worlds. It was useful, most of the time, but I didn't want to escape the real world right now.

Killian's eyes turned slightly hard as he watched my head move, but his grin remained. "Irish," he corrected. "I'm curious to know what you think a *boy like me* is. I'll tell you now, I'm nothing like that asshole Heathcliff, not with pretty blondes," he promised.

Something passed between us. In the silence that descended, something turned almost palpable. His ice blue eyes were locked on mine, and it was impossible to tear myself away from him. It was like falling into another one of my daydreams, but I wasn't falling alone. It wasn't me who chose to escape the world and venture into another offered by books or music. This was all him. Those ice blue eyes drew me in and had me tumbling away from everything. A promise lay behind them, a promise I didn't understand, but I wanted to explore.

"Shouldn't you be polishing hubcaps or sweeping out the garage, kid?" a deep voice shattered the moment, and I blinked rapidly as Killian lazily tore his eyes from mine.

He looked at someone across the car and lifted the cigarette in his hand. "Smoke break," he replied nonchalantly, as if whatever had passed between us hadn't actually happened, as if I'd dreamed it.

I stared at him as he gave me one last glance, which I clung to because the glance promised I wasn't dreaming or hallucinating. It promised a shared secret. An impossible connection, one that would only make sense in books because people didn't have that sort of connection from a five-minute conversation, not in real life.

I jumped when the driver's door opened and my mother sat down in the car, her blue eyes accusing.

I swallowed, fighting to get my breath under control. "What?" I asked innocently.

I hoped my voice made it seem like I had nothing to hide. It didn't work since I never hid anything from my mom. She was my best friend. I told her everything. Until now. Something, I wasn't quite sure what, warned me to keep this to myself and not tell the woman whom I completely adored and respected, to keep it between Killian and me, the stranger who I knew nothing about.

Mom raised a disbelieving brow as if my forehead was transparent and she could see every thought it contained. "Don't play dumb. That obscure Russian literature in your lap makes that act fall short."

I sat up straighter. I had to do better if I were to hide the truth of my feelings from her. The best way to do that was distraction and to rely on my mother's utter hatred for reading anything that wasn't based on celebrities.

"Leo Tolstoy is hardly obscure. He is considered to be one of the best novelists of all time," I informed her.

She rolled her eyes. "That book is fifteen hundred pages."

I raised a brow. "So?"

"So that book could be used to sink a small boating vessel, or as a weapon to knock out even the most hardheaded attacker," Mom said with complete seriousness.

I fought a smile. "I'm using it for its intended purpose."

She didn't miss a beat. "I doubt its intended purpose is to be sitting in the lap of a teenage girl while a teenage boy puffs smoke in her face."

My elation at maneuvering the subject quickly dissipated, but luckily, I was saved when someone called from the vicinity of the trunk of the car.

Mom pointed at me. "This isn't over," she warned.

I sank back in my seat the moment she left.

I didn't know what *it* was, this thing I had been so desperate to hide from Mom. I was almost ashamed at myself for being so adamant to hide it. My mom was not a person I hid anything from. But this was *mine*. This little feeling was mine to cradle, to treasure. I doubted it would go any further anyway; boys like Killian were not interested in girls like me. So I decided that I would just keep it to myself.

I sat in the car twiddling my thumbs for a couple of minutes, annoyed that the fact the hood of our car was up hindering my ability to peek at whatever was going on. Okay, hindering my ability to peek at Killian.

I thoughtlessly shoved my book into my bag—I usually treated my books with the deference they deserved—and yanked myself out of the car in order to insert myself in Killian's intoxicating presence once more.

Once I rounded the car, it was not just Killian's intoxicating presence I was faced with. Three other men in leather vests stood in a rough semi-circle around Mom. One seriously hot bald one was chatting to her with a smile on his face. It was not him I focused on, not even Killian, whose eyes cut to me when I rounded the hood. It was the biggest one in the group. The one who was scowling at my mom.

Zane.

We had met him a couple of days prior when he helped change our tire. He was our neighbor. He didn't say much and would scare most people, I guessed. His hulking form, multiple tattoos, his stormy gray eyes, and the general air about him screamed 'danger.' I was pretty sure that was his intention since I hadn't seen him smile in the small amount of time I'd been in his presence. He needed to smile. Some part of me instinctively knew this and felt comfortable with him. He deserved to smile. So I grinned wide at him.

"Zane," I greeted him in a bright voice. Nerves tingled down my spine at not only his hard gaze turning to me but all of the men who had been focused on Mom. I swallowed. I didn't need to look like a bumbling idiot in front of Killian, plus I was seriously excited to see Zane. I knew there was more to him than he appeared.

"I so thought you might be here. This is your club, right?" I asked, glancing around the garage to a large building to the side, noticing the flag flying above it. "I told Mom we should come in and say hello." I gave her a look. "But she didn't want to disturb you. Totally sucks about the car, but at least you're here and we can thank you again for the other day."

The gesture had resonated somewhere deep down. It had made me realize that would have been something my dad would've done if he had been around. At least the dad I imagined would. Maybe that was why I immediately liked Zane, despite appearances. He was a good guy. I sensed that, and I also sensed he needed someone to help just as we might need to be helped every now and again. Don't ask me where that thought came from either; I had no idea. I just knew it to be true.

A light bulb pinged above my head.

"You should come to the movies with us and we can treat you, as a thank you. Don't worry, we don't see girly stuff. We love action movies—the more unbelievable, unrealistic explosions and car chases, the better," I added quickly, needing to let him, and maybe the other men, Killian specifically, know that Mom and I were different. I didn't understand why I needed them to know that. I never said things in order to alter what people thought of me. Until now. A weird, instinctive part of me had the feeling that this was a pivotal moment, for Mom and I both.

Zane regarded me, although he didn't smile, but mine didn't falter. I knew he probably had to retain his street cred, or whatever. I had no such problems.

"Movies aren't really my scene, Lex," he replied.

My smile wavered slightly. I guessed it was a long shot.

The man with the bald head and tattoos snaking up his neck gaped between Mom and me. "Mom?" he repeated in disbelief. "No fuckin' way, that's your daughter?"

I swallowed a giggle at his blatant cursing. Mom never cursed in front of me. It was funny really. Every kid in school did, as well as every character in most movies we watched, but it was something she didn't do. So I followed suit; it was instinctual to mimic some of my mom's beliefs and habits. I didn't particularly like cussing either. Maybe it was a throwback from my favorite books; you didn't see Jane Eyre cussing like girls my age did these days.

"That's what they told me at the hospital," Mom replied dryly, and I noticed she had to tear her gaze away from Zane to address the man who spoke.

Something niggled in my belly at that gaze.

"You're shittin' me! There's no way you're old enough to have a kid," he argued.

This was not an unusual response when people found out Mom was my mom and not the sister she looked like. She had me young, like really young, and she barely looked old enough to have a kid, let alone a sixteen-year-old like me. We were basically imprints of each other. We both had white, curly blonde hair, though I wore mine longer and didn't tame it near as much as Mom did. We were both pale and petite, but I had a dusting of freckles along my nose that my mom didn't.

Freckles.

My stomach flipped at that thought and my gaze cut to Killian. His eyes bore into mine as if they had been on me the entire time.

"Tell that to the doctors who cut her out of me sixteen years ago. I'd like to think I didn't undergo major surgery for nothing," my mom responded in her—and my—trademark sarcastic manner.

I was surprised when all of the scary biker dudes around us

8

started chuckling at Mom's words. It wasn't that Mom wasn't funny, she was, but these men looked serious—hot, but serious. It was comforting to see they had a sense of humor; it made them less intimidating.

"To formally introduce you, this is the fruit of my loins, otherwise known as Lexie." Mom held her arms out, pointing to me as if she was presenting a prize bull.

I smiled warmly at all of them and did a little wave. "Hey," I greeted, feeling comfortable with them for some unknown reason. I was a friendly person, but I didn't always click with people straight away. These men, believe it or not, made me feel at ease.

Well, almost all of them. I could feel Killian's gaze on me. I definitely did not feel at ease with him.

"I'm Cade," a dark-haired, tall, and slightly menacing man replied, looking between Mom and me. His eyes seemed to be hard and soft at the same time. He was built, not as much as Zane, but big. And, like the rest of them, with the exception of Killian, he had various tattoos covering his body.

A blond man who was slightly leaner, but still big and had an awesome man bun grinned warmly. "And I'm Brock. Pleased to meet you both." He directed his grin to Zane, but it was more teasing. "You already seem to know *Zane.*" He emphasized his name; I guessed because he had first introduced himself as "Bull" when he changed our tire. I had refused to believe that was his actual name, and he explained, in clipped sentences, that it was his "road name." Zane was his real name. I liked it much better and felt it suited him more.

"Yeah, Zane totally saved our skin the other day when Mom got a flat," I explained since Mom seemed to have turned mute while staring at Zane. "Mom can't change one," I added, baiting her only a little.

My statement hit its intended mark and her gaze cut to me. "I can change one," she all but hissed at me.

I grinned at her. "Uh no, Mom, hence your suggestion to call AAA when we saw it," I teased.

She narrowed her eyes at me. "I had yet to consume an ounce of caffeine that morning, *doll*," she gritted out with a forced smile. "I barely had control over my fine motor skills, let alone be able to change a tire. I'm sure if the occasion arose again and I was properly caffeinated, I could change a tire, no problem," she informed not only me but the men in the group.

"I'm *so* sure." My tone may have been teasing, but I felt a little barb at the thought. I realized I didn't *want* my mom to have to do things like this alone. She deserved a partner, one who would help her with more than changing tires. I wanted happiness for my mom more than anything, especially since I'd be going to college in two years. I didn't want to leave her alone.

"Mullet photo," she hissed out of the corner of her mouth in warning. It was her way of urging me against things. It was a threat to post a photo of baby me in a mullet on the Internet for all to see. It was not pretty.

She moved her attention away from me and back to the men who had been watching our exchange. "So I'm just going to circle back to the good news portion of this announcement. You mentioned we could still make our movie, despite your dire diagnosis of Betty," she said to the man in the coveralls.

I hadn't been aware that our car was in dire straits. Then again, the sounds it was making weren't entirely natural. I wasn't exactly cut up over the turn of events. My eyes locked with Killian once more. Not cut up at all.

"Betty?" Brock repeated, jolting my eyes away from Killian's.

"Betty's our car," I answered for Mom once more.

"You named your car?" he asked in disbelief, looking at Mom.

"I didn't name her, Lexie did. She was ten and decided a car such as this required a name," Mom said quickly, embarrassment in her tone. It was unfamiliar. Mom never got embarrassed, even that time at a parent-teacher conference when she spilled coffee all down her white shirt, rendering it see-through. She had laughed it off and exclaimed, "I paid enough for this bra, at least someone gets to see it."

"I didn't technically name her," I corrected, leaning against the car. "I merely broached the concept of naming the car. You were the one who christened her Betty."

I may have been being slightly evil to my dearly beloved mother, but it was kind of entertaining seeing her flustered and also educating. Yes, these men were rather attractive and slightly intimidating with their biker cuts, but Mom wasn't easily intimidated. I had a weird feeling it was Zane doing this to her. I nurtured this tiny thought and the idea of Zane smiling at one of Mom's jokes.

"Only because all of the names you came up with were utterly ridiculous and didn't suit the car's personality," Mom shot at me, finding her tongue.

"A car has personality?" Brock asked, half choking on a laugh.

Mom thrust her hand out to the car in question. "This particular car does. Some obviously do not. Like a Toyota Corolla or Volvo, any make. A cherry red VW Beetle on the other hand...."

She didn't say any more; she didn't need to, I thought. Betty spoke for herself, though that was a sixteen-year-old girl's opinion; hot bikers might have other ideas.

"Okay, we're getting off-track again," Mom said, giving me a pointed glare. "The previews are lost to us at this rate, so we need to get back on track."

I was happy to forfeit our much-enjoyed previews to watch Mom like this and to sneak gazes at Killian every now and then, feel his eyes constantly on mine.

Cade shook his head. "I'm guessing there's no such thing as staying on track in a conversation with you two," he deduced, correctly. Mom and I had a tendency to go off on tangents when the mood took us. It was part of our charm.

Luckily, it seemed that the men thought this was an amusing quality and chatted warmly and even gave us a loaner car to take in the meantime. Since it wasn't quite ready for us to use, we couldn't use it to go to the movies. Lucky, the smiling bald one in the coveralls had not only offered to take us, but to come with us. It was obvious, even to someone as inexperienced with such things as me, he was interested in Mom.

It must have been obvious to someone with even more experience since Zane's face had turned positively stormy at Lucky's suggestion.

He had stepped forward and all but barked at Lucky, declaring he would take us. I didn't quite understand the dynamics of this gesture, but it filled me with warmth.

Zane didn't want Mom going to the movies with Lucky. That meant something, even if he spoke in grunts basically the entire ride to the theater and barely even smiled. He had insisted on paying for all the snacks and I caught moments of Zane glancing at Mom with something in his eyes. I'd even used my brilliant skills to make them sit together.

I had been completely and utterly pleased with myself when Zane dropped us back at the garage to pick up our loaner car after the movie. "See you later, Zane," I said with a grin as I opened the door. "You totally like it, I can tell. So you'll come next time as well?" I asked hopefully. Mom and I had a weekly tradition of going to the movies. It was nice having his silent presence with us.

He gave me a little eye smile, his hard eyes crinkling almost imperceptibly at the edges. He never smiled with his mouth, for whatever reason, but that was his way.

"Maybe, Lex."

I beamed at him. "Saaweet, catch you later," I called, jumping out of the truck.

My plan was to give him and my mom a moment together. Most of it, anyway. A little part of me hoped I'd see Killian once more. It had only been two hours. I barely knew him, but I was hungry for his gaze. My eyes searched the bays, which had a few people in coveralls milling about. I then moved my gaze to what I guessed was the clubhouse. There was a grassed area in the front, and a few men milled about, wearing the same leather cuts as Zane. I squinted to see better.

"Want me to go and ask them if they'd be willing to sit while you paint them?" a voice said at my side.

I jumped at my mom's presence. I had been unaware she'd gotten out of the truck so quickly.

I pasted a grin on my face. "I've got what I need. I'll do it from memory," I shot back.

She rolled her eyes and slung her arm around my shoulder. "Let's get you out of here before you decide to get yourself a motorcycle," she said, directing us away from the clubhouse.

I resisted the urge to glance over my shoulder in one last ditch effort to see him. He would have forgotten about me already, I was sure.

Chapter 2

I couldn't stop thinking about him. It was ridiculous. Boys were never on my radar, never even in my stratosphere. I read countless books about every subject under the sun, every great literary work I could get my hands on. The Bronte sisters, Dickens, Fitzgerald. I listened to every song that I considered necessary to my existence. Kurt Cobain. Bob Dylan. Jim Morrison. Stevie Nicks. All of the things that were a part of my soul, most of them were inspired by, sparked by, and created by love and infatuation. So I was familiar with the concept, in an abstract sense.

But never in my wildest dreams did I think I would actually be feeling something akin to what some of my favorite works had been inspired by. I was smart to know it wasn't love, that was positively ridiculous, but seeing his inky black hair and smoke drifting out of his mouth every time I closed my eyes was bordering on insane.

Mom had drilled me after we got home from the movie with Zane. Luckily, I was able to blow her off by speaking casually about Killian, which was not something that would normally work. My mom and I were in tune, and her hatred for literary greatness aside, she was sharp. She would have known there was something more that I was hiding about Killian.

That was if she hadn't been preoccupied with another man who had been at the garage.

Zane.

I knew she was also trying to hide whatever it was between them, but I wasn't an idiot, and though adults liked to think teenagers are blind to such things, I saw it. I saw perhaps more than Mom saw.

I saw Zane. I saw beyond that tough-guy image he seemed to hide behind. He had something haunting him. I couldn't even start to think of what it was, but I knew by the way he looked at Mom, she might be able to help. He might be able to help Mom with what haunted her too.

She thought I didn't see that either. She tried so hard to be happy and give me a life of laughter, which she did. I considered myself the luckiest girl ever to have a mom who doubled as a best friend and to have Steve and Ava, who weren't my blood but I considered grandparents. I treasured the love I had around me. But I also saw the shadows that crossed over Mom's face when she thought I wasn't looking and the funny way she looked at Steve and Ava when I had first asked about the father I never knew. I knew there was something deeper, something potentially ugly hiding in my mom's past, something she was most likely protecting me from.

I wished with the romantic wish that our lives might turn into some novel. That Mom and Zane would fall in love, and they'd cure each other and we'd make Zane smile again. We smiled and laughed all the time. Something told me Zane needed to smile and laugh too.

That's what I was thinking of when I shut my locker, how to match make my mom and Zane. So I jumped when I realized someone was leaning against the one next to mine.

Someone who I had been dreaming about.

"Freckles," he greeted, his eyes glued to mine.

"Um... Killian, hey," I stuttered, while shuffling my books in my hand so I didn't drop them at his feet like a klutzy idiot.

In one smooth move, my books were out of my arms and safely

stacked in his muscled ones.

The bell rang and he pushed off the locker.

"You don't have to carry my books," I argued quickly, aware that various kids walking past us were staring. Girls in particular. I knew they were most likely staring daggers at me. I didn't make friends easy, thanks to the fact I listened to my headphones or read a book at lunch. So I hadn't exactly clicked with a girl posse just yet. But I knew how the girls swooned over Killian. Everyone did. I had been hyperaware of him ever since that day at the garage a few days ago.

"What class you got?" he asked, ignoring my question and ignoring the stares we were getting. He seemed genuinely unaware; every ounce of his attention was on me. It was unnerving to say the least. People, especially teenagers, never gave you their complete attention. They were on their phones, or their eyes were half glazed over. Maybe that's why I preferred the small handful of friends I had back at my old school, that and Mom, Steve, and Ava. Maybe that's why I hadn't made any friends here yet.

"Calculus," I said automatically; I couldn't help the dread in my voice. I hated it with a passion. But I was also a perfectionist, so despite my distaste for it, I worked hard to get decent grades. I needed more than decent grades to get a scholarship.

Killian grinned slightly at something and turned in the direction of the class. "Let's go then. Wouldn't want you to be late for a class you're obviously itching to get to," he deadpanned.

I got into stride beside him. "You're hilarious. Anyone who actually likes calculus needs their head examined," I informed him seriously.

He gave me a sideways glance and our shoulders brushed against each other as we walked. The casual touch and his proximity seemed to make all of my nerve endings fizz as if I'd gotten a mild electric shock. I instinctively touched my hair to make sure it wasn't awry with wild static.

Killian followed my hands, his eyes intense. "Don't worry. Your head doesn't need to be examined. It's beautiful," he said softly. "Though I wouldn't be averse to examining it, if pressed."

My breath left me in a whoosh at his words. I actually tripped over my feet, like an idiot.

He stopped to catch me, no easy feat considering he was carrying my books. His hand grasped my elbow, and his eyes burned into mine. "Easy, Freckles," he murmured. "Don't want to be damaging that pretty head, do we?"

The moment seemed to yawn on forever, the crowd of students dissipating, everything leaving that moment like it did at the garage days ago.

"Shouldn't you be getting to your next class, instead of accosting our newest student, Mr. Decesare?" a voice jolted us out of our little universe once more. This one was stern.

My head snapped to the source of it, though I noticed Killian's eyes were still firmly on me.

A short man stood in front of us. Half of his head was bald, and he'd gone to great pains to comb over what little he had left. The result was not effective. His face was pinched, and somehow I was immediately reminded of a ferret. He was wearing an ill-fitting tweed suit and terrible, clunky, black shoes. He was also glaring at Killian like he was responsible for climate change. I vaguely remembered him as the vice principal. I couldn't for the life of me remember his name. I was in danger of forgetting my own when I was in Killian's presence.

"Mr. Decesare?" he repeated with impatience, eyes narrowing even more as Killian studiously ignored him.

I moved my gaze back to those eyes that were still staring at me; they twinkled slightly, and Killian gave me a small grin before he turned his head. He raised his brows at the vice principal with impatience of his own, somehow managing to look like he was the one disciplining him.

He didn't say anything, merely waited.

"Do you want another detention, Mr. Decesare?" the vice principal finally gritted out.

Killian grinned. "Not particularly," he responded.

The vice principal's cheeks turned red. "Well, I advise you get to your next class and subject some poor teacher to your insolence, instead of Ms. Spencer here," he instructed harshly.

I pursed my lips together in anger that wasn't familiar. I was immediately annoyed at the way he was talking to Killian, the lack of respect and downright hostility in his demeanor.

I stepped forward. "It's my fault," I explained. "I was lost, and Killian was helping me find my way."

The teacher regarded me warily. The sharp barb of hatred was gone from his gaze now that it was directed at me, but a shadow of it remained. On Killian's account, I guessed, for whatever reason.

His mouth turned into a cruel smile. "Well, I doubt Mr. Decesare would be much help, considering he barely goes to his own classes. You're probably more likely to get lost with him as your guide than going it alone." His gaze darted to the dwindling amount of students left in the corridor. He stopped one boy in a football jacket on his way past. "Mr. Louis, would you do Ms. Spencer the favor of escorting her to her next class?" he asked, though it wasn't exactly a question, merely a command with a question mark at the end.

"Mr. Louis" was a boy I'd seen around a few times. He was almost always surrounded by boys in matching football jerseys and various girls, most of them cheerleaders, and some of whom glared at me not five minutes ago when I had been walking with Killian. He was your quintessential jock—tall, handsome with wavy blond hair, tanned skin, and lean muscles. I didn't really like to categorize people like that, in stereotypes that never captured the complexity

18

of the human spirit, but it was hard when he seemed to fit it to a T. Everyone was more comfortable playing preconceived parts in high schools, ascribing to identities constructed for them.

His blue eyes ran down my body, and he showed me white teeth when he made it back to my face. "I'd like nothing more," he responded with a grin.

I felt Killian step forward, his heat at my back. My gaze flickered to him and any hint of the previous teasing, softness he had had with me disappeared. His jaw was hard and his eyes were glittering with fury.

"That's really not—" I tried to protest.

"I must insist. I have some business to discuss with Mr. Decesare," the vice principal interrupted me.

Killian took another step forward, slightly in front of me, first glowering at the vice principal in a way I didn't think he was capable of. It was full of menace. Of promise. It was not the way a teenager looked at an adult. The way he stared at him, Killian switched the positions of power somehow, exhibiting an aura of assertiveness, one that made the vice principal look painfully small.

"Those her books? I'll take those, thanks, bro?" Jayden—I thought that was his name—held out his hands to Killian, smiling at him.

Killian stared at him for a long moment, and I actually thought something—I'm not sure what—bad would happen. Then he seemed to shake himself out of it, purposefully turning to me, books still in his hands. He handed them to me pointedly.

"Catch you around, Freckles," he said. It wasn't a casual phrase the way most people used it. It was a promise.

We stared at each other for another long moment before he stepped back. I almost sighed out loud at the loss of him.

Jayden immediately stepped forward. "Should we go? Don't want you to be late. What class you got?" he asked as if the tension hadn't been stifling just moments before.

I tore my gaze away from Killian, who was still staring at me. "Calculus," I said finally.

"Sweet, me too," he said, sounding pleased. There was a slight pressure at my lower back as Jayden lightly touched me, turning us away from Killian and the vice principal, whom I held a serious distaste for.

I looked over my shoulder at Killian, who was flat out ignoring the vice principal and was glaring at Jayden's hand.

"Though Mr. Hazelton is a total prick at the best of times, I will thank him for giving me the opportunity to talk to the pretty new girl," Jayden said, causing politeness to kick in, which meant I had to look at him. Plus, I couldn't very well stroll down the corridor staring at Killian. I'd smack into something and look like an idiot.

I didn't really know what to say to something like that; luckily, he didn't seem to expect a response.

"Jordan," he said, pointing to his chest. Okay, not Jayden, but I was close.

"Lexie," I replied quietly, shuffling my books.

He nodded to them. "Want me to take those?"

I held them tighter. "I'm good," I said firmly. Stupid as it was, there was something decidedly intimate about the way Killian had taken my books. I didn't want it to be taken away with Jordan doing it.

He didn't seem offended, just nodded. "So, where'd you move here from?" he asked, doing a chin lift to a couple of boys who walked past us.

"Um, DC," I replied, not liking the smiles they exchanged when they looked from me to him.

"DC, sweet. You're going to find it pretty boring here in Amber. There's a lot less to do than in the big city," he informed me, directing us into the classroom.

"Boring's good," I told him.

He gave me a strange look, then sat us down amidst people who I didn't know, but he exchanged greetings with. I desperately wanted to sit off in the corner on my own where I could labor over equations in silence, but I didn't have much of a choice.

"Everyone, this is Lexie. She's new. Lexie, this is… everyone." He grinned stupidly as I felt various probing eyes on me.

I'd had it initially. This was a small town and I was new. People, especially high school kids, took notice. When I started here, people stared, making me feel slightly self-conscious. Hardly anyone actually came up and actively tried to make friends. Some were nice enough, chatty even, but I didn't come home with a huge handful of party invitations either. People didn't fawn over the new girl like they did in movies. I was quickly forgotten, in a way only teenagers could do. I was thankful for that.

Now it looked like I was suddenly remembered and I got a chorus of hellos, nice to meet yous, and various other questions from the two boys and girl who had surrounded us.

I hated it.

I was a social person, sure. My mom and I thrived off company, and we had a huge group of friends back in DC. I didn't have many from my school. Lydia, my best friend, was someone who I missed like crazy. There were a couple of others, but I didn't feel the need to collect friends like accessories. I didn't want that.

Now it seemed, I was the newest accessory.

••••

"So, what's the deal with you and Killian?" Jordan asked, tossing a ball that had appeared from nowhere as we filtered out of class.

"Killian?" Stacy, a dark-haired girl who was one of Jordan's friends, repeated, her eyes darting to me. They were not kind.

I was somehow being bustled to the cafeteria with a growing group of Jordan's friends and all of the attention was on me.

"Yeah, he had her books and he looked like he was going to fight me for them when I was showing Lexie to class," Jordan explained.

"He was carrying your books?" a girl I didn't know asked in disbelief. She was small, wearing a cheerleading uniform, and her chocolate-brown ringlets were separated into pigtails.

"He was probably trying to steal them. He'd steal anything that wasn't nailed down," Stacy shot in snidely.

I did not like her. I usually reserved judgment on people, a quality my mom instilled in me, but my mom would gladly have my back with a girl like this. There were girls like this in every school, it seemed. They made themselves appear bigger by making others smaller.

Anger crept up my throat at the way she was referring to Killian.

"He was just *carrying*," I emphasized that word, looking pointedly at Stacy before I continued, "them to be friendly."

She smiled cruelly. "You're new, and you seem... trusting," she began, using the word as an insult. "Killian doesn't have a friendly bone in his body, trust me," she said sweetly like she was looking out for me.

I had an almost uncontrollable urge to yank her gold hoop earrings out of her ears. I swallowed it, just in time for us to reach the cafeteria and for me to be ushered to a huge table.

Once more, introductions were made and I spent the rest of lunch fielding questions about my last school, and everything else that could possibly be interesting about me. I answered on autopilot, my gaze darting around the cafeteria for Killian.

I didn't find him. And I found myself immensely disappointed.

Chapter 3

The next Wednesday, I had commenced my plan to get Mom and Zane together. It was perfectly executed with a chocolate cake and an excuse to get Mom to deliver it. She just happened to be at home when I finished it, and I just happened to be on my way to meet a girl from English class, which meant I was unable to deliver it.

I felt very tempted to rub my hands together and laugh like an evil genius at my brilliance. Though, that would give me away. So, instead, I rushed out the door with English books in tow, giving my mom no choice in the matter.

I made it to the café in town feeling rather pleased with myself. I was actually looking forward to my study date also. I loved any chance to discuss Shakespeare, but I was also happy with the girl in my English class who had been assigned my partner.

"Gina!" I greeted with a grin as I breezed through the door. "Sorry I'm late." I sank down into the chair, heaving my bag onto the table.

She smiled shyly at me. "No problem."

Gina was quiet and definitely a fellow bookworm. She hardly said much, which was all right since I was happy to do most of the talking. I didn't make friends easy, but when I felt comfortable with someone, I engaged in word vomit like I did with my mom on a regular basis.

I felt comfortable around Gina. She was real, unlike Jordan and his friends, who I'd had to suffer two lunches with before I'd escaped them. I'd escaped them by sitting with Gina on the third day. Stacy had breezed past us like we were invisible. Jordan and a couple of the other boys and pigtail girl smiled hello, but no one stopped.

It was sad really, the way they clung to social hierarchy. Gina was pretty. She had long, coppery hair that was thick and shiny. Her green eyes were striking and took up most of her face, and she had beautiful clear skin. She was slightly overweight, and I thought she carried it well. She also wore glasses and didn't have a conventional fashion sense.

Therefore, she wasn't considered "cool."

As someone with less than conventional fashion sense—I was wearing high-waisted, patterned gypsy pants, a crocheted crop top, and had a feather hanging from a braid in my hair—and absolutely no desire to be chained to a way of acting or dressing in pursuit of "cool," I didn't give a damn at how Gina dressed. Nor how she stuttered over her words. Especially not the fact she carried a couple of extra pounds. She was friendly, sweet, and although she didn't say much, we got on.

"Okay then, let's get down to the nitty-gritty," I declared, yanking out a book. "But first, I need about a gallon of coffee, how about you?" I asked.

Gina nodded. "Make that two gallons."

I put my hand over hers. "Your love of Shakespeare cemented our friendship. Your love of coffee has made us soul mates," I said seriously with a grin.

••••

"Killian Decesare is staring at you," Gina hissed as we gathered our books, getting ready to leave.

It was two hours of intense study and thirty minutes of comfortable conversation later; we had agreed to call it a day.

I didn't have a chance to answer because her eyes bulged and her face turned pink. "He's coming over here," she declared in horror, quickly shoving things in her bag.

I felt him before I saw him, his heat stopping close to my shoulder.

"Hey, Freckles," he murmured almost in my ear. His eyes moved to the girl who looked like she might go into cardiac arrest. "Gina." He nodded with a smile.

Gina's jaw dropped open at the fact he said her name and she quickly hurried out of the booth. "H-hey, um, I've got to..." She pointed at the door. "Bye," she blurted before almost running out the door.

I followed her with my eyes before turning my attention back to Killian. I drank him in greedily. I hadn't seen him around school the past few days, and I hated to say it, but I looked for him around every corner. He looked as good as he did the last time I saw him. He was wearing dark jeans, a white tee, and a motorcycle jacket.

I saw his eyes touch the small sliver of skin showing at my stomach as I straightened after putting all my books in my bag.

"You scared off my study partner," I accused.

He shrugged. "It seems I have," he agreed. "You need someone to help you study, Freckles?" he asked, voice teasing.

I swallowed a grin. "No thank you, I'm done. I was just leaving, in fact." It was true, but there was nothing I wanted less in this world than to leave his presence.

Killian's eyes bore into me. "Where you goin'?"

"Home." Though I really wanted to say "Wherever you're going." I was afraid that might sound a trifle tragic considering this was the third—yes, I was counting—time I'd been in his presence.

He nodded out to the window. "I'll take you."

I followed his gaze out the window and let out a small laugh. I did it partly to hide the way my stomach dipped the moment I set eyes on the motorcycle he had nodded to. An image of me riding on the back of that, pressed up against him, came to my mind. My spine tingled at that thought.

Killian tugged on the braid in my hair. "Somethin' funny about my bike, Freckles?" he asked softly.

I shook my head slowly. "No, your bike is... awesome, for lack of a more eloquent word," I replied honestly. "The possibility of me riding it... not so awesome," I explained.

"Dad would bring out the shotgun?" he guessed.

"Mom would bring out the mullet photo, then murder me slowly," I corrected.

His brows furrowed together. "Mullet photo?" he asked with a small grin.

Crap.

He did not need to know about the existence of a photo showing a baby me with a mullet that Mom promised to show the world if I ever got on the back of a motorcycle.

"Nothing," I said quickly. "Nothing at all." I slung the bag over my shoulder. "It's a no to the ride," I said with disappointment.

Killian fell into stride beside me as I walked toward the door. I expected him to suggest not telling my mom; he had a 'screw the establishment and all authority figures' vibe about him, but he stayed silent.

"What are you doing?" I asked when I realized that we had left the coffee shop and walked straight past his amazing bike. I had let myself fall into yet another daydream being in his presence.

"Walking you home," he responded immediately, brushing his shoulder against mine.

I glanced at him. "But you'll have to walk all the way back here to get your bike. That's silly. I can walk home alone," I informed him, stopping on the sidewalk.

He stopped too, and he moved to face me, standing so close our bodies almost touched. Every part of me seemed to zing with electricity at the proximity. "I don't want you to be alone," he murmured. "I don't much want to be alone either, not when I've got the opportunity to walk with you."

I stared at him, stunned. I wanted to stay like that forever, this close to him. I also wanted more. I stared at his lips, licking my own.

His eyes hardened and he stepped back. He nodded his head down the street. "This way?" His voice was hard, the words flat. I noticed the cords in his neck pulsing, and his hands were balled into fists.

I idly wondered at his reaction. Was it my fault? Did I do something? I cursed my lack of experience. My lack of knowledge.

I nodded when I realized he was waiting for a response.

He started walking at my nod and I automatically did the same, not wanting to leave his side.

We were silent for a long while, long enough to leave the main street behind, and go into the neighborhood where my house was. For once, I cursed how small this town was. I wanted my house to be hours away, not minutes that seemed to be passing far too quickly.

"Your dad, where's he?" Killian asked suddenly.

I glanced at him; he was watching me intently as he walked. Not many people asked straight out about my dad when I alluded to the fact he wasn't around. They danced around the subject, asking vague questions, trying to probe the answer out of me so they didn't look nosy. I liked how Killian asked straight up, no bullshit.

"Your guess is as good as mine. Never met him."

Killian's eyes darkened, and he grasped my hand, squeezing it. "I'm sorry, Freckles," he said softly.

I focused on my breathing, on not doing something stupid like passing out at his hand clutching mine.

"Don't be sorry," I said finally, slightly breathless. "My mom, she's amazing. She's more than I could have ever asked for. I don't even notice that I'm meant to have two parents. She's crazy enough to be both the mom and the dad. Plus, I've got Steve and Ava."

I wasn't lying; weirdly, I didn't have a gaping hole where I thought a father should go. Maybe it was because I'd never known any different, maybe it was because I'd never felt like I was missing out on anything. Our home never felt incomplete. Mom filled it up. Steve and Ava filled it up.

"Though," I whispered, "sometimes I do wonder about him. About why he left us. Sometimes I have stupid dreams about him coming home and declaring he'd been held hostage for sixteen years or some other equally ridiculous reason for being absent from our lives." I paused. "Sometimes I do wish I knew why," I said softly. "I've never told anyone that." I'd never voice that particular dream to Mom; she clammed up whenever I even broached the topic of my father. I had seen the hurt on her face, even when I was too young to properly understand, so I stopped mentioning it. Now I was older, I wasn't quite as satisfied with vague answers.

I needed more. At some point, I'd demand it.

Killian's hand squeezed mine. "I'm glad, Freckles," he replied, voice hard, "that I'm the first person to get a piece of you no one's ever got."

My heart jumped at the statement, the feeling behind it.

I expected him to say more, but Killian was silent, looking down the street, though I guessed it wasn't the street he was truly looking at.

"What about your folks?" I asked, needing to know more about the elusive boy who had taken my mind hostage.

He kept staring for a long moment, long enough to make me

think he wasn't going to answer me.

"My old man died when I was a kid," he declared flatly. "Mom's a junkie. *Mom* isn't exactly the title I'd give her, but I'm mindful of not corrupting the gentle ears around me." He gave me a soft, teasing look.

I stopped walking at his words, causing him to stop too. It was either that or let go of my hand. He didn't seem too keen on doing that, so he stopped a couple of paces in front of me. He turned and moved back so his body faced mine.

My heart bled right there in my chest; his words had actually opened it up, the pain for him was so real. It was unexplainable really. I barely knew him, but I hurt for him.

His brows furrowed as he bent his head to meet my eyes. "What, Freckles?" he asked, eyes guarded like he was expecting something, something bad.

"I'm so sorry," I choked up, feeling tears filling my eyes. "I can't even imagine that. Having no one," I whispered, feeling a tear drop from my eyes.

His body jolted at my words and his face gentled. It was an amazing, mind-blowing transition. No one, no boy had ever looked at me the way he was looking at me right then. I didn't know people actually looked at other people like that.

He stroked my cheek, his touch featherlight, but it caused tingles to erupt from every inch he touched. "I've got people," he told me. "Got the club. They're my family. Wouldn't trade them for anything. Plus, I'm not alone right now." His thumb brushed away the tear rolling down my cheek. "You're too pretty to be sad," he murmured. "'Specially don't want you shedding any tears over me."

I quickly blinked away any residual wetness, suddenly embarrassed at my emotional display. It was my downfall. I'd been emotional ever since I was younger. I felt things deep in my soul. Books stayed with me for months after the pages were gone, and I heard the feeling in songs long after silence had descended. I was a creative person; I never truly lived in silence. It had never really bothered me. I'd just accepted it as part of who I was. Now I realized how stupid it seemed. I wanted to pull away from his touch. I also wanted to live the rest of my life in it.

I couldn't do anything though. I was paralyzed staring at him, drinking in every moment of... whatever this was. I didn't understand it, the thing between us. This tingling at the bottom of my belly at his every touch. This sort of yearning. The impossible need to kiss him.

Killian managed to shake himself out of it and stepped back, pulling on my arm gently so we were walking once more.

"The club," I said finally, after getting my emotions together. "That's the same one Zane's in?" I asked. Though it seemed like a stupid question because he had been at the garage that also served as their clubhouse. I was infinitely curious about the motorcycle club that everyone in town seemed to know about. My knowledge of motorcycle clubs was pretty lackluster, apart from what I saw in the media. I didn't get the feeling these were the bad guys the news painted out most motorcycle clubs as. The men Mom and I had met at the garage certainly seemed scary at first, but they were friendly, and I felt weirdly at ease with them.

Especially Zane. I knew he was a good person. Something inside me just knew.

Killian gave me a sideways look. "Zane?" He paused. "Bull," he muttered, almost to himself. "Yeah. Grew up in it, Freckles. They're good people, despite what anyone says." He sounded almost defensive.

I gazed up at him. "I know they're good people," I stated with a small smile. "You're in the club. So is Zane. They're good people."

Killian stopped once more, and I was glad because we had reached the end of my street and I really didn't want to stop talking to him or let go of his hand.

"You don't judge anyone on first glance, do you?" he asked, amazement dancing in his icy eyes.

I smiled again. "No, not until I've had the chance to get to know them and had a chance to make up my own mind, and not let other people make it up for me."

He gazed at me for a long moment. "Christ," he whispered. "You're so far from a normal sixteen-year-old girl. You're a different species than most of those airheads at school," he pointed out in disbelief.

I turned serious. "You don't seem like normal a seventeen-year-old boy," I countered. I had done some subtle digging and found out he was a year older than me.

"That's 'cause I'm not, Freckles," he responded, his voice flat. His face turned serious. "No one outside the club, 'specially not in that place full of idiots we call a school, has had a different opinion of me. Apart from you," he murmured. "I treasure that. I need you to be wary though," he warned. "The fact you didn't judge the club, anyone in it, is amazing, babe. But you need to be wary. Don't be certain of anyone else who looks rough around the edges. There're people who wouldn't hesitate to take advantage of a beautiful teenage girl's lack of prejudice. People who I'd have to beat up if they did so. I'd much rather be using my hands to hold yours than use my fists to get revenge on anyone who did that, Freckles."

I swallowed and regarded him with wide eyes. I didn't completely understand everything he said, but I was pretty sure he said he'd be beating up people for me. It was intense. Scary. Terrifying. Terrifying because I liked it.

His thumb and forefinger grasped my chin. "Need you to tell me you understand what I said," he commanded softly.

I didn't. Not really. But I'd most likely be obsessing over this conversation for the next twenty hours, so I was sure I'd understand later. So I nodded. "I understand."

His eyes searched mine. "I can't believe it," he muttered. "The fact you're so much more than I thought you were to start with. And, Freckles, I knew you were somethin' special the minute I laid eyes on you in that flowery dress strutting into school for the first time."

I gaped at him. My stomach dipped at his words and my heart threatened to beat out of my chest at the look in his eyes, how close he was standing to me.

He was going to kiss me.

His eyes darted to the left. He nodded his head. "That's your place."

I followed his eyes to my house at the end of the street. "Indeed it is," I agreed.

"Go to it, Freckles," he ordered. His thumb brushed my jaw and he stepped back. "I'll see you at school," he promised, giving me one long look before turning on his motorcycle boots and walking back toward town.

I stood there, staring at his retreating form, waiting for my heartbeat to return to normal, for my breathing to stop choking me.

As I did this, I realized something he said.

"The moment I laid eyes on you in that flowery dress strutting into school for the first time."

The first time I'd noticed him was days ago at the garage. I thought that was the first time he noticed me too.

Something scary and amazing settled in my stomach at the realization that he'd noticed me almost the day I got into town.

•••

"Mom!" I called, dropping my bag at the door and nearly skipping into the kitchen.

I felt like I was floating. Flying. I kept replaying every moment with Killian, my stomach squeezing at every new thing I took from the walk. The memory of his eyes, his thumb brushing against my cheek.

I couldn't wait to tell Mom. I wanted to keep it mine a little longer, but I didn't think I could hide how utterly ecstatic I was.

"Hey, kid," Mom greeted me with a weak smile.

I immediately stopped my skip and my smile froze on my face.

Something was wrong. Very wrong.

"The fact you seem that happy after spending that long studying Shakespeare makes me need to think really hard to make sure I didn't drop you on your head when you were an infant," she informed me. "No normal human is that happy after studying."

Mom and I engaged in almost constant sarcasm and movie quotes instead of conversation; it was our way. This time though, it seemed forced. Something had Mom feeling seriously down. She was trying to hide it, which meant she didn't want me to know.

Whatever it was had me instantly changing my mind about telling her about Killian. I buried my feelings of joy down quickly.

I sat down at the dining table in the middle of the kitchen. "No normal human eats—" I paused to do a mental count "—four packets of king size Reese's Cups and still looks like you, and also doesn't have diabetes."

Somehow, my mom ate worse than a teenage boy and was still petite and had beautiful skin. It was a mystery how it happened, though it meant good things for my future.

"Yes, well, here I am. The secret to girlish figures, beauty beyond compare, and excellent health... excessive amounts of sugar," she replied, grinning through chocolate teeth.

She was going to great pains to hide whatever had gotten her down. It niggled at me that she wasn't going to tell me, but I'd give her time, maybe she would. I sure as anything wouldn't be telling her about Killian now. A little part of me, an ugly part, was glad I'd found a reason not to. To be able to keep it just for me for however longer.

Chapter 4

"Calculus on your lunch break? My, we are living life on the edge, Freckles," a deep, teasing voice tickled my ear.

I jumped slightly, not so much in surprise, but at the way my body immediately responded to the familiar voice, to the feel of heat at my back. I turned to meet icy blue eyes, which were twinkling.

I grinned. "What can I say? I'm a rebel," I deadpanned.

He rewarded me with a grin that warmed my stomach. "Good thing I'm here then, to get you on the straight and narrow," he said, setting his tray next to mine.

I watched him sit down next to me. Like *right next to me*. My bare arm brushed his muscled one. It was closer than people normally sat. Way closer.

"I don't think I've ever seen you in the cafeteria before," I mused, my nerves making my voice shake.

He turned his body so it was angled to mine, so I got his full attention. "Don't think I've been in here for a year at least," he replied seriously.

My eyes popped out of my head. "Where do you spend your lunch break then?"

He shrugged. "Anywhere but the feeding trough. I usually go for a ride, hang out at the club."

"But you're not supposed to leave school grounds," I pointed out, like the complete nerd I was.

I felt red creeping up my neck the moments the words left my mouth, especially when Killian's lips turned up in amusement.

"What can I say, Freckles? I'm a rebel," he teased.

I barely resisted the urge to bury my head in my textbook. My eyes darted down for a moment. "Why are you here now then?" I whispered to math equations.

I felt pressure at my chin as Killian's hand grasped it so it tilted up and my eyes met his. "Found a very good reason to brave feeding time at the zoo," he murmured.

I blinked rapidly at the meaning behind those words.

"I'm glad," I whispered, blurting the thought before my mind could stop me.

Killian's eyes flared. "I am too," he said softly, then his eyes flickered down to my textbook. "For a multitude of reasons, one being so that I can ensure you don't fail calculus," he informed me, letting go of my chin.

The loss of his touch echoed through my body as my mind registered his words. I followed his eyes.

"They're wrong?" I groaned.

He grinned at me. "Spectacularly."

This time, I did put my head in my hands. "I'm going to fail, which means I won't get into college and I'll end up having to busk on the streets for money."

"Don't despair. You're unlikely to be destined for a life on the streets, not when you've got me," he promised.

I pushed my head out of my hands to watch him as he pulled the book away from me and glanced down at it, strands of his inky hair falling around his face. I had a desperate urge to run my hands through it.

"I've got you," I repeated his words, though I didn't mean to do it out loud.

His head snapped up and his eyes were intense. "You've got me," he repeated once more, and I knew he meant for more than a calculus tutor.

I wanted to freeze that moment in time and somehow make it tangible so I could tuck it away with my books and relive it over again. Unfortunately, reality made that impossible.

I tore my gaze away from his and my eyes darted around the cafeteria. The sound I'd been shutting out the moment I'd locked eyes with Killian came roaring back in. People walking past were giving us sideways glances. More than a few were straight-up staring.

I worried if looks could kill, Stacy's glare would stop my heart instantly.

"People are looking at us," I said quietly, moving my eyes back to Killian.

He didn't even glance around. "People are most likely lookin' at *you*, Freckles." His face hardened slightly. "Though I'd be happy if the jock for brains is currently looking this way. Maybe then he won't get any ideas that will make me have to divest him of some teeth," he said, only half joking.

I raised a brow at him. "What ideas would those be?"

His gaze darkened. "Many which don't bear repeating, but the main one being he doesn't realize how far out of his league you are," he declared. "Though, there's not one boy in this place who's even near that," he added.

I swallowed and heat crept up my neck at the way he was talking about me. Me. "Present company excluded," I whispered, unsure of where my boldness was coming from.

Killian's face froze and he was silent for a moment. "No, Freckles, present company is the one person at this school who has no business even being in your presence," he murmured, his voice rough. He paused. "But what can I say? I'm a rebel." His voice wasn't teasing like before, but my whole body warmed at the fact it meant he wasn't going anywhere. Not right now at least.

His face cleared. "Let's get to making sure you don't have a future on the streets," he teased, the moment leaving.

I forced a smile and tried my best to focus on the equations in front of me and not the muscled arm pointing to my mistakes and the boy attached to the muscled arm.

I failed spectacularly. But I would gladly fail calculus if it meant I got to spend every lunch break with Killian.

•••••

"Hello?" I called to the cavernous room.

No one answered. I paused for a second longer, just to make sure I was alone.

I wasn't necessarily hiding, per se, but Jordan had promised he'd save a seat at lunch for me, with a weird twinkle in his eye. I so didn't want to see what that was about. His friends and he seemed nice enough, on the surface. I didn't miss the pointed comments about people that walked past and didn't fit in their parameters of "cool." Nor did I miss the way Kyle had purposefully tripped a small, skinny redheaded boy who had scuttled past us the other day.

I especially didn't miss the comments Stacy had been handing out to me whenever I found myself in that group.

"Lexie, I love your skirt. It's so cool how you, like, don't even care that the whole boho look is so... done. You like it and don't let things like fashion stop you. It's groovy," she said sweetly yester-day.

I had failed to let that barb puncture me anywhere. I was comfortable with how I looked, and I wasn't going to let one comment from a petty girl affect me.

I had bitten my tongue when I really wanted to say, "I'm not one to be a blind fashion victim; otherwise, I'd be bumping into doors. How's your eyesight?"

Instead, I gave her a wide smile and thanked her. Then I'd made my escape as quickly as possible.

It was Wednesday. A week to the day I'd walked home with Killian. I'd spent four glorious lunch breaks in his presence, trying not to turn into a bumbling idiot when he spoke in his rough and low tone. Not that he spoke overly much. In between helping me with calculus, he asked me more questions about my life back in DC, and my favorite books and movies.

"*The Lion, the Witch and the Wardrobe*, that's your favorite book?" Killian asked on the fourth day, his eyes light and teasing.

I nodded, trying not to focus on how close his body was to mine. "I wish I could say it's *Ulysses* or *The Grapes of Wrath*. They're great, don't get me wrong, but it'll always be Narnia in my heart," I told him, failing to be embarrassed. "See, it was the first book Steve and I read together. Mom isn't exactly... into reading to put it lightly," I joked. "But Steve was the reason I found the love of my life." I paused to think about music. "Well, second love," I corrected. "So it'll always be the book that started it all." I looked at Killian, whose eyes were burning into mine, his face blank. I felt my neck redden. "You think I'm a big dork, don't you?"

Killian's expression turned intense and he shook his head slowly. "No, Freckles," he murmured, "the more I find out about you, the more you fascinate me." His voice was dark.

I had never looked forward to lunch more than I had those four days. I could barely concentrate in classes. It was ridiculous. I saw girls basically lose their minds over boys throughout my teenage years, and I'd always considered them silly for doing so. I'd been somehow proud of myself for not letting such things mess with my goals.

I had goals, but I wasn't exactly sure of what I wanted. I knew I loved reading. That music was my soul. That writing songs made the world melt away. Strumming the guitar felt like I was going into another world. I was also a realist. Love of music, talent for strumming a guitar, and a half-decent voice didn't guarantee a future.

Mom told me I could be anything I wanted to be. I didn't particularly want to be famous or rich. Sure, it would be nice. More than nice, I guessed.

I mainly wanted to be happy. Mom and I were far from rich. There were times in my childhood that I knew even giving me a dollar for a hot dog was impossible. I knew it was hard. But I never remembered being unhappy or feeling like I was missing out.

I didn't need money to be happy. I needed family. My books. And I needed music. If I could find a way to make a living out of that, great.

But the amount of talented, passionate artists that made a living were few and far between, so I had to work hard. My mom had such unwavering belief in me, and she had worked so hard to give me the opportunity to be anything and everything. I didn't want to let her down. I couldn't let her down. So I worked hard at school. Hard.

I didn't trouble myself with boys mostly because I was too busy to worry about them. Partly because I'd never met any who I thought were worth venturing out of my books for, untangling myself from music for. And another part, one that I was unlikely to verbalize, knew I'd never find one to measure up to the kind of love I'd grown up with. That Jane Austen, Margaret Mitchell, Fleetwood Mac, Billy Joel, and The Beatles had made so beautiful.

That fricking Walt Disney had tricked me into thinking was real.

I wanted the fairy tale. I wanted a love as deep as the ocean, as unyielding as the wind, stronger than diamonds, and as unpredictable as a volcano. I wanted a love that made me crazy and sane at the same time. The feeling that the world slipped into place the moment you laid eyes on that person. Your person. The one meant for you.

I wasn't an idiot. I knew that most likely didn't exist.

And if by some miracle it did, I didn't think I'd find it at sixteen.

I didn't *want to* find it at sixteen. I wanted to make it. Figure out where my life would take me first. I wanted to travel. I wanted to live first.

But here I was, at sixteen, no idea what I wanted to do and having seen only two cities in my life, and I had this wondrous elation that I found it. Ridiculous and stupid was what most people would say if I verbalized it.

Which was why I hadn't. Not even to my mom. I'd hardly admitted it to myself.

I had a cocktail of emotions threatening to explode, so I needed this empty room. The one I'd found when I was lost a couple of days ago. The one with the stage and the old piano in the middle of it.

It wasn't a guitar, but it was something. It offered me the solace, the quiet that music offered me.

I sat down and lightly traced my hands along the keys. I wasn't as good on the piano as I was with the guitar. With the guitar, I barely knew where my hands ended and the instrument began. But the moment I touched the keys, instinct took over and my entire body relaxed. I got lost in the music.

I started to sing "Breathe" by Pearl Jam softly at first, the words running through me like a river. Everything fell away but the music, and I was able to silence my unquiet mind.

As the last note of music flew off into the air, and my voice softly trailed off, I immediately heard all of the noise rush back in.

Literally and figuratively.

"Holy shit! You're like... *fucking amazing*," an excited voice yelled.

41

I jumped, nearly completely off the stool, my eyes snapping open.

"Good one, scare the living shit out of the girl. She'll run before we even get to talk to her," another, quieter voice scolded.

I watched a boy with spiky blond hair punch the one who yelled in the shoulder. He was wearing all black and had shoulder-length black hair. Despite being scared out of my wits, I appreciated his Joy Division tee. They were walking up the stairs to join me on stage, another with a beanie and who was seriously good looking followed silently, though he was grinning at me. They all were.

"Please don't say you've come here to murder me," I joked lightly.

All three of them chuckled. The one in the tee came to sit right next to me on the piano seat, not worrying about things like personal space with virtual strangers.

"If we murdered you, what good would you be to our band?" he asked. "We need you alive, kicking, and preferably singing." He furrowed his brows, looking at my hands resting on the keys of the piano. "We've already got a keyboardist," he mused, frowning at the boy behind him accusingly before turning his attention back to me. "Let's hope by some miraculous turn of fate you're a musical prodigy and play more than one instrument. You don't play guitar by any chance?" he continued, speaking so fast I could barely follow his train of thought. Luckily, I lived with a woman who spoke much faster than that and engaged in such banter my entire life.

"Only as well as I put one foot in front of the other," I answered with a grin.

He grinned back. "*Righteous*. It's serendipitous."

The one with blond messy hair leaned on the piano and smiled at me. He was handsome; they all were actually. The one beside me had hair that rivaled Killian's on the inky and shiny scale, though it was longer, brushing his shoulders. He was wearing multiple silver rings and a couple of chains around his neck. Though he was tall and skinny, his bone structure made him look like he could be a Calvin Klein model. The blond one had messy, short hair and was slightly more built than the one beside me. He was wearing a striped crew neck sweater, faded jeans, and Chuck Taylors. The silent one behind him was seriously hot. He had a beanie pulled low on his head, and his dark eyes were nothing less than smoldering. I envied the length of his eyelashes, and his jaw was hard and angular, his skin tanned. He was more built than the other two. His muscles were clearly visible considering he was wearing a black wife-beater and black jeans.

"Sorry, he missed his dosage today," the blond one informed me, nodding his head toward the boy beside me. "I'm Wyatt. This is Noah." He jerked his head behind him.

"I'm Sam," the one beside me cut in with a grin. "The most talented and best looking by far," he said confidently.

"Or maybe the loudest and dumbest," Wyatt teased.

Sam scowled at him.

I found myself feeling warm and comfortable in their banter.

"Lexie," I said, before they could engage in fisticuffs, as entertaining as that would be.

"We know," Sam said, moving his attention back to me. "A hot new girl comes to school? First thing I did was find out your name, address, and social security number."

Wyatt punched him in the shoulder once more.

He rubbed it distractedly. "I mean, nice to meet you," he said with a grin.

I couldn't help but laugh. "Nice to meet you too." My eyes moved to the other two. "All of you."

"I bet you're wondering why we're accosting you in the auditorium while you minded your own business, totally *owning* Pearl Jam," Wyatt asked.

I sat a little straighter. "The thought hadn't crossed my mind," I said seriously. "I just assumed you did this with all new students." Sarcasm just naturally came out of my mouth. I usually reserved it for people I knew and felt comfortable around. That was a handful of people. Now it seemed three more were added to that small group.

There were a couple more chuckles.

"We were actually coming here to practice." Wyatt nodded to the stage where a drum kit was hidden slightly by a curtain. Guitar cases leaned on it.

"You guys are in a band?" I asked, unable to keep the excitement out of my voice.

"Sort of," Wyatt hedged.

Sam jostled his knee. "Until now, the band was incomplete. We've needed a lead vocalist and another guitarist, and we're the only talented people in this burg. We'd given up hope... until now," he informed me with bright eyes.

I realized they were all staring at me. "You mean me?" I asked in disbelief.

Sam nodded rapidly.

"If you're interested," Wyatt added quickly. "We can jam together, now if you're free?"

"Yeah, so we can assure you we don't suck, which we don't," Sam told me.

I gaped at them. I'd never been in a band at home. The idea had been intriguing, but I didn't exactly have the confidence to go out looking. Plus, I was a rather solitary creature. I was happy reading, writing music, listening to it, singing, doing all of that alone. But right now, I couldn't think of anything cooler than making it with people.

I gave them a small smile. "I'll take you up on the jam offer, but I'm reserving my right to make sure you don't suck before I answer the band offer," I teased.

Sam pushed up rapidly off the chair, jostling me slightly as he stood. "Let's get to it." He was gone and at the drum set before I could even stand.

Wyatt winked and ambled over to a guitar case.

Noah gave me a warm smile that would have melted me had I not already been transfixed by another bad boy. "Welcome to the madhouse. Just a warning, once you're in, you'll never get rid of them." He nodded to the boys. "Believe me, I've tried," he joked, his eyes warm.

I smiled back, and before I knew it, they had me situated in front of a mic and we were singing. Each song melted into another as we seamlessly played together like it was natural, like we had for years.

Boom.

A band was born.

Chapter 5

I had a sort of psychic power. Well, not psychic, exactly. I couldn't read minds or move objects with the power of thought. I couldn't tell the future either. I could see what songs people needed. I believed in the power of music. To inspire, to communicate, to elate, to bring down, and... to cure. A good song, a song that spoke to your soul, could sometimes help repair a broken soul. Or at least act to soften the sharp edges.

So that's why I sang Cat Power's "The Greatest" in the garage Mom had helped me convert into a practice space for our newly formed band.

It had been a whirlwind since the Wednesday our little band was born. It seemed I'd spent every spare second with boys who were quickly becoming my best friends along with bandmates. After school, study periods, and lunch breaks were dedicated to playing. I loved it.

I thought I'd discovered the power, the beauty of music. Playing on my own with my guitar was one thing, but playing as part of an entire whole, playing with people who had the same passion as me was amazing.

It was then I realized that was exactly what I wanted to do. For the rest of my life, I wanted to make music.

It was a helpful distraction from the fact I hadn't seen nor heard from Killian since Tuesday.

Our school was small, the chances of me bumping into him

should have been high, but considering he wasn't in any of my classes and I spent all of my time practicing with the boys, I guessed it wasn't implausible I hadn't seen him. I had searched the cafeteria for his tall, leather-clad, and utterly delicious form without luck. I didn't have much time to actually look for him, considering we only were in there long enough for the boys to scarf down food and then we went to the auditorium to practice.

Though we had needed a real practice space considering Mr. Hazelton had found us on Friday when we were playing on a study break. We all happened to have study breaks together. Well, apart from Sam, but he declared he would rather "listen to Justin Bieber on repeat for the rest of my life instead of going to History class."

We had just finished a set that was fricking awesome, if I did say so myself, when Mr. Hazelton revealed himself, arms crossed and face pinched.

"Oh shit," Sam muttered from beside me.

"What do you think you're doing in here?" Mr. Hazelton snapped, addressing all of us.

"Um, hate to point out the obvious, Mr. Hazelton, but we're playing music. Practicing for our band's grand future," Sam drawled, grinning slightly.

Mr. Hazelton was not impressed. "I can see what you're doing, Mr. Kennedy," he snapped.

"Well, why did he ask?" Sam muttered under his breath.

Mr. Hazelton narrowed his eyes. "I can see what you're doing, but I'm lost as to the reason why you think it's an appropriate use of school property and your time," he continued sharply. "School is for bettering yourself, for making your future." He ran his gaze over Sam. "For *most* students at least. Wasting not only your time, but Ms. Spencer's is frankly unacceptable."

"Well, it's technically our study period and Mr. Hamilton gave us permission," I cut in, my voice friendly even though I hated Mr.

Hazelton ever since his exchange with Kill.

"I'll be speaking with Mr. Hamilton about letting students waste their time with such"—he scrunched up his nose—"trivial pursuits," he promised.

"A life lived for art is never a life wasted," Sam cut in, his own eyes narrowed.

Mr. Hazelton dismissed him with a condensing look. "I don't appreciate the flippant attitude, Mr. Kennedy. I want you all out of here before I slap you all with detentions."

He gave us one more warning look before turning on his heel and striding out.

"Bro, did you actually just quote Macklemore to Mr. Hazelton?" Wyatt asked in disbelief once the door had slammed shut.

Sam turned to him and shrugged. "Well, it's not like I can exactly remember Plato on the fly."

We were all quiet for a moment; then we burst out laughing, apart from Sam, who was watching us in confusion.

So, to avoid Mr. Hazelton's wrath, Mom and I set aside Saturday to convert our garage into a practice space. Mom had done it under duress and complained the entire time. She hadn't loved the idea of manual labor, but she was more than supportive of our band. She'd even convinced herself that she would be our 'Momager' when we hit the big time. It didn't matter she hadn't actually met the boys yet, nor heard us play, she supported me all the way. That was her.

But she had been different since that day a week ago. I couldn't put my finger on it. She still laughed, joked, and ribbed like normal, but there was an edge, something that seemed off. I couldn't ask because I couldn't verbalize what it was. So instead, I sang.

I got so lost in the song, in the lyrics, I didn't notice anything but the rhythm passing through me, the words.

It wasn't until silence descended and my mind started up again did I realize it wasn't just my mom who I was singing to.

"Did it sound okay?" I asked her, not noticing the figures in the driveway at first.

That was until one of them answered since Mom had gone mute.

"That was kick-ass, Lexie! You've got a great voice, girl," a loud voice exclaimed.

I jumped at the foreign, manly voice and my whole face flamed when I spotted the owner of it. More accurately, who the owner was standing beside. Lucky was the bald, tattooed man who we had met the day our car broke down, the one who could scarily believe I was Mom's kid and used a lot of swear words. Mom had told me his name when I'd asked about him. He was leaning on our car, along with Killian whose eyes were blazing into every part of me.

I immediately jerked my head down, fiddling with the strings on my guitar.

With the absence of him even for a few days, the memory of our connection seemed to be more and more in the realm of my imagination, and at that moment, I wasn't sure whether I'd imagined it. I didn't want to make a dork of myself by going bright red and gazing at him. Even more so, I didn't want to be educated on how wrong I'd be by looking into his eyes and seeing them empty of what had been there days ago.

So I kept my head down while Lucky and Mom chatted about the car, intent on my guitar strings like my life depended on it.

"So you going to audition for *American Idol* with those pipes?" a deep voice asked me, and it took me a moment to realize I was being addressed and the voice was closer than it had been before.

Lucky stood in front of me, hands casually in his pockets. He was seriously hot. Hotter than any movie star I'd drooled over with Mom in action movies. He was tall and totally rippling with muscles and tattoos. I guessed he had the ability to look menacing with tattoos covering him and creeping up his neck, his shaved head, and his cut. But he didn't. His eyes were light, and his smile friendly.

I couldn't help but smile back, focusing all of my attention on him instead of the boy who stood slightly behind him, instead of meeting the eyes I could actually feel on me.

"I don't think I've got any reality shows in my future," I replied brightly, swallowing my unease and my sick excitement that came with Killian's presence. "I'm happy to be in a garage with my guitar and my band."

"Band?" a raspy voice repeated before Lucky could answer.

Killian stepped around him, right in front of me, right in my bubble. I didn't have any choice but to look at him.

"I didn't even know you could sing like that, Freckles," he continued softly.

Lucky glanced at him and grinned even bigger.

I had told Killian about my love of music in our cafeteria conversations, but I didn't tell him the extent of it, nor how I sang or played guitar. I always felt it would be kind of pretentious to tell people I was "good" at singing. It wasn't something to boast about, to tell everyone about. It was me. A part of me just like my hands were a part of me. I didn't exactly go around telling everyone I had hands.

I nervously glanced at him. "It's new. Not the singing part, I've been doing that forever. The band part," I babbled.

Lucky slapped Killian on the shoulder. "Well, I can't wait to see this band. Anyone with a singer as pretty as you is bound for superstardom. Promise you'll get me Gwen Stefani's number when you hit the big time?" he asked seriously.

I couldn't help but giggle. "I'll do my best," I replied solemnly.

He rubbed his hands together. "Excellent."

Killian didn't seem to find Lucky as amusing as I did. He was too busy churning my stomach with the intensity of his stare.

Okay, it was safe to say I hadn't imagined it, whatever it was between us.

My stomach did a little flip at this realization.

"Sorry," Mom apologized as she rushed back into the garage, her eyes on us. Or more aptly, Killian. She quickly moved her attention to Lucky. "They were hiding from me." She handed two keys to him, the keys to the loaner car we had been driving since ours was getting repaired.

I couldn't help but roll my eyes and reluctantly moved my attention from Killian. I had to. Mom had crazy spidey senses; she would spot the way I was looking at him.

"We need a key rack," I informed her. Mom was forever losing our keys. I didn't like to think how many parties, movies, and dinners we had been late to because Mom had inexplicably left the keys in the microwave or some equally obscure place.

I watched her eyes narrow at the space between Killian and me, or more accurately, the lack of it before she focused on me. "We do not need a key rack."

I raised my eyebrows. "Where were said keys then?"

Her face lost a bit of its bravado. "They may have been in the freezer," she muttered.

Lucky laughed at this. I was not surprised, so I only gave Mom a triumphant look.

She glared at me and turned to Lucky. "Thanks for everything. I assume your company will send an invoice?"

Now that her attention was diverted, I snuck a glance at Killian again. He was still staring at me. He stepped a hair closer and I held my breath.

"Tonight," was all he rasped before Lucky's voice broke the spell one word and one look had weaved.

"We're off, Kill," he declared, jerking his head to the car at the curb.

Killian's gaze stayed on me for a split second longer. Then he lifted his chin in farewell to Mom, who was frowning at him.

Mom and I watched them go in silence.

"That anything I need to worry about?" Mom asked finally.

I jerked, escaping from the thoughts I had about whatever "tonight" meant, struggling against the butterflies for tonight.

"What?" I asked, feigning innocence.

She put a hand on her hip. "The mini hot guy who could teach college classes on smoldering looks," she stated lightly.

I rolled my eyes and moved my attention to my guitar once more. I couldn't lie worth a damn, especially to my mom. "Of all the things you need to worry about, such as climate change, corporate ownership, and your chances of developing heart disease, that is nowhere near in the realm of importance. It's nothing," I lied.

Mom stared at me; her gaze softened slightly. "I disagree, doll face. Things like planet Earth's inevitable demise and my own health pale in comparison to my little treasure. I'm biologically ingrained to worry about you. I'll do it until I'm old and gray and senile and telling my cronies in the nursing home about my rock star daughter," she said softly. "It's also my job to protect you. From fads like glittered eyeliner, to the dangers of over exfoliating, and broody teenage boys who have heartbreaker all but tattooed on their forehead," she informed me, frowning at the spot where Killian had stood.

I pushed up and wandered over to her. "I don't need protecting from such things. Especially heartbreak. I'm too busy concentrating on my future to worry myself about such trivial things," I lied.

Mom didn't believe me, but she stayed silent.

•••

"Okay, not only is your mom like a total MILF, but she's officially the coolest parent I've come into contact with," Sam declared. "I didn't think parents like her existed. I thought they were just some myth."

Wyatt glared at him. "Dude, you do not tell Lexie her mom's a MILF, not cool," he scolded.

Sam held up his hands innocently. "What? She is. I doubt Lexie's blind; she knows her mom's hot. Plus, it bodes well for you, babe. You're the spitting image of her. You're totally hot already, and you'll age well," he told me sagely.

Wyatt sighed and shook his head.

Noah grinned.

I giggled; I couldn't help it. "Thanks, Sam, I can sleep easy knowing that," I said dryly.

"Apart from being totally inappropriate, Sam is right. It's awesome we've got a practice space," Wyatt said, looking around the garage that would now be the band's home.

Noah nodded. "Seriously. Thank her. You're lucky she's totally supportive of this," he added in quietly.

The way his eyes hardened while saying this worried me slightly. I'd only spent a few days with these boys, but I was already connected to them. We clicked instantly. It was like we'd been friends for years, not days. So we hadn't exactly told everyone about our lives. They didn't talk much about their parents; apart from me, what teenager did? I knew I was an exception, thinking of my mom as a best friend.

I had an inkling Sam and Noah's parents were far from their friends.

"Yeah, she is, isn't she?" I said quietly, my mind in a hundred different places now the music had taken away the anchor.

"I'm totally down for us rocking covers and jamming out in the garage for now," Wyatt said, leaning against the wall. "But you also write some stuff, right, Lex?" he asked, nodding to the notebook that was never far from my person.

I reddened at the thought of anyone actually reading the songs I wrote. I never put them there with the distinct intention of letting anyone else read them. I only wrote them because I had to. Because it was necessary.

"Nothing good," I said quickly.

"I bet that's wrong," Wyatt argued.

"But, if you're not ready to share, that's sweet," Noah cut in, giving Wyatt a pointed look.

Wyatt nodded. "Sure, totally. Maybe we could all write some stuff together." He glanced at Sam. "Well, the three of us, at least. I don't think Sam has a long enough attention span to sit and write something longer than a text to the flavor of the month," he said with a grin.

Sam shrugged, not looking offended in the slightest. "I'm happy with my role in the band. Best drummer and sex symbol," he declared.

We all laughed at this and the warm feeling of having these boys encircled me like a cocoon.

"We better get our sex symbol home so he can get his beauty sleep," Wyatt said, slapping Sam on the shoulder.

They packed up their stuff. Then I got hugs good-bye, as was the boys' way. They were overly affectionate with me, treating me like I was a beloved sibling, which, being an only child, I loved.

"Catch you on the flipside, babe." Sam saluted to me, meandering toward Wyatt's beat-up car.

Wyatt winked at me.

Noah leaned in and kissed my cheek before he jogged to the car.

I watched them leave with a smile.

"Doll face! Can I turn your bedroom into a home theater or are you coming in here to sleep?" Mom yelled from the kitchen window.

I grinned. "I'm coming," I yelled back.

I slowly walked back to the house, my stomach in knots. It was tonight. The tonight Killian had whispered about. Tonight. No time, no inkling of when in the multiple hours classified as night as to when this would be. Vague. I didn't like my chances of sleep.

••••

I did sleep, as unbelievable as it was. Why was it always when you wanted to stay awake your eyelids turned into concrete cinderblocks?

The buzzing of my phone jerked me out of a troubled slumber. I was immediately alert and fumbling for it, knocking various things off my dresser.

KILL: Backyard

I scrambled out of bed, getting caught in my blankets and falling to the floor with a bang.

"Ouch," I hissed in frustration; then I froze. I listened to the silent house for any sign of my mom waking up and discovering me. After a few seconds, I was happy she wasn't going to catch me doing something I'd never done before, sneaking out of the house in the middle of the night. I moved.

I really wanted to turn on the light and apply an entire face of makeup, do my hair, and change into some attractive PJs.

I didn't want to risk it, and I was worried my pounding heart would give out if I did. So all I could do was blindly tie my wayward curls into a haphazard knot and wipe any residual drool off my face.

At least I wasn't wearing anything as embarrassing as my Harry Potter PJs. I had on soft pink bottoms and a lace-trimmed cami.

I quickly shrugged on a chunky gray cardigan and slipped my

feet into flip-flops before tiptoeing out of my room.

Every one of my nerve endings were on fire as I quietly closed the back door. I had never done anything like this. Never had the desire to do anything like this. Mom and I had an open relationship, so it was completely unnecessary for me to do things like sneak out. She'd never forbade me to do anything in my life, though I didn't think she'd approve of meeting with a boy in the middle of the night. I felt slightly sick at the prospect of disappointing her, of doing something like this.

Another part of me couldn't care less about this. All that part of me wanted was to see Killian. I searched our dark and seemingly empty backyard, the trees backing onto our property looking slightly ominous. A twinge of fear crept up my spine before I felt heat at my back.

"Freckles," a voice tickled my ear, and my entire body tingled.

Despite the familiar heat, the familiar voice, I jumped and turned. I couldn't see Killian very well in the dim moonlight, and it didn't help he was wearing all black. But the shadow on his face bathed in the dim light had me holding my breath at his dark beauty.

"You scared me," I whispered.

"You don't ever have to be scared of me," he murmured back, standing close, but not touching me.

I breathed heavily as we stood in silence. "What are you doing at my house in the middle of the night?" I asked finally.

His hand moved up to my bun and yanked the ponytail out softly so my curls tumbled around my shoulders. My heart pounded at his touch. "Needed to see you," he said simply.

I blinked at him. "You saw me," I pointed out softly. "This very day in fact." I paused, thinking of the fact it was past midnight. "Or yesterday, now."

"I didn't get to see nearly as much of you as I would have liked.

I've missed my little calculus student," he said softly.

I gazed at him. "Yeah, well, my grades have severely suffered from your absence," I whispered back, my eyes darting up to Mom's dark window, half expecting her to poke her head out and yell at me for being a terrible child. "Where have you been?" I asked when I was satisfied we were safe from discovery for the moment.

"Around," he replied cryptically. "You've got a beautiful voice, Freckles. Knew you liked music, didn't know you breathed it. That you owned it," he murmured.

Heat crept up my neck. People had complimented me on my voice before, many times. Not being arrogant or anything, it was a fact. But Killian saying it was somehow different; I treasured his compliment.

"Thanks," I whispered shyly, looking at my flip-flops.

His hand went to my chin, tilting it up. "Seriously, Freckles, you're destined for something great with talent like that. The world's gonna be a much richer place when it hears that beautiful voice," he told me in a rough voice.

I stared at his eyes, feeling like I could see them clear as day, despite the hazy moonlight.

"Your band, that's Wyatt, Noah, and Sam?" he questioned.

I nodded against the hand that was still at my chin.

He was silent for a long moment.

"Any of them hit on you?" he asked in a hard voice.

I blinked and couldn't help it; I laughed softly. "Dude, no. They're like my brothers," I informed him, screwing up my nose. I didn't want to let him know that Noah was gay. Noah had most likely not even admitted that to himself yet.

My chuckle died out at the meaning beyond his question and the hardness in his voice. The protectiveness.

"I doubt any red-blooded boy has fraternal feelings for you, " he informed me.

"I think you're so wrong on that score," I argued. I wasn't an ogre or anything, I knew that. But before whatever this was with Killian, I'd hardly ever had this kind of interaction with the opposite sex. Granted, Jordan was always flirting with me at school, but it was only because I was akin to a shiny new toy.

Killian's face lowered so I could feel his breath on my face.

Every inch of me froze, even my breath. My unquiet mind was suddenly silent.

"Trust me, being a red-blooded boy, I'm not wrong," he murmured.

We stayed like that, inches away from each other for the longest moment of my life.

I was certain he was going to kiss me. I wanted him to kiss me, more than anything in my entire life.

I felt his loss like a physical thing when he slowly pulled back.

He ran a finger through my curls. "Go back inside," he ordered hoarsely.

I stared at him. "I don't want to."

"Shit," he cursed under his breath. Then he was there, right there, his body taking up every inch of space around me, sucking up all the oxygen around me. His forehead rested against mine. "You need to go inside, Freckles," he whispered. "'Cause I'm not gonna be able to control myself for much longer. And I'll regret it. Hate myself for not being patient. For not waiting."

Then there was cold air where his warm body once was. I actually stumbled into the empty space.

"I'll see you at school on Monday," he promised.

Then, like a friggin' magician, he disappeared into the darkness.

I was guaranteed no sleep that night.

Chapter 6

ONE WEEK LATER

"Bye Mom! I'm going for a run," I called into the kitchen, putting my iPod on an armband.

Mom leaned against the doorjamb, eating a cookie and frowning. "I don't like you going running," she said in between bites. "It increases the possibility of you seeing a dead body. I don't want my baby scarred for life."

I looked at her. "I can't wait to hear the logic behind this one," I muttered. "How does me running equate to me coming into contact with a dead body?" I asked.

"Um, watch any crime show, baby doll. It's *always* the jogger that discovers the body," she told me as if I was slow for not making that connection. "Or the hiker," she added. "That's why we don't hike."

I raised a brow. "Oh, *that's* why? Not because you have the lung capacity of a ninety-year-old woman?" I asked sweetly.

She scowled at me.

I put my earbuds in my ear. "Good-bye, Mom."

"Just remember, if you see any stray body parts sticking out of bushes, do not investigate. Call the authorities," she shouted as I turned my back.

"Love you too," I replied, turning on my music.

I loved running. Exercise. Mom to this day cannot reason as to where this came from, or my preference to eat things such as fruit and vegetables. Most of the stuff Mom cooked came out of a package, and almost everything she ate was artificially flavored. I had no idea how she still looked as amazing as she did. I enjoyed exercise, no matter the fact my mom couldn't fathom that. I had a creative mind, one that was constantly on. It was only quiet when I was playing music, reading, or more recently, with Killian.

It was never silent while I ran, but pushing myself, feeling the burn in my limbs, somehow helped me to catalogue my wayward thoughts.

And wayward they were. It had been an amazing, crazy, and busy week. The night Killian visited me in the backyard was the night I got no sleep. Instead, I lay on my bed for what felt like hours, my headphones in, replaying every second of the small interlude in my head. I had had butterflies the entire rest of the weekend. I didn't tell my mom, for obvious reasons. And I felt guilty. Incredibly guilty for keeping such a big secret from her. My feelings and thoughts had taken up so much of my mind it was like they had become me. I was hiding a part of myself from my mom.

"What are you thinking about so intently, doll?" Mom asked me on Sunday night.

I jerked up. "Nothing," I said quickly, hoping my face didn't betray me. "Just homework stuff, band stuff," I lied.

She stared at me for long moments, as if trying to use her mom powers to read my mind. I did my best to look innocent.

"Don't stress too much about homework, baby doll," she said finally. "Life is far too short for that, and you're naturally intelligent; you get it from me. Plus, I need you here for emotional support while watching *The Walking Dead*," she added seriously, her eyes moving to the opening credits.

I let out a breath through pursed lips, feeling like I'd dodged some sort of bullet.

It was a pretty surreal and somehow terrifying moment when I realized that this, right here, was the moment I stopped telling my mom everything. That there was a piece of news, a piece of me that I couldn't—that I didn't want to share with her. I suppose every teenage girl had such moments, most likely before they were my age. I guessed a lot of them didn't think twice about keeping secrets from their mom. But it was different for me. She wasn't just a mom; she was my best friend. I was scared that this was something my mom wasn't a part of, somehow it was a grown up part of me, although most adults would dismiss what Killian and I had as not "real love." I knew better. With a certainty that came from ignorance I guessed, but a certainty nonetheless.

Monday at school, I was a wreck. Nerves chewed at my stomach and I'd gotten up at six for a run to attempt to quiet my mind. Then I spent an ungodly amount of time, even for someone raised by my mom, on my outfit choice.

It was another first for me, dressing to impress someone. I never did that. I dressed for myself, not to follow trends or pretend to be something I wasn't. Mom and I never had much money to spend on clothes, but that never stopped us. Mom was an expert at vintage shopping and getting bargains. I didn't think she intended on introducing me to boho/hippy style, but she never once told me I couldn't wear anything. She always let me be who I was.

I had experimented with looks, what teenager hadn't? But I'd never felt the crisis of identity that I read came with adolescence. I'd always known exactly who I was and was comfortable with that. I knew that had a lot to do with having a slightly crazy but amazingly supportive mom. She let me discover who to be and indulged my passion for music and books, even when she didn't understand it. I knew she scrimped and saved to get my guitar lessons before I had started teaching myself.

But that morning, I had tried on every item in my wardrobe with

Killian in mind. In the end, I put on khaki green, tight combat pants. They were way low slung, and I had to lie on the bed holding my breath to do them up. I had paired them with a white racerback tank, knotted at the front to show off a teeny bit of midriff. Not enough to raise school eyebrows or my mom's—I doubted that would be possible anyway. Then I slung multiple necklaces around my neck and tamed my wild curls so they tumbled down past my bra strap. I wanted to look effortless, but still hot.

I frowned at the freckles dusting my nose, then remembered Killian's name for them. I decided against covering them up with any makeup and just went for glossy pink lips and a swipe of mascara.

Of course, the no-makeup look took way longer than it was meant to, so I was subjected to Mom pounding on my door threatening murder and dismemberment if I made her miss Shelly coffee. We had discovered it the first day we arrived in Amber and Mom had proposed to Shelly, the maker of said coffee, that very day; it was that good.

Since I'd been up for hours, I'd already had two cups. Coffee was serious for Mom and me; we needed it.

I hustled out. "Sorry, sorry," I chanted, stuffing books in my embroidered backpack.

"Wow," Mom exclaimed, her eyes glancing down my body. "Oh to be young again and pull off things like belly-baring outfits and pants like that," she mused, her eyes dreamy.

See? No judgment. I would have to be wearing hot pants and a sequined bra to cause any disapproval.

I rolled my eyes. "You borrowed these pants last month," I reminded her.

She tilted her head, remembering. "Oh yeah. I did look good in them too."

"Don't ask me how you're the same size as me with the eating habits of a prize bull, but you are. I guess it bodes well for my future," I said, grabbing my lunch from the fridge.

Mom hustled me out of the house. "It will bode even better for your future if you hurry up so your mother can get caffeine into her ageless body before she expires."

I was not joking about the coffee.

She dropped me off and I spent the first few periods barely listening, barely taking anything in; my thoughts were on seeing Killian again. So I had wandered aimlessly into the cafeteria, trying to casually scan it for him.

"Hey, Freckles," a voice sounded from behind me.

I swallowed and turned slowly, my eyes meeting Killian's for a split second before his traveled down my body. I watched in amazement as they darkened. My belly fluttered at the way his gaze was a physical touch.

"Hey," I breathed.

I was totally happy about every moment spent over my outfit today. Killian returned his gaze to my face and his muscled arm moved up to lightly tug on my curl.

"Like your hair down," he murmured quietly.

The flutter in my stomach intensified so much I could almost feel it in my throat. The way he touched me, so casually, was intoxicating. I wanted more. I wanted to kiss him, almost more than my next breath.

"Lex!" a voice shouted.

I jumped as the roar of the cafeteria returned. I moved my gaze to see Sam waving me over to a table with him, Noah, and Wyatt. I chewed my lip.

Killian glanced in their direction, his eyes blank.

"We don't have to sit with them," I said quickly, though my heart dropped at the thought of my boys and my... whatever Killian was, not being able to coexist. I wanted deeply for them to get along.

I felt his hand on the small of my back and the area tingled. "No, Freckles. They're your friends. I'm not taking you away from them." He glanced at me as we walked over. "As much as I want you all to myself," he added darkly.

I swallowed visibly and blinked at him, trusting him not to guide me into any tables, considering I couldn't take my eyes off him.

"Hey, Kill," Sam greeted enthusiastically, standing to do some weird boy-fist-handshake thing.

Killian obliged. "Sam," he muttered back.

He lifted his head to Noah and Wyatt. Wyatt grinned at him. Noah regarded him more levelly but responded to the greeting.

We all sat and I was afraid of a yawing silence as the boys had some sort of stare down. I didn't know why I was afraid when Sam was around; he launched into an epic conversation the moment we sat down. Killian was friendly, engaging with all of them, and I spent most of the time soaking it all in. I had watched Killian at school. He seemed like a loner and didn't even register the existence of most people at school, though I'd seen him glare at Jordan a couple of times. He was distant, almost broody with everyone but me. And even with me, he liked it when I did most of the talking. But he showed another side of himself, making an effort with all of the boys, even Noah, who was bordering on downright rude. I especially liked the way he sat so close to me, close enough our thighs touched, and every now and then he'd brush a curl out of my face.

The bell rang and I was reluctant to be out of his presence. I was ecstatic, floating on cloud nine at the fact things were so easy, so natural with everyone.

"We've got English Lit, Lex," Noah declared, standing and staring at Killian.

"Bro, aren't you in my Biology class?" Wyatt asked Killian as they stood too. Wyatt was the same age as me, but he was seriously good at biology. By the sounds of it, he could be a doctor if he wanted. But he wanted to be a rock star, much to his parent's dismay.

Killian nodded, rising at the same time as I did, handing me my backpack.

"Thought so. I've seen you there a couple of times," Wyatt replied. "Should we head? I know Morton's damn near homicidal every time I turn up late," he said, frowning.

I was staring at Killian with narrowed eyes at the "couple of times," part of Wyatt's statement. I didn't have any classes with Killian, considering he was the grade above me. But I didn't like the idea that he cut classes. He was smart. I knew that he could easily get a scholarship to any college he wanted.

"Lex. English Lit," Noah reminded me sharply.

My eyes cut to him. "Yeah, Noah, I haven't forgotten."

"See you later, Freckles?" Killian murmured, his eyes on mine.

"Dude, we're going to cruise the music stores after school. Daddy needs a new bass," Sam cut in. "Come with," he invited.

"Rain check," Killian replied. "Got work."

Sam's face fell. "Well, that blows."

Killian shrugged. "It's not too bad." He moved his attention to me. "Bye," he said softly.

"Bye," I muttered.

He looked at me a beat longer then left with Wyatt, Sam trailing them.

I scowled at Noah as we walked in the opposite direction. "What was that?" I snapped.

Noah had the guile to look innocent. "What?"

"You doing your best impression of the ice queen Elsa," I retorted. "What's the deal? Do you not like Kill or something?" I asked, feeling crestfallen. Noah was my friend. The thought of him not liking Killian was painful.

His face hardened. "I don't know him well enough to like or dislike him."

I frowned at him as we walked into our English class. "Well, you could have a career in politics with answers like that," I said dryly, unpacking my books and placing them on the desk with a little more force than necessary. "I like him, Noah. I want you to like him too," I added softly.

Noah sat down, sighing. "I want to like him too, Lexie. But I also don't want you getting hurt."

I turned to him. "What makes you think Killian will hurt me?"

"I don't know," he hedged. His eyes turned from the front of the class and he lowered his voice as the teacher started talking. "He might not hang around anyone at school, his friends are bikers," he whispered, "but that doesn't mean he hasn't spent time with certain members of the female class."

My face must have paled as I felt the blood leave it rapidly.

Noah's hand moved on top of mine in a comforting gesture. "I'm not saying that to hurt you, Lex," he whispered quickly. "He's never been with... anyone like he is with you. But I'm protective of you. No matter how much Sam chats to him, so is he, and Wyatt. He'll need that entire biker gang he hangs around with if he does hurt you," he warned ominously.

I didn't get to say anything back as we earned a throat clearing and pointed look from the teacher.

Noah's face moved to the front of the class, and I continued to stare at his profile. There were many things to think of on what he just said. I felt sick thinking about Killian with other girls. Stupid, I know. He was hot and a teenage guy. Of course he'd dated before. Not everyone was like me and hadn't even been kissed at sixteen.

Hardly anyone was like me, I guessed.

It wasn't that that gave me the most pause. It was the way Noah's face had changed when he warned me about Killian hurting me. He was quiet and mild mannered. He may have had muscles, but I had never even seen an inkling of violence on my gentle friend. Until then.

I prayed I didn't see any more of the violence that hid beneath his eyes.

••••

It was a happy accident on Friday that I was walking into the school parking lot the moment a motorcycle roared in. Skipping may have been more of an appropriate description of what I was doing since I felt like I was floating around the school for the past week. How could I not be when I had lunch with Killian every single day so far. Sometimes we ate with the boys, but a couple of times he had directed me out onto the quad with a chin lift to the boys who gave me knowing winks. We had talked about everything and nothing those times. Sometimes he helped me with homework, but mostly we chatted about our favorite books, movies, and music, and got to know each other. The more I got to know him, the more I liked him. *Liked* him. So much so that I didn't think there was a moment of my day that he wasn't in my mind.

I stopped my journey to Wyatt's car and watched as Killian's bike rode toward me and pulled up beside me. I turned my body his way but stayed rooted in the spot as he dismounted, his eyes on me.

I couldn't help but drink him in, even though I was frowning at him. He was wearing his motorcycle jacket, which he basically lived in. A tight, white tee was underneath, hinting at the muscles I had only imagined seeing and touching. I bet any jeans label would pay millions to have Killian model the pair he was wearing, faded, not in the artificial way, but through wear. Black motorcycle boots stopped inches away from my fringed ankle boots.

I moved my gaze to meet his ice blue eyes. They were worried.

"Where are you going, Freckles?" he asked. "You sick?" His gaze ran over my face, looking for signs of illness, his hand going to my elbow.

I wanted to be touched by his concern. I was, a teeny bit, I could also feel myself getting annoyed. "I'm fine," I replied tersely. "Where have you been?"

"Where you going then, you cutting?" He smirked, ignoring my question. "My little Freckles would never break the rules, not without me at least," he teased.

I ignored the butterflies at getting called his. "I'm getting Sam's stuff he forgot. It's my study period and we were going to stay after school and use the auditorium for acoustics." We were braving Mr. Hazelton's wrath to do so. I usually hated breaking any kind of rules, but we had our music teacher's explicit permission, after he heard us play. He'd promised to brave Mr. Hazelton himself if need be. I had a feeling Mr. Hazelton wasn't well liked within the faculty.

"Are you only just getting here? It's almost lunch, if that great ball of fire in the middle of the sky hadn't already told you that." I pointed to the sky.

Killian grinned. "I'm aware of the great ball of fire and its position in the sky communicating time."

I didn't grin. "That means you're late."

"If it's almost lunch, I'm just on time," he countered, his eyes turning intense.

I stared at him, something stirring in my belly for some reason.

"Three periods come before lunch," I reminded him.

"Yeah, they're not important. Lunch is," he said, his voice hoarse.

My fingers tingled. "Lunch," I whispered, realization dawning.

Killian nodded. "Yeah. Lunch. With you."

I swallowed. "Where have you been this morning?"

He shrugged, looking sideways a moment. "At the garage.

They're short. Need an extra hand. I'm helping them out."

Without even thinking about it, I lifted my hand and turned Killian's chin so he faced me. "But you have school," I reminded him. "What about your classes?"

Killian's eyes blazed into mine. "What about them, Freckles?"

I dropped my hand quickly, registering that was the first time I'd touched him of my own accord. I hadn't worked up the confidence to do it yet. Apparently irritation helped.

Killian didn't let my arm fall to my side, as was my intention. He grasped it and linked my fingers with his.

"You need to go to them in order to graduate high school," I whispered, trying not to be distracted by his large hands engulfing mine.

He shrugged again.

I frowned. "Killian, you need to graduate high school, so you can go to a good college." I hated sounding more like a mom than my actual mom ever did.

Killian's eyes went blank and he dropped my hand. "You think I've got a chance at college, Lexie?" he asked in a flat voice.

"Yes," I replied firmly. "I do."

He shook his head. "That makes one of us," he muttered, glancing at his feet. "Guys like me, we don't belong in college. I'm only wasting my time here." He nodded at the building in front of us. "But Steg insists I do it if I wanna prospect. That place doesn't hold a future for me." He paused. "Well, at least it didn't."

There was a long, beautiful moment of silence as I realized his meaning. I couldn't address that now, though.

"You can be anything you want to be. You're smart. Really smart. You could be a frigging astronaut if you wanted," I exclaimed.

Kill grinned. "Got no desire to travel into space and see the stars up close, Freckles. I can see the only one that matters right here." He stepped forward so our bodies brushed together.

I gazed at him, my entire body going jelly at the proximity and the electricity between us. I blinked rapidly. "Don't do that," I snapped. "Don't distract me when I'm trying to have a serious conversation."

"I'm being dead serious, Lexie." His eyes were blazing.

I let the warmth of those words settle around me. "You can be anything you want to be, Kill. You might not have a mom who tells you that, but you can," I whispered.

His eyes hardened the moment I mentioned his mom. "The only thing I've ever wanted to be was a patched member of the Sons," he informed me. "Don't need a high school diploma for that."

I bit my lip, feeling profoundly sad that he was potentially throwing his future away for this club. It wasn't my place to judge. They were his family, and Zane was part of it. It wasn't my place to judge what was and wasn't suited for his future. If I really thought about it, I technically didn't know him that well. On the other hand, it was like I'd known him forever. Or as forever as I could fathom. It just got to me the way he talked about himself as... less. The way he dismissed himself.

"What if you change your mind?" I pressed softly. "What if you decide you want to get out of Amber? See the world?"

He searched my eyes. "I won't change my mind," he replied firmly. "You don't have to get on a plane to see the world, Freckles. Shit I've seen in my life, I know plenty about the world. Enough to know what I want from it." He stepped forward to clasp our hands together once more. "The only thing I've ever wanted was my bike, that cut, and the freedom that came with that. It's a short list, never thought it'd grow." He squeezed my hand. "Stand corrected, Lexie." His voice was almost a whisper, his mouth so close to mine I could feel his breath. He was going to kiss me. Finally. After all those almost kisses, after weeks of confusion and desperation, it was going to happen.

I even leaned forward slightly, preparing myself, my entire body pulsing from the realization. Then the bell rang, shocking me backward and Kill's eyes moved behind me, to where people would be filtering out onto the quad no doubt.

"Let's get Sam's shit. It's time for lunch," he declared, stepping back.

I let out a breath. That was the only time I'd actually dreaded the lunch bell. I was starting to think Kill and I would never actually kiss. We'd be stuck in this weird almost relationship limbo forever.

Chapter 7

My mind had wandered so far it took me a moment to realize my body had done the same. I stopped to catch my breath on a corner and looked around me. The neighborhood was foreign. Amber wasn't really big enough to have nice and bad parts of town. There were definitely streets with impressive houses, but no mansions or gated communities were around here. Our neighborhood was mostly full of family homes, apart from Zane's. And although they might not have been mansions, people took care of their homes. Took pride in them.

The houses around here didn't show that. Some looked like the residents took a passing interest in lawn maintenance; others looked like overgrown jungles. Paint chipped off most houses, as with the one in front of me. The lawn was mowed, but it was yellowing and patchy.

I guessed the house had been white at some point, but the weatherboard was faded to gray in some places and completely peeling off in others. There was a closed off garage, which was in a similar state of disrepair, but that wasn't what caught my attention. It was the motorcycle in the garage. It was familiar. I would know it anywhere.

My heart sank and soared at the same time. I knew who this debilitated house belonged to.

Out of the corner of my eye, I saw movement. I turned my attention to the front door, which had a very familiar, leather-clad body leaving it. Though I couldn't hear the slam, I watched the force behind Killian's body as he yanked it closed and then stormed down the cracked pavement toward his bike. Something must have told him he was being watched because his stormy gaze landed on me and he froze. Literally right on the spot.

I did the same. This was because of the purplish black shadowing underneath his eye and the bleeding cut on his cheek, which hadn't been there yesterday. Worry and anger, pure anger, bubbled inside me at the sight of it. I felt a distinct urge to know who inflicted violence on his beautiful face and a need to extract some sort of revenge on them.

Killian seemed to shake himself out of his paralysis and moved his stride toward me. I didn't move, didn't even take my earbuds out as he got closer. I merely stared at the bruise on his eye.

When he finally got to me, his gaze slowly went up and down my body. I realized I was not only sweating but wearing bright pink running shoes, bright pink short shorts, and a tight, white tank. I probably looked ridiculous and I guessed my face matched the color of my shorts.

His hands reached up to pull my headphones from my ears. "What are you doing here, Freckles?" he asked, his jaw hard.

"What happened to your face?" I replied, not caring about how terrible I most likely looked.

His eyes turned blank. He stepped back slightly. "Nothing."

"That's not nothing," I argued. "That's something. Someone hit you." My voice was small, quivering with anger.

"I'm fine. You should see the other guy," he told me, his tone didn't match the cliché joke. He was so far from laughing, or even smiling. This entire version of him was foreign to me. "What are you doing here? At my house. You shouldn't be here," he continued in the same foreign voice.

I felt myself redden more. "I was out running," I said, pointing out the obvious. "I wasn't paying attention as to where I was going. I had no idea this was your house." I glanced at it. "Until now," I continued, meeting his eyes.

"You should pay better attention." His voice was almost a growl. "You definitely shouldn't be running around this neighborhood, especially like that." His gaze flickered down to my legs for a moment. "You shouldn't be here. A girl like you doesn't belong here."

I blinked a couple of times to catch up with everything he was saying, to try to understand the coldness in his voice. "But you're here," I pointed out. "It can't be that bad." I tried to make my voice light.

My words had the opposite effect. He laughed without humor. The harshness of the sound almost made my body jerk. "You have no idea what you're talking about," he snapped. "Go home. Now, Lexie," he ordered.

I flinched at the way he was addressing me; it was so unlike him. My eyes flickered to the house once more and something clicked. He was embarrassed. Embarrassed for whatever reason that he lived here, as if there was a reason to be. And hot, broody boys like Killian weren't supposed to be embarrassed, so he was going for cruel instead.

I stepped forward, frowning at his head in concern. "Okay, I'll go home, but only if you come with me. Tell me what happened to your face, let me make sure it's okay. Patch up the cut," I said, my voice soft.

Killian stepped back, away from me. "You're going home. I'm sure as shit not coming. I've got places to be, Lexie. Stop trying to venture into stuff you don't understand. Go where you don't belong," he said in a cold voice.

"Where I don't belong," I repeated in a hurt voice. "You mean with you," I said slowly, my stomach sinking.

Killian nodded once. "That's exactly what I mean. A girl that wears that much pink, is that bright, does not need to be tarnished with my black," he said. "So go," he commanded.

I stood tall, not giving in to the urge to run, to let the tears at the back of my eyes fall at the harsh words. "No," I replied firmly. "You don't get to tell me where I do and don't belong. I'm not going anywhere."

Killian stared at me for a long moment, his face blank. "Fine," he said finally. "I'll go."

Then he turned on his heel and strode to his bike, mounting it and roaring off. I could only stare at him. He didn't even glance my way.

•••

"You sure you don't want to come with us, babe?" Wyatt asked after we'd finished our practice session.

I nodded. "More than sure. Mom and I have plans." Plans with a lot of junk food and trashy movies.

"Yeah, but it's Saturday night," Sam cut in. "Your mom's effing awesome, don't get me wrong, but this party will be sick."

I laughed. "I'm sure it will be, but parties aren't exactly my scene."

Sam looked utterly confused at this concept. "Parties are *everyone's* scene," he exclaimed. "You've got drinks." He held up a finger like he was preparing to list the qualities. "More than often, no parents," he said holding a second finger up. "Girls, music, and drinks," he continued, holding up four fingers. "What's not to love?"

Noah pushed his shoulder. "Bro, think of the girls you encounter at those parties, then think of Lexie," he instructed. "You think she has anything in common with them?"

Sam scrunched up his nose for a moment. "Other than the fact she's hot? I guess not."

Noah nodded and his gaze moved to me. "Don't worry, babe, that's a compliment. I'm not going to waste brain cells by going to that party either."

Sam's face fell. "What? You're not coming?" He turned to Wyatt. "Bro, please tell me the world makes sense and you're coming?" he pleaded.

Wyatt grinned. "Of course I'm coming."

Sam looked to the heavens. "Thank you," he whispered.

I looked to Noah. "If you're not going to this fabulous sounding party, want to come to movie night with me and Mom?" I asked. "I can promise a lot of sugar, a lot of C grade action movies, and almost constant commenting on said action films."

Noah grinned. "Sounds like fun, I'm in."

I beamed back. Noah was the quietest of them all and I worried about him. Even though he hadn't told me I was now certain he was gay. I was certain that no one knew. I also knew he had a hard home life. His mom ran out when he was a kid and his dad was no peach. If he was any fruit, he'd be rotten to the core, judging by the black eye that had only just faded on Noah's attractive face.

He'd shrugged it off when I expressed horror, but the boys had hard faces. Sam didn't have a grin anywhere in sight when he'd turned to me.

"Noah's dad's a fucking asshole," he'd clipped quietly in my ear.

Needless to say, I wanted to give Noah as many chances of staying out of his place as he could. And I genuinely liked spending time with him. Loved it in fact. I loved all of these boys. Already.

"We on for another practice tomorrow, Lex?" Sam asked.

"Yeah, I'm completely down," I replied, leaning against the sofa. Anything that would let me escape into the vortex that music offered me was welcome. Anything that helped me forget what happened this morning, that stopped the tears that seemed to be constantly at the back of my eyes.

I glanced to the boys. "As long as you don't have any other plans?" I added, noting we had spent ungodly amounts of time together.

"Like what?" Sam asked.

"Like working on that English Lit paper that's due Monday?"

Sam's eyes widened. "Homework? On a Sunday?" he declared in disgust. "No. As long as I have time to sleep off tonight's beers, I'm in. How about we grab lunch at The Point?"

The Point was one of the few grills in town. Lots of kids from school hung out there. It had great burgers.

"Sounds great," I said, smiling.

"Righteous." Sam grinned, hoisting his rucksack on his shoulder.

I walked with them to the curb, making plans for tomorrow and telling Noah what time to come over.

"Have fun tonight," I told them with a grin. "Don't do anything I wouldn't do."

Sam laughed. "Can't promise that, Lex, but I'll promise to have fun." He winked and got into the car.

Wyatt leaned in to give me a hug.

"Take care of him," I instructed in his ear.

Wyatt grinned at me. "Always do."

"See you tonight, Noe," I said to Noah.

He gave me a chin lift and all the boys folded into the car, tooting the horn as they sped off.

I smiled after them and my gaze moved across the street. I beamed at the open garage door and the huge form I could see in it.

"Zane!" I called out and jogged over.

I hadn't seen Zane around in what felt like ages and I needed to commence my matchmaking activities between him and Mom. I hadn't even heard how the cake went. It was that and I actually liked Zane. It seemed I forged instant connections with everyone in this town. The boys, Killian, and Zane.

"Hey, Zane," I greeted when I made it to his garage where he was working on his bike. It was a cool bike. I didn't know much but I knew it was a Harley and was pretty badass.

"Lex," he grunted out, nodding at me.

Most people would probably be put off at his monosyllabic greeting, but I didn't miss the slight softness at the edge of his eyes.

"I hope the noise didn't disturb you. We put soundproofing up, as not to brass off the neighbors, but I'm not sure how effective it is," I explained. I chewed my lip, hoping if he did hear us that he didn't think we were a complete mess. His opinion meant a lot to me. "Mom can still hear us from the kitchen," I continued. "I know because she texted me a draft of my Grammy acceptance speech." I met Zane's eyes, realizing how arrogant that sounded. "As a joke," I added quickly. "We're just a high school band. We aren't even that good yet, but Mom's delusions have us set for stardom."

Zane stared at me for a moment, his face blank. "A band?" he clipped, zeroing in on one statement.

Mental forehead slap. I'd been babbling about the band and he knew nothing about it. I nodded quickly, moving to touch one of the handlebars on his bike. It was the first time I'd even touched a motorcycle.

"Yeah, you see those guys leaving before?" I asked, referring to the boys.

Zane nodded curtly.

"That's my band," I exclaimed with a grin. I frowned when I realized I could only call them "my band" as of yet. "We still have to think of a name. It's kind of a sticking point between the guys," I explained, thinking of the few arguments Noah and I already had to mediate. I shrugged. "Creative minds and all that."

Zane didn't answer, but that didn't worry me. I wandered around his sparse garage, looking for something that would tell me more about him.

"You should come and listen to us once we get a little better," I offered, thinking of my matchmaking mission. I could even see if I could con him into staying for dinner. A dinner that I cooked, not Mom. I actually wanted him to like her, and her cooking would not make him like her. It may poison him. I reconsidered this. "Or maybe when we get our first gig," I added, thinking that might be safer. My eyes caught something that sparked my excitement. "Hey!" I exclaimed. "I didn't know you played!" I grinned at an old Fender case resting in a corner, gathering dust, which was sad considering what a great instrument it was.

There was a long pause. "Long time ago," Zane explained, his voice rough.

I turned to regard his blank face. I caught a glimpse of something in his eyes. Something I didn't understand but I recognized.

Pain.

I smiled at him. "You should come and play with me some time," I offered shyly. Music helped cure me of whatever pain I'd had in the past. Granted, nothing bad had ever really happened to me. Something had happened to Zane. I couldn't even think of what since my life didn't give me anything to measure that look in his eyes up to, but I guessed it was bad. I thought of something else. "Maybe you could even teach me some things," I mumbled, brushing some of the dust off the case. "Mom couldn't afford to get me regular lessons, especially after she bought me my guitar, so I've mostly taught myself." Then I realized what that sounded like. "YouTube's great," I added quickly. My eyes cut to him. "But it would be cool to learn off a real, live human being."

It would be more than cool. I'd get to spend time with Zane, and maybe get to know him enough to help him realize how awesome my mom was. I wasn't completely selfless; I enjoyed Zane's company. He was part of Killian's family too, a part of the Sons of

Templar. My stomach dropped thinking of that, of Killian. The boy who most likely didn't want to know me anymore.

"Yeah, kid, all right. Maybe," he answered, focusing his eyes back on the bike.

I grinned, full on beamed, inside and out. The heaviness in my stomach thinking of Killian was momentarily forgotten.

"Really?" I asked. "That is aces, Zane! I'm free, you know, whenever. Well, apart from when I'm obviously at school. But anytime after that. Seriously. Whenever suits you." Excitement made my voice speed up to how I talked with Mom. No regular people could normally understand me when I got like this.

Zane must have understood at least some of it because he nodded again.

I didn't mind that he didn't answer; I liked it actually. I wandered over to the space where he was sitting by his bike, looking at it for a second before sitting on the cold concrete.

Zane's blank gaze flickered in surprise before he masked it.

"You mind if I sit here and watch for a while?" I asked, my voice quiet and no longer filled with excitement. "Sometimes I just need a bit of quiet after the music makes up all the noise in my head."

I needed quiet more than anything at this moment. I needed the silence that Zane's presence offered. Thinking of Killian was not something I wanted to do.

Zane nodded silently once more, turning his attention to his bike. I sagged in relief at the fact he didn't tell me to go away. I didn't think too many big and scary bikers really liked hanging around with stupid teenage girls, but Zane was different. I knew that.

It was nice, welcome, the time I spent watching him tinker with his bike. I wondered if this was what other girls did with their dad's, sat with them while they did something, comfortable in silence.

I yearned for something like that, something I knew I'd never have. But Zane gave it to me, for that short amount of time.

Once I reasoned he'd be sick of me watching him, I stood to leave, loathe to let the noise back in, but knowing it was inevitable.

"Heard you," he stated, breaking the silence. His blank face met mine. "The band, you're good."

I beamed at him and felt the warmth of his words all the way home. It lasted a while, but not long enough.

Killian invaded my mind the moment I found myself back in my room and didn't leave the entire night Mom and Noah argued over which action stars would win in a death match.

I was afraid he'd never leave my mind. I'd be haunted forever.

The only way to quiet my mind was to write after the movies had finished and Noah had left.

Chapter 8

"Lexie, can I talk to you a second?" a sickly sweet voice asked.

I paused, counted to five, and took a deep breath. "Sure, Stacy," I said, closing my locker so I could see her face. "What's up?"

She tightened her ponytail and bit her pink, glossed lip. "It's kind of... awkward," she began with false nervousness. "It's about Killian. You're with him, right?" she asked with a light tone, conversational. Only I knew every word she was saying was carefully chosen.

My stomach dropped at her question. I didn't miss the glances and not so subtle barbs she threw my way when she could and the way her eyes followed Killian from across the cafeteria. I really didn't want to give her the satisfaction of knowing that after this weekend I didn't think we were anything. I didn't want to admit it to myself either.

"What about Killian?" I asked instead, my hands tightening around my books.

She moved her wedged heel closer to me slightly, her eyes darting around as if she was divulging national secrets. "Well," she started, her voice only slightly higher than a whisper, "I honestly normally wouldn't say anything, you know, poke my nose in where it doesn't belong."

I used all of my effort to hold in my snort of disbelief. Instead, I stayed silent.

"But, it kind of does belong, since I've had... *experience* with

Killian before." She looked me up and down. "Like I said, I wouldn't normally even go here, but you seem like a nice girl. I wouldn't want you to fall for Killian like so many other girls did and then get hurt when he kicks you to the curb."

I guessed *so many other girls* translated to her.

I couldn't restrain my irritation anymore. "Spit it out, Stacy," I snapped, surprised at the sharpness of my voice.

Stacy was obviously surprised as well because her head reared back slightly and she raised her eyebrows. The look of fake concern rippled on her face a moment, revealing the smugness underneath. "I just wanted to tell you, that as soon as Killian gets what he wants... you know"—she gave me a meaningful look—"you're dust. You become invisible. He's only after one thing."

She opened her mouth, no doubt to spout more false friendship and concern crap. I had no patience for it.

"Maybe he is only after one thing because you only give him one thing," I informed her. "Now I appreciate your concern. You're a true friend. But I've got to get to class."

I didn't even wait for my words to filter through her hairspray and into her brain. I pushed past her and stormed to my next class.

I was fuming. I had never talked to anyone like that before. Been outright rude. My mom might have been eccentric in her child-rearing methods, but she'd always taught me to be polite. She'd also taught me the importance of having a backbone. I wasn't going to let the resident bitch—every school had at least one—try to sabotage whatever there was with Killian.

If there was even anything.

Which, after the weekend, I doubted would be anyway.

That's where my mind was the entire morning, thoughts swirling around my head. Stacy's words were like slow-working poison. They had hurt at the start, but the logical part of my brain had shoved them aside as weapons of a woman scorned.

I was anything but rational when it came to Killian, I was discovering. So I chewed them over my entire history class. I may have had little to no experience when it came to boys, but I knew what Stacy was alluding to.

Sex.

I'd never had it, obviously. I'd never even been kissed. Not properly. A couple of sloppy and inexperienced boys didn't count. I knew the mechanics of it. And the specifics. My mom had me at fifteen; she gave me my first sex talk when I was twelve. She had urged me to be sure, to be absolutely sure for my first time. I was lectured on every kind of birth control on the market and Mom had insisted I come to her before I did anything. She'd also urged me to be celibate until I was thirty. That was something I knew wouldn't happen, but I hadn't considered it happening anytime soon. It didn't bother me; I didn't think about it like most girls my age did. I'd sometimes wonder idly about when my first time would be, but it was hard to give it specific thought when no boys showed interest in you.

Until now.

Killian hadn't even kissed me yet. He'd had opportunities. Plenty. But he hadn't. Why hadn't he? Did he not think of me that way?

The thought chilled my blood. I knew he thought of us more than friends, and I sure as heck did. I wanted to kiss him more than anything. I was desperate to touch him, have his arms around me. I wanted more than kissing. At some point. Way in the future.

I found myself in the hallway, on the way to the cafeteria without even really remembering most of the morning. I had functioned on autopilot, my mind running a thousand thoughts a second.

My step stuttered. The cafeteria. The possibility of Killian. Of seeing Stacy stare with satisfaction if he ignored me. I couldn't do it.

I turned on my heel with the intention of going to the nurse's office to fake some sort of bug when I almost collided with a tall body.

"Whoa, Lexie, you almost bowled me over," a voice joked, hands going to my upper shoulders to steady me.

"Sorry," I muttered, my eyes meeting Jordan's.

He shrugged. "No big. I've been hoping to run into you, just not literally," he said with twinkling eyes.

I smiled weakly, unable to muster up any effort to engage in witty banter.

"I'm going to beg, in fact," he continued, "for your help on this English lit paper. I'm seriously screwed. I'll get down on my knees if you want."

I couldn't help but grin genuinely. "Jordan, the English lit paper is due last period."

"I know. That's why I think the universe is showing me pity, putting you in my path. If you could sacrifice your lunch to help this poor shmuck, I'll be your slave for the rest of time," he said, eyes pleading.

I perked up. "Maybe the universe is looking out for both of us," I muttered, my eyes on the cafeteria doors.

"What?" Jordan asked, confused.

"Nothing," I said quickly. "The library's this way, in case you hadn't noticed." I pushed his large body away from the cafeteria.

Jordan's eyes brightened. "You'll help me?"

I nodded. "We'll help each other."

Jordan may have been grateful for our meeting, but I doubted he'd be as grateful as I was. I'd never been happier being someone's tutor.

••••

I made it through the rest of the day without somehow running into Killian or Stacy, a miracle I thanked the universe for. Unfortunately, the universe couldn't quiet my mind; I didn't escape thoughts of them.

This turned me cranky. I was never cranky. I was a happy person. I had a happy life. It was always full of laughter, music, and books. I was angry I was becoming the girl who was sitting in class, not listening while she brooded over a boy. A boy she barely knew. Who she hadn't even kissed.

"Lex, where were you at lunch?" Noah asked softly as we set our books down on our desks.

I sat down. "I was helping Jordan with his English paper," I replied, my eyes on the front of the class.

There was a pause, a long one. I moved my gaze to see Noah regarding me with one brow raised.

"Jordan," he repeated.

I nodded. "That's what I said."

"Since when are you and Jordan study buddies?"

"Since today," I snapped, moving my attention away from his knowing gaze.

"This wouldn't have anything to do with the fact we had to eat our lunch with a very silent and very broody Killian today, does it?" he asked casually.

My head snapped back to him. "You had lunch with Killian today?"

He nodded. "We all did. He was mighty curious as to where you were, considering Sam informed him you were, indeed, in the building. Curiosity quickly turned to concern when you didn't reply to any of our texts," he said. "I'm surprised he didn't arrange a search party or put out an announcement on the loudspeaker system."

I fumbled into my bag, looking for my forgotten phone. I wasn't someone who was glued to it. Its main use was for music. I hated texting and wasn't hugely keen on social media. Unbelievable for the generation I belonged to, I knew, but that was me.

"It's dead," I declared, looking at the blank screen.

"Phones away, Ms. Spencer," a brisk voice ordered.

I glanced to the front of the class. Mr. Lindon regarded me with a raised brow. I felt multiple eyes on me. "Sorry," I muttered, throwing the useless piece of technology into my backpack.

Noah squeezed my hand. "You okay? Do I need to get out my shotgun?"

I gave him a look out of the corner of my eye, waiting for the teacher's attention to go off me before I replied. "You don't have a shotgun."

"I'll find one if need be."

I patted his hand. "I'm fine," I reassured him quietly.

I could feel his disbelieving face out of the corner of my eye, but he didn't say anything more. Although, he doodled on a piece of paper, with "Shopping list" at the top. Underneath he wrote, "Shotgun."

When I glanced at it, I let out choked laughter, which earned me another disapproving look from the teacher, but it lifted my spirits.

●●●●

I stepped out into the warm sunshine, thinking I had somehow made it through the day, helped immensely by my friend.

"We'll meet you out front," Noah had told me before we parted ways for last period. "Since you went MIA at lunch, you weren't able to hear the news." He grinned. "That's bound to perk you up to your original level."

I hated surprises. "What news? Tell me now."

Noah shook his head. "Sam will kill me if I don't wait for all of us.

See you after school," he called, turning down a hall.

"Tell me now," I shouted after him, a couple of people giving me sideways looks.

Noah merely grinned at me over his shoulder and threw up a peace sign.

So I hadn't actually used all of my brainpower to think about Killian, only about 80 percent. The other twenty I wondered about the "news."

"Freckles." A voice beside me hampered my escape.

I felt his heat at my side and I gave myself a split second before I met his eyes.

"Kill," I greeted, my voice flat. My eyes immediately went to the fading bruise at his eye, and I had to ball my hands into fists to stop myself from reaching up to stroke it.

"I missed you at lunch," he said quietly, stepping closer to me.

I held my breath. It was an exquisite pain being this close to him with the cocktail of emotions simmering beneath my surface.

"You didn't reply to my texts either. No ones. I was worried."

I looked up at him. "My phone died."

Killian's brows furrowed as he gazed into my eyes. "Where were you?" he asked quietly.

I pursed my lips. I didn't want to tell him. He wasn't exactly Jordan's biggest fan. I didn't know how he would think about my tutoring services being extended his way. Then again, who cared what he thought? He was the one who'd been rude to me, who I hadn't heard from until today. Now I don't even get an apology. I opened my mouth, but someone beat me to it.

I felt pressure on my shoulders from behind me. "Just a reminder, I'm your slave for the rest of time," Jordan's voice sounded in my ear.

Killian's body went hard in front of me.

"Thank you for your excellent tutoring skills, Lexie Spencer,"

Jordan said. He obviously didn't notice the furious glint in Killian's eyes because he leaned in and kissed my cheek before winking at me and sauntering down the steps, followed by a group of people who waved and smiled at me.

Stacy did not wave, nor did she smile. Her gaze was locked on Killian and me. It was smug, considering Killian's jaw looked like it was going to shatter.

"Tutoring?" he gritted out, eyes on the back of Jordan's football jersey.

"You attempting to shoot laser beams out of those baby blues?" I joked.

Killian's eyes snapped back to me. "You were with him at lunch?"

I cocked my eyebrow up. "I wasn't aware it was illegal."

"He took you away from having lunch with me. He should be shot," he declared seriously. "He took away my chance at apologizing," he added in a softer voice.

Killian's dark gaze threatened to dissipate my bravado. I was in danger of melting at his feet. But I didn't. I couldn't. Though his gaze and his words made my heart pound, I was still pissed. Pissed at not just him and his over-the-top reaction to Jordan, but pissed at myself for letting him have such an effect on me.

I stepped back. "You don't possess my every lunch break, Killian. I'm sure I'm not the only girl you're having *lunch*"—I emphasized the word—"with. I've got to go." I turned and started down the steps, willing the boys to appear.

Killian caught up with me, firmly gripping my arm to stop me at the bottom of the steps by the curb. "What are you talking about, Lexie?" he growled, his brow furrowed.

I yanked my hand out of his grasp. "I know I'm not too hot at this." I nodded my head between us. "I'll admit I have terrible experience with boys. Terrible experience meaning no experience." I paused and took a breath. "I thought I was different, this was something different. Special," I whispered, glancing at my feet. I found my strength and looked back into his ice blue eyes. "I'm not going to be another girl on the assembly line."

His glare turned murderous. "Freckles, what are you talking about? This is—"

Luckily, the universe wasn't finishing intercepting emotional bullets for me because a car screeched up beside us on the curb.

"Get in, loser. We're going shopping," Sam called, hanging out the window with a grin. "You can come too, Kill, though it'll be a squeeze," he told Killian, not registering the body language between us.

I stepped fully away from him. "No, Killian won't be coming with us. He's busy," I said icily.

"Lexie—" His eyes darted to the car.

"Good-bye, Killian." I quickly opened the door before he could stop me.

I watched as Killian stared at the car as Wyatt sped off.

Noah frowned at me from across the seat. He opened his mouth to ask about that little scene, I was sure, but luckily Sam cut in.

"Did you tell her?" he shot at Noah, twisting around in his seat.

Noah dragged his gaze from me. "Since you threatened to stab me with your drumsticks if I did, no," he responded dryly.

I grinned despite myself.

Sam's excited gaze cut to me. "You are not going to believe what I have done for us," he exclaimed. "Seriously, you're going to want to marry me, have my children, name a statue after me—"

"Short version, Sam," Wyatt instructed, his voice teasing. I didn't miss the serious glint in his eyes as he glanced at me in the rearview mirror.

"Dude, this news needs an intro, for dramatic effect," Sam drawled. "Okay." He lifted his drumsticks and pounded them on the head of the seat. "We've got a gig!" he yelled after an appropriate amount of buildup.

I raised my brows. "A gig?"

Sam nodded rapidly. "Yes, because I am a god among men, I know people." He waggled his eyebrows.

"Technically, *I* know people," Wyatt cut in.

Sam glared at him. "You know them, but it's my terrific charisma that got people feeling like doing us a favor," he snapped. "People who know people who know people who own clubs. Clubs where record execs have been known to hang. A certain club that is willing to turn a blind eye to the fact we are a smidgeon under age."

"If you call five years a smidgeon," Noah added in.

Sam didn't respond, only gave him a glare before turning back to me, a smile immediately returning. "So tell me how much you love me."

I leaned forward and kissed his head. "I love you so very much, Sammy," I told him seriously. I did. Not only for the gig, which I was totally psyched about, but for distracting me from my pounding heart, sweaty palms, and buzzing mind.

His cheeks reddened slightly, but he grinned. "Yes, well, I'm sorry to break your heart, darlin', but I'm saving myself for all the groupies I'm bound to have. Probably a good thing we nip our affair in the bud right now. I'm quite fond of my face. I don't need Killian rearranging it. What's the deal with you two? You're boyfriend and girlfriend, right?" He spoke rapidly; I was impressed.

My stomach dropped at his question, and my mouth went dry as I searched for an explanation. I could feel both Noah and Wyatt's knowing eyes on me.

"Anyway, that's why we're going shopping," Sam continued, luckily not waiting for me to answer. "We, meaning me, need to construct our image," he declared.

"Your image?" I repeated.

Sam nodded.

I couldn't help it, I burst out laughing, the feeling warming up the body that had felt ice cold before.

"Okay, let's talk options," I said, rubbing my hands together.

Luckily, the rest of the ride was taken up with talk of wardrobe and set lists.

"Your mom gonna be okay with this, Lexie?" Sam asked as we got out of the car in Hope, the town over from Amber.

I thought a second. Would any parent be happy about their underage, teenage daughter playing in a club at 11:00 p.m. at night? "Yeah, she'll be fine," I told him. I didn't doubt it. Mom, more than anything, wanted to help me achieve my dream. She also knew I was the furthest from a rebellious teenager as you could get. She trusted me.

"What about your guys' folks?" I asked as we walked in the door of some rock vintage shop.

Sam snorted. "I'm sure my dad will give his complete approval from his position passed out drunk on the sofa," he said.

"I'll have to sweet talk them, but I'll be good," Wyatt added in.

"My dad will be glad to have me out of the house. I doubt he'll notice I'm gone," Noah muttered.

My heart fell that two of my boys had such rough home lives. I couldn't imagine not having a supportive parent.

I didn't know how it could be possible, but we had the most amazing afternoon, each doing our own fashion show with equally outrageous outfits.

I found myself thanking my stars. I might not have Killian, but I had my boys. I prayed I'd find a way to be okay with that.

••••

KILLIAN: Backyard

The text didn't wake me up. I was already wide awake. The afternoon with my boys had chased away the feelings dredged up by Stacy and Killian, but they all came hurtling in with the darkness.

I didn't even think. I threw the covers back and shoved my feet into sequined Ugg boots. I left my hair wild around my shoulders and didn't even put a jacket over my lacy tank. I was that eager to see him.

I didn't think of the shame or the guilt I felt sneaking out of the house without my mom's knowledge. I rushed down the stairs after closing the door quietly, aiming for the dark figure with his back to me.

"Kill, I—" I started to say the thing that I had come to realize moments ago.

I was cut off by Killian turning around and clutching the sides of my head, bringing his mouth down on mine. I was paralyzed for a split second, taken completely unaware by the feeling of his mouth on mine. Then I relaxed into his touch, his arms circling around me as his lips coaxed mine open. They opened automatically, letting him in, letting the fire explode in my body at being subjected to such an amazing kiss for my very first time.

I felt his loss the moment his lips left mine. He didn't move far away, resting his forehead on mine. I could only see the dim outline of his body in the darkness, but I felt his eyes on mine.

"I was going to wait," he murmured in a husky voice. "Wait till out first proper date to do that, till you were ready. But seeing that asshole putting his mouth on you today, I had to claim yours. To make sure it wasn't his touch that lingered on you. That I would be the only one kissing you for the near future."

I breathed into his mouth, my body still burning a thousand flames. His arms were tight around my hips and I drank in the feeling that came from this.

"Wow," I whispered in response.

"Just wow?" Killian asked. I could feel the smile in his voice as his hands flexed against my waist.

"Wow may be a small word but it encompasses a lot," I stuttered. "Give me a second," I whispered dreamily.

"I've got you in my arms. I'll give you a lifetime," he murmured back.

"Not helping," I told him.

He chuckled and I felt the vibration through my body.

"No one's ever kissed me before," I admitted finally.

A hand moved up to cup my jaw. "Know that, Freckles. I don't have much—a car I built up with my dad, my bike. Thought they were the most precious things I had in this world." He paused and brushed his lips against mine once more. "I was wrong. You giving me that, me having that, it's the most precious gift I've ever gotten. Mine."

I couldn't fathom all of this was happening right now. My stomach was a mess of butterflies, of joy, of fire.

"We need to talk about whatever that was today after school," he murmured, his arms still tight around me.

I stiffened at the reminder of that, of Stacy's words.

Killian didn't miss this. He didn't miss anything. His arms flexed around me and he leaned back to grasp my chin and face it toward him in the dim moonlight.

"Freckles," he probed.

I blinked up at the dark silhouette. "It was nothing. Silly," I said, hoping to dismiss the subject altogether.

"You were upset. So that's not nothing. That's never nothing," Killian argued.

I sighed, feeling warm and cold at the same time. His words, the sentiment behind them, warmed my heart, but the echoes of Stacy's words battled against that warmth.

Killian rubbed my arms, his hand leaving my chin to warm them, as if he sensed the battle inside my head. Inside my heart. He waited patiently for me to find the words, as if he had all the time in the world.

"Stacy just said some things about... what you wanted from me. About how it was something you took from other girls and then dropped them, forgot about them," I said, my words tumbling out in a rush. I hoped, if I said it quick enough, they wouldn't settle into the air like a weight.

Wishful thinking.

Killian's whole body went taut, and I could almost feel the change in his emotions; his fury was that physical.

"She said that?" he gritted out.

I nodded slowly. "Not those exact words, but that was the gist," I whispered.

Killian's hands moved from my arms to cup my face so his nose brushed mine and I could feel his breath on my lips.

"Someone that bitter, that empty, could never know what I want from you," he rasped, his voice hard and soft at the same time. "That I'd never take anything from you. I want to give you every-thing. The fuckin' world." He paused, breathing heavily. I, for one, wasn't breathing, his words like actual oxygen. "Nothing. *Nothing* would make me forget about you, Freckles," he promised fiercely.

We were silent for a long time, his head resting against mine, his words chasing away every single echo of doubt in my mind.

"Promise you'll never let ugly words make you forget that," Killian whispered.

"I promise," I whispered back.

Killian landed a featherlight kiss on my lips, electrifying my entire body with the small gesture.

"We've got more shit to talk about," Killian continued, like his words hadn't just rocked me to the core. "But we're not doing that in the middle of the night when you don't have a sweater on." His hands rubbed my arms.

"I'm not cold," I protested. I was burning hot. His arms were better than any sweater ever invented.

"Yeah, well, I don't want my girl getting sick," he said. "Plus, I don't want us sneaking around in the shadows. You need to be in the light, Freckles."

"Is that what I am?" I asked quietly. "Your girlfriend?"

Killian brushed hair from my forehead. "No, not until I take you on a proper date. One your mom knows about," he replied, staring at me.

I chewed my lip. "What, so we can't be boyfriend and girlfriend until you've formally asked my mom?" I asked, dumbfounded.

"Already consider you my girl, Freckles. Have since the moment I laid eyes on you. Want to take you on a proper date so your mom knows, so the world knows your mine. Only mine."

My heart thrashed against my chest with those words, with being in Killian's arms. Being his freaking girlfriend.

He bent his head to kiss me softly once more. I melted into him immediately. Too soon, he pulled back. "You need to go back inside," he murmured against my mouth, rubbing my arms. "Tomorrow we'll talk about today, about everything you said. And I'll give you a proper apology for Saturday, an explanation," he promised.

"You don't have to apologize," I said quickly. I feared he could burn down my house and, as long as he kissed me after, all would be forgiven. It was a dangerous thought.

Killian squeezed my arms. "I'm givin' you an apology. You deserve it. You didn't deserve that shit," he told me firmly.

He kissed my forehead. "Inside, Freckles," he ordered.

I stayed for a moment, staring at his dark form. "Thank you," I whispered.

"For what?"

"For giving me the most precious gift, the most perfect first kiss in the history of first kisses." And before I could feel exposed by hearing the words outside my head, I turned and rushed back into the house.

I was in danger of skipping into the house, but I was mindful of my sleeping, ignorant mother upstairs. At least I thought she was upstairs. As I danced quietly around my dark room, I peeked out onto the dark street and saw my mother's form exiting Zane's house and rushing across the street.

I gaped at what I was seeing, then quickly closed the blind.

"Holy crap," I whispered to myself.

Mom. Coming out of Zane's in the middle of the night. In her nightie.

I grinned.

Totally awesome.

I went to sleep with a smile on my face.

Chapter 9

I walked into the cafeteria more nervous than I had been any other day of my life it seemed. The memory of Killian's lips on mine was playing on a loop in my mind and my lips still tingled from his touch. I wanted to see him, badly. Another part of me didn't want to see him. Whatever we talked about today, however it went, it couldn't match up to the fantasies I'd built up in my mind.

"Lexie!" a male voice greeted me, just not the right one.

I turned. "Hey, Jordan," I said, hoping my disappointment wasn't visible.

He smiled warmly at me, rubbing the football he always seemed to have with him. Not a cliché or anything.

"So, when would you like me to commence duties of being your faithful servant?" he asked.

I laughed. "Your servitude is totally unnecessary. I was glad I could help."

He frowned. "Well, I just couldn't let you sacrifice your time without giving you something in return," he mused. "How about I buy you dinner and then we can talk about me potentially getting regular sessions with you? In exchange for weekly pizzas?" he asked with a hopeful glint in his eyes.

I paused. I didn't mind Jordan's company, much. He wasn't the type of person I'd chose to hang out with. Conversations with him were always surface, kind of like social chewing gum. You went through the motions, but in the end, you got nothing out of it. I didn't mind helping him out with his homework either. But I wasn't a complete dummy when it came to boys. I knew an ulterior motive when I saw one. I was the new girl, a novelty for boys in a small town. It didn't really have anything to do with my personality, for Jordan at least. Killian... well, I hoped with every part of me it was another story.

"You need a tutor, I suggest the yellow pages," a rumbling voice answered for me, much less diplomatically than I could.

Speak of the devil.

Jordan's smile dimmed as Killian stepped beside me, his arm purposefully going around my waist.

"Hey, Freckles," he murmured, his mouth brushing my hair.

"Hey," I whispered, locking eyes with him for a split second before his gaze turned hard and he directed it at Jordan, whose eyes were on Killian's hand.

He was not the only one fixated on that glorious limb. My mind buzzed with his casual touch, his show of affection and if I wasn't mistaken, possession. The kiss last night had signaled a pivotal shift.

"Sorry, dude, wasn't aware you spoke for Lexie," Jordan said. His tone had an edge that I didn't think he was capable of.

"She's quite capable of speaking for herself," Killian replied blandly. "But I'm just saving her the trouble. She'll be too busy to be tutoring jocks, considering she's got her band and school taking up her time, oh, and me," he said.

Jordan's eyes narrowed at Killian.

"Kill's right," I cut in, not wanting a brawl to start on my account. "He's just not very articulate or tactful." I gave him a pointed look. "I'm sorry, Jordan. I don't mind helping you out now and then. I just can't commit to regular sessions," I said, deciding to skirt around an outright no, especially since Killian was being so brutal.

Jordan's face turned soft and easy. "No problem. I can wait until you're... less busy," he said, a double meaning behind his words, reminiscent of Stacy's the previous day.

"Once he gets what he wants, you're invisible."

Killian's form tightened beside me. "Consider her busy for the remainder of your high school career, which may be long, consider you'll no doubt have to repeat eleventh grade."

And before Jordan could respond, Killian snatched my hand and walked us off.

"Sorry," I mouthed over my shoulder, feeling guilty for the slightly hurt and confused look on Jordan's face.

"Kill," I scolded, smacking his shoulder. "That wasn't nice."

"I'm not nice," he replied briskly.

"You're nice to me," I countered, only now realizing he was directing us out of the cafeteria and outside to the grassed area various students camped out on when the weather was nice. Or they wanted to smoke.

"You're the exception to the rule, Freckles," he murmured, squeezing my hand.

"You're nice to my boys," I argued as he led us away from second-hand smoke and rowdy groups of students.

"I'm civil to them," he corrected, shrugging off his jacket. His eyes met mine. "Again, because of the exception to my rule."

He laid the jacket down on the grass and gently pulled me down. My heart stuttered at the small but meaningful gesture.

I pursed my lips. "Was it necessary to be like that with Jordan?" I asked, sitting next to him and pulling my lunch out of my bag. I didn't have much interest in it, but I thought it might be good to have some sort of distraction for my hands. Hands that itched to run through Killian's hair, to return the easy affection that he was showing. I wasn't confident enough to commit to such affection. Yet.

"Yes," he replied, leaning back on his elbows.

I raised a brow, showing the fact I wouldn't accept a one-word answer. "He needs the tutoring, trust me."

Killian grinned. "I'm sure he does, Freckles. Just not from you."

I frowned at him. "I'm unsure if that's your decision to make." I paused for dramatic effect. "No wait, I'm certain that's not your decision to make."

To my surprise, Killian didn't seem irritated by my tone or accompanying glare. He merely leaned forward, shaking his head, and grasped my neck, leaning in to kiss it.

"As much as I wish it was my decision to make sure you aren't in the presence of jerks who have absolutely no interest in your tutoring skills, it's not. I'll just have to make sure you are more interested in spending time with me, and I can assure you I have no interest in your tutoring skills either." His hand flexed slightly at my neck at the same moment as my stomach flipped. "I'm interested in a whole lot more than one part of you. The entire whole, in fact," he murmured, his voice low. We exchanged an electrifying stare before he leaned back again. "That is, as long as you're not purely using me for my calculus tutoring skills," he added in a light tone.

I felt incomplete without him in my bubble. I focused on my lunch instead.

"Well," I hedged, with a small grin. "It's not just that," I conceded. "I'm also mighty interested in your hair-care routine."

Killian stared at me a beat then burst out laughing. I watched the beauty of him while actually laughing. I'd never seen that before. Sly grins, yes. Straight up laughing? No. And I was responsible for it.

He stopped, shaking his head. "Well, I'll have to keep that little gem close to my chest in order to stretch out our time together," he replied, chuckling.

I nodded. "You must," I agreed, forking my food into my mouth.

Killian's eyes went to my Tupperware container. "Freckles, what is that?" he asked, leaning forward and inspecting my lunch like a foreign insect.

I finished my mouthful self-consciously. "Lemon quinoa chicken salad with basil dressing," I answered, hoping none of that basil was currently residing in my teeth.

Killian's wide eyes returned to my face. "Quinoa?" he teased.

I jutted my jaw out. "It's the super food of the Aztecs," I defended my lunch choice.

Killian shook his head, chuckling. "Jesus," he muttered.

"It's good for you."

"It looks it," he agreed, but he made it sound like not a good thing.

I leaned forward, passing my container and fork to him. "You cannot express that much contempt for it without trying it," I declared.

He stared at the container and then me, not moving. "I trust your word, Freckles," he said, smiling.

I didn't reply, merely shook the container at him. Mom expressed the exact same opinion of my "healthy habits." She said it like eating healthy was equivalent to sniffing glue—until she tried them. I was a good cook, if I did say so myself.

Killian sighed dramatically, leaning forward to snatch the container from me, making a show of slowly bringing my fork to his mouth.

"I don't have cooties," I snapped.

Killian paused, his eyes turning to me. "I'm well aware of that," he said, eyes blazing.

I felt my cheeks redden at his meaning. I didn't say anything and he put the fork in his mouth, nose screwed up. He chewed and swallowed, then looked to my fork and to me.

"This is good," he said in amazement, forking more into his mouth.

I grinned triumphantly.

"Like really good. You must be a good cook, making something like 'quinoa' taste like this," he said, handing the container back to me.

"You kind of have to be, with a mom that considers defrosting pizza cooking," I replied with a grin.

His face quickly lost its teasing smile. "Yeah, that's one better than mine, Freckles. Pretty sure I existed on cereal until I learned how to cook for myself, till I was old enough to earn money for groceries." He paused. "Which was about a year after my dad died. Only time I got hot meals before that was when Evie dragged me to her and Steg's for dinner, which was often. Still is."

I lost my smile at the same time as he started speaking. I put my container down, forgotten. "Kill, that's—" I started in a broken voice.

"That was my life, Freckles," he interrupted. "Unraveled pretty quick after my dad passed. My mom's weak. She was a crappy mom when dad was alive, but she functioned, barely. Enough. After he died..." He trailed off, shaking his head. "She damn near forgot I existed. It's no great loss to me," he said, meeting my watery eyes. "I got the club. They're the only family I need. Gave me a job. Showed me the way around a motorcycle. Cade was the one who gave me the piece of junk I repaired enough to be rideable." He spoke reverently of this "Cade" who I'd only met once. He was the president of the Sons of Templar MC, the family Killian was talking about.

"It's 'cause of them I can feed myself, and I belong to something more. That my life isn't completely in the gutter. I'm not spillin' all this to get your sympathy," he said, wiping a tear from my cheek. "Just your understanding, your forgiveness."

I blinked. "Forgiveness?" I repeated in disbelief. "There's nothing to forgive. Kill, none of this was your fault."

"None of that was my fault," he agreed. "The way I treated you last weekend was." His voice was hard. "You're the only completely good, completely beautiful thing to come into my life since I was twelve. It... screwed me up, seeing my beautiful thing so close to the ugliness I tried to shield you from," he said, glancing off to the side. "I didn't want that, that ugly anywhere near you, Freckles. Shit, I spent the whole weekend arguing with myself over whether I should even be with you, drag you down, taint you with being with someone like me."

I moved forward, so I was on my knees in front of him, unable to hear him speaking about himself like this. "Kill—"

"This," he interrupted, pointing at the faded bruise on his face, "is from me fighting off my mom's dealer from taking advantage of her while she lay passed out on the sofa."

I flinched the moment he said the words, my heart breaking at the image of this, my mind unable to fathom something like that even happening. It happened in the movies, in news stories, not real life. Not the real life I was used to.

Killian leaned forward and touched my cheek with his finger. "See," he whispered, "even telling you that screws with the beautiful world you're a part of. Ripples it, tears it. The fact I've got shit like that in my life, that it could somehow bleed into you..." He paused, his face turning hard. "I can't accept that, Freckles."

"Stop," I commanded. "Stop that right now, Killian."

Killian didn't say anything, more out of surprise than anything else, I guessed.

"There's a lot wrong with what you just said. First, I need to tell you something. My mom's parents were alcoholics. She was brought up in a trailer. She had a rough childhood. I don't know the specifics, 'cause she isn't too hot on repeating them at story time." I paused. Mom told me the bare minimum of her upbringing and only had released those particular details last year when she felt I was old enough to handle it. I idly wondered what else she was hiding that she didn't think I was old enough to handle.

My mind moved back to the current moment. "Out of all of the people in this world, my mom is the most important to me, the most special. She's my best friend. I'm guessing here, but I think she had the same upbringing as what you've been unfortunate enough to have." I swallowed the razors that scratched at my throat at the thought of my mom having to deal with thoughts like the ones Killian was vocalizing. Ugly, untrue thoughts brought on by people who were supposed to protect you from such things.

"The most important person to me, who I love and respect above all else, was a part of this world that you seem to think separate than mine. This upbringing that somehow makes you think it defines who you are. You're right. It *does* define who you are. But it doesn't make you bad. It makes you more beautiful than I could ever be for growing up in that ugliness and turning into... you," I said softly.

Killian stared at me for a long moment, a moment that almost seemed separate from time. His eyes were so fierce. Then he leaned forward, and with extreme gentleness, he clasped my face and kissed me. His mouth moved slowly, patiently, chasing away the sounds of people around us, chasing away the demons that came with the conversation. There was nothing. Only me and him.

"I'm glad I met you, Freckles," he said when his mouth left mine, his forehead resting against my own.

"Ditto," I whispered.

I didn't think I could ever be gladder to have met a person in my entire life. A person who was quickly becoming a huge part of my world.

••••

"I'm going to vomit," I declared.

A large hand slipped into mine, squeezing it. "You're going to be great. We're going to be great," Sam promised me. "Please don't vomit. It'll ruin my outfit. This is our debut. I'm establishing myself as the most attractive and fashionable of the group," he added with a grin.

I let out a choked laugh that seemed to grate through my dry mouth.

Another hand slipped into mine on the other side. "We'll be right there with you, Lex," Noah murmured, nodding to the stage that we were meant to be playing on in about one minute.

I nodded, my eyes locked on the spot I was going to stand. In front of people. A lot of them.

"Breathe," Noah reminded me.

I sucked in a strangled breath.

I thought of all the people out there. Then I focused on one. My mom. The one who promised me it was going to be great, that I was great. The one who supported my dream. I wasn't going to let her down.

Then I thought of someone else. Someone who wasn't out there. He was in my head though. It was like he'd purchased prime real estate in the landscape of my brain.

Killian.

Earlier today, I had been standing in the middle of my bedroom looking at my entire closet scattered on every surface in my room. Why hadn't I bought a new outfit when we were shopping earlier today? I had nothing!

I was about to burst into tears or let out a petulant little scream when a knock at the door made me jump about five feet.

I considered not answering it. I was not in a state for human interaction, and my traitorous mom had gone away somewhere, promising she'd be back soon. What kind of mother left her daughter in the midst of such a crisis? Surely there was someone I could report her to.

A second knock had me moving to answer the door.

"Killian," I exclaimed in surprise when I yanked it open.

His gaze flickered over me and then he met my face with a grin. Shoot.

I was wearing a Gryffindor T-shirt and gray jersey shorts. My hair was piled into a knot on my head, and I was not wearing a scrap of makeup.

"This is never going to work," he declared seriously.

My mortification quickly melted away and was replaced with dread at his words.

"What?" I asked in a small voice.

"Me and you. See I'm more of a Hufflepuff man myself. There can only be one victorious house," he proclaimed, still serious.

I stared at him for a full moment then burst out laughing. Like full-on, side-stitch laughing. There might have been an edge of hysteria to it.

When I got myself together, I saw that Killian was staring at me, his grin gone.

"Thanks," I said, slightly breathless. "I needed that."

He stepped forward off the doorstep so he was close to me and he grasped my forearms lightly. The space where his skin met mine felt electric. "I need to do that more often," he murmured.

"What?" I whispered.

His hand reached to touch the side of my eye. "Make you laugh. You're beautiful at any given moment of the day, but when you laugh?" He shook his head. "I must say, it feels great to be the one to be responsible for that."

My belly flipped at his words, at his proximity. I didn't even care Mom could return home at any moment and see this. I hadn't asked her about a date with Killian yet. I was too nervous. I was also mindful of whatever she had going on with Zane, so I was waiting for the right moment.

"Your gig's tonight."

I nodded.

"You nervous, Freckles?" he asked softly.

"I was," I whispered, eyes on his. "Until now." Nerves didn't seem important when Killian was right there. Everything seemed insignificant apart from this immediate moment.

Something moved behind his eyes at my words and his hand flexed at my forearm. "You don't have nothin' to be nervous about, Lexie. I don't have any doubt in the world my girl's gonna rock the roof off that place."

I swallowed. "What if I suck?" I whispered my greatest fear. "What if I freeze or fall over on stage or forget the lyrics to Pearl Jam?" I babbled in horror. "Any rock band that forgets the lyrics to Pearl Jam has dug their own grave."

My freak out was silenced by lips on mine. Killian's lips. Every single thought left my body as he kissed me, slowly, gently, his arms going around my waist.

When he pulled away, I felt like I might float off if it wasn't for his hands holding me.

"You're not going to suck," he promised against my mouth. "It's physically impossible for you to be anything more than amazing."

"You're amazing," I blurted without thought.

My mind caught up with my words. *Shoot. Who says that?*

Killian grinned against my mouth. "Glad you think so, Freckles. It ups my chances of being able to stick around you for a bit longer."

"Chances are already through the roof," I replied instantly. With him, I didn't even think about playing hard to get or cloaking my true feelings. I had no choice but to be honest, whatever we had was too special to be tainted by dishonesty.

Killian didn't reply; he merely searched my face, that intense look returning.

"Good," he said finally. He kissed me softly on the mouth once more. "Break a leg, Freckles," he murmured, then his warmth was gone.

I stood there stock-still and watched him saunter back to his bike and roar off.

"Lexie," a voice jolted me back to the present.

I focused my gaze on Wyatt, who was standing in front of me, guitar slung over his shoulder. He was grinning, a light of excitement in his gaze.

"You ready to rock the roof off this place?" he asked.

I gazed at him, then looked at the two other boys at my side. Noah handed me my guitar.

I took it and slung it over my shoulder. "Yeah, I'm ready."

Chapter 10

"**H**oly shit, that was awesome. We were awesome!" Sam all but yelled as we walked into the room backstage.

I was grinning from ear to ear. I was afraid my heart was going to beat out of my chest and my feet didn't seem to touch the floor.

Sam stood in front of me, his hands grasping my shoulders, shaking me slightly. "You fucking *rocked*, my girl! Seriously, apart from me, you carried the whole thing," he declared, yanking me into his arms for a quick hug before he released me, pacing around the room, smashing his drumsticks on every surface.

Wyatt grinned and gave me a quick kiss on the cheek. "You were brilliant, babe," he said on a slightly quieter decibel. His eyes were almost glowing. "I think this was a pivotal point for us," he predicted sagely.

I smiled at him, then to Noah, who was relaxed on the sofa, his eyes lazy but a grin painting his face.

"We were *all* great," I said to them. "That was—"

"Like smoking weed, doing a tequila shot, and having sex all at the same time," Sam finished my sentence as I trailed off.

We all looked at him. He looked mildly chastised. "Or what I imagine it would feel like doing those things, considering I'm underage and all that," he quickly backpedaled with a grin.

Wyatt rolled his eyes and Noah shook his head. I giggled slightly, but I felt a small twinge at the fact I hadn't done any of those things. Not that I particularly wanted to drink tequila or smoke weed. The other thing... I hadn't thought that would be something that I'd think about. But now I felt a weird tingle at the base of my stomach as I touched my lips, thinking of Killian's on mine.

That's what being on stage felt like. Not exactly kissing Killian, but the same principle. Everything fell away but the moment. I felt like there was no world outside of that, that this, that moment, it was natural, who I was. Where I was meant to be.

"And," Sam continued, unaware of my being lost in my head, "did you see the freaking guys from the Sons of Templar were here?" He was pacing around the room with electric eyes. He stopped and regarded each of us. "The Sons of Templar," he repeated as if we didn't hear him. He threw up his hands. "The fuckin' badass bikers who basically rule our town came to watch us play? Like what? This will do awesome things for our image," he declared.

"Like we have an image," Wyatt interjected with sarcasm. "Dude, this was our first show. It was kickass, I grant you that, but I doubt the biggest badasses this side of the country came here to see a high school band. More likely they came to drink beers or pick up chicks."

I chewed my lip. I had a different theory. While I was on stage belting out music that seemed to become a part of me, I didn't notice much. My eyes caught my mom's watery ones once or twice, but other than that, the crowd was a big blur. Apart from the line of hulking men at the bar. One man in particular. Zane. I'd been spending more time with him since I'd sat with him a few weeks ago. I'd pop over when I saw him in his garage and Mom was at work. We didn't really say much; I just sat and watched him tinker with his bike. He'd explained some of the mechanics of it, and I even helped him with some stuff. For the most part, I just enjoyed the silence. My life was never quiet. Mom and I talked all the time. It was a constant stream of dialogue, even when we watched movies. School was the same, especially with Sam as one of my best friends. When I wasn't talking to people, I was listening to music. Or reading. That was meant to be quiet, I supposed, but characters came alive in my head, speaking, shouting sometimes. It was the same when I was writing songs. My head was loud, sometimes deafening with the thoughts demanding to be put to music.

So those moments with Zane, I had come to treasure them. I felt a connection with him. I saw something in him I didn't understand. It was pain. I could see that much. But I couldn't understand the depths of it. I couldn't fathom the sort of agony that I thought I glimpsed behind his eyes. I had hope, some romantic hope that had been birthed from my world of fiction, that Mom could repair that pain. That he could repair the pain I sometimes saw in her.

She hadn't told me about... whatever they were yet. I didn't want to push her. But I wanted, more than anything, for them to become... something.

"Wait," Sam said, eyes shooting to me. "Isn't your mom like, friends with them. The Sons of Templar, I mean. Dude, is she dating one of them?" he asked with childlike excitement.

Wyatt punched him. "Bro, you can't ask Lexie something like that about her mom. Actually, I don't think you should be allowed to talk about Mrs. Spencer anymore," he decided.

Sam rubbed his arm. "What? It was a compliment. Have you seen their old ladies? They're hot. Mia's joining some prestigious ranks," he continued.

"Stop talking, now," Wyatt commanded tightly.

I giggled, I couldn't help it. I went to sit on the sofa beside Noah, who slung his arm around me and squeezed me tightly.

"You were seriously awesome, Lexie," he murmured in my ear.

I grinned at him. "Right back at you, Noe."

Sam and Wyatt were still arguing in front of us. Wyatt was attempting to lecture him on the social niceties around referring to people's moms as MILFS. Again.

Noah looked at them, shaking his head. "This is our future." He nodded his head to them. "Acting as mother and father to two petulant children."

"In addition to being wildly rich and famous," I added dryly.

Noah nodded. "Of course."

I laughed and rested my head on his shoulder. "I wouldn't have it any other way," I whispered.

"Me either," Noah replied.

Wyatt gave up on Sam and sat beside me on the sofa, muttering to himself and glaring at Sam.

My eyes moved to the doorway and I leaped off the sofa. "Mom!" I yelled, launching myself across the room and into her arms. "That was awesome," I exclaimed, pulling myself from her arms. "We totally rocked this place."

Mom's eyes were twinkling and I knew she was about to cry.

"Hell yeah," Wyatt interjected, causing Mom to jerk slightly.

"I think I carried your asses," Sam teased. "It'll definitely be me on the cover of Rolling Stone. I'm the best looking," he informed the room.

Mom's tears were a memory thanks to my crazy friend; her face erupted in a grin.

I poked my tongue out at Sam—a gesture of love in my opinion.

Mom smiled at him and then moved her gaze around to rest on Noah for a moment. "You guys are definitely the best band I've seen live," she declared with pride.

I raised an eyebrow. I didn't think Mom spent much time at rock concerts, but the pride in her voice was evident. I felt a happy heat at the bottom of my stomach at this.

"Thanks, Mrs. S." Sam grinned at her. "We totally appreciate you bringing us here and not getting all parental about the venue and time. We just gotta rock—you know, no rules," he drawled like he had been performing concerts for decades, not minutes.

I rolled my eyes at him but smiled. I was thankful for my mom. For the fact she let us do this and brought us here. I knew not many parents would do that.

"Okay, guys, the only reason I'm not getting all 'parental,'"—she air quoted Sam's articulate term—"is because we're blowing this joint in T minus two on account of the fact your delicate teenage sensibilities are yet to be corrupted by what's in this bar, and I'm afraid long-term exposure could be dangerous for your music career and Clay's reputation. Get your stuff," she ordered with a grin.

Because we knew how lucky we were, underage high school kids playing in a bar, we hustled with her request. We had to be well-behaved or at least maintain an illusion of good behavior in order to be invited back, that's what Sam said. He had all sorts of ideas for our "reputation" that he intended on building. I helped them gather everything, not paying too much attention to Mom chatting to the club owner, Clay. I did notice he was standing pretty close to her. I felt a weird sort of irritation at that as I put my guitar in its case. Clay was nice; he was awesome in fact, letting us play at his bar. He was okay looking for an older guy, I guessed. He was tall and not as muscly as the hulk-like Sons of Templar men. He had silver in his black hair. He worked it, in a gruff, George Clooney type of way.

That didn't irritate me. He wasn't right for Mom. Zane was. It was a completely irrational thought. I had no idea about what was going on with them, but it didn't matter.

"She's not fuckin' going anywhere with you," a deep voice brought me out of my ponderings.

I looked up and struggled to fight my grin at the owner of the statement with trademark profanity.

Zane stood behind Mom, like right behind her, glaring at Clay. I didn't exactly understand where Clay was meant to be going with Mom; maybe he'd asked her on a date. Whatever it was, it seemed like that would happen over Zane's dead body.

"Holy shit," Wyatt muttered, his eyes on the glaring match between the two men.

"Dude, as much as I'd love to see it, please don't let Bull go postal on Clay. We need him for our career," Sam whispered in my ear.

Zane yanked my mom to his side and slid his arm around her neck. My eyes widened, and somewhere I did a little happy dance at what this gesture meant.

"Called it," Sam muttered from beside me.

I ignored Sam and let that little warm feeling that sparked from my mom's look of pride earlier and Mom and Zane in such a position grow bigger. You didn't think they'd fit. My mom wasn't tiny, but Zane dwarfed her. She looked glam in her black dress and high-heeled boots. He looked gruff and dangerous covered in tattoos and wearing all black and his motorcycle vest—cut, whatever. But they did fit.

"Zane!" I said, hitching my guitar on my shoulder as I made it over to the little huddle that Mom had going on. "I'm so glad you came! This gig freaking ruled!" I said with a grin.

Zane's attention stayed on my mom for a split second, and then his eyes moved to me. He released Mom and took my guitar off my shoulder with much more ease than I ever handled it. It may have been like an extension of my arm, but it was heavy. My heart bloomed at the simple gesture. It was something a dad would do. I knew Zane wasn't my dad. I wasn't delusional, but it felt nice to have something so small feel so big.

Zane's big hand moved to yank one of my curls lightly. His face was blank, but he did one of those eye smile things that he only did with me and, when she wasn't looking, my mom.

"You were great, Lex," he told me, his deep voice a soft rumble. "Got a lot of talent, girl."

I beamed at him. People said that to me all the time, but coming from him, someone who mattered, someone I wanted to think would matter to our family, it meant everything.

"Dude, you're in the Sons of Templar?" Sam interrupted the moment. "That's like... freaking sick!"

I couldn't help but smile. Only Sam would call one of the biggest, baddest bikers I'd ever met "dude."

Zane's attention moved to one of my best friends, his eye smile gone. His face was hard, scary even. Sam didn't seem to blanche at all, but I deflated. I found myself wanting, more than anything, for Zane to like and respect my boys.

"Okay, let's get out of here, guys. You've all got parents to get home to, who I'm sure will think I've taken you to a rave if I don't get you back soon," Mom said, clapping her hands together, her voice interrupting the glare Zane was sending at Sam.

I breathed a sigh of relief. My mom was a superhero at that moment.

Clay opened the door, the boys, Sam most so, hustled out pretty quickly. I lagged behind a bit, waiting for Mom and wanting to say good-bye to Zane.

Clay was staring at my mom, despite the glare Zane had directed back at him.

"Offer's still good, babe. Call me if you change your mind. Regardless"—his eyes cut to me and I swallowed at being involved in whatever this conversation was—"I've got her covered."

I looked to Mom. I had no idea what this meant. She looked just as confused, albeit a smidgeon more panicked than I felt.

Zane looked to me, his glare slipping away for a spilt second before he turned to Mom. "Take Lexie to the car," he commanded.

"Zane," Mom protested, looking between him and Clay. I guessed she was worried about potential fisticuffs.

"To the fuckin' car, babe," he said, his tone brokering no argument.

I smiled on the inside, despite the tense atmosphere. It was cool hearing Zane call Mom "babe." That meant good things. Maybe not at that moment, but for the future, I was certain.

Mom grabbed my hand after a small stare off with Zane. "Let's go to the car, baby girl," she said, a forced lightness in her voice. "Let the men have their... conversation." She gave Zane a meaningful look and murmured something in his ear.

I grinned on the inside once more.

"Why was Zane so angry at Clay?" I asked with false innocence once we'd gotten into the parking lot.

Mom looked behind her. "Angry? He wasn't angry. He's just a big, bad biker. They act angry with everyone. It's their way of communicating. They've got their own language, like German. To the outsider, it seems like they're constantly arguing, but it's just their way. Call it alpha male speak."

I rolled my eyes and shook my head at her as we reached the car.

●●●●

I lay in bed, wide awake, unable to sleep. That was partly because my phone kept lighting up with texts from the boys.

> SAM: We need a name. We're obviously going to be world famous. We need a name to reflect our future stardom.
>
> WYATT: How about "Music & Tonic"?
>
> SAM: Be serious. Do you even want a Grammy?

That wasn't the only reason I couldn't sleep. I was jazzed. It was like I'd had four coffees. Or a million. I couldn't sit still; my mind was whizzing like a million bees were stuck in there. I was scribbling thoughts onto my notebook, sure half of them would be complete nonsense on rereading in the morning. I was also waiting. Waiting for the text, not from Sam or Wyatt, but from Killian. I'd carefully chosen my mint green pajamas and had tamed my previously rock star teased hair, leaving it down because I knew he liked it.

I had no doubt that he'd come.

But then 2:00 a.m. came and went.

Then 3:00 a.m.

Then came the doubt.

Chapter 11

You would think the day following a successful first gig played by my band would have had me floating on cloud nine, that I would be wandering around with a smile on my face.

This was not the case.

I had been up since some ungodly hour because sleep didn't give me the solace from my mind. I couldn't lapse into dreamland when my eyes always seemed to be peeking at my phone, waiting and hoping it would light up. It wasn't healthy. It was downright desperate in fact. I was more than a little angry at myself. So I decided if my mind couldn't be healthy, my body sure as heck would.

Hence me being up before the sun, ridding our house of coffee on the thought that it was bad for both Mom and me and green tea was much better. I would have rid the house of junk food as well, had our cupboards had something more than a tub of peanut butter.

We ate out a lot and hadn't gone grocery shopping in a while.

I thought about going for a run but deduced my traitorous feet might take me past Killian's house, and I'd cement myself in becoming a crazy stalker. Instead, I decided on a kickboxing DVD which turned out to be a bad idea when my mom stumbled down the stairs and glared at me.

"How are you related to me?" she muttered at me in disdain. I responded with a cheerful greeting. Mom was not a morning person, and I was.

I had to be cheerful. I couldn't exactly tell Mom the reason for my unhappiness, which in turn made me even more unhappy for keeping secrets from her. She then nearly murdered me when she found out I'd thrown out all of our coffee. She refused to speak to me and marched out of the house wearing a mismatched outfit, declaring she'd exorcise me if I continued to torture her by giving up caffeine.

Luckily, I'd been forgiven when I apologized by text and promised to give her a villa in Tuscany when I was rich and famous. She rewarded me with a latte for my trouble. I was kidding myself if I thought I could live without caffeine.

I had multiple texts from the boys all morning asking to hang out. I blew them all off, feigning homework and sequestering myself in my room. I didn't even open a textbook. Instead, I shoved my headphones on, listened to Bob Dylan, and wrote songs.

I only left my sanctuary when Mom popped her head in.

"Pizza and Ryan Gosling?" she suggested with a grin.

I nodded. "Sounds perfect." I did my best to smile convincingly.

She didn't seem to notice my performance. Her eyes cut to my desk and the various screwed up bits of paper.

"You finally short-circuited one of the wires up there, Jimmy Neutron?" she asked, nodding to the paper. "I wouldn't worry, kid. It's inevitable for a teenager to have some sort of physical reaction to doing homework on a Saturday," she said in distaste. "Even the Rain Man."

I jumped up, hoping she didn't look too closely at the offending bits of paper. "Just calculus, you know how much I hate it," I said quickly, walking to the door and out into the kitchen. Mom followed me.

"Why such a subject is taught at school is beyond me," she said. "If they wanted to torture the youth of today, waterboarding is much less painful." She winked at me and picked up the phone. "One or two?" she asked, referring to the pizzas.

I raised my eyebrows.

She nodded somberly. "You're right. What was I thinking? Three."

"And garlic bread," I added, needing to drown my sorrows in cheese and carbs.

"This isn't my first rodeo, sister," she replied, phone to her ear.

I smiled at Mom, happy that I had her to distract me. Movie nights and pizzas might not help the insistent thoughts buzzing through my mind, but it might silence them just a smidgeon.

●●●●

I lay in bed that night, full of pizza and Ben and Jerry's, unable to sleep. I should have been exhausted, considering the lack of sleep I'd gotten the night before, but my mind wasn't giving me that. I had the exquisite torture of dissecting every moment Killian and I had two days previous, looking for where I went wrong. It was miserable.

My phone buzzed and lit up my dark room in the midst of some of my darker thoughts. I stared at it with a scrunched up nose, knowing it would be Sam or Wyatt arguing over band names, as they had been all day.

I sighed and reached over to it, preparing to try to play peacemaker. My heart leaped into my throat at the name and accompanying message.

KILLIAN: You awake, Freckles?

I typed back frantically and sent my one-word response.

ME: Yes

I stared at the screen and bit my lip. Shoot. I shouldn't have responded that quickly. It was almost midnight on a Saturday night; if I was awake, I should have led Killian to think I was doing something interesting and fun that made immediate reply impossible and less tragic.

KILLIAN: Backyard.

The moment my eyes read the word, I scrambled out of bed so quickly I caught my feet in the sheets and tripped over, smashing my hip on my side table.

"Ouch," I half yelled as pain blossomed in my hip. "Ouch, ouch, ouch," I repeated, hopping around the room.

I wasn't worried about making noise, considering I'd heard Mom leave about half an hour ago. I had smiled as the door closed. I knew exactly where she was going. To Zane. The only thing that quelled my happiness was the fact she was sneaking. That she was keeping it a secret. She knew how much I liked Zane. I couldn't for the life of me understand the cloak and daggers act. Then again, I was performing an eerily similar act and couldn't even understand why I was doing it.

The pain in my hip subsided enough for me to yank on pink Ugg boots and a dusty pink, chunky sweater over my gray leggings. I made myself take a quick look in the mirror to run a hand through my wayward curls and leave them down.

I paused with my hand on the doorknob, taking a deep breath.

Do not act eager or desperate. Demand an explanation for radio silence, I told myself.

I stepped soundlessly down the steps leading to the backyard, squinting into the darkness.

"Freckles," a voice greeted from beside me as a figure seemed to materialize at my side.

I jumped and placed my hand on my pounding heart. "Jeepers creepers," I whispered in shock.

Killian stepped even closer, his hand in his pockets. I could see his half grin illuminated by the kitchen lights I had left on. "Did you just say 'jeepers creepers'?" he asked in a light tone.

My cheeks reddened. "No," I replied in embarrassment.

Killian stepped even closer to me, though he didn't touch me; his hands stayed in his pockets. "Yes, you did. My little Lexie says 'jeepers creepers,'" he murmured.

I lost my breath momentarily at the "my little Lexie part" of that sentence. "It's instinct," I protested. "Mom doesn't curse. I've picked up some of her... replacement words."

Killian was so close I could feel the heat of his body. "Don't be embarrassed," he said, voice turning husky. "It's adorable." He paused. "I like that for you. Your mom protects you from cursing." There was an edge to his tone and my heart sunk a little, realizing that his mom didn't protect him from anything, definitely not something as trivial as cursing.

His hand came up to brush my jaw lightly. I held my breath in some sort of attempt to prolong the touch, to get the most out of it. "Someone as pretty as you doesn't need ugly words around them, coming out of their mouth," he decided.

I pursed my lips. I had always felt self-conscious over the fact I didn't swear. Yet it was another thing that Killian seemed to accept. To like.

"Well, if I want to protect myself from the dangers of curse words, I'd have to find a new band, considering their vocabulary, but that's not likely to happen anytime soon."

There was a long silence, one that made me anxious to fill it up and also keep empty at the same time. I was itching to ask Killian as to why I hadn't heard from him, why he turned up at my house in the middle of the night. But I didn't.

"Yeah, Freckles, after Friday night, I don't think you'll be getting rid of those guys anytime soon," he said finally. "They need their superstar if they want to go anywhere."

My heart skipped a beat. "You were there?" I deduced.

"Of course I was there," Killian said, his hand trailing down my arm to engulf my hand. "I wouldn't have missed it for the world."

I tried to think with his thumb rubbing against the back of my hand. "I didn't see you. Why didn't you come and say hello?" I asked finally.

"Didn't want to draw attention to myself, considering Clay knows me and knows that I'm a couple years shy of being allowed in his bar," Killian explained. "It was your night. To have with your friends, your family," he added.

I frowned at him in the darkness. "And you," I corrected. "You're my... we're friends, aren't we?"

Killian's hand tightened on mine. "We're more than that, Freckles."

I ignored the flip my belly did at this. "Good. Well, that means at our next gig, I expect you front and center," I commanded.

Killian chuckled softly. "Your wish is my command."

I paused. "If you were there, how come..." I paused, not wanting to sound like the crazy kind of girlfriend, if that was what I was.

Killian's hand went to my chin. "How come what?"

I stared at him. "How come I haven't heard from you?" I asked in a small voice, really hoping I didn't sound tragic.

Killian's hand cupped my cheek and he sighed. "Sorry, babe. I've had some shit going on with my mom." He put a finger on my half-open lips, predicting my question. "I'll tell you about it tomorrow. This time's too precious to pollute with her."

I stayed frozen as his hand lingered at my lip for a split second, his thumb brushing along it.

"Long story short, I've been busy. Ordinarily, I'm never too busy for you. This was an exception. The only one there'll be," he promised.

I swallowed. "You could've used that thing that was invented to inform people that they're busy," I said softly. "You know, a modification on Alexander Graham Bell's invention?" I teased lightly, mostly to disguise the hurt I felt, despite his beautiful words.

Killian paused, then sighed again. He rested his head on mine for one glorious moment before responding. "I'm not used to this," he murmured. "Having to check in, to *want* to check in. To think about someone every second I'm awake. I'm not exactly good at it."

"I think you're doing pretty well," I whispered.

"When it comes to you, 'pretty well' ain't gonna cut it."

We were silent once more as I bathed in his words. Something clicked in my head. "Tomorrow," I said suddenly. "You said we'd talk about your mom tomorrow. What's tomorrow?"

"Tomorrow," Killian said, brushing my cheek, "is our first date. Our first proper date."

My heart skipped about a million beats at this. "That's pretty short notice," I said finally. "What if I was busy?"

I saw half of Killian's attractive face smile. "You busy tomorrow night, babe?"

I was silent for a moment. "No," I said finally.

He full-on chuckled, bringing me into his arms. His lips pressed on my head and I sank into his arms. He smelled amazing, musky with a faint lingering of cigarette smoke. Even though I hated the things, I liked the residual smell on Killian.

Too soon, he pulled me out of his arms. "Your mom gonna be all good with this, Freckles?" he asked, his voice a little flat, cautious.

My stomach dropped at the fact I hadn't told her. I wouldn't be telling Killian this; I was mindful of our conversation on the quad.

He felt unworthy because of his upbringing, no matter how much he tried to disguise that fact. Me not telling Mom about us would strike a personal chord with him. It would hurt him. I was not doing that. I felt a little sick at the thought.

"She's fine, ecstatic actually," I lied.

I almost felt Killian's disbelieving look. "Your mom is 'fine' with you dating for the first time? Dating a boy with a motorcycle?"

"Considering she's dating someone with a motorcycle, she can't pass too much judgment," I replied, going for evasion instead of a straight-up lie.

Killian's body stilled. "She's dating someone with a motorcycle?" he repeated slowly.

I nodded. "Although she's trying to keep it on the down low. She didn't count on my keen skills of observation." I paused. "Or my insomnia, meaning I caught her sneaking across the street," I corrected myself.

There was a weird energy to the following silence. "Insomnia?" he repeated in concern. There was a pause. "Across the street?" Killian repeated my words in a clipped tone.

"Yep."

"To Bull's?" he clarified.

"One in the same."

"Shit," he muttered, disbelief evident in his tone.

"Why is that so surprising?" I asked. "Granted, he and Mom aren't exactly the most compatible, considering he is almost mute, and I'm surprised her vocal chords haven't given out by how much she talks. Still, he's a man and my mom's a catch," I said a little defensively.

Killian rubbed my arms. "It's not your mom," he reassured me. "It's Bull and, well, any woman," he said vaguely.

"What? Is he gay or something?" I asked, not believing that for a second. Apart from the little fact of Mom's midnight visit where they were not likely to be playing checkers, there was the way Zane looked at her. Granted, I didn't have much experience in that area, or any, prior to arriving in Amber, but I knew that was not how a gay man looked at a woman. That was how a very straight man looked at a woman. Kind of how Killian looked at me.

Killian barked out a laugh before he quickly silenced it. "No, it's not that. It's...." He trailed off.

I perked up. "It's just what?"

Killian shook his head and kissed my nose lightly. "Nothing, Freckles."

I frowned, sensing there was more to this particular story, but the nose kiss did a lot to distract me.

"Tomorrow night," he murmured, his mouth close to mine.

"Yeah, tomorrow night," I breathed.

The moment was held in some kind of beautiful limbo that seemed to last forever and for no time at all at the same time.

Killian pressed his mouth to mine, his lips moving gently as he kissed me lazily, gently, as if I was made of glass.

"Get some sleep," he commanded softly.

Yeah, like that was going to happen. I was going to inspect my entire wardrobe for date attire then most likely have a nervous breakdown over the fact I'd never been on a date before and the prospect of telling my mom.

"Okay," I whispered.

Killian kissed my forehead and he stayed in that spot, and I realized he was waiting for me to go into the house. I regretfully extracted myself from his warm presence and wandered to the house. I stole a glance over my shoulder.

"Night," I called softly.

"Sweet dreams, Freckles."

Chapter 12

My prediction leaving Killian last night proved correct. I stayed awake another couple of hours after he left. First, it was because it seemed like my body had been zapped with electricity and I needed to find an outlet—excuse the pun. So I had scribbled into my notebook, tried to read, then did some yoga. I had done all this floating on a wave of happiness with a small edge of dread at finally telling my mom. I wasn't nervous about what she'd say. She was my mom; she was cool. Although she may not like me dating, she'd never forbid it. I was absolutely terrified that she'd immediately hate Killian for what she thought he was. What he projected to the world. The smoking, motorcycle-riding, devil-may-care attitude that came with this persona he'd built to keep the world out. He may have seemed like your quintessential—disgustingly attractive—bad boy on the surface, but he was so much more than that. I needed Mom to see beyond the surface. See what I saw. Her approval meant everything to me.

So sleep was lost until the early hours when my mind had quieted enough to drift off with music playing in my ears.

My adrenaline roller coaster had obviously taken its toll on me when I woke up near noon the next day. I managed to yank myself out of bed and dreams of Killian to stumble to the coffee pot, then the living room.

"Hey there, sleepyhead," Mom greeted, glancing up from the TV, smiling.

Still half asleep, I didn't respond. I snuggled up to her on the sofa, just needing to hug my mom. Her arm went around me and we both watched the TV, content in silence. My sleep-addled mind realized these moments would become few and far between. I was growing up. Hugs with my mom weren't the only kind of affection I was coming to know. I was discovering a different kind, the kind that turned you into a woman. It was a melancholy thought, the final farewell to the last of my childhood.

"Your body finally realized that it's a teenager and can't get up at 6:00 a.m. after a night on stage," Mom observed.

I sipped my coffee, out of necessity and to stall while my thoughts settled. The last morning hugs with Mom wasn't the only things that signified the passageway into womanhood. It was the secrets. The fact Mom was oblivious to the reasons for my lack of sleep, for my late rising.

"I'm not planning on commencing said lifestyle until I learn how to function without eight hours of sleep," I said finally, moving my mind away from such serious thoughts on such little amounts of caffeine.

"As long as coffee is the only substance you abuse to get you through lack of sleep, that's fine with me," Mom said, running her fingers through my hair.

"Okay, should I throw out the cocaine that I scored on Friday night?" I asked seriously.

Mom pretended to ponder. "Just leave it on the nightstand," she said finally.

I sipped my coffee, smiling. We might be saying good-bye to some things, but our sarcastic banter was something we'd have forever, regardless of our ages.

Mom's hands continued running through my curls. "Got something to talk to you about, kid," she said, her voice lacking any previous humor.

I glanced up at her. She was serious, her face slightly nervous. I knew exactly what this subject was going to be. "Does it start with a Z and end with an 'ane?" I asked.

Surprise flickered over Mom's face. "You've got more brains than I give you credit for, doll face," she teased.

I tapped my head. "Not just a hat rack." That and I caught her in the act. I reasoned I would've had a less concrete instinct on the subject of the two of them, but I still would've noticed. "Mom, it's like totally obvious. Even the guys in the band saw it," I explained. "I saw it way before that."

Mom's eyebrows raised and she chewed her lip uncertainly. Nice to know where I got that particular habit from. "And you're not mad? Don't have questions?"

The uncertainty in her voice had me sitting up and placing my coffee down so I could give her my full attention. "Mad?" I repeated in disbelief. "No way, I'm ecstatic! You deserve someone, Mom. You've had years of bringing me up, working your butt off to give us this." I gestured around our eclectically designed living room. I glanced back at her. "I was always worried you didn't have someone. Now I get it. You were waiting for the right person. Zane's your person," I told her with confidence. Maybe I felt confidence because I had an inkling of what it was like to find your person. As crazy as it was, my age, our limited amount of time together, none of it mattered. Killian was my person.

Mom looked at me with twinkling eyes; then she shook her head. But not to my statement, to some internal thought. "Yeah, kid, he's my person," she murmured. She clutched my hands. "But you're my one and only, you know that, right? My main person. No one ever knocks you off that spot," she promised.

I blinked away any prickling of tears at her words to roll my eyes. "Well, duh. I'm like the most amazing daughter ever. Even a hot biker couldn't knock me off that spot," I responded. "Plus, I'm your meal ticket for when you retire. You need to stay on my good side." I smiled at her, happiness radiating from me at the fact she'd finally told me, the fact my mom finally had her person. The thought of her revealing her secret made the issue of my date with Killian that more pressing. I swallowed that. Mom needed to have some time digesting what just happened.

I stood up. "Got homework to do," I declared, which was actually correct. I'd neglected it for far too long. I needed to get it done before... tonight. I glanced at Mom and my eyes prickled once more. I'd never realized how badly I wanted this for her, this happiness, this feeling. Maybe I never realized it because I never understood what she'd been missing out on the years she spent bringing me up, working her ass off. Now, I knew.

"Glad you're happy, Mom," I told her quietly.

She smiled. "Was always happy, kid," she replied firmly.

I thought on it a second. She was right. She was always smiling, laughing, content. Happy. But there was a different kind of happiness that came with what I guessed she and Zane had. I winked at her and quickly left the room. I felt like skipping. I'd always been happy too. Mom gave me a beautiful life. We may not have had material things, sometimes it was a struggle, I knew, but it was a good life. We had Ava and Steve, and we had each other. Now we got more. I sat down at my desk and got started on my calculus homework with a huge smile on my face.

••••

It was time. Calculus was done. English Lit was done. Even biology was done. My room was cleaned. I'd procrastinated enough. Almost my entire afternoon was spent doing it. I'd taken a break to go and chat to Amy, Rosie, and Lucy, women who were not only exceptionally beautiful but super nice too. Amy was married to

Brock, and I was pretty sure Rosie was Cade's sister. That was another thing that made me happy, Mom having friends connected to Zane and the Sons of Templar. Amber seemed to have welcomed us with open arms.

I just needed to bite the bullet.

I dragged my feet to the living room and leaned against the doorjamb, watching Mom fold laundry for a second before I built up the courage to speak.

"Mom?" I said finally, in a small voice.

She glanced up at me. "I'll give you a hundred dollars right here and now if you agree to fold the laundry for the remainder of your time living at home," she said seriously.

I screwed up my nose, happy for the respite from my intended topic. "That's like one hundred dollars over two years. That's like... fifty bucks a year." I raised my eyebrow. "That's slave labor. Even Cinderella would have gotten more pocket money than that," I informed her, sitting down on the sofa.

"Cinderella got fancy shoes and a prince for a husband out of the deal," she shot back.

"So in addition to the hundred dollars, you're going to wave a magic wand to get me horrifically uncomfortable shoes and a prince for a husband?" I clarified.

Mom shook her head. "Of course not. I don't need a wand to give you horrifically uncomfortable shoes. Just check out my closet. Fashion is pain," she declared. "And on the prince front, I don't doubt your ability to snag one of your own, though you better hurry up. All the good ones are getting snaffled up," she teased.

I swallowed, my throat was sandpaper. Mom had unintentionally veered us back to my dreaded topic.

"What's up, sweetie?" she asked. She knew me too well.

Just do it. "I was wondering..." I dragged out the words, twisting my hands together. I glanced up at Mom and took a breath. "Well,

I've got a date," I said quickly, my whole body sagging with relief as soon as I spoke the words.

Mom seemed to sink back in relief too. "So no tattoo?" she asked weirdly.

I gave her a look of horror. How could Mom get a tattoo out of that? "Of course not. I'm only sixteen."

Now that she seemed to be comforted by my lack of ink, she grinned. "Thanks for reminding me. I would have forgotten otherwise."

I needed to make sure we didn't veer off track like we did so often. "So the date, it's okay with you?" I clarified.

"Of course it's not okay with me," she replied, and my stomach dropped. "I'd rather you become a spinster and lived with me until you were old and wrinkly, but I knew it was a long shot," she continued, quelling my panic. "So I guess it's okay as long as you're home by ten and don't get frisky." Her tone was light, but I knew Mom was serious about that particular detail. "So who's the lucky guy?" she asked with a smile.

My heart pounded even thinking about him.

"Killian," I told her, smiling. I couldn't help myself. Since telling Mom we were going on a date, it was real. Like properly real. I had a strange yearning to cartwheel across the room. I suppressed the urge, mainly because of the way my Mom's face dropped a smidgeon.

That fear came back at the look on her face. The fear that she wouldn't like Killian. Such a thing would likely split me in two.

"He's not taking you on his motorcycle, is he?" she asked, with an edge to her voice.

I patted Mom's hand in an effort to reassure her. "No, Mom, he knows your rule. He's got a car."

My efforts to reassure her seemed to backfire. Mom raised her eyebrows in suspicion. "A car and a motorcycle? How does a teenage kid afford that?"

I bristled at what was thinly veiled by her words. "He didn't steal them, if that's what you're saying," I snapped, feeling protective over Killian and irrationally annoyed at Mom immediately pigeonholing him.

She held her hands up in mock surrender. "I didn't say anything of the sort."

"That's what you were thinking," I retorted sharply. "He built the car from the ground up with his dad, and Cade gave him the motorcycle to do up when it was a pile of junk," I explained, needing Mom to know the context, to know there was more to him than what she thought.

Again, my efforts went awry.

"You know a lot about the kid for someone who hasn't been on a date with him," she teased with a raised brow.

My mouth suddenly went dry once more, with guilt. "Yes, because we talked first. Had actual conversations. Became friends. Isn't that what you taught me to do?" I asked defensively, mostly to hide my guilt over the fact we'd already surpassed the "friend" stage.

"Take a chill pill, dude. I was only teasing," Mom said with a grin. "Let's move along to the most important question."

I eyed her skeptically, waiting for more attacks on Killian's character. Or waiting for the question "Where do you buy a shotgun?"

"What?" I asked finally.

Mom grinned. "What are you wearing?"

••••

"Okay, out," I commanded, directing Mom to the door.

She had the audacity to look offended. "What? Why?" she

whined.

"Because you are absolutely no help," I informed her, with my hand on my hip.

She put her hand on her chest. "I take that as a personal affront, an attack on my very character. My fashion prowess is highly sought after, and you're getting it for free and trying to get rid of me? Well, I never!"

I regarded her. "Your fashion prowess may be sought after, but you keep asking to borrow things instead of actually helping me pick an outfit," I pointed out.

"You should take it as a compliment. You've got great taste and a highly covetable wardrobe. Comes from your mother, of course."

I held back a smile. "Out," I commanded.

She pretended to jut her lip out. "Okay, okay. I'm just a call away if things get overwhelming." Her eyes turned serious and she rested her hands on my shoulders. "You could wear a paper sack and still be too beautiful and too good for any boy," she said quietly. "Please don't though. We've got a reputation to uphold," she added, giving my shoulders a squeeze and leaving the room.

I sank back onto the bed when she left, staring at the ceiling. I was still for a moment before I grabbed my phone and put it to my ear.

"I've got a date," I blurted as soon as my best friend answered.

"Holy shit, a date?" Emma repeated, not bothered by my lack of greeting.

"Yep. In—" I paused to look at the time on my phone "—less than two hours. I have no idea what to wear, what kind of makeup to do, what to say, and what to do with my hands. Did I mention I have no idea what to wear?" I babbled, feeling panic creep up my throat. "Oh my God. I can't go on a date. I'm canceling."

"Breathe," Emma commanded calmly.

I paused, doing as she said.

"Okay, now that you're not in danger of going postal, I need you to fill me in," she ordered after a moment. "Last I heard from you, you had an awesome gig and I was gearing myself up to have a rock star best friend and to potentially have a fling with one of your bandmates."

I had kept Killian and my... thing a bit of a secret, even from Emma, my best friend. The closest person I had in my life in addition to Mom and Ava. We didn't talk every day, but when we did talk, it was for hours and we'd talk about everything under the sun.

Except Killian.

I felt a little blossom of guilt at keeping this secret.

"You can't have a fling with any of the boys," I snapped. "It would turn ugly and I simply couldn't stand the drama."

"Don't change the subject," Emma ordered, knowing me too well. "Date. Boy. Spill."

I sighed and, like my mouth had a mind of its own, I did just that, spilled every last detail of my... thing with Killian.

"And now that we finally have an official date, everything seems different and new, and I feel like I might vomit," I finished, breathless.

There was a pause at the other end of the phone, a long one.

"Wow," Emma said finally. "I want to be raging at you, my best friend for keeping such a colossal secret from me for so long, but I also have an urge to do a happy dance around the coffee shop I'm currently standing in, regardless of the hot barista who will think I'm a dork for doing so."

I braced. "Which one's winning out?"

I didn't get a response, but I did hear the unmistakable sounds of Emma's happy dance.

I grinned.

"Okay, I'm back. You totally owe me because the barista

definitely thinks I'm an insane person. You're taking back the ban on the bandmates," she declared.

"The ban stands."

She sighed dramatically into the phone. "You better introduce me to Prince Harry when you play for the Queen for her 100th jubilee," she relented.

I grinned wider. "Done."

"Okay, so it sounds like we don't have much time, so I can't talk as much as I would like to about this Killian character," she said quickly. "I will say one thing. I'm happy for you, Lexie. Ecstatic. You've always been a knockout, and the idiots at school were always too blind chasing empty-headed teenagers to notice. It sounds like you've found one who knows you're worth noticing."

I sucked in a breath. "He's the one worth noticing."

"Uh-uh, none of that. You're the catch. He better treasure you, or I'll come down there and beat sense into him myself, after Mia does of course," she stated. "We'll have a debrief after. For now, go to your closest, get your favorite pair of faded jeans that make your butt look good and your bell-sleeved, plunge-neck Free People blouse."

I pushed myself off my bed and retrieved the items.

"Got them?" she asked.

"Got them," I confirmed.

"Good. Now you'll borrow your mom's dusty pink wedges to go with this amazing outfit," she declared. Emma knew both Mom's and my closets almost as well as we did, considering our home was like a second home to her. She didn't have the greatest home life, so Mom made sure she was always welcome for sleepovers and dinners as often as possible.

"Hair," she mused. "Bohemian fishtail," she decided finally.

"Killian likes my hair down," I informed her.

There was a pause. "Well, this is the 21st century, and we do not do our hair in accordance to male preferences. We do it according to fashion," she replied.

I couldn't help but giggle. "Yes, ma'am."

"Don't go heavy on the makeup. You don't need it. Just mascara, some highlighter, blush, and pale pink gloss. That stuff I gave you, so it doesn't smudge when you guys kiss," she instructed, having a lot of experience testing kiss-proof gloss. She was nowhere near as inexperienced as me on the boy front.

"You're a lifesaver." I felt slightly less like losing my lunch.

"It's what best friends are for."

"You need to come down and stay. I miss you more than anything," I choked out, having a serious bout of homesickness for my friend. I didn't actually miss DC, just the people in it.

"As soon as I rake up enough cash, I'm contemplating moving down there," she joked.

I noticed an edge to her voice that had me worried things with her parents might be getting worse, But I didn't get time to question her on it.

"We will talk tonight, or at the latest tomorrow. For now, go and make yourself pretty, not that you aren't naturally like that, bitch," she teased. "Love you long time."

"Love you longer," I whispered back, before hanging up.

I stared at the outfit on the bed and took a breath. "Okay, let's do this," I muttered to myself, swallowing my butterflies.

Chapter 13

I only had one shoe on when I heard knocking on the door. I rushed into the living room, hopping as I attempted to put my other shoe on.

"I'm not ready, I'm not ready," I chanted in distress. "Answer the door, Mom. Stall him," I ordered before darting back into my room.

I managed to get the other shoe on while rushing back to my room without doing myself permanent injury. I shoved some items into my fringed purse and moved to face the mirror. I had done as Emma instructed and tamed my curls into a loose fishtail braid, which tumbled down one shoulder. I had torturously made it so various curls wisped out, as if of their own accord. My makeup was light. I decided against the blush, knowing my body would be doing the job of that particular cosmetic product as a result of my nerves. I just dusted some glittery shadow on my lids and swiped mascara. I quickly applied my candy-floss-colored lip gloss and pulled at my top self-consciously.

It was kickass. Mom and I had fought over it at a discount store. I'd won. It was gypsy and boho and way more me. The sleeves were long and flowy, but the print was delicate. It clinched in at the waist and draped down past my hips. It was the neckline that had me pausing. I usually wore a cami underneath, but I had decided against it tonight, so I was more than aware of how plunging it was. I wasn't exactly lacking in the chest department, but I'd never shown so much of it, on a date no less.

I jolted out of my thoughts. It was too late to change anyway. I took a deep breath, trying not to pass out, trying to shut up the hundred and one thoughts swirling through my brain. I succeeded in not passing out, but the thoughts wouldn't be quiet.

There was nothing for it. I slowly walked out my door and padded toward the living room, hearing the low murmuring of voices. I really hoped they were getting on, and Mom had not threatened to kill him or anything equally ridiculous.

My thoughts stopped the moment I reached the living room. The moment Killian's eyes locked on mine. He stood from the sofa, not taking his eyes off me.

At that moment, my mind was quiet. The intensity in his gaze made everything else insignificant. It made me feel like I was ten feet tall. Like I was beautiful. Like I was his.

"Freckles," he murmured, his eyes traveling down the length of me. "You're beautiful," he declared as his eyes met mine once more.

A flame burnt up my neck and onto my cheeks at his words and his soft, husky voice, in front of my mom no less. I was glad I'd forgone the blush.

I watched silently as he crossed the room and grasped my hand. "Have her home by ten, Mia," Killian told Mom, tearing his eyes away from me.

I had a split second to take him in. He looked amazing, like usual. He was wearing faded blue jeans and a Grateful Dead tee that I coveted immediately. I also appreciated the heck out of the way it hugged his muscled torso. He wore his trademark leather jacket, despite the warm California weather.

Killian gently pulled me out the door. I waved at Mom over my shoulder. She grinned sadly, and then we were outside.

I didn't think of much as Killian dragged me across our lawn in the direction of his car.

My eyes traveled across the street where Zane was swinging off his motorcycle. His blank and serious gaze was locked on Killian, or maybe Killian's hand, which was intertwined with mine. I gave him an exaggerated wave and a smile. Killian, who had been watching me, followed this gesture. He gave Zane a chin lift before taking us to the passenger door of his car and opening it for me.

I smiled up at him. "How chivalrous," I said.

Killian's returning smile was electrifying. He tipped an imaginary hat.

I giggled as I got in the car, and he closed the door after me. While he rounded the car, I looked over at Zane, who was staring,— no, glaring over at Killian. I didn't have time to think about that because Killian was in the car and we were moving. It was right then that I realized I'd never been in an enclosed space alone with Killian before. We'd had lunch together multiple times in a cafeteria full of people. We'd been alone together, but that was out in the open, surrounded by space. Now the fact we were actually alone, just the two of us, was all the more evident. I felt butterflies and fiddled with my hands nervously, unsure of what to do, what to say.

Killian's hand reached over to grasp mine and he pulled it over to rest it on his thigh. I glanced up at him, and he gave me a long look before returning his attention to the road.

There was silence, but it wasn't uncomfortable. Far from it. It was like we were both bathing in each other's company, not needing words.

"Where are we going?" I asked finally as Killian directed the car out of town and up an unfamiliar road.

Killian glanced at me. His hand momentarily left mine to change gears, and I felt awkward having my lonesome hand on his muscled thigh. Just when I was about to yank it back, his hand closed on mine once more, giving it a squeeze.

"Wait and see, Freckles," he murmured.

I screwed up my nose. "I don't do well with surprises." I hated surprises. I unwrapped and rewrapped my Christmas presents every year. Mom had yet to find out.

Killian grinned. "It's not a surprise. It's a wait and see."

I glared at him. "Potato, potahto."

He chuckled and shook his head, lifting our intertwined hands so he could press his lips into my hand. I lost all motor skills at this gesture. I sure as anything forgot about my hatred of surprises. He could have taken me skydiving for all I cared at that moment.

"Impatient are we?" he murmured.

"No," I replied, my voice husky. "I'm just not the hugest fan of surprises."

Killian looked forward. "Duly noted."

I followed his eyes and the structure illuminated in front of us. The parking lot was full with cars, despite it being a Sunday. The fancy script on top of the all-glass restaurant overlooking the ocean read "Valentines." I'd heard about this place; it was the nicest restaurant in Amber. Not that that was saying much; Amber didn't boast many restaurants, but people actually traveled here to try it. I couldn't help myself as Killian parked, my eyes on the crowded tables, but be a little disappointed. The thought of going to such a nice restaurant was touching, but I didn't want to be around people. As mentioned, apart from a handful of midnight meetings, it was never Killian and me. I wanted those moments of blissful limbo when everything fell away. I wanted them to last longer than a blink of an eye. I wanted it, yet I was terrified of being alone with him, but a good kind of terrified, like the kind I felt when I was on stage on Friday.

Hence the disappointment. I sat up a little straighter. I wouldn't sulk or make my disappointment known. That would be bratty and spoilt. My mom didn't raise me like that.

A little tug on my hand moved my attention to Killian. Meeting his eyes, I had a feeling he had been watching me the entire time I was taking in the scenery.

"You good to wait here for a couple of minutes, Freckles?" he asked softly, surprising me. "I would've picked this up before I got you, so I didn't have to waste any time on this date not being with you, but it's on our way."

I gaped at him a moment. "You mean, we're not going in there?" I asked, nodding my head to the restaurant.

Killian's face didn't change, but his eyes seemed to harden just a touch. "No. You disappointed?" he asked with an edge to his voice that hadn't been there before.

"No, I'm happy," I said quickly, without thinking. *Shoot*. "I mean, this is nice, lovely actually," I backpedaled, fearing I sounded like the brat I was determined not to be. "But..." I trailed off, unable to find the words.

Killian surprised me by smiling. "But it's not us," he finished for me.

I sagged in relief. "No, it's not us," I agreed. It was strange that we could make that distinction when the 'us' was brand new and this was our first official date, but that was the way it was.

Killian looked at me for a long moment, his eyes liquid, the hardness of before was gone. "I had planned on going the traditional route and waiting until the end of the date to do this. Fuck traditional," he muttered.

Before I could ask him what he was talking about and be surprised as this was the first time he had cursed in front of me, he wasn't across from me anymore. He was there, right *there*, not just right in front of me, but kissing me. It happened so quickly, I instinctively kissed him back, then got lost in the kiss that was different than others we'd shared. I felt like it was my first kiss all over again. There was everything in this kiss. Only me and Killian, but it was everything. I didn't know where I ended and he began.

As quickly as it started, he was gone. Not truly gone, both his hands framed my face and his mouth hovered above mine.

I stared at him through my lashes. "Fuck traditional," I whispered.

Killian's body jolted at my words, and then he shook his head. "Jesus," he muttered against my mouth. "I have a feeling you're the end of life as I know it."

"Is that a good thing?" I asked.

Killian's hands tightened just a smidgeon. "Yeah, Freckles. It's a good thing."

I let out a breath of relief.

Killian smiled at me. "Sit tight for two minutes, 'kay?" he murmured against my mouth, rubbing his nose against mine.

"'Kay," I breathed back.

Killian looked at me for a moment longer, and then the air emptied as he leaned back over to his side of the car and knifed out.

I sank back against my own seat and watched him round the hood then followed the back of his body as he jogged into the restaurant.

I touched my lips absently and then fumbled into my bag for my phone, aware of the time pressure.

"It's over already? Shit, babe, I'm sorry. What a waste of a good outfit. I'll be happy to deliver some creative form of punishment to his door if you give me the address," Emma answered.

"What?" I whispered. Then I caught her meaning. "No, the date's not over yet."

"Then what are you doing calling me?" she asked in confusion. "Is he sitting there watching you talk on the phone? Lexie, I know you haven't been on a date before, but you must know that's a major *don't*."

My gaze darted to the door, aware Killian would be walking through it at any moment. "Stop talkin. I don't have much time," I hissed.

144

"Oh my God, he hasn't kidnapped you, has he?" Emma asked in panic. "Blink twice if he's kidnapped you. No, shit, I can't see you blink. Say periwinkle if you're being held against your will."

I let out an exasperated breath. "Em, shut up. I'm not kidnapped or having a bad date," I said quickly. "I think I'm having the best date in the history of all dates. He's already kissed me and told me I'm the end of his life as he knows it."

There was a pause. "Well, shit," she said finally.

"Shit's right," I agreed. "So I just wanted to call and tell you if I'm a drooling mess after having been overwhelmed with... all of this, I love you. And thanks for the outfit choice. He loves it. I think that may have been the reason for the kiss."

"Honey, it has nothing to do with the outfit and everything to do with the girl inside it," Emma said softly.

I caught a glimpse of Killian's jacket in the doorway. "He's coming back. I've got to go." I quickly hung up the phone and shoved it in my bag. I laid my palms on my thighs as Killian got back in the car. He reached back and placed two amazing smelling bags in the backseat.

His eyes found mine. "You good?"

I nodded. I was more than good.

He smiled. "Good," he muttered, turning the car on and putting his muscled arm behind me to back out of the lot. As soon as we were back on the road, he snatched my hand once more. It went willingly into his hold. He hadn't turned back to town. Instead, he turned further up the rise, a road climbing so the hills were on one side, the ocean on the other.

"Where are we going now?" I asked, glancing out the window.

"Your hatred of surprises a reason for that question?" Killian teased.

I glanced back at him, thinking. "No," I said. "Actually, I don't really need to know where we're going. I'm happy if we don't go anywhere but right here." I only realized after I said it that my sentence didn't make much literal sense. "Right here" was fluid, considering we were in a moving car, but I meant right here with Killian.

He seemed to get my meaning because his eyes blazed into mine before he turned his attention back to the road.

I reluctantly tore my gaze away from his profile. Though I could look at him for days, I guessed it would be a tad weird to keep staring at him while he drove. I turned my attention to the road. We were high, and dusk was just hitting the sky, turning it into an explosion of colors, with the waves and twinkling sea below it. It was beautiful. Though I liked my previous view.

We lapsed back into our comfortable silence and Killian pulled into a dirt road that took us toward what I guessed would be some kind of lookout.

"Aren't you worried about your car getting dirty?" I asked him as we traversed the road. I knew how much pride he put into this, that he built it with his dad. He treasured it. It was also clean, something strange for a teenage boy's car.

Killian quickly glanced at me. "Cars get dirty, babe. That's life. It's not clean or simple. You're not livin' it right if it is," he declared.

I stared at him, surprised at such a profound answer to such a simple question. "But your car's always clean," I pointed out.

"I clean it," he responded simply.

I couldn't help it, for some reason, I burst out laughing. When I found my breath again, I looked at Killian. "I would happily forgo this route if I could spare you the time of having to clean your car."

Killian gave me another sideways look before parking his car at a grassed area boasting a beautiful view of the ocean and horizon beyond. Normally, I'd be transfixed with such a view, but the way Killian gave me his full attention, nothing else existed. I reasoned I could be sitting in front of the Mona Lisa and still prefer the gaze I was locked in right now.

"Some things are worth getting dirty for, Freckles. No matter the clean-up," he murmured. We stared at each other for a long beat. "Plus," he said with a grin, releasing my hand to reach to the backseat. "Maybe I'll be treated to watching you wash it for me. Got a bikini?" he teased.

I laughed again. "In your dreams, buddy."

Killian gave me a look, one that made my stomach feel strange and my lips tingle. Then he handed me the sweet-smelling bags. "You take these. I'll get the rest."

I was about to ask him what "the rest" was, but he got out of the car. I followed suit and stood gazing at the view, not sure of what I was meant to do with these bags.

"Follow me, Freckles," his voice rasped in my ear.

I jumped slightly, not realizing Killian had even been behind me. I did as instructed as he led us out to almost the edge of the cliffed area and he laid down a big checkered rug and cooler.

It was only then it clicked. I usually was much quicker on the uptake, but Killian took up all my headspace prior to now. "A picnic," I whispered. "You made a picnic."

Killian looked at me, gently taking the bags from my hands. "Technically, I didn't *make* the picnic, considering my boy Jase hooked us up with the food. I'm merely serving it up in a different location," he corrected, pulling containers out of one bag and plates out of another.

I watched with a fluttering heart. "You made a picnic," I repeated softly. "It's perfect."

Killian set the containers down on the blanket before straightening back up. "Glad you think so. Though I'll admit, I have selfish motivations. I want you all to myself, no interruptions, no one else. Just you and me," he declared, stepping forward to grasp my hips.

The gesture and the words were amazing and would have made

me feel great if it wasn't for the pressure he exerted in the wrong place, causing me to ruin the moment by letting out an unintentional mew of pain and flinching from his grasp.

Killian's face instantly turned hard; all the soft disappeared. He stared at me in concern. "What? Did I hurt you?"

I stepped forward, touching his hands to reassure him. "No," I told him quickly. "I hurt me. I just forgot about it. Don't worry. I'm fine." I hoped he wouldn't take it any further, so I didn't have to embarrass myself.

Killian frowned. "You hurt yourself? Where? What happened?" he asked in a brisk voice.

I sighed and my face flamed. "I was a little... eager in getting out of bed last night and may have had a tussle with my bedding. A tussle I lost and the edge of my bedside table won," I said in a small voice.

I held my breath, expecting laughter. When I didn't get it, I looked up. Killian's face was inscrutable. "Show me," he commanded.

I sighed and lifted my top up, still feeling the flame of a blush on my cheeks. I exposed my hip and the purplish bruise above my low-riding jeans.

Killian hissed in a breath as his featherlight touch brushed against my skin.

I blushed for an entirely different reason this time. This wasn't his hand on my face or my arm. It was a more... intimate spot.

"Jesus, Freckles," he muttered, his eyes on the bruise, his mind obviously not in tandem with mine. Then again, he wasn't as inexperienced as me. Such a touch probably wasn't a big deal to him. I felt a stab of pain more severe than my hip at this.

"It's fine," I reassured him. "I bruise easily." My hands were still holding up my top and I was aware his fingers still brushed the top of my hip.

His ice blue eyes met mine. "I'll remember that," he said. "I'll make sure to take extra care, so I don't bruise you." His eyes stayed locked on mine and his fingers trailed along my hip. I sucked in a breath and his eyes changed; a heat entered them, and I knew his thoughts mirrored my earlier ones. His hand snapped back to his side and I let go of my top.

"Let's eat before it gets cold," he said in a husky voice.

I cleared my throat. "Good idea."

Then we ate, spoke little, watched the sunset, and enjoyed each other's company.

••••

"You seriously expected to go to Hogwarts?" Killian asked.

I nodded. "Checked the mail every day on the days leading up to my eleventh birthday and combed the skies for owls," I told him seriously.

Killian's body vibrated next to mine. He lifted our intertwined hands up toward the sky. I regarded them in the moonlight with the backdrop of the night's sky above us. We had long finished our amazing meal and were laying on our backs, side by side, looking at the stars and telling embarrassing childhood stories. Well, I was telling embarrassing childhood stories. Killian was merely listening and asking the appropriate questions.

"What did your mom think of this?" he asked when he had finished chuckling.

"I didn't tell her, of course," I said. "She could have been a Muggle. I didn't want to jeopardize my chances of going to the most prestigious school in the wizarding world just because of my big mouth."

Killian didn't just chuckle this time, he boomed with laughter, the sound ringing in the silent air. It was nice. He may have been laughing at me, but I didn't mind. I liked making him laugh, either with me or at me. I didn't think he'd had many opportunities to laugh in his life.

"Of course," I continued, "I came to the sad realization I wouldn't be going to Hogwarts soon after I turned eleven. When I told Mom a few years later, she was immensely disappointed that I didn't tell her. She told me she would've fashioned a letter herself to avoid my disappointment."

"And what would she have done when little Freckles had her bags packed, waiting to go to school?" Killian asked, his tone light.

I turned my head to regard his profile. "I asked that exact same question. She said she'd find a way to get us to King's Cross and watch as I ran into the divider between platforms nine and ten."

Killian let out another bark of laughter. "Jesus, your mom's crazy, babe. In a good way."

I nodded. "The best way."

The silence we had enjoyed a lot of tonight descended once more, but I wasn't eager to bathe in it as I had been, reveling in Killian's body next to mine, our intertwined hands.

"What happened with your mom this weekend?" I asked quietly.

There was a long pause as Killian sighed and rubbed his thumb over the back of my hand. "What always happens," he said finally, his voice flat. "The shit she puts in her body landed her in a mess I had to clean up. Though it was not just me who had to clean it up. The club is burdened with her crap too. They've got a residual sense of loyalty to my dad, even though he's five years in the dirt."

I paused for a second. "Maybe it's not just your dad they're loyal to," I whispered. "Maybe it's his son, the one who said himself the club is his family."

"Family or not, they shouldn't have to deal with that ugly stuff."

"Neither should you," I told him, anger bubbling up at the sense of responsibility a seventeen-year-old boy had to his addict mom.

The boy I liked. A lot. "But that's what family's for. Not just to enjoy the good times, to band together in the ugly."

Killian turned his head to mine. I could almost feel the weight of his gaze in the darkness. "How'd you get so wise, Freckles?"

I smiled at him. Even if he couldn't see me, I couldn't help it. "I've just got experience with family. One that isn't blood but love you like they are, no matter what."

Killian squeezed my hand. "Steve and Ava? They aren't your grandparents?" he asked.

"Yeah, they are," I replied. "They just aren't Mom's biological parents; doesn't mean they aren't my grandparents. They took Mom in when she was a kid and I was a baby. Gave her a job. Gave us a family. I've never thought about them as anything else. Family isn't about a last name. It's about a feeling."

Killian squeezed my hand. "I'm glad you've got that, Lexie. You deserve to have that."

I squeezed his hand back. "I'm glad you've got the club," I whispered. "You don't just deserve that, you deserve more."

Killian leaned over so his body hovered over mine and his hand rested lightly on my hip. "I've got more, Freckles," he said against my mouth.

Before we could say anything else, his mouth settled over mine and he kissed me. It was like the kiss in the car, different than any other one we'd ever had. Heat built in my stomach as the kiss lasted longer than any other we'd ever had. Killian's hand on my hip felt like a branding iron and his body hovering over mine swallowed me into beautiful oblivion. I didn't think about anything but how I could live in this moment forever. That I could kiss Killian forever.

I made an embarrassing sound at the back of my throat to protest his lips leaving mine. They didn't go far. He still hovered above me, and I could feel his fractured breathing on my face. His body tightened and he was still and silent, lingering like that for a split second. Then, to my dismay, he sat up, gently pulling me with him.

"It's almost ten," he said in a flat voice. "We've got to get you home."

And without even looking at me, he stood and gathered the scattered containers.

I was confused at the distance that seemed to yawn in front of us when we had been so close moments before. I pushed myself up, rolling the sleeves of his leather jacket up so I could help. I inhaled the scent of him for a moment. He'd given it to me when the night air began to bite through the thin fabric of my shirt. Just like the movies.

Though now the movie-like perfection of our date was shattered as we packed up in silence. I fought back tears as Killian barely looked in my direction when he grabbed the things I handed him, walking to the car to put them back.

I followed him, doubt crippling me as he opened the passenger door to let me in. The silence followed us from the outcrop into the car as he navigated the dirt road in the darkness and led us back onto the winding road at the top. I fiddled with my fingers the whole time, sneaking glances at him. When the headlights of another car illuminated his face, I saw it was tight and hard, and his knuckles were white as he gripped his steering wheel.

I couldn't stand this anymore. "Am I a bad kisser?" I blurted, red creeping up my cheeks the moment the words left my mouth.

Killian's head snapped to me for a second. "What?" he clipped out.

"Am I a bad kisser?" I repeated, completing my mortification, but I was determined. "Because this was... wonderful, until the kiss and now you're not speaking to me."

Killian didn't answer, but the atmosphere in the car changed, and he pulled off the road, parking on the shoulder, just before we entered town proper. He turned off the engine and leaned over to clasp my neck.

"In no universe could the way you kiss be described as bad," he murmured, his voice rough and soft at the same time. "Kissing you, Freckles, tasting how sweet you are..." He trailed off, his hands flexing at my neck. "It's good. The best kind of sweet I've ever tasted in my bitter life. That's the problem," he explained.

My heart was beating out of my chest as his words chased away the doubt, but I was confused. "How is that a problem?" I managed to choke out.

"It's a problem 'cause I don't have experience with sweet, with good. I've just realized how precious that is. How precious you are. How different to me you are. You're innocent."

I blushed even more. In fact, I was pretty sure my whole body turned crimson. He knew. Of course he knew. I'd told him he was my first kiss.

"It's nothing to be embarrassed about," Killian said firmly, reading my mind. "It's beautiful, babe. I just need to remember that. Go slow. Savor the sweet."

My breathing quickened. That was pretty much the most beautiful thing anyone had ever said to me. It's like every scene from my favorite love stories had jumped off the page, melded together, and formed this boy.

"So I'm not a bad kisser," I stated, deciding not to articulate just how much I was tumbling, falling for him.

Killian paused and I felt his smile. "No, Freckles. You're not a bad kisser." He kissed my head and leaned back over. "Now that we've clarified that, I need to get you home so your mom will let me take you out again. 'Cause I plan to. A lot," he said, his voice firm.

I smiled as he pulled back onto to the road, and of its own accord, my hand found his and rested both of ours on my thigh. It felt strange, beautifully strange being that bold.

Too soon, we pulled up outside my house. The lights blazed and I had no doubt Mom would most likely be pressing her nose up against the window. I moved my glance to Killian, who was staring at me—no, not at me, into me. I felt like he could see everything. It was ridiculous, I knew. It was our first date. But then again, things like this didn't adhere to things as trivial as logic.

"So I'm going to have to give Guinness Records a call," I told him seriously.

Killian's face changed, and he looked confused but amused. "I don't follow, Freckles."

"Well, they're going to have to knock some poor shmuck off the top and replace this as the best first date in the history of their records," I explained with a smile.

Killian grinned, and then he glanced over at my house. "You can't say things like that when I can't kiss you. Don't think your mom would want to see that," he joked, though there was a heat in his eyes.

I smiled shyly. I felt a little triumph over the fact the things I said made Killian want to kiss me, that he was saying things like that. To me.

He leaned over and kissed my head, lingering for a moment. "See you at school, Freckles," he murmured.

I glanced at him through my lashes. "Yeah, school," I repeated, having trouble stringing a sentence together.

After tearing myself away from the car, I struggled not to look at him over my shoulder the entire walk to my door. I knew he was watching me because I didn't hear his car roar away until I had sunk against the closed door.

Chapter 14

The next day, I woke up with a smile on my face, which remained the entire morning at school as I seemed to float from class to class. I had known that last night was amazing, special, beyond anything, but Emma had cemented it when I called her when I got home.

"Tell me again about what he said when he pulled off the road when you asked if you were a bad kisser," she had commanded dreamily.

I had told her. In detail. Twice. I had gone from wanting to keep the secret of Killian and me just between us to needing to dissect it with my girlfriend. A girlfriend who, I might add, never spoke dreamily on the phone. So I knew I'd fallen into something special. It didn't matter we were both in high school, and you weren't meant to find such things at this age. That most people would brush off such notions on account of my age and inexperience. None of it mattered. Not when I just knew.

Killian was leaning outside the door as I left calculus, not holding any books or maintaining any illusion that he was here for school's intended purpose. In fact, when his eyes found mine, I had the ridiculous notion that I was his purpose for being here.

He stepped forward, taking my books out of my hands and slinging his arm around my shoulder, kissing my head. "Hey, Freckles," he greeted, oblivious to the multitude of stares we were getting, like it was just him and me and no one else existed in the universe.

"Hey, Kill," I replied, deciding to follow his lead and let the various stares melt away. "Did you actually attend any classes this morning?" I asked as we entered the cafeteria and Killian directed us toward what was ours, the bands, unofficial table.

He grinned down at me. "Yes, in fact, I did," he said with a grin.

"Why do I feel like that's not true?" I teased as we sat down at the empty table.

"Why, I'm offended you think so little of me, Freckles," he replied in mock hurt.

"It's not how little I think of you. It's how little *you* think of the educational institution," I shot back.

"Oooh, first domestic," Sam cooed, placing his tray down on the table. "Twenty bucks on Lexie," he told Wyatt, who sat beside him.

I scowled at him.

"I can be the one to back up Kill," Wyatt interrupted. "He was at biology this morning, much to Mr. Morton's dismay."

"Dismay?" I repeated, placing two containers on the table. I handed one to Killian.

He raised his brows at me in question.

"Lunch," I explained. I didn't want it to be a big deal, me making lunch for him, but the way his eyes turned liquid made me think it was a big deal to him. In a way that made my stomach turn warm.

"What? We're your beloved bandmates and the key to your success, how is it Killian gets that"—he nodded to the container—"and we're stuck with a mysterious and disgusting hamburger, which may or may not contain meat?"

I grinned at him. "'Cause Killian's prettier than you," I joked.

Sam's eyes widened as if I'd actually hit him.

Killian's hand went to my neck and he pulled me close. "You can't call me pretty, Freckles, damages my street cred. Go for hauntingly handsome if you must," he murmured in my ear, his breath tickling my neck.

He released me with a grin and I flat out laughed.

"What's so funny?" Noah asked, setting his tray down, looking between Killian and me skeptically and reluctantly returning his chin lift.

Sam turned to him. "Be honest. Who do you think's more attractive, me or Killian?" he asked, ignoring Noah's question.

Noah's face paled and I knew why. "Why are you asking me?" he asked, his voice hard.

Sam didn't catch the change in atmosphere. I didn't think anyone did, apart from me. I was the only one who guessed at Noah's secret.

"Because," Sam drawled, "Lexie has informed me that Killian is better looking, therefore he gets lunch made while we are risking heart disease and food poisoning with this muck."

Noah's face changed imperceptibly and his shoulders relaxed. "Lexie's dating him. I think that comes into the equation."

Sam frowned. "That's not answering the question.".

"For fuck's sake. Killian's better looking," Wyatt said through a mouthful of food. "I'm not saying that 'cause I fancy you, bro," he reassured Killian, who was grinning. "It's on the information that you've snagged the hottest girl in school."

Killian's hand found mine.

"You think I'm the hottest girl in school?" I asked in disbelief.

Wyatt raised his eyebrows. "You passed a mirror lately?"

Sam nodded. "Hottest in school. By far," he agreed.

Noah nodded. "Never thought I'd say this, but Sam's right," he said between bites.

I rolled my eyes, fighting my blush. "Whatever," I brushed their comments off.

Killian leaned into my ear once more. "Not just the school, Freckles. Whole town," he murmured before turning his attention to the lunch I made him.

"Okay, what were we talking about? Mr. Morton's dismay, I believe," I addressed the table, changing the subject.

Wyatt laughed. "It was gold, Lexie, I tell you. I've never seen his face get that red."

I glanced at Killian. "What did you do?" I asked, waiting for a story of how he set a curtain on fire.

Killian shrugged, turning his attention to his lunch. "Merely pointed out the shortcomings of his hypothesis," he mumbled.

"You did more than point out shortcomings. You totally called him out on his mistake. Bro, you could teach that class," Wyatt expanded.

I raised my eyebrows and felt a pang at my first guess.

Killian shrugged again. "He's an idiot. It's not hard to see that."

Wyatt seemed to sense Killian's reluctance to talk about how brilliant he was, so he changed the subject. I found Killian's thigh under the table and gave it a squeeze. His dark gaze settled on me. We stared at each other a moment, then were dragged into conversation by Sam.

I floated on cloud nine for the rest of the day.

••••

"You're willing to delay shopping in order to talk to a boy?" Mom asked in horror.

I grinned at her and patted her arm, not responding, but turning so I could call the boy in question.

Mom had picked me up from school and decided to take us shopping in Hope, the next town over. She merciless teased me about how I looked lovelorn and dreamy. I barely argued. I was too busy floating in happiness. Her teasing was good-natured, and no disapproval seemed to lurk underneath it. Only disapproval in me delaying shopping in order to invite Killian to the movies later on.

"Freckles," he greeted after I had dialed.

"Hey, Kill," I said, looking at the shop window. "You're not busy are you?"

There was a pause and a clanging in the background. I guessed Killian was at the Sons of Templar garage, where he worked every day after school and on the weekends.

"Never too busy for you, Lexie."

I smiled at the store window. "Well, I hope that means you can come to the movies tonight with Mom and me. Though, I think it's only fair to warn you you've never had a movie experience quite like one with the Spencer girls. It's life changing," I informed him.

I expected a chuckle at the other end of the phone, but there was only silence.

Shoot.

"You want me to come to the movies with you and your mom?" he asked finally.

My stomach dropped. "Yeah, I mean, only if you want to. You don't have to. I understand if you don't want to come," I said, quickly trying to hide my disappointment.

"I want to come," he replied, with something strange in his tone I couldn't distinguish over the phone.

I sagged in relief. "Okay, good. I'll text you the details. I've got to go before Mom has me drawn and quartered. We're shopping in Hope, and I've committed the crime of calling you instead of letting her loose on the general public," I joked.

"You're in Hope?" Kill bit out, his voice hard and alert.

My smile fell slightly. "Yeah, why?"

I was sure I heard a muttered curse. "Nothing, Freckles. It's just... you remember what I said about not trusting anyone else wearing a cut?" he asked tightly.

"Yeah," I replied, slowly, confused. "Why? What's going on?"

"Just make sure you do that, Freckles. I'll meet you in Hope as soon as I can get away," he promised.

"Okkkayy," I dragged the word out, feeling something prickle at the back of my neck at his words, at the urgent tone.

"Be careful," he commanded.

"Yeah, I'll be careful not to let my mom empty the whole store," I joked, not knowing how much trouble we could get into in a vintage clothing store.

Killian didn't laugh. "I'll be there as soon as I can," he promised. Then he hung up.

I screwed up my nose, staring down at my phone. I shrugged my shoulders. I guessed sometimes boys were a mystery. When I turned, I wondered whether Killian was damn clairvoyant. In front of me, speaking to Mom, were a cluster of men who were wearing motorcycle vests like the cuts the Sons of Templar wore. Though they were nothing like the men I'd met at the Sons of Templar. They were rougher, a lot rougher.

I stepped forward. "Mom?" I asked, not wanting to show the extent of my uneasiness in front of men like this.

I felt the weight of various gazes on me, and my skin crawled.

"Hey, sweetie. Shit, you're almost as pretty as your momma," a bearded man greeted me, his beady eyes focused on me.

I swallowed, giving Mom a quick glance. I met his eyes with what I hoped was confidence. "Thanks," I replied.

I didn't miss the way Mom had positioned her body in front of me as if I needed protecting. I had never been this uneasy before, with the realization that Mom most likely couldn't protect me, or either of us, against any of these guys, if my first impression of them was anything to go by.

The bearded man moved his attention to Mom. "You need to let Bull know he shouldn't be letting his woman and her pretty little daughter walk the streets alone. It's not safe for girls like you," he said. I didn't miss the falseness of his concern, the threat that lingered underneath it. "Let him know you ran into Logan and we're happy to keep an eye on you both." I felt his eyes move to me once more. "More than happy," he added.

He tipped an imaginary hat at us, and just like that, he and the men with him turned their backs and sauntered to their motorcycles on the curb.

Mom and I both stared at them, and Killian's warning rang in my ears. It was my first experience of encountering people who made me truly feel unsafe. My first time understanding that the bad things on the news and in the papers actually happened to people. Actually could happen to me.

● ● ● ●

"Those guys today, they were bad guys, weren't they?" I asked Killian as he handed me popcorn, putting his hand on the small of my back while he managed to juggle two drinks. It was impressive.

His dark gaze found mine as we walked toward the theater. "Yeah, Freckles," he bit out the answer. His voice was soft but his face was granite.

It was just me and Kill at the movies. Mom was at home with an angry-looking Zane. A murderous-looking Zane. He turned up at the store in Hope about an hour into our shopping expedition. Along with what looked like half of the club, who escorted us all the way home. Yes, escorted us. I wasn't an idiot; I knew what this meant. What Kill had obviously told Zane and that it must have been something serious to have him turning up to a vintage shop and going home with us. I hoped he wasn't mad at Mom, like he looked like he was when we left for the movies after Mom declared she and Zane needed to have a "chat."

"That guy, Logan, he said he knew Zane," I continued as we

walked.

Killian's jaw hardened once more. "He doesn't. Not yet at least. Soon he'll know him really well."

I stopped just outside the doors to our theater. "What does that mean?" I asked, turning to him.

Killian regarded me. "Nothing, babe. Let's just watch the movie."

I stood my ground. "We're not going to watch the movie until you answer the question," I declared. I was serious. I was willing to give up the latest Bond film for this stare down.

Killian seemed to see this in my eyes because he sighed in defeat and gently took my elbow to direct us to a seat. I sat silently, raising my eyebrow expectantly.

"What do you know about the club?" he asked, his hand resting on my thigh.

I shrugged. "Not much. Just that guy Cade is the president and that Zane's in it. That they're your family. That it's about motorcycles and brotherhood."

Killian's face changed as I spoke, some of the hardness melting from his eyes. "Yeah, brotherhood. That's the core of it, babe. Family, loyalty as well. It's a world, an alternative to the one that society tells us to live in. It's one where you can be free. Sometimes freedom comes at a price. Sometimes freedom means breaking chains disguised as laws."

"You mean that the Sons are outlaws? Criminals?" I clarified.

Killian's eyes turned guarded. "One of many words for it, Freckles. Outlaws are just people livin' outside those chains I described before. I know there was a time before I was old enough to understand, a time when they were so far outside the law they made their own chains. Chains that almost strangled the club. That left scars." His eyes burned into mine, and I sensed there was a story behind that. A big one. One I wouldn't hear on a seat outside a movie theater with a bucket of popcorn in my hands. I was getting

162

the CliffNotes version.

"With Cade as president, they've broken free of those chains. We have," he corrected. "The club is never going to be contained, be chained by anything. But they're not going to do stupid shit that lands its members behind bars, not anymore," he said.

I chewed over his words. "To live outside the law, you must be honest," I murmured.

Killian smiled. "Bob Dylan's never been more appropriate."

My eyes widened at him. I was surprised he knew that. Most people our age couldn't even name one of his songs, let alone quote him.

"I listen to real music, Freckles. The kind without computer generated bullshit," he clarified.

"Well then, you're perfect for me," I joked.

"Nah, babe. You've got that the wrong way around."

I shelved that comment for later when I could fawn over it in the safety of my bedroom. For now, I needed more information.

"So the men in Hope, how do they fit into this? Apart from making stupid comments to me and Mom," I continued.

Any softness in Killian's eyes turned to granite. "They what?" he clipped. His voice was quiet, almost a whisper, but there was something about it that scared me. It scared me because it wasn't the look of a boy. It was the look of a man. A very dangerous man.

"Nothing," I said quickly, hoping I could tame the beast I unwittingly unleashed. "Stupid stuff that sleazy guys say."

The storm that descended over Killian's face told me I should not have said that. "You're sixteen," he clipped out. "They've got no business saying anything to a fuckin' sixteen-year-old. More importantly, you're mine. They're not just gonna meet Bull; they're gonna become acquainted with me," he declared, his voice full of menace.

I didn't even have time to suggest and maybe fawn over the

"mine" comment. I placed the popcorn down and clutched his hands. "If that means what I think it means, you are not going to," I commanded.

Killian's face was blank. "You don't get a say."

Oh, no he didn't. I leaned back, pursing my lips. He had just unleashed a monster of his own, one that I didn't even know resided inside me. "I don't get a say," I repeated in a quiet tone.

It looked like Killian was going to say something, backpedal most likely, if the look of realization on his face was anything to go by. I didn't give him the chance.

"So is this because I'm a girl or because I'm an entire year younger than you so I should somehow respect my elders?" I asked.

Killian regarded me. "It's neither. It's club business," he said cryptically like that was an answer.

"I don't get how it's 'club business'"—I finger quoted—"when my mom and I were the ones to encounter the douchebags on bikes. If anyone has the right to go and give any kind of beat down, which I'm not saying anyone does, it would be me and Mom."

I ignored the way Killian raised his eyebrows in amusement at that statement.

"Furthermore, I'm not sure how a five-minute exchange requires this much reaction, nor do I understand why Zane turned up shopping, and we had a bevy of motorcycles escorting us home," I continued, building up steam. "Putting aside that mystery, the fact that I'm at the epicenter of this entire debacle, and it's my boyfriend who is talking about engaging in a *conversation*, which I'm guessing is a euphemism for fight, with grown men, definitely means I get a fricking say," I declared, scowling at him.

Killian didn't flinch in the face of my rage. I guess I wasn't surprised. He was just declaring war against an entire motorcycle club. A teenage girl's wrath was nothing against that. I didn't expect him to smile. For his eyes to glow.

"First time you've called me your boyfriend, Freckles. I like it."

I widened my eyes. "*That's* what you got out of that?" I asked in disbelief. I stood up, fuming with anger I wasn't accustomed to. "I need to leave before I try to drown you in that bucket of popcorn," I declared, nodding my head downward.

Kill's hand caught mine before I could even take one step. He gently pulled my body to him. "I'm not letting you storm off," he murmured. "As cute as you are when you're angry, I'm not sure I like the end result of you trying to get away from me."

"Well, your solution to that conundrum's easy. Don't make me angry," I retorted. "You don't like me when I'm angry." I couldn't help myself, even in a serious moment; I couldn't stop my *Hulk* references. I blamed it on my mom. She found a way to mention the *Godfather* when she was angry.

I could tell Killian was fighting a grin, but I had to give it to him, his face stayed serious. "I have a feeling I'll like you any way I can take you," he responded. "But I'm sorry. I didn't mean what I said the way you took it. It's hard to explain to someone who hasn't grown up with the club at their backs, belonging to the club. But when you're a part of the club and someone screws with you, the club hits back. As one collective fist. And we pack a punch, Freckles. Bull claimed your mom. I've claimed you. It means you're family. We've got your back." He stroked my face. "It's because of your connection to the club these guys even bothered you, so it is our responsibility to make sure that doesn't happen again."

I stared at him, my anger melting away as quickly as a punctured balloon deflated. "The club will make sure," I clarified.

Killian nodded.

"The *men* in the club. Not you. Promise me. I don't want you getting hurt," I pleaded.

Killian's face was hard. "I can take care of myself, babe."

I nodded. "I know that. But I can't. I can't handle the thought of you getting hurt because of me. Promise me."

Killian stared at me. "You gotta understand, Freckles, I'm prospecting for the Sons as soon as I turn eighteen. I won't be able to sit this kind of stuff out. Not in the future."

My stomach lurched at the thought. "That's the future. This is now."

He shook his head and kissed my nose. "It doesn't bode well for me, my inability to say no to you," he murmured.

I grinned. "But it does bode well for me, grasshopper."

Kill chuckled and reached down to grab our forgotten snacks. "Let's get you into the movie before you convince me to do anything else," he ordered.

"Like sell your soul to the devil?" I teased.

"Someone already owns that, Freckles, but it sure as hell isn't the devil," he muttered as we walked into the dark movie theater.

On account of the movie having already started, I didn't get to respond to that. But my hand did grasp his the entire time.

Chapter 15

"You know if the wind changes, your face will freeze that way," Mom observed from the door.

I looked up from my homework. "I'm smiling. What's the problem with that?"

She pushed forward and landed herself on my bed. "People that smile all the time are creepy. Like Ted Bundy type creepy. I can't have you walking around the house like that. I'll have to sleep with one eye open, just in case you snap."

I swiveled my chair around to face her. "Walk around like what? Happy?"

She nodded. "Yes. It's not healthy. I'm worried for you. No teenager should walk around constantly happy. Aren't you meant to wander around all broody and angry at the world?"

I laughed and pushed off my chair, moving to lie beside her on my bed. "Would it make you happier if I listened to death metal and slammed doors a lot?" I asked seriously.

Mom pondered. "Yes, yes it would," she deadpanned.

I laughed. Mom grasped my hand. "All jokes aside, doll face. I'm happy you're happy. Is it the boy?" she asked softly.

I thought a moment. Since the weekend, since the movies, it felt like Killian had spent every spare moment with me. He worked every day after school, but he would always stop by after, more often than not, staying for dinner. Mom accepted him into the fold easily, ribbing him as she did me. He didn't seem to mind. Though he never said much, he always had a half grin on his face. When the band was over, he'd either take off on his bike while we practiced or lounged on a sofa in the garage watching us. Or more accurately, watching me.

"Yes and no," I said finally. "He makes me happy. But it's not just him. It's my boys. The ones who are like brothers. The fact I get to make music with them, and it's good. It's Amber. This little town is like home already. It's that Steve and Ava are coming to visit in three weeks." I squeezed her hand. "It's my mom is happy. That she has her person," I whispered, turning my head to glance at her. "When does Zane get back from his run?" I was kind of peeved he had to take off before I even got to see him and Mom as a couple. A "run," Killian explained, was going off for days to weeks on elusive "club business."

Mom's face went blank, and she squeezed my hand before sitting up abruptly. "I'm not sure, doll. Biker missions are top secret. I'm more apt to get the nuclear launch codes than Zane's return date," she joked.

I narrowed my brows at her as she stood up. Her humor seemed forced. My heart stopped for a second, dread replacing the joy that had been there moments before.

"Is everything okay, Mom? With you and Zane I mean?" I asked, sitting up.

Mom smiled brightly, but it didn't reach her eyes. "Everything's fine," she reassured me, her voice going high at the end. "I've got to go make dinner if Killian's coming over, which I assume he is considering it's been approximately four hours since you last saw him. He'll be having withdrawal symptoms."

I smelled something fishy with her eagerness to leave. "Make dinner?" I repeated.

She scowled at me. "Ordering Chinese means making dinner," she said defensively.

I sighed, pushing up off my bed. "*I'll* make dinner. Something that doesn't come in a box to ensure my mom and boyfriend don't get scurvy," I replied.

Mom gave me a look. "I eat fruit," she protested.

"Name the last time you ate something with nutritional value," I challenged.

Mom screwed up her nose and followed me into the kitchen silently, obviously wracking her brain. "I had a pink starburst yesterday!" she declared triumphantly.

I craned my head around the refrigerator door. "Candy in no way counts," I informed her.

"It was strawberry flavored," she argued.

"*Flavored,*" I emphasized the words as I pulled out vegetables. I held up a carrot. "Does this foreign object look familiar?"

She pretended to think. "Don't tell me, don't tell me," she chanted sarcastically.

I rolled my eyes. "Are you going to make yourself useful and helpful?"

Mom nodded, making her way to the refrigerator I just closed. "You bet your cute butt I am," she replied, reaching in. "I'll be consuming my entrée of fruit salad." The door shut and she held up a bottle of wine. "Grapes," she said with a grin.

••••

"How did Mom seem at dinner?" I asked Killian, fiddling with my guitar. "Do you think she seemed weird?"

Killian glanced up from where he was seated at my desk. He was allowed in my room on the proviso the door stayed open, and he stayed off horizontal surfaces, on Mom's instruction.

"Is that a trick question?" he replied, fighting a grin.

I pushed my hair off my face and scowled at him. "No. I'm

169

serious. I thought she's seemed... off since last week. I'm worried it has something to do with her and Zane. Have you talked to him?"

Killian raised his brows. "Babe, he's on a run," he told me as if I didn't know.

"I know that. But phones exist," I pointed out. Though Kill barely used his apart from texting me now and then, asking if I was busy or telling me he couldn't come over on rare occasions.

"Yeah, but do you really think Bull and I call each other and gab about our days and his love life?" he asked, his eyes teasing. "You actually have to talk in order to use the phone."

I narrowed my eyes. "Zane talks," I defended, feeling protective.

Kill shook his head. "Barely. Not to anyone, apart from you and your mom," he said quietly.

I chewed over this, absently strumming my guitar.

"Don't worry, Freckles. I'm sure all's well in the land of Bull. As well as it can be. I can tell you it's been better than it has been in memory since you and Mia entered his life," he told me.

I glanced up at him, feeling a smile creep onto my face. Kill's words reassured me.

"Now can we stop talking about your mom's love life and can you play me something?" he asked.

My smile got bigger. We had gotten into a ritual when Kill came over. Sometimes we'd do homework. Correction, *I'd* do homework, he'd either sit watching or helping me, or read a book. Kill didn't do homework. Or we watched a movie with my mom. Kill quickly understood how serious we took movies and how emotionally invested we were in characters on *The Walking Dead*. He'd slotted into the process effortlessly. He even comforted me when I thought Glenn was dead, not even acting like I was a crazy person for getting emotional over a fictional character.

But whatever we did, we finished the night with me playing and singing. I'd felt self-conscious at first. When I was in my room singing and playing, that was when I was most me. When everything was stripped raw, and I projected my true self while I got lost in the music. The way he'd looked at me after I'd played "Like a Rolling Stone" by Bob Dylan had curbed all my fears and scared the crap out of me. It was like he understood music was my soul, my everything. Somehow he inserted himself into that piece of my identity. Secured his own place.

"Any requests?" I asked.

Kill leaned back, crossing his arms. "Nah, babe, anything you play is beautiful."

A blush crept up my cheeks and turned my head down, strumming. I started to softly sing Alice Kristiansen's cover of "We Don't Eat" and soon found the courage to move my gaze up and lock my eyes on Killian's ice blue ones and not tear it away. I sang the entire song to him, and we entered that space that was just ours. The one where the present was the only thing that mattered. The past and future were inconsequential. A distant memory.

A weird sort of loss settled over me as I sang the last word and silence roared louder than my strumming.

The electricity in the air crackled between Killian and me as neither of us said anything.

"Can the songbird of our generation keep it down? I'm trying to watch *Toddlers and Tiaras*. You're ruining the trashmosphere." Mom cut the moment away from the door. She glanced at Killian. "That's trashy atmosphere. If you're gonna hang with the Spencer girls, you need to know our language," she informed him. Her gaze flickered back to me. "That was beautiful, kid. No surprises there." She gave me a sad smile then pushed off the doorway. "*Toddlers in Tiaras* is calling to me. I'm coming, Honey Boo Boo," she said to an imaginary person in the living room. "Also, it's your friendly timekeeper reminding you it's 9:53. Say your good-byes, kids. You have to survive an entire night without each other," she proclaimed dramatically.

"Good-bye, Mom," I said, glaring at her.

She gave me a pageant wave then disappeared.

Killian looked at me. "Seems normal to me," he said. "Well, your mom's version of normal."

I poked my tongue out at him and placed my guitar on the bed, padding over to him. I lifted myself up to set my butt on the desk and swung my feet. Killian snagged my hand and twirled his fingers against mine.

"You nervous for Saturday, Freckles?" he asked after a moment of silence.

I looked up from my inspection of our intertwined hands. His large calloused one engulfed my tiny one. He had the hands of a man already.

"Nervous?" I repeated. "No way. I'm excited. I can't wait to meet the rest of your club. The people you call family."

Saturday, Rosie, Cade's sister, was throwing a big barbecue at her place, one that the entire club and its extended family would be going to. I hadn't been to anything connected to the club yet, and I couldn't wait. I was fascinated by the world that Kill told me about, about their way of life. I couldn't wait to see it in the flesh, to experience it. I also wanted to inject myself into the family Kill considered blood like he had here. On that thought, my stomach dropped.

"Are you nervous?" I asked in a small voice. "For your family to meet me? That I won't fit in there?" I never felt uncomfortable in my own skin, and Kill never made me feel like that, but I wanted so desperately to fit into Killian's life, I felt uncertainty. I hated it.

Kill's face turned hard, but his eyes were liquid as he pushed off the chair and stood in front of me. His hands pushed my hair off my face and cupped my jaw. "Anywhere that I am, that I belong, automatically comes with a place for you," he murmured. "You don't need to fit because there's no way you can slot in anywhere. You're one of a kind, Lexie. I'm proud as shit to be introducing you as my girl on Saturday, don't forget that."

I gazed at him. "'Kay," I replied like a dummy.

Killian smiled. He bent his head to brush his lips against mine. "Got to go now," he mumbled against my lips.

"Unh-unh." I made a sound of protest at the back of my throat.

"See you in the morning," he continued.

"You'll bring coffee?" I asked, finding coherent thought.

Kill chuckled. "I value my life, so yes."

I grinned at him. That was another routine we'd fallen into. Kill drove me to and from school every day, dropping me off before he went to work at the garage. When he'd learned about mine and Mom's addiction to Shelly's coffee—the woman who owned the café in town—he had brought us each one every morning.

Mom had declared she was going to name her first-born child after him the first morning this happened.

"You already have a first-born child and her name is Lexie," I reminded her.

"Names can be changed. Your new middle name is Killian," she decided with a grin, then winked at Kill. That moment was when Kill broke through whatever residual doubts Mom had over him. Caffeine was the surest way to my mother's heart.

"Gonna go to sleep hearing your beautiful voice in my ear, Freckles," he whispered, bringing me back into the moment, "like I do every night." He kissed my head and then he walked out of my room. I listened to him say good-bye to Mom and then smiled.

I was definitely looking forward to Saturday.

•••

I threw up my hands. "Nope. I give up. You're going to have to chauffeur me around until the end of time," I moaned, sinking my head onto the steering wheel. The steering wheel of Kill's car, which he was attempting to teach me how to drive. So he had been subjected to my utter inability to control a motor vehicle.

"Remind me to murder my mother when I get home," I said, my voice muffled. "It's all her fault I'm in this situation. If she hadn't opened her big mouth, you'd still be blissfully ignorant about this." I waved my hands above my head. "And I'd still have some dignity intact." Mom had told Killian about the fact I was yet to learn how to drive after the incident in Hope. Killian had promised to teach me, and he had the afternoon off work, so we began lessons. They weren't going well.

"Freckles, take your head off the steering wheel," Killian ordered, a hint of laughter in his tone.

"No," I sulked.

"Lexie," he warned.

I huffed out a breath and did as he asked, scowling at his grinning face. He pushed a hair out of my face.

"You reconsidering our relationship status now that you know I'm an idiot?" I asked seriously.

Killian's grin disappeared and his hand went to cup my cheek. "Don't ever want to hear you talking that way about yourself, joking or not," he ordered. "I also don't want to hear crazy talk about me reconsidering this." His thumb ran along my cheek. "That's not gonna be happening anytime soon," he promised.

I blinked at him through my lashes, all of my mortification forgotten.

"Now, start the car again. Remember to put your foot on the clutch. Go slow, Freckles. We ain't in no rush. Actually, I'll be happy if you stall a hundred more times, if that means I get a hundred more moments in the car with you," he murmured, his hand leaving mine.

I blinked at him again, my brain turning to wonderful mush.

"Babe, start the car," he reminded me softly.

"Right," I whispered. "Just a warning though," I said, shifting my attention to the pedals and turning the car on, "you're gonna have to give me at least five seconds grace every time you say stuff like that."

"Stuff like what?" Killian asked, playing ignorant.

I looked at him with my hand on the ignition. "You know what."

I had to give it to him, he looked genuinely unaware. "No, I don't."

I sighed and worked up the courage. "Stuff like what you just said. The beautiful, romance-novel-type stuff. Stuff that makes me fall," I whispered, not able to break eye contact with him.

His face turned inscrutable. "Fall where, Freckles?" he rasped.

"Fall into you, into this," I whispered, my voice barely audible.

He stared at me for a long moment then leaned forward and pressed his mouth to mine. He pulled back after kissing me, hands at either side of my face. "Just a warning, babe, you're gonna have to be prepared for me to kiss you when you say shit like that," he murmured against my mouth.

"Like what?" I whispered back.

His eyes searched mine. "Shit that makes me want to fall all over again."

He sat back in his seat like he hadn't just rocked my world.

"Start the car, Freckles," he commanded softly.

I let out a breath. "I think I'm gonna need ten seconds," I told him.

He didn't say anything, but I saw a small grin on the side of his mouth.

••••

175

"Havin' fun, Freckles?" a deep voice tickled my ear.

Shivers descended down my spine in the best way as I turned around. I grinned at Killian.

"You scared all the kids away," I observed, watching the little toddlers disperse at the entrance of my boyfriend all dressed in black.

My boyfriend. I never got tired of saying that. The boy towering over me, looking at me with those ice blue eyes that seemed to be as deep as the ocean itself. As if the ocean itself was focused on me.

"Good," he muttered, stepping forward to clasp my wrist. "I've been waiting for a moment with my girl for eternity." He paused, his eyes briefly leaving mine. His hard stare turned empty and dangerous as he regarded his biker brethren. "Which may have been good since I had time to educate my future brothers where their eyes should not be straying," he gritted out, his own gaze moving down my body. "Though, I'm fighting a losing battle," he muttered, his eyes deep again. Dark.

I blushed, happy that he seemed to respond so well to my outfit choice. Who knew my budding biker boyfriend would appreciate a vintage, multicolored, embellished cropped jacket over a flowing, white, lace dress that stopped well above my knee?

I regarded my slouchy-heeled ankle boots, unsure of where to look. His hungry gaze made my stomach go wild. His hand went to my chin and moved it up so I made eye contact with him.

"Proud as anything, Freckles, to let these guys know you're mine. Shit." He shook his head. "Can hardly believe it myself. But I'm happy to stay sleeping, if I'm dreaming that is."

My breath left me. Kill waited the five seconds we talked about, not minding the silence while the party roared around us. How could he be so broody and mysterious and sometimes downright mute and then say such eloquent, beautiful things? I liked to think of myself as well-read and a songwriter to boot, but I'd have trouble reciting the alphabet if you asked me now. Killian seemed content, watching me, one hand cupping my cheek, the other rubbing at my wrist.

"Kid," a savage voice shattered the moment and I jumped at the roughness of the tone.

My face broke into a huge grin to see Zane was the owner of that bark. He stood a reasonable distance away, but his eyes were latched on Killian. He was also the owner of the murderous look that Killian was receiving. I guessed it was likely to bring grown men to their knees. Not Killian. He stared right back.

"Steg needs to talk to you," he growled. "And those hands need to be off Lexie."

Kill's hands dropped to his sides and I could actually feel the anger pulsating through him. I could tell he wanted to argue, but even someone as brave as Kill was no match for Zane.

His eyes snapped to me, the anger falling away. "I'll find you later, Freckles," he murmured purposefully before giving Zane one last scowl and storming into Rosie's house. I watched his back for a second, and then my excitement gave way to my longing. I beamed at Zane's hard face and ran over to him. I didn't even think. I threw my arms around his huge body. I'd missed him. Two weeks I hadn't seen him, hadn't been able to wander over to his garage to seek his quiet company, to feel my head clear as we strummed together.

"I'm so glad you're back," I murmured into his cut, inhaling the leather smell.

His huge hands settled lightly on my arms, and he gently pulled me back to inspect me at arm's length. "Good to be back, Lex," he clipped. His face was blank, but his eyes smiled. He may not say much, but I knew warmth lurked underneath his tone, way down.

"Did you have a good run? Or ride? Or whatever." I waved my hand. "Where did you go?" I asked him, rapid-fire.

"Bit of everywhere, Lex. New Mexico, mostly."

"But you're home now," I pointed out.

Zane nodded. "There's no place like home."

My smile widened. "Did you just quote the *Wizard of Oz*?" I teased.

"The wizard of what?" Zane questioned. Zane's face remained blank, but he didn't show any notion of being annoyed at having been stuck talking to a teenage girl at a biker party. He seemed... happy. Well, his version of happy, which made me ecstatic. Maybe we could do it. Mom and me. Make him happy. More specifically Mom, but I hoped that I contributed too.

I grinned. "Don't play dumb. Every person on planet Earth knows *Wizard of Oz*. Dorothy, the tin man? Flying monkeys? Witches? Sparkly shoes?" I reminded him.

Zane raised his eyebrows in a way that said, "Do I look like I watch movies about sparkly shoes?"

"Oh my God. You haven't watched the *Wizard of Oz*," I declared in shock. "Right, okay. Game plan. You'll come over to our place tonight with snacks, lots of snacks, and we shall rectify the situation."

My grin fell short as Zane's attention moved from me and focused on something over my shoulder. His face turned hard and the light left his eyes. I followed his gaze. It was focused on Mom. She had her phone to her ear, and my stomach dropped when I laid eyes on her. I didn't know how I knew exactly, maybe it was the frozen blank look on Mom's face, but something was wrong. Really wrong.

Zane's hand went to my chin. "You stay here, Lex. I'll see to your mom," he told me firmly.

"But," I argued, needing to know, needing to make sure she was okay.

"I got her, darlin'," he declared.

I stared into his eyes, something mingling with the dread,

something warm at the fact that Zane did "have" Mom. I nodded silently.

I watched Zane stride over to Mom, my body frozen in its spot. Some weird psychic part of me knew that whatever was on the other side of that phone, even Zane couldn't fix.

I was right.

Chapter 16

Dread seemed to swallow me up, to paralyze me as I watched Mom's face contort in pain and her collapse into a chair as if her legs just stopped working. Zane crouched in front of her, ripping the phone from her ear.

"Lexie, honey, how about we go inside?" a soft voice suggested.

My gaze flickered to Gwen, Cade's seriously pretty and nice wife. She regarded me in concern, her eyes flickering at where mine had been resting moments ago.

"I-I've got to talk to my mom," I said, my voice dry.

"Sweetie—" she protested, but my wooden legs had already moved me away from her and toward Mom and Zane. It was rude, walking away like that, but that instinct, that same one that told me something was very wrong, told me to do it.

I made it within hearing distance to hear an unfamiliar voice. It sounded vaguely like my mom, but it was wrong. Different. Ugly. Pain had contorted it.

"Ava bakes brownies," she choked out. "Who would want to hurt a grandma who bakes brownies?"

My blood turned to ice at her words. My heart started beating so loud I could hear it in my throat.

"Mom?" I choked out.

Both her and Zane's heads snapped to me. I actually flinched when I saw the entirety of mom's face, which had been obscured by Zane. Like her voice, I barely recognized it. It was the same basic shape, the same hair, nose, and mouth. But it was wrong. Something changed it, ripped through it without breaking the skin.

Mom pushed off the chair she was on with what looked like a massive physical effort. Zane was almost glued to her back as she came to stand in front of me.

"Doll face, let's go home," she murmured, trying to herd me toward the street.

I couldn't move. Not from this spot. This was the very last place I had stood where everything had been okay. If I moved from this spot, I'd fall off, into whatever had ripped my strong and beautiful mom apart with one call. I needed to stay in this happy spot, but I also needed to know.

"No," I argued. "I want to know now. Tell me what's going on."

Zane stepped forward, strength radiating from his strong form, yet none of it seemed to leak into me. "Lex, listen to your mom. We'll get you home and you can talk there," he murmured. His face had softened and his eyes were light once more. Not with a smile. With pity. Concern.

"No," I choked out. I had to stay in my spot. I was terrified I wouldn't be able to handle it anywhere else but this spot. I didn't know why, but I just knew.

"Freckles," a soft voice rumbled in my ear, and I felt Killian's heat at my back, his hand at my elbow.

I wrenched it from his grip. "No, Kill," I croaked. I couldn't even look at him. My eyes were glued in one place. "Mom?" I probed.

Mom moved forward, right in my space, her hands moving to cup my face. It was bad. Whatever it was, it was bad.

"It's Ava and Steve," she whispered, her eyes glittering with pain.

It took a moment for the words to filter through my brain. Then they got there, and pain zapped through me like a physical thing, at Mom's tortured voice saying those names.

"They're going to be okay though?" I pleaded. They had to be okay. Whatever this was, it could be fixed. It could get better.

There was a pause. A pause that stretched on so long I knew. I knew, but I wouldn't believe it. Not until my mom spoke in a voice so drenched with pain. Then I did.

"No, baby," she choked out.

Two words and everything in me froze. It was like someone hit pause on my brain. Though everything still moved around me, Mom pulled me into her arms. She murmured words that barely penetrated, muffled words that sounded like I was listening from underwater. Words that filtered through and told my brain what my broken heart already knew. Ava and Steve were dead. It was then I was surrounded by the arms that were meant to make everything better that I hit play again. Then I realized Mom couldn't make this better. Nothing could make this better.

My body shook uncontrollably; pain stabbed into me like a million needles. I didn't even know it was possible to feel a yawning emptiness and all-encompassing agony at the same time. Until now. I couldn't hold my weight up any longer and my legs buckled beneath me. I wanted to sink to the ground, to melt into some puddle of nothingness, of blackness where this wasn't real. Where I realized that this was just a terrible, terrible nightmare and I would call Ava and laugh about it.

I'd never hear Ava laugh again. Or see Steve's eyes crinkle at the corners when I sang country songs with him.

I didn't sink into the ground as I yearned to. Instead, I went up, up into a hard body that smelled familiar of leather. That held strength. Safety. I buried my head in the leather of Zane's cut and clutched it as hard as I could, wanting to escape inside it.

"I've got you, Lex," he murmured into my hair.

Those words were the last thing I heard before I fell into the abyss.

"You think you can walk into the house, baby doll?" a soft voice filtered through my foggy, pain-drenched mind.

I lifted my head from Mom's shoulder, blinking. We were in our car, in front of our house. I didn't even remember the ride. I only remembered the pain. I glanced at Mom. She was trying to be strong for me. I had to be just as strong for her. So I nodded.

"That's my strong girl," she cooed, kissing my head lightly. "We'll get through this, doll face, promise you," she whispered.

Prior to this terrible day, I was likely to believe almost anything my mom promised me, my faith in her was that unwavering. But right now, grief seemed to have stripped away everything I had been certain about. It had torn through my world like a tornado, destroying everything in its path. Only rubble remained.

Mom cupped my cheeks, bringing my face close to hers. "When your life has been full of light and happiness, the first eclipse that casts a shadow over it seems like it's going to last forever. But it won't. It doesn't. The light will come back, shine brighter than ever, and you'll be the stronger person for it," she promised.

Her words penetrated the darkness that had cloaked itself over my soul. A tiny logical part of my brain realized the truth in that statement. People survived. People lived through loss every day. But that was *people*. Others. I didn't realize how hard their struggle was, appreciated from my golden throne of happiness, not realizing that one phone call could topple me off.

I met her eyes and nodded once more. I had to cling to something, so I decided to cling to those words. I clung to her, burying my face in her chest, hoping beyond hope that my mother's arms, which had healed everything in the past, could heal this.

"Let's get my girls inside," a deep voice declared.

Zane. I had forgotten he was even here. That he had driven us here. He gently grasped my arms, lifting me out of the car and setting me on my feet. Without hesitation, his huge arm went around my shoulders and directed me to the house, my mom was on my other side, clutching my hand.

Had this been any other moment, my heart would have filled with joy at Zane calling us his girls, at him injecting himself seamlessly into our family unit, like he'd meant to be there all along.

This wasn't any other moment.

Joy seemed like an abstract, distant concept. A fairy tale that would never be real. Not now. Not when I knew what the world could do. How could you feel joy when you knew what true pain was like?

•••

When I woke up, it took me a second to remember. I forgot. In those blissful moments between sleep and consciousness, I forgot. When I sat up, touched my feet to the carpet, grounded myself in the stark reality, I remembered. The pain wasn't likely going to let me forget.

I clutched my middle for a moment, trying desperately to hold myself together. You couldn't feel this without splitting in two. Without falling apart. Tears streamed down my face as I remembered them. The last time I'd seen them. The last time I would ever see them.

Ava kissed my head, her beautifully made-up eyes filled with tears. She squeezed my upper arms.

I grinned at her. "Don't cry, Ava. It's only a short five-hour plane ride away," I said. Then my own eyes filled with tears. I had never been further than twenty minutes away from Ava, my grandma. My second mom.

She pulled me into her arms, and I inhaled her signature perfume that filled me with nostalgia and comfort.

"We'll come and visit all the time, I promise," she murmured against my head. "I intend on being on a first-name basis with all stewardesses on the flight. I'll be making the trip that often," she promised, pulling me back.

I smiled, wiping my eyes. "Probably easier to just buy a jet," I deadpanned.

She nodded seriously. "I'll look into it." She stroked my cheek. "Steve and I are so proud of you, honey. You and your mom both. Couldn't be prouder if we tried," she whispered.

"Don't say that," Mom whined from behind her. "That'll give her a complex, a big head. You've got to knock her down a bit, so she reaches her true potential."

Ava laughed. "Okay, Steve and I are only moderately proud of you," she amended, playing along. She was well acquainted with Mom and my specific brand of humor. She should be, considering she was partly responsible for it. You wouldn't think it. She wore her hair in a demure chignon every day, wore slacks and designer court shoes and sweater sets. It was part of the charm.

"Stop hogging my little chickee," Steve complained from behind Ava, putting his hands on her shoulders. His green eyes twinkled, and his tanned face stretched into a grin. He was almost completely gray, but his masculine face held hardly any wrinkles. Mom teased him constantly about it, saying he slathered it in expensive face creams to get that result. He took the ribbing in stride. Like I said, he was used to it; Ava was his wife. Mom was, for all intents and purposes, his daughter.

Ava kissed my cheek, wiping the lipstick that no doubt transferred onto my cheek after doing so. "Love you, baby girl," she whispered.

"You too," I whispered back.

Ava gave my arms one last squeeze and moved to say her good-byes to Mom.

Steve stood in front of me and ruffled my head. "You gonna keep your mom in line for me, chickee?" he asked.

I grinned up at him. "I'll try my best, but you know that's a full-time job and I have to attend high school too."

Steve nodded. "Yes, I agree. She's a lost cause, I fear," he agreed somberly. "Just do your best. Make sure she doesn't burn anything down, most importantly my hotel."

I laughed. "I can't make any promises."

Mom and I were moving to Amber, California so Mom could manage Steve's newest purchase, a boutique hotel on the beach. Steve owned many around the country, which was how Mom came to meet him and Ava almost sixteen years ago. She had left home, for reasons I didn't fully know, and found a job with them. They took pity on the teenage mother and gave her a job and a place to live. They also gave her a family. Gave me that.

Steve pulled me into his rough embrace. "I'll miss you, kiddo," he murmured in my ear.

"Get working on that jet. It'll make things so much easier," I told him when he let me go.

I had intended it as a joke, but he nodded, giving me a thoughtful look. "I'll do that."

My eyes popped out. I shouldn't be surprised, not only were Steve and Ava really wealthy, Steve would do anything for Mom and me. I wouldn't put it past him to do something rash just so he could come and see us whenever he wanted. I didn't think he was actually rich enough to buy a jet, but he'd spend his last dollar for us.

"Regular air travel will do just fine," I said firmly.

Steve grinned. "Fine's never good enough for my girls."

"Will Amelia and Alexis Spencer please come to the gate, this is your final call," a voice called over the loud speaker.

I turned to Mom, my eyes wide. "Mom! You said we had plenty of time," I near screeched, gathering my bags.

She shrugged, grinning. "We do."

I gave her a look. "We don't. The lady on the speaker just said so. Why did you do this?"

She hitched her bag over my shoulder. "I love it when they call your name. It's like we're celebrities," she mused.

I gaped at her. "We'll be the most hated people on the plane," I corrected.

Mom didn't look worried. I clutched her hand, dragging her away from Steve and Ava.

Steve merely shook his head, pulling Ava into his arms.

I gave them a distracted wave. "Bye!"

Ava blew us a kiss. "Bye, babies."

I sobbed as I realized I was rushing. It was the last time I ever saw them, and I hadn't even said a proper good-bye. I was too busy worrying about what a plane full of strangers would think of me. I didn't even say I loved them, tell them how much they meant to me.

My entire body shook. I could almost smell Ava's perfume. But I knew I couldn't. It was a dirty trick my mind was playing on me.

The buzzing of my phone pulled my attention away from my sorrow for just a moment. With bleary eyes, I regarded the screen, looking at the time first. It was nearly 6:00 a.m. I had slept since yesterday afternoon. Why couldn't I have slept for longer? Until the pain didn't feel like it was going to destroy me?

I had multiple texts and multiple missed calls.

Most were from the boys in the band; someone must have told them.

SAM: Shit, I don't know what to say, Lexie. I'm crap with emotional stuff. I just wanted to let you know I'm sorry.

I'm here and can get my hands on liquor from my dad's liquor cabinet.

WYATT: Killian called me. So sorry, babe.

NOAH: Here for you. Just call if you need to talk. We love you.

KILLIAN: I don't know what to say to make it better, Freckles. Wish I could take away all your pain. Call me when you can. I'll be there as soon as you need me. I know you won't want to talk. Won't want the noise. I know you just need your music. Your soul.
You're my soul, Freckles. Listen to this and remember that. Always.

Attached to his text was a link. I put my headphones in and pressed play on the song Killian sent me. "Knockin' on Heaven's Door" by Bob Dylan. Of course. Bob Dylan was ours. When the song finished, tears streamed down my cheeks. I curled up on my bed and put the song on repeat.

Chapter 17

I couldn't stay on my bed any longer. I couldn't call Killian either. All I wanted was him to make it all better, to take it all away. I needed his quiet presence. But I also couldn't stand the thought of it. Of presenting this raw, stripped part of myself to him. I didn't even know how to be around myself. So I shrugged my cardigan on and picked up my guitar, slipping outside into the brisk morning air. The walls might have been suffocating me inside, but I felt vulnerable in the open air. I curled up on one of our lawn chairs, jostling my guitar so it sat in a playing position. My hand hovered over the strings. I couldn't think of what to play. It felt foreign in my hands. I was lost. Tears dripped down my face. Music couldn't even fix it.

I heard the door open and shut behind me. I didn't move, didn't flinch. I expected it to be Mom, to face her grief as well as my own. Zane's huge form came to stand beside me instead. I expected him to say something, to ask if I was okay, to make me lie and say I somehow was.

He didn't. He didn't say a thing. He just loaned me some of his strength with his silence.

"I'm not going to wake up, am I?" I asked him, resigned. "This isn't a nightmare. It's real."

His large hand came up to the back of my neck and gave it a gentle squeeze. "It's a nightmare," he disagreed. "Not one that you're going to wake up from, but one that's going to end," he promised, his voice rough.

I blinked at his words, wishing, hoping I'd believe him.

"Have you heard of dementors?" I asked finally, not looking up at him. I didn't wait for him to answer. "I'm guessing you haven't, considering they're a fictional character in *Harry Potter* which you're even less likely to watch if you haven't even seen the *Wizard of Oz*," I continued, flinching at the memory of the last conversation we had. Everything from this moment on would be split into before and after. Before was when I was under the illusion that life was easy, that bad things happened, but to others. My life was only sunshine. Bathed in the light of blissful ignorance, of a stupid happiness that I would never have again. Then there was the after. The now. When I knew the truth.

"See, dementors are things that come along and suck every piece of happiness out of a person's body. Strip them of every good memory until there's eventually nothing left, making them believe the possibility of happiness is utterly impossible." I paused. "That's what this is," I choked out.

Zane moved in front of me, kneeling and grasping my neck so his gray eyes met mine. "Even in the cruelest of worlds, there's not a reality where something would take away your possibility to be happy again. I'll make sure of that," he declared. "Not gonna lie to you; this is shit. It's hard. Hopefully, the hardest thing that's ever gonna scar your life. But scars fade. They heal. You'll heal, girl," he promised.

I stared at him, blinking. Then I burst into tears, diving into his body and sobbing against his tee. He put his arms around me, letting me drench him with the ocean of my tears. He kissed my head and pulled back slightly.

"How about we go and I'll make my girls some breakfast?" he asked softly.

I wiped my eyes. "Your girls?" I repeated. "Are we yours now,

Zane? Are you here to stay?"

Zane's face turned hard. "You and your mom, that's what you are. I'm not going anywhere, Lexie."

I smiled a sad smile, then got up to follow him into the living room.

• • • •

I sipped my second coffee of the day, watching Zane crack eggs into the pan. He had insisted he be the one to do the making of the breakfast. I leaned on the counter, watching him. I didn't want to admit it to myself, but I didn't want to be too far away from him. I felt safe with him. The demons behind his eyes understood the ones I had been introduced to.

My mind flickered to someone else I felt safe with. Killian. I hadn't replied to him yet. I didn't know what to say. I didn't know what to say to any of them. If I wrote back, acknowledged their sympathy, that would make it real. Zane wasn't giving me sympathy, which meant he didn't recognize my grief. He was giving me support and strength, but not sympathy. It was an important distinction. One it seemed my very sanity relied on.

I regarded his profile. I had to look up to do so. Way up. Killian was taller than me, and I had to stand on my tiptoes to even come face to face with him. Zane towered over me. His entire body was a huge wall of muscles and vibrant tattoos. My eyes trailed the colorful designs covering his arm.

"Do they mean anything?" I asked finally, nodding to the ink.

Zane's gaze flickered down to them. "They mean everything, Lex."

I screwed up my nose at him in confusion.

His eyes did their smile thing, not before I noticed the demons lurking behind them. It seemed I could see them easier now that

191

the film of innocence had been ripped from my gaze.

"They're reminders," he added as if to clarify.

It didn't clarify much. "Reminders of what?"

Zane's body was tight. "Of life. Of death. Of everything in between."

I nodded into my cup. "Something permanent when everything in life seems so temporary," I murmured.

Zane's head snapped up and his gaze locked on mine. There was something in his stare; it was almost... pride. "Sixteen years old and you're wiser than 80 percent of the planet," he muttered.

I smiled. It was not a happy smile. If this feeling of heartbreak was what it took to be wise, to understand life, I'd trade it in a second for a lifetime of ignorance and confusion. For Steve and Ava. I'd give up my voice, my fingers, my ability to read, to sing, to listen to music for them. For a respite from this.

"Do you think we should wake Mom?" I asked, worried about her state of mind. I needed to see her. To make sure she was still here.

"We'll let her sleep, Lex. She'll wake when she's ready," Zane replied, his voice soft.

I liked the way his face changed when he talked about Mom. The gentle way he spoke about her. I loved that for her. She needed that right now. We both did.

"Either that or her body will go into caffeine withdrawals," I attempted a joke, but I was afraid it fell dangerously flat.

I wondered if I'd ever feel the same about joking again. About laughing. How could I laugh when Steve and Ava were dead? Gone.

"Do you believe in heaven, Zane?" I whispered, desperate for someone to tell me that they weren't just gone. Snuffed out of existence. That would be unbearably cruel.

Zane's body jolted at my question, and he moved the pans off the burner and turned to face me. His large hands cupped my cheeks, swallowing my face.

"Not sure about God, girl. Don't believe in something that would cause so much pain to people who deserve a lifetime of happiness."

My heart dropped at his words. I knew one person saying God wasn't real didn't make it so. But this person, Zane, I considered him to hold authority, more wisdom than my own. Because if pain equaled wisdom, he was likely to be Yoda in a cut.

"But I do believe those people, those good people, go somewhere better, somewhere they deserve," he continued, giving me a beacon of hope.

I blinked away the prickles at the back of my eyes. "You think Steve and Ava are there?" I asked. Pleaded.

"Know it, darlin'," he told me with a resolution that had me believing.

That's what I clung to. That tiny beacon. It'd be my lighthouse in the blackened storm that was my tortured mind.

●●●●

"T minus twenty and we're out the door, baby doll!" Mom shouted down the stairs. "That's how long it's taking Zane to acquire a 'cage'—whatever in Channing Tatum's name that is. I guess it's biker slang for car. Why they don't say *car* is beyond me," she continued to yell.

I wanted to smile. I really did. I even tried. But I think my face just turned into a weird sort of grimace like I was having a stroke or something. Mom was trying. Really hard. She was trying to hold it together so it was more okay for me to fall apart I guessed. Luckily, neither of us actually had the time to consider falling apart since, after our breakfast, Mom put the three of us on the next flight out to DC. Yes, *three*. Zane was coming too.

He had declared there was "no fucking way in hell" his girls were doing "this shit alone." Yes, his girls. Mom hadn't even said a word to the sheer amount of profanities in that sentence. I thought she was grateful to have him coming. I knew I was. I was terrified of what would happen if he left Mom and me alone with each other, mirrors of our grief. I was terrified of Mom not having someone to be strong for her, so she didn't have to be the one doing it.

"I'm ready, Mom!" I yelled back, sinking into the sofa, staring at my phone. I had bitten the bullet and messaged everyone back. I took the cowards way out and sent a mass text to all my boys, including Killian, informing them of my imminent and open-ended trip to DC. Everyone but Killian had texted back.

There was a pause and Mom appeared at the top of the stairs. She had two armfuls of clothes and only one sock on. "How are you ready? Did you pack?" she asked in disbelief.

I nodded. "Yes, Mom, I packed."

She scowled at me. "Seriously, how I spawned someone so organized is beyond me."

I tried my smile thing again. "Need some help?"

A knock sounded at the door.

"No, I've got a system. Your organized brain would mess it up," she informed me. I knew for a fact her "system" was shoving as many clothes as possible in a suitcase and using sheer force of will to get it closed.

"You get the door," she nodded to the foyer. "It'll be Zane in his 'cage.' Early," she stated like it was a capital offense. "What kind of biker is punctual? Educate him on my utter abhorrence for that term while you're there," she instructed, turning on her heel.

I sighed, abandoning my phone and hope for Killian's reply for answering the door.

I lost my breath when I opened it. I almost lost my knees. Killian stood at the other side of it, his eyes somehow confronting me with my own pain. We stared at each other for a couple of moments.

Then, without even realizing I was doing it, I threw myself into his arms. They circled around me instantaneously, burying me in his chest. I sank into it, breathing in his scent and letting myself relax into the safety of his embrace and escape into the little world of limbo that he created when he was with me. His lips pressed into my hair.

"I'm so sorry, baby," he murmured.

I didn't say a thing, just clung to him. I didn't cry; I couldn't. I was past the point of tears at that moment. My pain was so deep my body didn't even react to it, so it just froze.

Killian held me in his arms for an indefinite amount of time before he gently, as if I was made of china, pulled me from his arms just enough so he could gaze into my eyes.

"Gets to me, Freckles, that I can't protect you from things that hurt you like this. That I can't do anything."

I regarded him, eyes clear. "You just did," I whispered.

His eyes turned liquid and his thumb brushed my lip gently. The rumbling of an engine had us both looking to the curb where an SUV parked behind Kill's bike. Zane climbed out of it, his eyes on Kill. Instead of walking toward us, he slammed the door and leaned against it, crossing his arms. Kill's jaw tightened at this strange action that you obviously had to be a boy to understand.

He turned back to me, any trace of hardness gone the moment his eyes touched mine. "Know you gotta leave. I want you calling me, Freckles. Texting. Whatever. Just check in. Talk to me. Any time. I couldn't leave without letting you know you've got me," he murmured. "You don't need me. I know you're strong enough to get through this without me. But I'm not gonna let that happen."

He leaned in to kiss my head, his lips lingering there for a moment. "Soon as you get back, I'll be here," he promised.

"Okay," I whispered.

He pulled back and I found myself desperate not to let him go.

But I did. As soon as his body left mine, the agony of the world rushed back in. I watched as he strode over to Zane, got real close, clipped a couple of things to him I couldn't hear, then turned to his bike without waiting for an answer. He gave me one long, meaningful look before he roared off.

I took a deep breath. It was broken and sucking in the air felt like sucking in broken glass, but I repeated the process.

"You ready, Lex?" Zane's deep voice asked.

I glanced up at him. "Yes," I lied.

••••

It was the funeral. The most horrible, despicable moment in my life. Walking into the church and seeing two coffins beside each other. Coffins. And two of the most important people in my life were in them. Lifeless. Nothing.

My step had stuttered, and I stopped right there in the aisle, my eyes locked on them.

"Doll face?" Mom whispered, her hand squeezing mine.

I just kept staring, feeling numb, feeling like I might vomit. Feeling like I must have floated into someone else's life. This couldn't be my life.

"Lex," Zane murmured, his hand squeezed the back of my neck.

I took a breath of those glass shards in the air.

"Courage, dear heart."

Steve's voice cut through the shards of glass. No one else could hear it, I knew that. No one else needed to hear.

I used all of that courage to put one foot in front of the other and walk to the front of the pew and sit down, Zane and Mom on either side of me.

Mom kissed my head. "I'm so proud of you, Lexie," she whispered. "They were too. You know that, right?"

I moved my gaze to look at my mom. "Only moderately proud though, right?"

Mom and I surprised each other by erupting into a fit of hysterical giggles. Zane's arm circled around the both of us. I rested my head on his shoulder.

"Lexie!" a voice called after the service had finished.

I yanked myself out of Zane's arms and turned towards the familiar voice. Emma's tear-stained face came into view, and I didn't hesitate to run into her embrace.

"Em," I murmured, my voice breaking and the tears flowing.

"I'm so sorry, babe," she said into my hair, her voice thick with tears.

Ava and Steve and been family to Emma too. Emma had been my best friend since forever and because her parents were not good people, Mom, Steve, and Ava made sure she spent a lot of time with us. She was part of our family, and I'd only felt okay with leaving her here in DC knowing Steve and Ava would look out for her.

Now they were gone.

Fresh tears erupted at that thought, and Emma squeezed me tighter as if she sensed them. She finally pulled out of my embrace, rubbing under her eyes.

"Why I didn't wear waterproof mascara is beyond me," she exclaimed, her voice croaky.

I smiled a sad smile and squeezed her hand. Emma wasn't always good with emotion, and she always had to cut it off with sarcasm or a joke. She had a hard exterior, which was necessary growing up with her parents, but I knew a soft heart lay underneath.

"Hey, Em," Mom's soft voice greeted from behind us and her arms circled both of us.

There was only silence as Mom gave her silent strength.

When she finally released us, Emma's black-smudged eyes widened at the form that had pulled Mom's body into his.

"Holy crap," she muttered.

I giggled, somehow, despite the fact my heart was shattered.

"Emma, meet Zane. My..." Mom trailed off as if she didn't know what to call Zane.

"Emma's my best friend," I explained, jumping in to save Mom.

Zane gave her a nod, his eyes warming just a tad.

She gaped at him. "Wow," she muttered. "I mean, nice to meet you," she added quickly.

Mom smiled through the tears in her eyes, and even Zane's eyes brightened just a bit.

We started the walk to where they'd... bury Ava and Steve. Emma linked her arms in mine.

"How you going, Lex?" she whispered, her voice tortured once more.

"Shit," I said simply. I may not have cussed before. When I was the innocent Lexie. The one who didn't think there was any reason to use ugly words. Now I realized that there were situations that were so horrible they needed words just as harsh to describe them. Emma was the only one I could be truly honest with. I didn't want to tell my mom how much my life felt like it was falling apart. She was trying so hard to hold it together. Zane was holding her together.

"I j-just can't believe they're gone," I stuttered, my voice choking with tears.

Emma squeezed my arm. "Me either, Lex," she replied. "I don't know what to do, what to say, to make you feel better."

I squeezed her arm this time. "Nothing," I whispered. "Just being here is good. I've missed you so much."

"Missed you too, Lex."

I didn't have time to talk more to my best friend because we reached the place where we'd bury two-thirds of the most important people in my world.

I had my guitar in my hand. My fingers hovered over the strings. I hadn't played it since before. Before the split between then and now. I hadn't been able to. It was like I had forgotten how. Maybe it was because music was my soul and right now my soul was broken. I couldn't play with a broken soul. I looked out onto the cluttered headstones beyond the two corresponding holes in the ground where Steve and Ava were going. Together. Side by side. They'd have each other. I had to play. I couldn't let them go down into the ground in silence. Without saying good-bye. I knew they couldn't hear words of good-bye coming from my mouth right now, but maybe they could hear them if they were coming from my soul.

"Courage, dear heart."

Without thinking, my fingers moved, brushing against the strings. I held my chin high and started to sing "Over the Rainbow," my voice clear, hoping it would carry to the heavens.

●●●●

"Murdered?" I repeated, my voice tasting bitter with the word coming out of it.

Mom squeezed my hands, her face blank, trying to be strong for me. But she couldn't mask what was in her eyes. The pain. The agony.

It was only now, sitting in the hotel room late after the funeral that I thought to ask how Steve and Ava died. You'd think it would have been something I'd have asked early. A pretty important detail. But when grief blankets your mind like a heavy and poisonous fog, you forget about everything but the pain and the fact that two people you love are gone. You don't focus on the how.

"Yeah, baby," she whispered.

I felt it. The pain. The agony. There was something else. Fury. White-hot and so foreign I didn't quite understand the strength of it as it filtered through my veins.

Murdered.

Someone had purposefully come in and snatched them out of this world. Stolen them. They snuffed out two people. Two people who were the kindest, funniest, best people I knew.

My family.

Someone had come in and stolen that, plunging a dagger into my heart.

"How? Why?" I choked out.

Mom flinched then she stroked my face. "Baby doll, you don't need to—"

"How?" I interrupted her, my voice like a blade through the air.

Mom paused and sucked in a deep breath, looking to the ground before she met my eyes. "They were shot, honey. We don't know why," she said, her voice barely a whisper.

Shot.

I felt as if a bullet passed through my own body with this knowledge. Images from TV shows, crime shows, from books came into my mind, of people getting shot dead. The blood. The empty eyes. I tried to picture Ava and her Chanel suit covered in blood. Steve's twinkling eyes empty. I wondered if it hurt. If they hurt when it happened. How long that pain lasted for. It seemed at that moment, my head was too heavy to hold up with that knowledge, so I let it fall. Then I sucked in a tortured breath and used all of my strength to pull it back up.

"Have they caught them?" I asked, meeting my mom's eyes.

Mom shook her head slowly.

I gritted my teeth. Then I looked up to Zane, who was standing close behind my mom, his hand on the back of her neck. His face was blank too, but his eyes were soft, different than they had been. More open. Since that day, that horrible day at the barbecue, something had fallen away, a shutter, and he openly showed, in his Zane way, how much he cared.

It was nice seeing that. More than nice. At any other moment, it would have been. Right now, it seemed nothing in the world would be nice ever again. That happiness was akin to a fairy tale that only children believed in. Because in a world where you lost people you loved, when people could kill people and not get caught, how could happiness exist?

I stood up on shaky feet and Mom darted up to grasp my hands. "Baby doll?"

I stepped out of her arms. "I just need...." I trailed off. What did I need? A time machine? A lobotomy?

Killian. At this moment, I needed him, and he was thousands of miles away.

"To be alone," I continued.

Mom didn't look happy about this, but she nodded.

When I met Zane's eyes again, he gave me a long look then grabbed me so I was engulfed in his large body, his arms going around me. I sank into his embrace and let myself feel some of the safety that he seemed to radiate.

He kissed my head and let me go silently. He didn't need to say anything.

I left the living room of the hotel we were staying in and padded into my bedroom. I lay on the bed, staring at the ceiling, trying to quiet the echoes in my mind.

Murdered.

Shot.

The words swirled around like poison in my brain. I didn't know how I was going to keep on living, keep on breathing, knowing what I knew, existing in a world without Steve and Ava.

So instead of focusing on what my world didn't have, I thought about what it did have. Mom. Emma. Zane. Killian. I held onto those thoughts, those memories. And somehow, they were my life raft, keeping me adrift in that sea of poison.

Chapter 18

ONE WEEK LATER

"**We don't have to go in**," Kill murmured, squeezing my hands. "I can take you any-where."

I glanced from the brick building to our intertwined hands resting on his thigh. My eyes moved to his, which were locked on me in concern. "I know you can," I replied.

His hand flexed in mine.

"But," I continued, "I've got to go in there at some point. Get back to living life. To reality," I said, resigned, scared, bleeding on the inside. It would be hard, but nothing was harder than the past week, than watching them bury two-thirds of my family.

"So proud of you, Freckles," Kill declared, his eyes glowing.

I smiled at him. I was getting better at making it look real. At actually feeling it on the inside. "I couldn't do it without you," I told him.

I was telling the truth. The past week, I may have lost two of the most important people in my life, but two more appeared. They didn't fill the gaping hole that was left, they never could, but they helped me forget it was there and believe it might not always hurt so much.

Zane was our rock. He was with us every step of the way. He didn't say much, just gave Mom and me his silent strength, taking care of us. It felt right to watch him sling his arm around Mom's neck, hold her hand, murmur to her softly, and even stay in the suite in our hotel with her. It wasn't weird or uncomfortable like I thought it might be when Mom inevitably got a boyfriend. It was right.

Kill might not have been there like Zane was, but he didn't let me go through the day without calling, without texting, without letting me know he was thinking of me, that he was there. It felt strange having someone other than Mom, Steve, or Ava being so concerned about me. It was a blissful sort of strange. *I* mattered to him.

I'd always thought of myself as a peaceful person. I believed in peace and harmony, and tried to live my life turning the other cheek, but the need, the thirst for vengeance trumped everything in the past week. I needed them to pay. I needed to know that these terrible things and the people that did them couldn't go unpunished.

Mom had given me a long talk about how the police would take care of it and how justice would be done the right way. I'd nodded in the right places and said what she wanted me to say, but I didn't want justice done the right way. I wanted revenge.

Kill leaned across his car and kissed my mouth lightly. "You could do it without me; I got no doubt about that. But you're not going to," he promised, repeating his sentiment from last week.

I smiled against his mouth. "Good," I murmured.

Kill gave me another quick kiss and moved out of the car. I gathered my books and clutched the outstretched hand that came from the passenger side where Kill had opened my door.

••••

"Lexie!" a voice yelled from halfway down the hall.

I turned and Sam near bowled into me. His arms circled around me and he lifted me into the air.

"You're back," he exclaimed once he put me down.

"Good spotting," I replied.

He grinned, then his smile disappeared completely as he remembered the reason for my absence. It would have been comical if not for the pity in his eyes. "I'm so sorry about Steve and Ava, babe," he said on a much quieter and somber decibel than I was used to. He grabbed my hand and squeezed it.

"Thanks," I whispered back.

Kill and I had arrived late this morning, so we had walked through the nearly deserted halls when he walked me to class. I had thought all of the stares I got when I entered my first class were on account of my tardiness, but now I realized every second person was giving me a sideways glance.

"I take it everyone knows?" I asked, resigned to having to field even more sympathy from mostly nosy teenagers, or at the very least this uncomfortable gawking.

Sam glanced around and started walking us to our next class, one we had together while he spoke. "Nope," he replied. "We, meaning Killian, made the executive decision to not share your personal life with the gossip mill. You've had mono," he told me with a wink.

"Well, at least that explains why I look like hell warmed up," I said.

Lack of sleep and grief and shed five pounds off me without me even noticing. My drapey pants and formally tight cropped tank were now hanging on me. I had tried to cover my dark circles with concealer this morning, but it didn't really work.

Sam stopped us outside of class. His face was serious. "You look great. On your worst day, you look better than any of these idiots." He nodded his head to Stacy, who was conveniently walking past us. She scowled at him, but for some reason, smiled triumphantly at me before disappearing into class.

"Thanks, Sammy," I whispered, deciding not to waste time on the motivations behind that smile.

"Anytime, Lex. Though I expect you to return the favor and inflate my ego when needed." He winked, walking us into class.

I laughed and it was totally genuine. "Yes, because your self-esteem is about to hit the floor," I replied, putting my books down. "If your ego inflated anymore, you'd go into orbit."

Sam shrugged. "Self-confidence is endearing."

"I think the word you're meaning is arrogant," I countered.

He merely grinned at me.

I grinned back and thought I might just survive this after all.

•••

Sam was babbling at my side about our next band rehearsal as we walked into the cafeteria. "Only as soon as you're ready," he added, his eyes regarding me in concern.

I stopped us. "Ready?" I repeated. "I'm more than ready. I need to play."

He grinned. "Good."

His grin fell and turned into a scowl at someone behind me.

"Lexie, I'm glad to see you're feeling... better," Jordan said, coming to my side, not acknowledging Sam.

It was something I noticed, Jordan and most of his friends barely spoke to my boys. I reasoned it because of their egos. My boys were much more attractive than any of those jocks and so much more complex, which was why simple minds couldn't understand them. Therefore, they ignored them.

"I am, thanks, Jordan," I replied with a tight smile. I didn't want to talk to him on principle. If you were a jerk to my boys, you were a jerk to me. But despite that, Jordan was always nice to me. Nice with an ulterior motive, but nice nonetheless. Mom and... Ava had trained me too well in basic manners to be rude outright.

Jordan stepped closer to me and Sam's face turned into a grimace at this. Jordan gave him little notice.

"Look, just between us," he stage whispered, "I know you didn't actually have mono." He raised his eyebrows knowingly.

My stomach dropped and I swallowed lead. But something about his tone made me realize he didn't know the real reason. Jordan wasn't callous enough to bring up the subject if he knew about Steve and Ava. He thought it was something else.

Sam stepped forward, his hand on my elbow. "Okay, we're done here. You're late for your steroid injection," he informed him.

Jordan finally glanced at Sam. "What, now Killian's dropped her you trying to get in there?" he asked with callousness I previously had thought him incapable of.

Sam dropped my hand and tried to get around me, his face wild. I'd never seen him angry. I didn't realize my carefree friend could even muster up fury. I knew now, he could. I quickly put my hand on his chest, stopping him.

"Sam, don't. It's not worth it," I murmured.

Sam's nostrils flared and his eyes were locked on Jordan. "Trust me, Lex. It'll be worth it," he informed me. His voice was injected with fury, but he didn't push against my hand.

I met his eyes. "Go and sit down," I ordered, nodding to our empty table. Noah and Wyatt obviously hadn't arrived yet.

Sam's face turned hard. "I'm not going anywhere until he goes," he hissed through his teeth.

"I need to have a chat with Jordan, and you need your hands in order to hold drumsticks. You don't need to break them on his head," I told him.

Sam gave me a long look before he cursed under his breath and reluctantly turned to our table.

I whipped my head around at Jordan, who had held his ground, his chest all puffed up, grinning at Sam's retreating form. "What's your deal, Jordan?" I hissed at him.

Jordan's grin left and he stepped forward to me, right in my space. His hand came to my elbow. "I'm just trying to look out for you, Lexie," he informed me. "You've fallen into the wrong crowd since you got here."

A raised a brow. "And you're assuming you're the right crowd?" I asked sarcastically.

Jordan's hand tightened at my elbow. "I'm not a criminal, like your biker ex."

My hackles rose and I tried to pull out of his grip unsuccessfully. "Kill is not a criminal and this conversation is over," I informed him.

Jordan looked genuinely surprised at my anger. "You're still defending him after he used you?"

I paused, stopping my struggle. "Used me?" I repeated. "He didn't use me. I have no idea what you're talking about," I said, genuinely confused.

"He did what he always does. He took what he needed from you. You held out longer than most, I'll admit. But when you gave it up, he gave you up. Don't worry. I would never do that," he promised.

I gasped. Blinking rapidly at him as the meaning of his words shot through me. That's what he thought? That's why everyone had been staring at me in the halls? Because they thought I'd had sex with Killian and he dumped me, and I'd been wallowing in my sorrow ever since? Tears prickled my eyes. This was too much. My emotions were raw, exposed to the nerve. Something that normally wouldn't affect me, the opinions of small people, threatened to bring me to my knees. I was about to rip myself out Jordan's grasp and run from his ugly words and attempt to run from my own feelings, but someone else beat me to it. In an instant, his hand was gone, and before I could understand what was going on, he was on the ground, clutching a bleeding nose.

"What the fuck...?" he mumbled out through the weird gurgling sound.

Killian's body obstructed my view of him, and his hands cupped my cheeks. "You okay, Freckles?" he asked softly, fury dancing in his eyes.

I nodded silently. He had just punched him. Right in the face. Right in the middle of the cafeteria.

Killian's head turned but his hands stayed at my cheeks. "You breathe in her fuckin' direction again, I'll break both your kneecaps," he growled, promise in his tone.

Jordan was being pulled up by his friends and silence had hung heavy in the previously bustling cafeteria. They all glared at Killian, shifting from foot to foot like they were going to turn this into a full-on brawl. My stomach dropped, but Killian didn't seem to flinch.

"I'd take another step forward only if you want to forfeit this season on account of the team's asses being handed to them," a casual voice said from behind me.

I turned my head in Killian's hands enough to see Wyatt, Sam, and Noah standing slightly behind us. Wyatt's stance was almost relaxed, but his face was carefully blank. Sam was the same; his fists clenched to the side. Noah was the worst. The veins in his muscled arms protruded from the tension he was holding in his body. He was glaring in a hate-filled gaze at the team. I didn't know if this was on account of things that happened just now, or more deep-seated issues he held close to the chest.

What I did know was my boys were standing up for me, having Killian's back. It petrified me, the thought of them going to blows because of me.

"Kill—" I began in a whisper, intending to try and stop the epic stare down going on.

"What's going on here?" a sharp voice cut through the air, and the crowd of students parted as Mr. Hazelton descended upon us. His eyes ran over Jordan, his bleeding nose, then Killian.

"My office. Now, Mr. Decesare. Mr. Louis, get yourself to the nurse then the same for you." His gaze flickered to me. "And you Miss Spencer."

Killian's form tightened. "She has nothing to do with this," he ground out.

Mr. Hazelton narrowed his eyes. "I didn't ask you to speak, Mr. Decesare. My office. Now."

Killian stared him down for a long second then moved his hands down and clutched my shaking fingers, pulling me gently along beside him.

Dread pooled in my stomach, not for me, for Kill. Mr. Hazelton had it out for him, and I worried this might be the last straw.

••••

I was sitting on the bench outside the vice principal's office, fiddling with my hands, staring at the closed door both Killian and Jordan had disappeared behind. Jordan's nose had stopped bleeding but it was swollen, and blood spattered his white tee. He hadn't even glanced at me as he walked past. He became very fixated on the very door I was willing to open with my mind. I jumped when it did just that. Jordan emerged first. This time he looked straight at me. I was surprised to see a sort of apology in his eyes. It was followed by a mouthed, "I'm sorry," before Killian pushed past him and came to kneel in front of me.

"Are you kicked out?" I whispered in worry.

To my surprise, he grinned. "Nah, babe. They're not gettin' rid of me that easy, not when I've got renewed motivation to go to all my classes," he murmured, his hand at my neck.

"Mr. Decesare, if you'd release Ms. Spencer, I'd like to speak to her," Mr. Hazelton stated, distaste clear in his tone.

Killian stilled slightly at the voice and didn't comply immediately. He gave me a long look. "I'll be right here, waitin' for you, Freckles," he promised.

"I'll be fine," I reassured him.

He stood, pulling me gently up. "I know," he agreed, "but I'll be here just the same."

He gave my hand a squeeze before taking the seat I had just vacated. Mr. Hazelton held out his hand, gesturing for me to go into the room.

"Firstly, I have been made aware of the reason for your absence, Miss Spencer. I'm sorry for your loss," Mr. Hazelton said to me as he sat across from me at his desk. He sounded anything but sorry, but it was obviously the required start to this conversation.

My heart stuttered and I glanced around the room. Everything was painfully arranged and organized. Not a speck of dust anywhere. No photos either. Figures. You'd have to be crazy to want to be married to... that. I swallowed my distaste for the man and met his eyes.

"Thank you," I replied, jutting my chin up.

He laid his hands out on the desk, his beady eyes running over me. "Mr. Louis has informed me he slipped in the cafeteria, and that's how he sustained his injuries. Mr. Decesare merely helped him up. Is that what happened, Ms. Spencer?" he asked. "Before you answer, I will let you know that lying to authority figures is not a good habit to get into. I know that must have been encouraged, given your... connection to Mr. Decesare, but I'd advise against it," he warned.

My hands balled into fists on my thighs. I met his gaze. "And how would my connection to Killian have anything to do with honesty?" I asked tightly. "He's the most honest person I know, and I don't think a teacher implying otherwise is professional. Or appropriate,"

I added icily. I had never spoken this way to anyone in my life, but I found myself burning with the need to defend Killian, regardless of the hierarchy in the situation.

Mr. Hazelton leaned back, raising a brow. His mouth turned into a thin line at my words. "Careful, Ms. Spencer," he warned. "I understand your situation, so I'll let that comment go. Answer the question," he ordered. "Is Mr. Decesare and Louis's recounting of the incident correct or not?"

I sat up straighter. "Yes," I replied. "That's exactly what happened."

Mr. Hazelton stared at me for a long moment, then shook his head. "We both know that's not what happened, Ms. Spencer. Though there's not much I can do about it considering the two involved parties aren't telling the truth. I'll be watching Mr. Decesare carefully. Very carefully. And by extension, you, Ms. Spencer," he promised. "I'd hate to see a young woman have her record tarnished by a troublemaking boy."

"Watch away, Mr. Hazelton," I replied, standing. "If that's all, I've got classes to get to."

He narrowed his eyes at me, and his nostrils actually flared in fury. Then he relaxed, waving his hand at me. "Go, go," he almost spat. "I'd be careful who you spend your time with, Ms. Spencer, it could ruin your entire future," he warned as I turned to the door.

I paused, glancing back at him "I wholeheartedly agree, Mr. Hazelton. I'll be sure to keep away from Jordan," I replied sweetly. I didn't wait for a response, merely pulled the door open and left the room.

Kill pushed off the chair the moment the door shut behind me. "Are you okay, Freckles?" he asked, putting his hands lightly on my hips when he made it over to me.

I smiled at him and nodded. "Fine. But Mr. Hazelton is an asshole," I hissed the word.

Killian reared back in surprise and slung his arm around my shoulder, directing us out of the office. "That he is," he agreed. "The asshole didn't do anything that requires me to call Bull and suggest we take a visit to his house later on tonight, did he?" he asked.

I glanced up at him. "No. Nothing that I couldn't handle," I added.

Kill nodded, his jaw hard.

"You're joking, though?" I asked. "If I had said yes, you wouldn't actually do that, would you?"

Killian glanced down at me. "I look like I'm joking?"

I gaped at him. "But... he's a teacher."

"He's an asshole. One who hurts my girl. Doesn't matter the job title, age, or anything. Anyone who does that answers to me," he declared.

Okay, wow.

He sat us down under what I had considered "our tree" out on the quad. I was thankful he didn't take us anywhere near the cafeteria or anyone in there.

"That's why you punched Jordan," I surmised, still confused over the reason for the fight in the first place, the things he said.

Killian's jaw tightened and he flexed his fingers. "That's why I'm plotting Jordan's murder," he ground out.

"Okay, now you're joking," I teased, looking up at him. I gazed into his ice blue eyes. They were hard. "You are joking," I pressed.

His hand went to my cheek. "Freckles, you've just been through a week of hell, just been broken, and he spews that shit on you?" He shook his head, eyes dancing with anger.

"Yeah, he didn't know that," I said in a small voice, unsure of why I was defending him.

"Doesn't matter," Kill bit out. "He should never have spoken to you like that in the first fuckin' place."

"Yes, but I feel like murder is a little obscene," I joked. I paused, glancing at him. "Please don't murder anyone on my account," I requested, half serious.

Kill's hands tightened. "I'd do anything on your account."

My heart clenched in my chest. We stared at each other for a long moment. "Why did Jordan lie for you?" I asked.

Killian sighed, pushing his hands through my hair. "'Cause despite his actions, he's not a complete idiot," he declared. "He may be a tool, but he's not a nark."

I raised my eyebrows. "Is this some kind of bro code?" I joked.

Kill gave me a serious look. "No one narks on the club. Even Jordan knows that."

I gaped at him again. "This has to do with the club?" I asked in disbelief. "But this is high school."

Kill shrugged. "Doesn't matter. It's about principle."

"Okkkaayy." I drew the word out, trying to grasp the concept in my mind. I knew the club had pull in town, respect, but I didn't realize how far the arm extended.

"The stuff Jordan was saying, where did that even come from?" I asked, changing the subject.

Kill's face turned to granite. "No clue. But I intend to find out."

"Thought you two would be here," a voice interrupted Killian's no doubt Liam Neeson worthy speech.

We both glanced up, and Wyatt, Sam, and Noah all deposited themselves on the grass.

"So, that was fuckin' intense," Sam declared, grinning. "You expelled, bro?" he asked Kill.

Kill shook his head.

Sam's face fell. "Well, that sucks," he murmured.

I sharpened my gaze. "How exactly does Killian *not* being expelled suck?" I asked him sharply.

"Isn't it obvious? He has to stay in this red brick prison for six more months," he declared, pointed back to the building.

I couldn't help myself, I laughed.

Wyatt rolled his eyes. "Jordan didn't roll on you?"

Kill shook his head again.

"Smart," Wyatt murmured.

"Obviously not that smart. He said that shit to Lexie in the first place," Sam bit out, humor gone from his face. "You okay, babe?"

I reached out and squeezed his hand. "I'm fine, Sammy. Just confused. Where did all that garbage even come from?"

All three of my boy's faces hardened. "We can answer that," Wyatt interjected, his voice tight. "A certain empty-headed teenager took it upon herself to put two and two together and get crazy. She took your absence and Killian's damn near murderous disposition and made her own conclusions, which she spread around the school as fact."

"Stacy," I hissed, a red film dispersing over my eyes. "That little troll." I stood rapidly, my eyes glued to the brick building. I was halfway across the quad before Kill caught up with me, stopping me.

"Whoa, Freckles," he murmured, standing in front of me.

"Get out of my way, Kill," I ordered, trying to squirm out of his grasp.

"Not until you tell me what you're plannin' on doing," he argued.

I met his eyes. "I'm going to have a long overdue conversation with a member of the student body."

Kill fought a smile. "Is this conversation going to involve hair pulling?"

"If it is, you have to wait for us so we can film it," Sam called from behind Kill.

"I'm not going to pull her hair," I told him. "If I was going to do anything, I'd chop the entire lot off," I corrected, and Kill full-on smiled now. "I'm going to educate her on what is and is not her business. You and me being firmly not."

Killian's smile left him. "I'll be doing that," he gritted out. "Don't you worry. I got you, Freckles, and I'm not going to let you dirty yourself by stooping down to her level. I'm more than happy to do that."

"This is a girl thing," I told him. "It's got to be me."

Killian frowned. "Lexie, this is your first day back. You shouldn't have to deal with this shit."

"I shouldn't," I agreed. "In a perfect world, I wouldn't. But this isn't a perfect world. I'm more than aware of that. Now please let me go so I can go and unleash a can of verbal whoop-ass on a certain biatch."

Kill regarded me, then he complied. "My kitten has claws," he murmured.

"You haven't seen the half of it," I promised, then resumed my journey.

The bell had just sounded and I knew exactly where Stacy would be, which was perfect, considering I had a shadow following me back into the building. Any other time, I'd be happy for Kill's presence, but I was telling the truth. This was girls' business. So it was more than appropriate it would happen in the place Stacy reapplied her makeup at the end of every lunch break. Kill didn't even get to stop me as I strolled in to the girls' restroom, his face tight and slightly helpless as I closed the door. Stacy was leaning forward into the mirror, touching up her eyeliner. Her eyes cut to me the moment I stormed in.

Her face turned soft. That kind of false soft it had when she approached me at my locker those weeks ago. "Lexie—" she began.

I advanced on her, glaring. "Nope," I hissed, getting right in her face. "You do not get to speak in this moment. You don't get to spew any more of your lies or false concerns," I declared. "I have no friggin' clue what your parents did to screw you up to the point that you think it's appropriate to mess with other people's lives." I looked her up and down purposefully. "Or whatever issues lie underneath all those overpriced and honestly tacky clothes. That's not for me to waste brainpower on. That's for you to pay thousands of dollars for therapy in the future. What I'm here to tell you is that my life and my relationship with Kill is none of your business."

Stacy looked shocked. "Lexie, I don't know what you're—" She tried to play innocent.

I cut her off again. "Don't play dumb, Stacy. We both know you're a lot of things, but not that," I said sharply. "No matter how much you try to convince the world that head is empty, it's full of bitterness and ugly thoughts. That's not my problem. All that ugly will eventually reach the surface thanks to a little thing called karma. My problem is you making up lies about me. That's not something I'd usually worry about, but when that lie causes people to get hurt, that's too far," I declared.

"Lexie—"

"Not finished," I cut her off. "You decide to make yourself feel better by making people feel worse. That's evil, but it's not up to me to change. You involve me or Killian once more, I'll make sure to change it. Trust me, you won't like how I do that," I promised.

Stacy lost the innocent look on her face and her expression turned snide. "What, are you threatening me, Lexie?" she asked. "I'm so not afraid of a hippie-wannabe loser."

I laughed in a humorless way that I didn't recognize. "I don't care whether you're afraid of me or not. I know you're not stupid enough to be so fearless in the face of the Sons of Templar, and you've screwed with a member of that family, so I'd be careful."

Her eyes went wide at this, and I was happy to see my words hit their mark. I didn't know how appropriate it was to be using an outlaw motorcycle club in high school drama, but I knew how much Zane cared about me. He made that clear this past week, taking care of Mom and me when we couldn't take care of ourselves. He was protective, in an intense and kind of scary way. Kind of like

Kill. I knew neither of them wanted to see me hurt. I wasn't sure if it was wrong to capitalize on that or not, but I didn't have the energy to do anything else. Loss and sorrow had drained me, exhausted me.

I didn't let Stacy see that. I gave her one more glare before storming out of the bathroom.

Kill pushed off the wall he was leaning on the moment I emerged.

Sam looked at me. "Not a scratch," he exclaimed. "Knew you'd own her." He sounded proud.

Kill took my head in his hands. "Not cool, Freckles, venturing the one place I can't go," he bit out. "Though I'd brave even the girls' bathrooms for you," he added, his eyes twinkling with amusement amidst concern.

"No need for you to venture into such scary territory," I reassured him, walking us away before Stacy could come out.

"You okay?" he asked, pulling me into his shoulder.

"No," I replied honestly, making his arm flex. I gazed at him, then to Sam and the boys who were trailing behind us. "But I will be."

Chapter 19

I was drooling. I really hoped I wasn't drooling. I quickly wiped the side of my mouth as inconspicu-ously as I could.

Nope, no drool.

I didn't know how it was possible because in front of me, right in front of me, was the most beautiful sight I'd ever seen. Killian. Shirtless. I barely heard the crash of the waves or the boys arguing about something. There was only Killian. He was wearing cut-off black sweats that slung low on his hips. Way low. Low enough so I could see every inch of his muscled torso. Every defined, carved ridge. I knew he was muscled. I had run my hands along his arms and chest many times. I had felt his strength, but it was quite a different thing to see it, see those muscles free from the chains of clothes.

He had been chatting to Wyatt, laughing about something when, as if he had some sixth sense, he turned his head. I had stopped slightly before the edge of the pier where the boys were congregated. We had decided to forgo the confines of the garage this Saturday afternoon and go swimming. We lived five minutes from the beach but never made the most of it. And Killian had the afternoon off, so of course he came. Wherever I went, he went, and wherever he went, I went. We had been attached at the hip since I'd gotten back from DC. I wouldn't have been able to breathe if it had been any other way. Knowing how quickly people I cared about could get taken away meant I wanted to clutch the ones I had left as tight as I could. I would have moments when fear paralyzed me, stilled me with the realization that it could happen. Any moment the phone could ring, and my heart could break all over again. Killian chased away that fear with his kisses, his gentle touch, and his liquid eyes.

Mom did it too with her smiles that conquered the grief and her strength. And Zane. I knew he gave that to her. And the smiles. He may not have smiled yet, but he was the reason for a lot of Mom's. He was part of our life now. He stayed at our home every single night and I didn't even question it. It was normal, where he was meant to be. He never said much, but that was because Mom and I said enough. Said it all. It was nice to have his silence balance out our loud. He didn't need to speak to show me what he felt for Mom. I could see it. My sixteen-year-old eyes saw it clearer than ever. Maybe it was because I knew what it was like to be in love. He didn't have to speak to show how he felt for Mom, and he definitely didn't have to speak to show how he felt about Kill. Since Zane was at home every single night, it meant he had to put up with Killian every single night. He would glare at him any moment he was in his presence, a glare that would most likely make any man run screaming.

Not Kill. He didn't blink at it. Or act like it bothered him.

It bothered me, more than a little. I cared about Zane. A lot. About how happy he made my mom, about how happy he made me. About how he somehow turned the three of us into a family.

I needed him to like Kill. Because Kill was my family too. My future. I was certain of that.

I finally tore my gaze upward to meet Killian's face, to get my mind back in the present moment. His icy blue eyes burned into mine. Literally burned my whole body.

I had slipped my yellow kaftan off at the pile of clothes the boys had haphazardly thrown at the edge of the wharf. This meant

Killian's eyes ran over every inch of my exposed body. I had never blinked at wearing a bikini before, never felt... naked. But right now, with Killian's hungry gaze rippling over my body, I wanted to cover up, and at the same time, I wanted more. I wanted that feeling of him devouring me with his eyes to last forever.

I managed to unstick my feet and walk on unsteady legs toward Kill and the boys. Wyatt's gaze followed Killian's, obviously wondering why he was flat out ignoring him. He grinned knowingly when I reached them.

"Cute bikini, Lex," he observed in a light voice.

I blushed. Kill did not. His head turned to Wyatt and he looked like he might just strangle him right there on the spot.

Wyatt laughed in the face of the fury and gave Kill a reassuring tap on the shoulder. "Don't mentally plot out where you'll bury my body just yet," he teased. "I've got my own girl to ogle." He nodded to one of the many girls that were on rotation, currently laughing with Noah. "I'll just go and do that." He winked at me and sauntered off. I gave his broad, muscled back an appreciative glance. But only the way I guessed a sister would notice their brother's body, with a fraternal kind of realization that their sibling was attractive, nothing further. It was the same with all of them.

Wyatt yanked the girl—Tillie, I thought her name was—into his shoulder. I could never keep track. He and Sam always had new ones on the go. Some were from school, most from the next town over. Smart. Most of them were perfectly nice girls, albeit a bit ditzy. I liked Tillie. I really hoped she lasted. But I didn't have high hopes.

My gaze moved back to Kill, whose jaw was hard as he stared at me. I grinned shyly, searching for something to say. But the look in his eyes muted me. I'd never seen such... hunger in it before.

Kill stepped a hair's breadth away from me, his hands lightly resting on my bare hips. I held my breath. We'd been this close before, closer in fact. But not like this. Not with my bare skin under his hands and his perfect, naked torso inches away from me.

"Jesus," he muttered, his jaw clenched. "Looking at you right now, Freckles, I've never been more conflicted," he said. His eyes flickered down my body once more. "All I want is to put you over my shoulder and take you away to make sure I'm the only man to see—" he glanced down "—this."

My belly did a somersault at the huskiness of his voice, the electricity in it.

"Then, I want everyone to see how fuckin' gorgeous my girl is," he continued. "Kiss you until you can't breathe so everyone knows what this beautiful creature is. Mine." His mouth dipped to brush against mine. He didn't kiss me though, merely touched his mouth to mine before pulling back. "What do you think I should do?" he asked, eyes twinkling.

As I gazed at him, my heart was pounding through my chest. I'd wanted Kill before, but this was different. I *wanted* him. I didn't know what to do. To say.

"Um, either of those options is... enticing," I whispered, and Killian grinned. "But... I've got a better idea." My eyes flickered behind me.

Kill raised his brow. "I'm intrigued."

I reached forward on my tiptoes, placing my palms lightly on his hard chest. He sucked in a breath as I laid my lips gently on his. Just before the kiss got any deeper, I put pressure on his chest and shoved him backward. In any other moment, this would not have worked. But Killian was not expecting this, not now. The look of surprise on his face as he tumbled backward into the water was almost worth losing his mouth on mine. His body. Almost. But I had to. Because I had to get him out of my proximity before I climbed all over him like an idiot. He landed in the water with a splash and the boys barked out laughter from beside me.

"That was fuckin' *awesome!*" Sam exclaimed, his eyes darting to where Killian's head had popped up.

Killian pushed his wet, inky hair back and glared at me. "You're going to pay for that, Freckles," he warned in a dark voice.

I grinned at him. "I don't see how," I replied tartly. "You're down there and I'm up here. Seems I have an advantage."

His eyes turned darker, and with speed I didn't know he had, he swam forward toward the dock. I tottered back, preparing to run, but I hit a hard wall of muscle. I turned to Noah, who was grinning.

"Traitor," I hissed at him.

I whipped my head back around, my escape route now blocked. I had intended on trying to run around, but I got distracted. Very distracted by a wet Killian pushing himself onto the dock. My eyes locked on the way the veins in his sinewy forearms pulsed as he did so. Then I found out his six pack looked even better dripping with beads of seawater. I realized I was standing there like an idiot. I managed to turn and dart around Noah, who was standing with his arms crossed but, I only made it about two steps further. Strong arms circled my middle.

"Not so fast, Freckles," a voice murmured in my ear.

I squealed as he deposited me over his shoulder with ease and threw me into the water. I was submerged in the chilly water, which worked well to quell the pulse of desire I had been fighting previously.

That didn't last long when water splashed on my face as a form dived in beside me. Killian pulled me to his body once he surfaced. I instinctively wrapped my arms around his neck, and he kept us afloat effortlessly.

"Hey," I whispered, our faces inches away.

His eyes were liquid. "Hey," he murmured back. His hand brushed my wet hair from my face. Then he bent his head to mine and kissed me. Really kissed me. I got so lost in the kiss I was sure I would have sunk if it wasn't for Killian's arms around me.

I jerked my head back when a splash sounded next to us. Kill did the same, but he didn't let me go. His hands tightened.

Sam surfaced not too far from us. He shook his head. "Got to keep it PG kids," he chided. "I've got delicate sensibilities. Young and impressionable you see."

I threw my head back and laughed, and Kill even chuckled.

Sam's eyes went back to the water's edge where two girls about my age were running into the water. "Ah, if you'll excuse me, I've got to go and corrupt my delicate sensibilities." He paddled over in the direction of the girls.

I laughed again, watching him swim toward the unknowing girls.

My eyes flickered back to the wharf where Wyatt was lying on his side, chatting to Tillie. Noah was reading a book, leaning against a post of the pier. His eyes met mine and he smiled. He had well and truly warmed to Kill now, and all was well in the world.

I turned my head back to Kill, who had been watching me the entire time. "I like this," I informed him. "You hanging out with us. All of my boys together. Having fun. You being here instead of the garage and acting almost like a real teenage boy, not a broody, biker man."

Killian's face turned hard to read. "You don't like the broody, biker man?" he asked, his voice teasing.

"Yes," I whispered. "I like him a lot. A lot a lot. Which is why I like it a lot when he forgets about his worries and forgets to be broody and has fun once in a while too."

Killian smiled, more than Zane. That wasn't saying much. But he usually only smiled at me. Sometimes at something stupid Sam or my mom said, both had rivaling, ridiculous senses of humor, which meant you had to be a cyborg not to find them amusing. But this was still rare with Killian. He didn't speak much to them either. He'd have boy grunting conversations with the boys, silent macho man speak with Zane, and clipped but friendly banter with my mom, but nothing like he was with me. It was like he was two people. The person he showed to the world and the one I got. The one who spoke tender, beautiful words, kissed me slow and gently, and treated me like the world's greatest treasure.

Kill's hands tightened around my waist. "Baby, I'm always havin' fun when I'm with you. Always happy."

I frowned at him. "What about when you're not with me?"

Killian grinned. "Then I'm thinkin' about you, so I'm also happy."

I screwed my nose up at him, but my heart flew at the statement. "I think about you too, when I'm not with you."

Kill rested his head against mine. "Good."

"I worry about you," I continued.

His head left mine and he touched my jaw. "Don't you worry that pretty head about me, Freckles. I'm fine as long as I got you," he declared. "And I plan on having you for a good long while."

●●●●

"Mom!" I yelled as Kill and I walked in the door, hand in hand.

We had spent the rest of the afternoon bathing in the sunshine on the dock, letting the air dry us, and joking and goofing around with the boys.

"Kitchen! Doll," Mom's voice called back.

I went to go into the kitchen, but Kill's hand yanked me back. Before I could I ask him what he was doing, his mouth plastered over mine, kissing me with a ferocity that matched the look in his eyes when he first saw me on the dock.

"What was that for?" I asked, catching my breath.

He regarded me. "Just needed to kiss you."

We stared at each other for a long moment.

"Doll! You get lost in the labyrinth that is our house? Do I need to send a search party?" Mom called out.

Kill grinned at me; then he led us into the kitchen.

Mom smiled knowingly when we entered. "Oh, not the labyrinth that is our house, but the labyrinth that is the boyfriend. Hey, Kill," she greeted warmly.

"Mia," he replied, nodding. His eyes went to the beautiful woman at the table, jostling a toddler on her lap. "Gwen."

She beamed at him. "Hey, Kill. Lexie, honey, beautiful as always," she said, eyes light.

Gwen was seriously the nicest and prettiest person I'd seen in real life. She was petite, with a small baby bump and a killer fashion sense. She let me borrow her designer stuff for our first gig. Her accent was kickass as well; New Zealand I thought it was. She was clad in designer gear head to toe and looked like she belonged in New York or L.A, not Amber. She certainly didn't look like she would be married to the president of an outlaw motorcycle club. Then again, Cade was smoking hot and I could totally picture them together.

The toddler struggled off her lap and she let her down. The beautiful little girl darted over to Kill, stretching her chubby arms up to him. "Ill, Ill," she called in her little baby voice.

Killian's whole body turned soft, and he let my hand go and bent down to take the little girl in his arms. "How's the little pipsqueak today?" he asked, nuzzling his nose against the little girl's button one. She giggled wildly and attached her hands to Kill's inky hair. I watched transfixed at Kill's gentle manner with her, with his easy way, his obvious affection.

"Jaw off the floor for a moment if you will, Lexie," Mom teased. "Gwen's got something else that will make you lose your little mind."

My gaze snapped to her and Gwen, who were both grinning at me watching Kill. Shoot. That was embarrassing.

I walked to the fridge, grabbing a coconut water for myself and a soda for Kill. Mom and Gwen each had glasses in front of them. "Oh yeah, what's that?" I asked, handing Kill the soda.

He jostled Belle into one arm so he could take the can. "Thanks, babe," he said softly.

I gave him a warm look before turning my attention to the table.

"Sit if you will, young grasshopper, and Gwen will explain." Mom held her arm out to the table.

I complied. Kill did the same, setting Belle in his lap, where she seemed content yanking at his hair. He didn't seem to mine.

I turned my attention to Gwen. "What's up?" I asked with a grin.

"Well, I've got a favor to ask you," she began.

"Sure," I replied.

Mom shook her head. "Not good form to agree to a favor without knowing what it is," she chided. "What if she wanted a kidney? Now you've already agreed, which means you're screwed."

I rolled my eyes. "You want a kidney, Gwen?"

She smiled. "Not today, but who knows, I enjoy cocktails. I might be needing a young untainted one in the future," she deadpanned, obviously right on track with Mom's brand of humor. Luckily. Most people thought she was crazy.

"It's mine and Cade's two-year anniversary coming up soon," she explained.

"Congratulations," I said. I meant it. They were pretty much the most awesome couple ever. Apart from Mom and Zane, of course. And maybe Amy and Brock. Okay, so top three. Cade kind of reminded me of Killian. He was hot, of course, despite the fact he was way older than me. But he was what I imagined Kill might grow up to be. Tall, muscly, dark features. Broody and almost scary. Until you saw him with his wife and daughter. Until you saw him look at them like they were the reason the world was spinning. It kind of reminded me of the way Kill looked at me. Something inside me yearned for that to be my future. Me and Kill. I chased that yearning away in surprise. I didn't need to be thinking about that now.

"Thanks," Gwen replied, bringing me back to the present. My gaze flickered over to Kill, our eyes met, and I quickly focused on Gwen.

"So we're having a party at the club next week, as you know," she continued.

I nodded. We knew. We'd been invited. We'd been pulled into the fold ever since that terrible day at Rosie's. Ever since Zane became Mom's. Mom spent a lot of time with the women, and they popped over and invited us around to their beautiful houses.

"Well, I was hoping we could hire you and your band to play at it," she said. "Before you break out and we can't afford you," she joked.

I gaped at her. "Are you serious? You want us to play at your party?"

She smiled and nodded. "Dead serious. We heard you play at the club. You guys are something special. Even the men said so. Lucky won't shut up about how you're setting him up with a 'hot MILF.'" She winked. "I don't have the heart to tell him she's with a country singer."

Mom laughed. "Yes, because that's the only thing stopping him," she scoffed.

Gwen grinned. "So will you? We can pay you, of course—"

"You'll do nothing of the sort," I interrupted. I felt strange at the idea of someone actually paying us to do something we loved. Strange that Gwen was even asking us, a high school band, to play at her anniversary. At Cade's club. Zane's club. Killian's club. My eyes cut to him, jostling Belle on his knee. His eyes met mine and he smiled.

"Yes, we will," Gwen argued. "I can't have the club violating child labor laws."

"Trust me, we don't consider music labor. We consider it a necessity to our existence. It can be my anniversary present to you," I added when it looked like she was going to argue.

Gwen pursed her lips. "You drive a hard bargain, Miss Spencer," she said finally.

And just like that, we had our second gig, one that I thought might change our lives forever. Little did I know just how much at the time. And not for the better.

Chapter 20

"Stay in the car, Freckles. I'll be two seconds," Killian said, opening his door.

I gave him a look, unbuckling my seatbelt. "Yeah, like that's going to happen."

His face turned hard, and he put his hand on my thigh, not in the tender, belly squishy way like he usually did, but to keep me in place. Though I'll admit, my belly did squish, just a little.

"Lexie, you're not comin' inside," he said harshly.

"I've never been in your house. Met your mom. It's got to happen sometimes," I protested.

Kill's jaw was hard. "Not if I have anything to do with it," he bit out. "My house, my mom..." He paused, his hand flexing at my thigh, almost to the point of pain. I didn't say anything. I could see him fighting something in his mind. His ice-hard eyes met mine. "It's not something I want you to think. Not how I want you to think of me. I don't want you having to touch that shit, to have that shit touching you."

My hand covered his at my thigh, my heart breaking just a little at his tone. At the look in his eyes. The shame. It was a peek at the vulnerability he only showed to me. That he barely showed. But I knew it haunted him.

"You want to know how I think of you?" I whispered. "I think you're one of the best people I know. The smartest. The most loyal. Definitely the most broody.." I paused "Well, apart from Zane," I amended with a small grin. I pried his hand off my thigh and moved it up to my lips so I could kiss it softly. "Nothing in there—" I nodded to the house "—could make me think any less of you. It could only make me think more of you, if that's possible. Make me love you more."

Killian's entire body froze at my words and I realized what I'd just done.

Shoot.

I'd actually just told the boy I had only been dating for a couple of months that I loved him.

Shoot, shoot, shoot.

What did I do in this situation? I was such a big idiot!

I dropped his hand immediately. Instead of it flinching away from the clingy, arguably crazy girlfriend, it cupped my cheek roughly, yanking my head forward, and Kill touched my forehead to his.

"What did you just say, Freckles?" he rasped, his eyes glued to mine.

I blinked rapidly, my heart pounding so hard I thought it might explode out of my chest. "I-I," I stuttered.

"You love me?" he asked in a voice so full of disbelief, so full of vulnerability that it made my heart stop right there in my chest.

Everything in me stilled and I gained beautiful clarity. "Yes," I said in a clear voice. "I love you, Killian Decesare."

There was a moment of complete stillness as my words filled up the car. Filled up my soul.

"Fuck," he muttered. He closed his eyes for a long moment, and when he opened them, the raw emotion in them had tears clogging up my throat.

"For the last five years, life has given me nothing but shit," he whispered. "No gifts, no breaks, no respite, now I know..." He paused. "Now I know why. Been eating that shit so I could get given this gift." His hands tightened at my cheeks. "What I'm holding in my hands. Hearing those words, it's worth the five years of shit. Hell, it'd be worth fifty."

Tears rolled freely down my cheeks. Kill wiped them away with his thumbs.

"Gotta kiss you now, Freckles," he muttered. "Gotta taste those words on your lips."

"Okay," I whispered.

I barely got the 'kay out before Killian's head bent and captured my mouth. I expected the kiss to mirror the tenderness of his words, of his gaze. It didn't. It was ferocious. Relentless. Unlike anything I'd ever experienced in my life. Like nothing I ever thought I'd experience. I couldn't get enough of that kiss. I was angry at the confines of the car, the angle making me unable to press my body to his.

Kill seemed to sense my frustration, or felt it himself because he let out a sound at the back of his throat and lifted me with ease across the car so I was in his lap. Our lips didn't stop moving the entire time. It seemed I didn't breathe the entire time. I pressed myself as close as I could to him. I couldn't get close enough. It was like I wanted to crawl inside his skin. That's how frantic I was.

Kill's hand went to my neck, pulling himself back slightly. We were both breathing heavily.

"As much as I hate to say it, and trust me, it almost physically pains me to do so, but you need to get outta the car, Freckles," he ordered, his voice thick.

It took me a couple of seconds to understand his meaning, and despite the electricity coursing through my veins, I blushed.

I leaned back, moving to climb out the driver's door. Kill's hands at my neck didn't let me go. Instead, he pulled me in for one more gentle, open-mouthed kiss. He held me for a moment longer, then released me.

I climbed out on shaky feet, a little scared my knees would buckle. I managed to stay upright for the short amount of time it took for Kill to knife out of his car and grasp my hand firmly. He eyed the house in front of us, his jaw hard.

"Let the record state I'm firmly against this," he muttered.

"So noted," I replied, squeezing his hand.

He gave me a quick glance, swore under his breath, then stepped his motorcycle boot forward.

It was only as his hand circled around the doorknob that I realized he hadn't said he loved me too.

••••

It was dark inside. I shouldn't have been surprised. Walking up the cracked front walk, I had noticed all the curtains were drawn. The outside of the house was in a state of disrepair. The white paint was peeling, and half looked like the sun had melted it. On either side of the cracked pavers were forgotten flowerbeds, overgrown and scattered with what looked like dead roses. I was fascinated with them before I moved my gaze to the lawn. It was the only thing that hinted that someone was taking care of the place. Though it was yellowing in places, it was freshly cut.

"This you?" I nodded to the lawn.

Kill merely shrugged.

He was silent when we got into the dark room, which smelled of cigarette smoke. It took a couple of minutes for my eyes to adjust to the darkness as Kill closed the door behind us. We had walked into a small living room. It was sparse, only a sofa with a faded floral pattern, a couple of old lazy boys, a coffee table, which was littered with various bottles, and a TV, which was blaring with infomercials. The walls were bare, but there was faded rectangles where I assumed pictures used to hang.

My heart clenched at this. My mom decorated in pictures. Every inch of our fridge was covered in snapshots—selfies of us from two weeks ago to photos of me at two years old. They scattered the walls, and there was a framed photo on almost every surface. I'd say about two-thirds of those photos had either Steve or Ava or both of them. I had stared at them for hours when we'd gotten home for DC, trying to understand that was the only place they existed now, in a little frame, in a static image that captured a moment in time and turned them into a memory. It had hurt my soul staring at those photos. Destroyed it. It still hurt looking at those photos. And I did. Every single day. The only thing that hurt more would be not seeing them. Not recognizing those moments, those memories. Which is what I suspected happened here.

I squeezed Killian's hand.

He didn't make any notion he had felt it. He just dragged me forward, past a kitchen that was to my left and down a dark hallway. None of the walls held a single picture, but I could see the skeletons of the frames.

I heard the dull thud of music coming from a closed door to my right, just off the living room. By the way Killian scowled at it, I guessed it was his mom's. He quickened his pace and took us to the room at the end of the hall, yanking me in and closing the door behind us.

Unlike the rest of the house, this room was bathed in light. A huge window opened up to the yellowing backyard, a wire fence, and a house beyond it. Not the best view, but it was daylight at least. I stepped further into the room as Kill let go of my hand, eyeing me with a blank look on his face, as if he was inspecting my reaction.

The room had one thing in common with what I saw of the rest of the house. It smelled of cigarette smoke. But it was faint and mixed with the wondrous, musky aroma that was Killian. That was the only similarity. Where the house was bare of anything resembling memories or personality, Killian's room exploded with it. His unmade bed was shoved in the corner of the small room, and a weight bench and bar were at the end of that. Across from that, under the window and spanning the length of his room was a bookshelf stuffed with books. Bursting with them. I wandered over, running my hand along the slightly rusting weight bar that had a scary looking dumbbell on it.

I glanced back to Kill, raising my eyebrow. "Do you even lift, bro?" I deadpanned.

The blankness on his face shattered and he grinned, shaking his head, still not saying anything, still standing there with his arms crossed, watching me. I tore my eyes away from his to look at all of the books crammed into every spare space of the case. On top of it was frames. A lot of them. I picked one up at random. In it was a small boy with shaggy, inky black hair sitting atop of a huge motorcycle. He looked tiny on the monster thing. His little boy face was stretched into a huge grin, and large hands spanned his shoulders. A man wearing a Sons of Templar cut stood behind him, his head slightly tilted down, laughing at the little boy. He had the same inky black hair as the boy, though his was streaked with silver at the sides. He wore it long, brushing his shoulders. The same strong jaw was obvious in profile, even under the thick stubble covering half his face. He was big and tall, with muscles protruding out of his white tee and a slight belly jutting over his thick belt buckle.

He was looking down at the little boy with the most open and beautiful look of love I'd ever seen.

A single tear trailed off my cheek and splashed on the glass.

I felt heat at my back. He didn't touch me, but his breath brushed at my neck.

"Your dad," I whispered, not looking down.

235

"Had me on a bike before I could walk," he murmured in answer.

"He's handsome," I pointed out, "like his son."

Killian didn't say anything.

"He loved you. Very much," I continued.

Killian stayed silent.

I carefully placed the picture down, looking at each and every one of the others. There was one of the large man cradling a tiny baby in his tattooed arms, a tear visible on his stubbled cheek. Another with a gangly, skinny boy with a backpack on, all in black, his arms around his dad's waist and father's around his shoulder. They were both flipping the bird to the camera.

I smiled.

The next didn't have a little boy in it, just the man, surrounded by other men in the same cut, standing outside a familiar clubhouse. Then there was one with a roughly twelve-year-old Kill standing out the same clubhouse with the same men. A couple of women were in it too, one I recognized as a younger Rosie. Another slightly older woman was tucked into Kill's dad's arm, her hand on Killian's shoulder. I didn't recognize her. She had bleached blonde hair that tumbled around her shoulders, and even in the picture I could see she wore a lot of makeup. She was pretty in a hard sort of way. I might not have recognized her, but I recognized those ice blue eyes. Unlike her sons, even in this photo, they were empty.

My eyes moved to a newer frame, and I let out a little gasp at the picture inside it, mingled between his precious memories of his dad. My hand was shaking when I picked it up.

"When did you get this?" I asked, turning my head.

Kill was so close I almost brushed his face when I met his eyes. They weren't empty. They were full. To the brim.

His hands rested on my hips lightly. "'Bout a month ago," he replied.

I gaped at him then back down at the photo. My fingers traced over the faces. My face. Kill's profile.

It was taken on one of the rare times Kill was caught off guard. I had enlisted Noah to sneakily take a photo of us on my phone. I needed it. Memories. Evidence. He had gotten a perfect one between sets when we were practicing one Sunday. Kill had been sitting watching.

It was right after I'd sang "Church" by Hozier and he had walked up to me and kissed me, right in front of the boys.

Sam and Wyatt had wolf-whistled and I had pulled back, blushing slightly, but smiling. I just happened to move my eyes in Noah's direction and the camera he was directed at me. So he caught the lazy, blissful smile on my face and Kill's profile, staring at me. Both of his hands were at my neck; my guitar was slung over my back. It was the wallpaper of my phone. I had meant to get it processed, but I hadn't gotten around to it yet.

"How did you get this?" I asked him in a soft voice.

His hands flexed at my waist and he nuzzled my neck. "Got it off your phone when you didn't notice," he replied into my neck.

"How do you know my passcode?" I accused, not that it was really an accusation. I didn't exactly have secrets hidden in my phone.

"Babe," he said, lifting his head. "It's Bob Dylan's birthday," he told me as if it was obvious. It was, but only to people who knew me. Really knew me.

I couldn't find it in me to even be a little bit annoyed at this. I was too busy trying not to burst into tears.

I carefully put it down and turned in his arms, running my finger down his stubbled jaw. He was getting more like his dad every day. Turning into a man. My finger traced his mouth for a second. His hand came up and circled my wrist, turning my palm up so he could kiss it. When he released it downward but keep our fingers intertwined, I reached up to press a gentle kiss on his mouth.

"Your dad would be so very proud of you, Killian Decesare," I whispered against his mouth.

Kill's body stiffened and his eyes seemed to shutter over. "He'd be proud of the fact I managed to snag a girl way out of my league. Out of my stratosphere," he stated, his voice tight with forced humor.

I frowned at him as he kissed my head and released our hands so he could step back.

"I don't know where you get that notion, but you are very mistaken," I informed him.

He regarded me. "Agree to disagree."

I huffed out a frustrated breath and glared at him. That only made him grin.

"You're cute when you're angry, Freckles."

I rolled my eyes. "Do what you gotta do," I ordered, waving my hands at him. "We've got to get to the club soon. I can't be in a bad mood because of my boyfriend's stubbornness. I need to be mellow enough to diffuse whatever argument Wyatt and Sam will no doubt be having." I turned my back to him and heard his chuckle but ignored it. My eyes settled on the wall across from his dresser. There were a couple of Rolling Stone and Grateful Dead posters, but my attention was glued to the frame in between them and what was in the frame—a worn, weather-beaten, and faded leather cut, one with a familiar patch. The Sons of Templar MC. The club that was his family. The thing most likely responsible for Kill being who he was today. The boy I loved. I loved the club for that alone. I also loved them because they welcomed us like family. Because Zane was part of it. Kill was going to be one day too. The thought filled me with warmth. Then something else, something colder, settled in the bottom of my stomach.

Kill's place will always be with the club, the voice told me. *Where does that leave you and your dreams of exploring the world?*

I swallowed the ugly thought and turned back around quickly. Any effort to rid myself of such thoughts paled in comparison to what stripped any cohesive stream of consciousness from my brain.

Killian shirtless.

He had come home to change before the party, and I had caught him right in the middle. His muscled back was corded and defined. Broad. He turned around and faced me, a shirt in his hand. He froze when he saw my gaze.

I gulped as the air seemed to turn thick enough to chew. Killian and me. In his bedroom. With a closed door. With a bed. With a shirtless Killian gazing at me like I was dinner and he hadn't eaten in weeks.

I swallowed roughly. We had never gone further than making out. A lot of the time it was very intense making out, but just making out. He hadn't even tried to go to second base. He seemed to sense my resistance, my need to go slow. I was split in two. I wanted more. Craved it. Even dreamed about it and woke up with pulsing blood and sweating. But I wasn't ready. Not for that. I was scared, terrified in fact that he'd get sick of waiting. Someone like Kill... with all of his experience. He'd get sick of waiting.

Then there was the other side of the coin. What if I gave into those fears? Conquered the fear I had of going further? What if he really did walk away after that? The logical part of me knew he wouldn't. I knew how much I meant to him, even if he didn't return those three little words. I knew. But it wasn't logic. It was pure terror. Because I was certain, more certain than I had been about anything in my life, if he walked away, he'd be leaving me in pieces at his feet.

Killian had been watching me this entire time. His eyes still held that hunger, but his brows furrowed in confusion as if he was trying to read my mind. He shook himself out of it and yanked his white tee over his head while walking to me. Safely clothed, he brought me close to his body, his hand under my chin, tilting my neck up.

"You look terrified, Freckles," he murmured, searching my eyes.

"I am," I admitted. I couldn't lie to him. Not in here, surrounded by his memories.

"I'll never hurt you, Lexie. You know that, don't you?" he asked softly. "It would be impossible. To hurt you would be to end me," he whispered. He cupped my cheek. "That means I'm never gonna pressure you. You're never gonna feel that with me. I'll wait for as long as you want. Forever if need be." He smiled against my mouth. "Though I don't like to think what state I'd be in at the end of forever." He paused. "I'd be okay as long as you're by my side."

I stared at him, licking my lips. "You don't—you won't want... more?" I croaked out. "You won't get sick of having... less?"

Kill's hands tightened at my neck. "You are not less," he declared in a rough voice, his eyes burning into mine. "I'll never want more, 'cause I've got more. Okay?"

I gazed back at him, looking for a lie in his eyes. I couldn't find one. "Okay," I whispered.

Kill kissed my head. "Good. Now let's get out of here before my mom jerks out of her stupor," he said, his face shuttered once more.

I clutched his hand. "You know I'll have to meet her sometime, right?"

He regarded me. "Sometime," he agreed. "A sometime I plan on being far in the future," he declared, opening the door.

We walked past the door with the thumping music; this time it was ajar.

I heard Kill's curse in front of me. As we entered the living room, his whole body went tight. His hand squeezed mine hard enough to hurt. I didn't say a thing, mostly because I was staring at the woman standing in the middle of the room swaying.

240

She blinked a couple of times in our direction. "Killian," she almost spat out his name.

Kill yanked me to his side, positioning me slightly behind him as if to protect me from this skeletal woman.

"Liz," he bit out.

The woman in front of us looked nothing like the photo in Kill's room. This was a shadow of her. The living corpse of her. I could only recognize her from the eyes. Killian's eyes staring at him, though they were clouded and full of contempt. The woman in the photo had been hard, that was for sure, but she was pretty, in that rough sort of way. This woman could not be called pretty. She was... I couldn't even find the word. Her yellowed hair was lank and in need of a major shampoo. It hung in greasy clumps around her face. Black regrowth spread over almost her entire head. Her eyes were smudged with hastily applied kohl. A smoke hung out of her lipstick-smeared mouth. She had on a white, stained, lace-trimmed camisole, exposing bony arms with red splotches all over them. Gray sweatpants hung off her bony hips.

"Who's your friend?" she asked in between cigarette puffs. Her eyes ran over me. "She's pretty," she added. It wasn't a compliment; it was an accusation.

Kill held me so tight I feared my fingers might break. Luckily, he let out a huge sigh, and the pressure relaxed a little. "Liz, this is my girlfriend Lexie. Lexie, this is Liz," he bit out.

She stepped forward, dropping ash on the floor as she went. She didn't even notice. Kill stiffened even more as she came closer to us.

"Liz?" she spat out finally. "You're not even going to introduce me as your mother?"

Kill glared at her with a look so full of hate I almost didn't recognize it. "No, I'm not because you're not my mother. Haven't been for years," he growled. "We've got somewhere to be." He dragged me toward the door.

Liz stepped slightly in front of us, crossing one hand over her stomach, the other going to her mouth, casually taking a puff of the cigarette.

"Get out of the way, Liz," he ordered, his body shaking with rage.

"You ashamed of me? That it? You don't want me to spend time with your pretty little girlfriend?" she asked bitterly.

"Yes," Kill replied. "That's exactly it."

Though her eyes narrowed, I thought I glimpsed hurt beneath those features. It disappeared quickly. She shook her head. "You think you're somethin'," she hissed. "Somethin' 'cause you hang around with that... *club*," she spat the word, "that killed your father. Let me tell you something, they're just a pack of losers. That's what you are too, for spending your time with them." She moved her venomous gaze. "I was young and pretty like you once. Then I made the mistake of attaching myself to his father. Ruined my life. Stole it. Stuck me here in this shithole of a town. Get out while you can. That's my advice," she said, taking another smoke, almost leisurely.

In an instant, Killian was gone, his hand no longer in mine. He had advanced on his mother. He didn't touch her, but she backed up to the wall all the same. Her forgotten cigarette crunched under his motorcycle boot.

"You will never compare yourself to Lexie again," he hissed, getting in her face. "You don't even deserve to exist in the same species as her, a fuck up of biology. And you never speak about my father again or the club. Don't blame them for turning you into what you always were." He looked her up and down in disgust. "You do, I'll make sure I stop payin' our fuckin' bills, move into the clubhouse, and make sure you ain't got nothing," he threatened.

She glared at him. "You're my son," she accused.

Kill turned his back on her, reaching out for my hand. I gave it to him immediately.

"Another fuck up of biology," he said harshly, opening the door and yanking me out behind him. He made sure to reach around and slam the front door before taking us to his car. He opened the door for me.

I paused. "Kill—" I started in a soft voice.

He didn't look at me. "Get in the car, Lexie," he commanded in a harsh voice. Nothing like the hate-filled one he spoke to his mother in, but one that made me flinch just the same.

He slammed the door of the car, his hands white as he gripped the steering wheel so hard. "Seatbelt," he barked at me.

I jumped again, doing as he commanded. The moment I clicked, he put his arm at the back of my seat and reversed out the back of the driveway at a high speed. He was not wearing a seatbelt. We pulled away from the house with a screech and drove toward the outskirts of town to the clubhouse in silence. Not comfortable silence. Stifling silence. Full of fury. I didn't know what to do. What to say. I'd never seen Kill like this.

He wasn't even looking at me. His furious gaze was locked firmly on the street leading us toward his club. The only family he had. I completely understood that now. His hands were tight on the steering wheel. He never had both hands on it. When he drove me anywhere, which was almost every day, one hand was always intertwined with mine or resting lightly on my thigh.

I gingerly reached my hand over to land it on his knee. "Kill—" I tried to break the silence again.

"Don't touch me, Lexie," he bit out, still not looking at me.

I jerked my hand away like it had been scalded. Tears burned at the back of my eyes. Not at his anger, not completely at least. Mostly it was the anger, the pure fury balled up so deep I hadn't noticed it. At his mom. The look he had given her, the way he had spoken to her, it shocked me. I didn't doubt from what I'd seen that she'd deserved it. The way she looked at him, spoke to him, sickened me. I thought of my mom treating me like that and I tasted bile.

"Fuck," Kill hissed under his breath. He slammed on the breaks and pulled off onto the shoulder. We were almost at the club now. There weren't any residential areas around, and we had parked on the side of a vacant, overgrown lot.

Kill didn't waste any time. As soon as the car was off, he was out. I jumped as the door slammed and he strode off into the middle of the lot, his palms on the back of his head.

I watched him for a moment then got out of the car. I slowly walked to where he was standing, stock-still. I knew he heard me approach, but he didn't turn, didn't speak. I waited.

"You see?" he rasped finally. He turned and I almost flinched at the blank look on his face, the pain only I could see underneath it. "You see now?" he asked, keeping the distance between us. "What I come from? The filth?" He shook his head. "My mom spouts that evil stuff on the regular, Lexie. I've come home multiple times to her on the edge of OD. More often than not with some loser there too." He sucked in a breath. "That's my mom. And your mom... she doesn't even fuckin' curse," he half shouted, shaking his head. "Jesus Christ," he muttered. "Might be an evil bitch, but Liz, she's right, you're too good for me—"

"Stop talking," I commanded, stepping forward, putting my hand to his lips. "If your care at all about me, about hurting me, you won't say another word." I waited a moment, my hand still at his lips before moving it down. He stood motionless, staring at me.

"You thinking so little of yourself, it breaks my heart," I whispered. "Your mom is not you. That"—I threw my arm out in the direction we came from—"doesn't mean a fricking thing." I stepped even closer and put my hand on his heart. "This does. What's in here is what matters. What's in those photos you've saved of your dad. You're not your mom. You're not even him. You're you. And you're amazing. I'd wager your dad had a lot to do with building that foundation. But you're the one responsible for the skyscraper."

Kill was frozen for a second. His hand moved to cover mine. "No," he murmured, "if anyone's responsible for building me that high, I'm looking at her."

I gave him a long look. "Agree to disagree."

To my complete surprise and utter delight, Kill grinned and pulled me into his body, kissing my head.

"Let's get you to the party," he murmured finally, after he'd held me in silence for a moment. "Not scared of much, Freckles," he informed me, letting me go and grasping my hand to walk back to the car. "But I am afraid of Gwen if I make the lead singer late to the party."

I laughed. It was easy, genuine. At that moment, I knew everything would be okay.

Who knew how very wrong I could be about that.

••••

I was floating, soaring higher than the clouds. We had just absolutely rocked this party. We even had the bikers dancing. Bikers. Big bad Cade even came up. Granted he just held his pregnant wife tight and swayed to the music, but I'd take that. Mom had gotten up and danced with Gage, one of the men I'd met today. He was big, menacing, and hot like most of the other men. Though his muscled arms were riddled with scars, and something was unnerving about his eyes. Not in a bad way, at least not the way he directed it at us. He was easy and friendly. I had a strange feeling those eyes could change with those he didn't consider friends or family.

Looking out at the crowd beyond me, I knew that's what this leather wearing group was. Family. My eyes touched on Zane, who was sitting at the very back of the picnic tables, not talking to anyone. He certainly wasn't dancing. I doubted anything would make him dance, not even Mom, no matter how much he cared about her. Which, by the way he was glaring at Gage laughing and dancing with her, was a lot. I met his eyes and grinned while I sang "Scar Tissue" by the Red Hot Chili Peppers. He didn't grin back, of course, but I was almost certain the sides of his mouth turned up.

We were rocking. The best we had sounded. We should be, considering how much we'd practiced.

Sam had been like a drill sergeant. "Dudes, these are the most baddest of all badasses in the state, maybe in the country. If we fuck this up, I may as well get myself a banjo and become a country singer. I'll never be able to be a self-respecting rock star," he had told us.

It was safe to say he was jerky with nerves as Kill and I had arrived, hand in hand. I didn't even have time to meet anyone before he pounced on us.

"Detach, lovebirds," he ordered, yanking my hand away from Kill, who glared at him. Sam, to his credit, ignored this or was too distracted to notice. "You're coming with me," he announced, "to go over last minute set lists and sort your tuning." He yanked my guitar from Kill's shoulder. "You"—he pointed at him—"will go far, far away where you can't distract Lexie. You may be scary as shit when it comes to her, but don't test me when it comes to my music."

I cracked a small smile.

"This isn't funny," he snapped at me.

I nodded somberly. "I'm sorry, you're right," I agreed. "It's not like this is, I don't know, a *party* or anything."

Sam did not find me funny, but luckily my boyfriend did.

Kill chuckled and kissed my head. "I'll come find you soon," he promised, turning away.

"No, you won't," Sam called to his shoulder. "She'll come see you when I say she can."

Kill ignored him and I snorted with laughter. Sam took me by the shoulders and maneuvered me through the group of mostly unfamiliar bikers, though a few gave me chin lifts. I smiled at them all.

"Bro, take a chill pill. You bump into one of these guys, you can kiss your nads good-bye," Wyatt warned, looking up from the guitar he was tuning.

He put it down to lean in and kiss my cheek. "Hey, babe," he greeted with a grin.

"I will not take a 'chill pill' or any mind-altering substance that hinders my godlike ability," Sam hissed at him.

"Godlike ability?" Noah repeated, jumping down from the makeshift stage and knocking his fist with mine. "Good to see you're keeping humble, Sam," he remarked dryly, slinging his arm around my shoulder.

Sam scowled at him. He then proceeded to order us around and make sure everything was perfect. We had just enough time to talk to Gwen and for all the boys to droll at Amy before it was time to start our set.

We started with old school rock, Led Zeppelin and Pink Floyd, and then moved on to some other stuff. Kill sat in the front of the scattered picnic tables, chatting to men, sometimes playing with kids, but his eyes always seemed to be burning into me. I smiled at him, big and wide, as often as I could and sang every word to him. Music could cure anything. I hoped it would help chase away his demons.

It was getting to our last song. Sam had violently insisted we don't play any "pussy shit" that would damage our precious street cred. But Gwen had specifically requested the song, and he turned into a puddle at her feet, pregnant or not.

"It's the accent," he said afterward. "She could ask me to chew off my own fingers in that accent and I'd do it."

So that was why I starting singing Ingrid Michaelson's "You and I." It was perfect for the sunny day. I was happy, deliriously so. The black mark on the day from Kill's mom melted away with one of the most beautiful songs ever. My mom was happy, dancing and throwing her head back laughing. Zane wasn't happy watching Mom dance with another man, but he was happy with her.

My eyes rested on Kill.

I was happy.

Deliriously so.

Then the world exploded.

Chapter 21

I hadn't even noticed the bikes fly into the parking lot at the edge of the grassed area where the party was being held. Had I, I probably wouldn't have thought anything of them. There were bikes everywhere. I barely saw them.

I saw these ones the moment they started shooting, opening fire on the crowd. The crowd with little children, with families. My family. I watched, paralyzed in horror as bullets flew through the air, hitting people. People must have been screaming, I guessed, but I couldn't hear them. I couldn't hear anything but the shots.

I kept staring at those men on the bikes. The ones with the guns.

This must be a dream. This can't be happening. Stuff like this doesn't happen, I thought dimly.

Something whizzed past my cheek and I realized this was real. People were shooting. People were *dying*. Right in front of me. I was standing in front of it watching.

Then I wasn't standing anymore. Suddenly, I was on the stage, flat on my back, Killian was on top of me, covering every inch of me with his body, his hands circling over my head.

"Get down!" I heard him roar to someone behind us.

My boys, I thought. Oh my God, someone was shooting.

Mom. Zane.

Zane would take care of her. I had to believe that. These bullets couldn't take her away from me. It wasn't the end of the world, as much as it sounded like it. Killian's body on top of mine, his smell, it calmed me. I was safe. Kill was here.

Suddenly, there was silence. Not complete silence; there was the screech of tires and people yelling and crying. But it was silent compared to the deafening gunfire that had filled the air moments ago.

I was pulled up to sitting. Kill's face was pale as he ran his hands frantically over my body. He wasn't setting it on fire like normal. There was no hunger in his eyes; it was almost desperation.

"Lexie," he said urgently, making me think it wasn't the first time he'd called my name. "Baby, you need to tell me if you're hurt anywhere?" he asked softly, his eyes locked on mine.

I blinked, understanding his question. "No," I said quickly. "The boys...." My head whipped back and dread filled my chest.

"We're fine, babe," Sam called in a shaky voice.

"Lexie good?" Noah called urgently.

Killian pulled me gently to my feet. "She's good," he said, relief clear in his tone. He quickly surveyed the area around him. I couldn't do it. Not at that moment. I was terrified of what I'd see. If I kept my gaze on Kill—living, breathing Kill—it'd all be okay.

"You guys go and help get the kids inside," he barked at them.

He cupped my head in his hands, resting his forehead on mine for a split second. "You okay, Freckles?" he whispered.

I couldn't speak. I could only nod.

Kill didn't say another thing. He led us to the side of the stage and jumped down first, then held his arms up to me. I rested my hands on his shoulders, letting him grasp my hips and set me down on the grass. I still couldn't look anywhere. I could hear it all. The people crying, the urgent barked orders. The sound of someone's heartbreaking sobs. Sobs that echoed in my soul.

This isn't happening, I chanted.

I finally found the courage to move my eyes and everything in me relaxed as my gaze landed on my mom. In Zane's arm. Living, breathing.

"Mom!" I cried, pulling out of Kill's arms to sprint over to my mother.

I buried myself in her arms, needing them more than anything at that moment. More than Kill's. I needed my mom. For her to make it better. I was five years old again, believing with every fiber of my being that my mom could fix anything.

"You're okay," she whispered to me softly.

I sagged against her arms. I was okay.

• • • •

"So is anyone else craving fried chicken something wicked?" Sam asked the group of us huddled in the corner of the Sons clubhouse. There was silence as Noah and Wyatt just looked at him. "No? Just me, okay then," he muttered.

I smiled weakly at him trying to lighten the mood, trying to normalize something in this situation, despite the fact his face was as white as a sheet. Despite the fact there were people in this room with gunshot wounds. There was a man outside. Dead. *Dead.*

I shuddered in Killian's arms and he tightened his grip around me, kissing my head. I snuggled deeper in his arms; the silent presence was the only thing that had me breathing evenly. That and the fact my mom was across from me. Not suffering from a gunshot wound. Zane wasn't here, but I knew he was okay too. The people I cared about, my people, were okay. Others weren't so lucky. I thought of the dead man and the woman who had to be dragged away from his lifeless body by Steg, an older man that Kill spoke of fondly. She was in the corner, staring blankly into space, a glass of clear liquid in her hands. Evie, Steg's wife, was sitting near her.

There were no smiles. Everyone in this room was either wearing blank faces of shock, pain, or anger. Anger mostly came from the men in the leather cuts. It simmered underneath, but it was barely hidden. I peeked up at Kill. His jaw was hard, his eyes shuttered and carefully blank. He sensed my eyes and looked down at me. His eyes immediately softened.

"Are you okay?" I whispered before he could speak.

His eyes narrowed at me. "That's my line, Freckles."

"The man that..." I trailed off. "The man that died. He was your family," I said softly.

Kill's body went hard and his arms flexed at my words. His eyes went above my head, not staring at anything in the room, nothing I could see at least. Most likely something only he could see. Ghosts.

He only nodded sharply.

I reached up to cup his jaw. "I'm sorry, Kill."

Before he could say anything, his eyes focused. On something. On someone. I turned my gaze.

"Mom," I exclaimed, moving out of Kill's arms to move in front of my mother.

She gave me a small smile and squeezed both my hands. "You okay, doll face?" she asked quietly.

I nodded. "I'm fine," I lied. I was far from fine. I was close to freaking the F out, but I didn't need Mom to know that. It would deepen the line between her brows that became pronounced when she was worried.

She gave my hands a squeeze and looked over my shoulders at the boys. "How about you guys?"

Sam gave Mom a shaky grin. "Totally fine, Mia." He paused. "Well, freaked the fuck out, but fine," he altered his original statement.

Wyatt and Noah both punched him in a synchronized move. Sam's face was contorted in pain.

"Dudes," he whined. "What in the ever-loving shit was that for?"

Wyatt glared at him. "Watch your fuckin' language."

I couldn't help but smile a little. Mom full-on grinned at the boys. "If there was ever a time to use that word, it'd be now," she told them. "Consider me giving you my explicit permission to swear as much as you find appropriate for the rest of the day," she deadpanned.

All three boys grinned back; even though they were shaky, they were grins. Only Mom could do that, make them smile after they almost died.

Her face went serious. "I've called all of your parents. I think it's safe to say they are all freaking the F out." She paused, her eyes soft. "Apart from yours, Sam. I'm sure they will be when they find out. I just couldn't get hold of them."

Sam shrugged. "I would imagine my own house could get shot up, and Dad wouldn't be likely to care as long as he didn't spill his beer," he responded, feigning nonchalance. "That's if he was conscious. Fifty-fifty chance there."

Mom's line between her eyes deepened. I knew how much she had come to care about my boys and considered them family. She knew about Noah and Sam's parents and the problems they had with them. Well, she knew some. I would expect she would apply to adopt them both if she knew all. It looked like she was considering that right now.

"You can come home with us," she declared. "After we get the all clear, of course." She glanced over at Cade, who was in a man huddle, though his eyes touched on us.

"Thanks for the offer, Mia," Sam replied. "But I'm gonna head home and steal a couple of my old man's beers and try to chill the... heck out," he replied. His eyes bugged out. "Shit," he muttered. "Any chance you can forget you heard the 'beer' part of that plan?"

Mom's eyes twinkled slightly. "One time. It's the only 'get out of jail free' card on that one, kid," she told him. "But if I hear it again, or if you involve my daughter in the underage drinking I know nothing about, I'll personally come to your house and shave your entire head," she warned. She knew how attached Sam was to his mop and her threat had the intended effect.

Sam blanched slightly and nodded. "Yes, ma'am. I mean, no, I won't ever do that," he stuttered.

Wyatt shook his head and muttered something that sounded like "idiot" under his breath.

Mom turned her gaze to me. "Gotta talk to you for a moment, doll."

"Okay," I replied, noting something in her tone.

She glanced around the room, eyes narrowing a small sofa that was currently vacant. She led me to it. I knew Kill was behind us. He sat on the arm of the sofa when Mom and I sat in it. His hand went to the back of my neck.

Mom glanced at him and smiled. "Guessing you're now Lexie's shadow until the end of time?" she teased lightly, but she seemed glad.

The hand at the back of my neck squeezed. "Not lettin' her out of my sight."

Mom nodded as if this was exactly what she expected. Then again, she lived with me; she was my mom, and she knew exactly how much Kill meant to me.

Her eyes moved to me and they turned serious. "I've just been speaking to Cade," she began, her voice gentle. "Honey, I hate to ask this. I hate all of this." She glanced around the room, her eyes settling on a man getting a bleeding arm bandaged. "That any of this is even happening," she said after a pause. "That my little girl had to be involved in this."

I reached out and squeezed her hand. "I'm okay, Mom."

She smiled sadly at me. "Yeah, and your very okayness is creeping me out, like a lot. You're braver than your mom, kiddo.

Stop showing me up," she teased lightly. She sucked in a breath. "I need to ask you, Lexie. When... when it happened, you were on the stage."

Kill's hand tensed at my neck.

"I was on stage," I confirmed, confused at this turn of events.

"Yeah, honey, so you had the best—" she cringed "—view. Cade wanted me to ask you if you saw anything," she clarified. "They've already spoken to the boys. They were a bit behind you so they didn't see much." Her face was hard, and I had the feeling she was not asking me of her own volition. "No one expects you to see anything, hon. If you didn't... good," she declared finally.

I got it. The reason for my mom's tight form, for the way she seemed to physically hate saying the words. Kill's body stilled behind me, and I noticed the way Cade was looking at me across the room. They wanted to know what I saw. Who I saw. They wanted revenge.

"Yeah, I saw," I replied quietly.

Mom sighed, her face falling into what was close to despair. She closed her eyes a second, then opened them again. "You up to telling Cade what you saw, baby girl? I'll be there the whole time."

"So will I, Freckles," Kill declared tightly from behind me.

I nodded quickly. "Yeah, I can talk to him."

Mom tore her gaze away from me and gave Cade a little nod that seemed to signify something.

So that's how I ended up in the room off the common area, the one with the word "Church" over it. There was a long oak table taking up most of the room, surrounded by seats. One bigger than the others sat at the far end of the room. A gavel, like the one judges use, sat on the table in front of that chair. I had a feeling this room was not intended for teenage girls and their moms. Then again, an anniversary party had not been intended to turn into a bloodbath either.

I was sitting on a chair with Kill beside me, his hand in mine. Cade and Brock leaned on either side of us on the table. Mom was close behind me, chewing her lip.

"Sweetheart, you just tell us what you saw. This all gets too much, you stop. We won't mind," Cade told me, his hard face turning soft.

Brock, the tall and equally menacing blond biker covered in tattoos, had the same soft look on his face. They were being patient and kind with me. Even though I guessed they were furious. I smiled at them. They were good people.

"It's okay," I replied. I took a deep breath and thought back to the moment the shots had started, the moment I'd stopped singing, frozen in place. I would have gotten lost, gotten terrified in that horrible memory had Kill's hand not been in mine, serving as my anchor. In my mind's eyes, I saw the bikes. The men on them, the guns in their hands. My heart sped up. "They were covered," I said, remembering the bandannas jerked up to their noses, the helmets covering the rest. I glanced up at Cade. "Their faces, I mean," I clarified. I thought back. "But they had bikes," I continued, trying to remember exactly what they looked like. "Kind of like yours, like Zane's, but not as cool," I attempted to joke and smiled. Kill squeezed my hand. I tried to think about the labels on the bikes, but couldn't. I furrowed my brows. "Couldn't say what make they were, but they definitely weren't Harley's," I said, hoping that would be at least helpful. I had paid a little bit of attention when I was sitting in the garage with Zane, and I listened when Kill talked about how there was only one motorcycle he'd be seen on. A Harley. So I knew a little. Not enough, it seemed.

Both Brock and Cade looked surprised at me. I couldn't be sure, but Brock seemed almost impressed. I couldn't say why; I wasn't being much help.

"Lost Knights," Brock muttered, glancing at Cade.

I had no idea what that meant, but Kill's form stiffened beside me.

Cade nodded. "Maybe." His eyes were hard, but they softened when they looked back to me. "Anything else, honey?"

Something came at me. An image of the men. What I saw before Kill had jumped on stage.

I nodded. "The vests," I said, thinking of every detail I could see in that memory. "Leather like yours but with a different patch. I don't know what it was, but it had red in it," I continued, remembering the splash of color sticking out in my mind. I sat up straighter suddenly, my mind snapping into place. I'd seen that bike before, one of them at least. "The bikes," I half shouted. "I knew they were familiar, but I just remembered where from." I glanced at Mom, who was watching me with a line threatening to become permanent between her brows. "You know that day in that vintage shop in Hope?" I asked.

She nodded, her face seemed to pale.

"That's where I know them from. They're the same ones. I'm sure of it," I said, turning back to Cade and Brock. My blood turned cold at the idea Mom and I had been so close to... murderers. Spoken to them. I shivered.

My words seemed to turn the air in the room electric. Brock's mouth turned into a grim line. Kill's hand was tight on mine.

Cade's face was looking into the distance; it was full of menace. That menace disappeared the moment he shook himself out of it and turned to me.

"Thanks, honey, you did great," he declared, looking like he was about to move from the room.

"You don't want me to tell the police, do you?" I asked them quickly. The police had been called, of course they had, but I knew the relationship between the club and the police. I didn't exactly know the details, but I knew it wasn't good.

"Lexie...," my mom said from behind me, full of something I couldn't place.

I turned to look at her horrified face. "No, Mom, it's okay," I reassured her. I turned back to Cade and Brock, who were staring at me in what I could best describe as shock.

I wasn't thinking of that. I was thinking of the woman's tortured sobs over that man. The grief I felt in my soul for her. The life that was stolen away, when I knew how precious life was. I was thinking of Kill losing his dad, and that man in the cut only becoming a memory in a photograph for that woman. Like Kill's dad. Like Steve and Ava.

"I get it," I told Cade and Brock. "The police probably won't find them. Even if they do, there's a chance they might not even go to prison." I paused. I wasn't an expert, but I knew that the law was never certain with these things. "Not all of them anyway. "But you—" I stared at Cade. "You'll find them, won't you?" It wasn't really a question.

Cade nodded slowly like he didn't know what to say.

I nodded right back. "Right, well, that's that then," I declared. I didn't need to know what would happen afterward. I just needed to know the people who tried to steal the most precious things from my life, that stole it from someone else, would pay. I didn't even know where this vengeful thought came from. I was certain if I hadn't lost Ava and Steve, I wouldn't be so clinical about this. I'd have doubts. But I wasn't that Lexie now. The before Lexie. The after Lexie saw the world much differently.

Cade was still staring at me. Then his body did a little jerk, and to my utter amazement, he bent down to kiss my head gently. As quick as he did it, he had straightened once more. I knew what it was. A silent thank you. His eyes cut to Mom for a moment. Then he and Brock, who winked at me, left the room.

Kill leaned into my ear. "You're amazing, Freckles," he

murmured. "So proud of you."

I turned to him and shrugged. "They're your family."

• • • •

Everything was black. I was blind. I couldn't see a thing. But I could hear. I could hear it all. The deafening shots. Then they were gone. Then I heard screams. Sobs.

I jerked awake, blinking rapidly at the dead quiet, dark room. Arms tightened around me.

"Freckles?" a worried voice murmured.

It took me a moment to register where I was. On the sofa. It was the last place I remembered being after we had finally made it home. Mom, Kill, and I. We also had a man on a bike following us. Kill had immediately led me to the sofa, deposited me in his arms, and turned the TV on. We barely said a thing.

The TV wasn't on anymore. It was the middle of the night, if the lack of light was anything to go by, and I was reclining on the sofa, my head on Killian's chest.

I must have fallen asleep. That didn't surprise me. I'd ridden on adrenaline for most of the afternoon. I was bound to crash. I was surprised at the fact it was the middle of the night, and I was waking up on the sofa in Kill's arms.

"You're still here," I whispered.

Kill's arms tightened. "I said I wasn't lettin' you out of my sight," he murmured into my hair.

"And Mom was okay with this?" I asked in confusion.

Mom wasn't strict in any sense of the word, but she was firm when things came to Kill. I had a curfew, I had to have the door open when he was in my room, he wasn't allowed in there when Mom wasn't home, and he most definitely wasn't allowed to sleep over.

Kill stroked my head. "Yes, but I'm under strict instructions to deposit you in your bed and come back to the sofa if you were to wake up."

My whole body stiffened at the thought of leaving Kill's arms and being alone in the darkness.

Kill must have noticed this because he pulled me up his body and positioned me so I was looking at the silhouette of his face in the darkness. "I'm not doin' that, Freckles," he reassured me, stroking my jaw. "I respect your mom. Her rules. Won't break them. Apart from the one that tells me I have to let go of my girl. The girl who I watched bullets fly past. Who I could've lost." His hand cupped my cheek. "I can't let you go, Lex. Not now. Not in the darkness when I'm terrified of letting you go. I'm scared you're going to fall apart in my arms," he admitted roughly.

I laid my hand over his. "Your arms are the only thing holding me together," I whispered. I leaned forward, pressing my lips to his. I needed to kiss him more than I needed anything else. The kiss deepened quickly and Kill's hands tightened around me. He moved on the sofa so he was lying flat on his back, and I was on top of him. I gripped his neck and his hands circled my hips as he deepened the kiss.

Suddenly, his hand was at my neck and he pulled back slowly. "Breakin' one rule already, Freckles," he rasped. "Can't burn them all. Can't take advantage of you like this."

I frowned at him in the dark, my blood pulsing hot. I wanted him. To feel alive. I just wanted more than anything to feel alive, to make sure Kill was real. But I sighed and rested my head against his chest. He laid his hand on the back of my neck. I was silent for a long while, happy to hear Kill's heart beating against my ear, and feel his chest moving up and down with breath. My head snapped up.

"You jumped up on stage," I blurted. Kill didn't say anything, so I kept going. "In the middle of a hail of gunfire, you jumped on stage," I continued in horror. In the midst of everything yesterday, I hadn't thought back to the moment. The moment where Kill shielded my body with his own. Against bullets. Bullets.

Kill's hands went to my neck. "Of course I did."

I knew he couldn't see me, but I raised my eyebrows. "Of course you did?" I repeated. "You could have got shot. You could have...." I trailed off, unable to entertain *that* thought, let alone give it life by uttering the words.

"Freckles, you were standing in the middle of the stage, frozen. Bullets flying around you," he murmured. "What did you expect me to do?"

"Not run in front of bullets," I answered immediately.

His hands tightened. "It wasn't a choice, babe. Not when faced with the alternative.".

"Which was?"

"Having any of those bullets hit you." His voice sounded tortured. "Have one of them take away the only thing that holds me together. If that had happened, it may as well have hit me too." He paused. "Wasn't a choice, Freckles," he repeated.

I sucked in a breath; it was strangled and hard to swallow. "You can't," I choked out. "Promise you won't do that again," I demanded.

"Can't do that," he replied immediately. "I'd promise you anything in the world, but not that. As long as my heart's beating, I'll be doing anything and everything humanly possible to keep you from harm."

I paused, the weight of his words hitting me like a tsunami. "Keeping you from harm is keeping me from harm," I whispered. "So remember that next time you jump in front of bullets, 'cause the same goes for me. If anything hits you, it hits me too."

Kill pulled me to his face, touching my lips to his softly. "Not planning on running through any more bullets in the near future,

Lexie. Sure as shit aren't planning on having you anywhere near them." He moved slightly, positioning me so I was tucked at his side, the sofa at my back. I pressed my head into his shoulder automatically.

"Now sleep," he ordered. As if such a thing was possible after everything that he'd just said. But surprisingly, right there in his arms, feeling safer than I ever had in my life, I fell. Fell right into the depths of Killian. Down a rabbit hole I hoped never to return from.

Chapter 22

TWO DAYS LATER

"Can I play you something?" I asked Kill.

He looked up from the car he was working on. "You need to even ask, Freckles?" he replied, his eyes liquid.

I smiled at him, slinging my guitar over my shoulder.

We were in one of the bays in the clubhouse garage. It was the first time I'd come here since the shooting. I had been feeling sick about coming back the entire drive over. But the alternative, being without Kill, was worse. I knew my attachment to him was bordering on unhealthy at the moment, but I couldn't help it. After everything that happened, I needed him. I couldn't have another person in my life taken away. Kill didn't seem to mind. In fact, he seemed to need me just as much as I needed him. He was the one who suggested I come to the garage with him after school since he had to work.

As if he had sensed my mood, he had sat in the car silently for a moment, holding my hand after we pulled into the parking lot. I stared at the grass area and the picnic tables. The place where a man had died. The blood was gone, but that didn't mean it wouldn't have sunk into the ground, tattooed that spot with death. I glanced to either side of us. Bikes were parked in a line. In a line where bikes, different from these ones had roared into the lot and shot at people. Shot at me.

"I can take you home, Freckles," Killian said, breaking the silence, his eyes locked on me in concern.

I knew he was waiting for me to have some form of breakdown. I was pretty sure Mom was too. You don't exactly come out of something like that unscathed. Even Sam had been quiet. But I was okay. Apart from the past two nights I had jerked awake in the darkness, terrified. I could have let the nightmares creep into my days and corrupt the daylight. I was determined not to. That would be letting them win. I wouldn't do that.

I leaned to grab my bag of books. "No," I declared. "This is your home. This is your family. I'm not letting something take that away from me."

Kill reached over to grab my books. His other hand touched my cheek. "Did I tell you today how magnificent you are?" he asked softly.

I grinned. "Not today, but the sentiment's welcomed."

He smiled and shook his head.

So we had walked along the lot, hand in hand. A couple of men waved to us, some smiled. I smiled and waved back. When we reached one of the bays next to the office, a man stepped out of it.

He was tall and wearing a leather cut. He had a graying goatee. I recognized him. Steg. Kill had told me he used to be president until he was shot a few years ago. Yes, shot. He had been shot protecting Gwen, who had almost been shot too. Yeah. The party wasn't the first time the Sons had seen blood. Been covered in it. It was something I didn't quite understand, but something told me it wouldn't be the last time either.

"Kid," Steg nodded to Kill, approaching us.

"Hey, Steg," Kill greeted him with respect. "Lexie's gonna sit with me while I work. That all good?"

I hid my surprise. Kill never asked permission to do anything. If I had been in doubt about what this man was to him, I wasn't now.

Gray eyes settled on me. The man in front of me was scary, no doubt. I thought those eyes had the possibility of being cruel. But they softened as they locked with mine.

"Course that's okay. I don't blame you, keeping a pretty one like this close," he remarked, his eyes twinkling. They turned serious and he stepped forward. "This one's special too. Heard what you did for the club, little lady. We don't take somethin' like that lightly, loyalty," he informed me. "Takes a lot to impress me, but color me impressed."

I blushed a little. "It was nothing."

Steg's hand came under my chin. "Wasn't nothin'," he said firmly.

I swallowed. "You're Kill's family."

"And you're Killian's, which means you're family too."

Kill's hand spasmed in mine at this.

Steg's eyes turned light again. "You just come and get me if he gives you any trouble, little lady. I'll make sure to kick his ass for you." He winked.

I smiled at him. "Thanks, I'll keep that in mind." I glanced at Kill. "Though I don't think he will."

Steg's face turned serious. "Yeah, I don't think so either."

Then he turned on his heel and left.

"He's nice," I remarked as Kill walked us into the garage.

He stopped us and turned to me, his eyes wide. "Nice?" he repeated. Then he surprised me by throwing his head back and laughing.

As beautiful and rare as the sight was, I frowned a little, confused. "How is that funny?"

Kill dropped my books and placed my guitar case against the wall, grabbing my hips. "Steg is a lot of things, Freckles," he murmured. "Nice appears nowhere on that very long list."

I shrugged. "He was nice to me. Therefore, he's nice."

Kill gave me a long look. "Yeah. Not once have I seen him warm to anyone that quickly. He was right. You're special. Not that I didn't already know that," he murmured, pushing my hair behind my ear.

I blushed. I could never get used to that. Those things he said. The way he looked right into me.

Luckily, he set me up at a small table across from a car on stilts, or whatever they were called. It was perfect for me to do homework on, as long as I didn't mind a little grease which I didn't.

I didn't get to focus much on my homework at the start because Kill had yanked off his shirt, revealing the tight wifebeater underneath that showcased his muscled body. He then stepped into coveralls, tying them at the waist.

His dark eyes met mine once he had done this. "Eyes on the books, Freckles," he instructed in a husky voice.

I swallowed and quickly complied before I ran over and pounced on him. It had taken me a long time to actually see the words on the paper. I quickly finished my homework, Kill and I working in compatible silence. Every now and then a man would walk past, saying hello to me, chatting to Kill for a while and then leaving.

But at the moment, it seemed we were the only ones in the whole garage. So I started strumming and softly singing "Monsters" by Katie Sky.

I sang it because of all the things that had been haunting me over the past few weeks; the way Kill's mom had treated him was the worst. He never spoke of her again, and I had tried to bring the subject up once. He had gently but firmly steered us off the subject.

"I'm not wasting breath talking about her. I'm certainly not lettin' you waste yours," he had growled. Then he had effectively silenced me by kissing me.

I hadn't missed the hurt in his eyes. I didn't know how to fix it, and it hurt me. So I decided to do the only thing I could, use the one thing I knew cured my soul. Music.

I lost myself in the words, but never took my eyes off him. As soon as he had heard the first few verses, he had pushed up from the hood of the car and stood still, staring at me.

I sang the last words of the song, hoping they would somehow repair the hurt that was buried so deep in the boy I loved.

There was silence as the music left the air, the echo of its meaning the only thing lingering in the air.

Killian's face was blank. He held himself so still, but his eyes burned into mine.

"Freckles," he choked out, stepping forward.

Clapping echoed in the garage. "Woo! That was fuckin' great. Can you do 'Enter Sandman'?" A cheerful voice asked.

Both my and Killian's gaze cut to the origin of the voice. Lucky stood at the edge of the garage, grinning. Gage was beside him, not grinning. His eyes were locked on me. Not really me, but the words I had sung more likely. I had a feeling they reached more than one damaged soul.

"She's not a goddamn jukebox," Killian bit out, wiping his hands on a rag.

Lucky's smile didn't dim. "Whatever, bro," he said. "I'm down for anything. She's got a great voice and I'm done with work for the day." He pushed himself up onto the trunk of the car, swinging his boots the way a small child would, though he could never be mistaken for a child. Not with his tattoos, his cut, and his millions of muscles. Okay, maybe not millions.

I smiled at him and at Gage, who was leaning against the side of the garage door, his arms crossed. He didn't look anywhere near as eager as Lucky for more, but he didn't look like he was going anywhere either.

"Lexie, you don't have to play for this clown," Kill exclaimed from beside me.

"Watch it, kid. I'm much bigger, not to mention more attractive than you, and you need a unanimous vote to get patched in," he warned, but his tone was light, the way an older brother might threaten a younger one.

Kill crossed his arms. My eyes got distracted for a moment with the way his veins pulsed as he did so. "What do either of those things have to do with you voting me in?" he asked.

Lucky grinned. "Nothing, I just needed to make sure everyone in this room knew that."

I giggled slightly and began strumming my guitar. I let the notes of Lucky's requested song fill the air and the sounds of their fighting silenced. I played a couple more songs and, to my surprise, drew a small audience. I guessed I should have felt self-conscious at that many rough bikers paying such rapt attention to me. I didn't. It felt easy. Normal. I didn't know if that was due largely to Killian by my side or that I considered these men family.

••••

"You're amazing," Kill muttered as we pulled up outside my house.

I turned to him. "Yes, I know. What specifically has made you acknowledge this at this moment?" I asked with a grin.

Kill didn't smile. "I'm serious, Freckles," he declared, his eyes on me. "That song...." He trailed off, seeming to get lost inside his head a moment. "You singing it took my breath away, Lexie," he murmured. "You playin' for my brothers like it was nothing, like it was somethin' you do every day, that was amazing. I'm always proud to call you my girl. That moment, thought I'd burst with it. Pride."

I stared at him and felt tears swimming in my eyes. He wasn't finished.

"I know why you sang that song, Lexie. What it meant. It meant a lot, babe."

I knew that was all I was going to get. Kill didn't shy away from telling me how he felt about me, though I had yet to hear those three little words. But he didn't tell me how he felt about anything else. We had stood side by side at the funeral of the man who was shot, and he had been emotionless and silent almost the entire time. When I tried to talk to him after, he had dismissed me, not cruelly.

"It's done, Freckles. He's gone. In the ground," was all he said.

So what he was saying now, what he wasn't saying, meant a lot.

I leaned over and placed my hands on his chest and kissed him lightly on the lips. Well, it started out lightly. Like most of our kisses lately, it went wild quickly. Kill's hands clutched my hair, pulling it slightly. He made a sound at the back of his throat as his forehead rested against mine.

"Go inside, Freckles," he ordered in a husky voice.

I leaned back a little so I could look at his whole face. "You're not coming in for dinner? The only cooking Mom's doing is reheating a lasagna I made in advance. Even she can't ruin that," I said, teasing.

"Not tonight." He sounded apologetic. "Got club stuff," he continued cryptically.

I raised a brow. "Club stuff?" I repeated. "Would you like to elaborate on that?"

Kill sighed. "I'd like to, but I can't. Sorry, Lexie. It's club business."

I narrowed my eyes. "But you're not even technically a member yet. You can't patch in until you're eighteen."

"I was born a member," Kill replied. "Patch is a formality. I'm a Son by blood. I'm not stayin' out of what happened over the weekend. What put you in danger. Steg knows that."

Blood. My stomach dropped. "This business, it isn't going to put you in any danger, is it?" I asked.

269

Kill's hand tightened at my neck. "Don't worry, babe. I'm gonna be fine," he promised. Then he pressed a firm kiss to my mouth. "I'll see you tomorrow."

I guess that was Kill's way of telling me to get out. I was irritated at this. "Yeah," I bit out, and before he could yank me back in, I grabbed my bag and guitar and climbed out, restraining myself from stomping up the driveway. It took greater restraint not to look back at the car that was idling at the sidewalk. I did it, slamming the front door behind me.

I dropped my stuff at my feet and let out a little sound of frustration.

"Uh oh, frustrated teenager sounds," Mom declared, emerging from the living room to lean on the doorjamb. "Has hell frozen over and are you finally transitioning into a teen monster?"

I frowned at her. "No, it's just Kill being... Kill."

Mom grinned, but the spark in her eyes was lost. "I've got to talk to you, doll," she said, her voice strange.

I immediately stiffened. "What?" I was bracing like I always did these days. I had a feeling it had to do with the fact I hadn't seen Zane since the shooting, and Mom making excuses as to why. I knew he'd be out with the men, finding who did this, so I hadn't been worried. I'd been worried about him getting hurt, that was it.

Mom directed me into the living room, and I understood why I braced, why my intuition had sparked. That was because she was intent on shattering my already fractured world. She told me we weren't going to have anything to do with the Sons of Templar anymore, not just the men I'd played to and laughed with not an hour ago, but the women who I'd started to think of as family.

"This club, these people, they live in a different world," she explained. "A dangerous world. One with bullets and guns. They're not bad people. They're some of the best people in fact," she said, her eyes far away for a moment. Then they focused on me. "But a world of bullets and guns is not one my baby girl is going to be a part of. I can't have my most precious gem in this world put at risk because of who I chose to date. So I'm not seeing him anymore. *We're* not seeing them anymore. Any of them," she said firmly.

My stomach dropped, tumbled it seemed. Her words were slowly sinking in, the meaning behind them. The fact she was forbidding me from seeing people. People I had grown to care about. People that had started to fill the void created by the loss of Ava and Steve. They'd never replace them, but it was something.

My breathing stopped and my head snapped up to her.

Killian. Killian was a part of that world, the one she was talking about. She could not be seriously trying to tell me I couldn't see the boy I loved anymore. She wouldn't stop me from seeing him. Nothing could.

She seemed to read my mind, and she leaned forward to squeeze my hand. "I like my baby girl breathing and happy which means I'll not take away the boy who helps that happen. The boy who jumps in front of bullets to save my girl. He's never going to be out of your life. I know that. I wouldn't do that to you," she promised.

She was saying it like she was giving me a gift. Doing me a favor. *Letting* me have one person when she took away everyone else.

And Zane. The man who I knew was family. He was Mom's *person*. She was telling me we had to cut them out of our lives, just like that.

"You can't do that!" I yelled when she told me Zane wasn't going to be in our lives anymore. Along with the entire family that I'd become so attached to. "He cares about you—he cares about us. *He needs us*," I screeched with tears streaming down my cheeks. How could Mom not realize just how much Zane needed us? How could she be so callous and selfish? "He's got no family without us. He's playing guitar with me," I added through my tears. He was playing with me. Music was helping. Not as much as Mom was, but it was helping him. I couldn't take that away from him. Mom couldn't take that away from me.

Mom stepped forward and grasped my arms. "He'll be okay," she promised.

For once, I didn't believe her. I didn't care about the pain on her face or the tears in her eyes. I didn't care about any of it. I was too angry.

I ripped myself out of her arms. "He won't," I hissed at her. "I hate you," I whispered, my anger making me use words I knew would hurt her. I didn't wait to see if they'd made their wound. I turned and ran out the door, tears running down my face.

I didn't stop until I was far away and puffing. I looked around. I was in a park, and my eyes were blurry and stinging from tears. Somehow, some miracle meant my pants had pockets and my phone was in one. I fumbled with the screen and put it to my ear.

"Freckles," Kill's deep voice greeted.

"Ki-Kill," I sobbed, not being able to catch a breath. I sank down onto a bench behind me.

"Lexie," he clipped, his voice instantly alert. "What is it? Are you okay?"

I hiccupped. "I need you," I choked out.

"Tell me where you are, baby," he requested urgently.

I glanced around and was able to tell him my location.

"I'll be there in two minutes," he promised.

My tears had gone by the time he got there, but my anger wasn't.

"Freckles," his deep voice was tinged with concern, and he yanked me into his arms as soon as he made it to me.

"What happened?" he asked, pulling back, his eyes running over me, looking for an injury.

I sniffed and brokenly told him about Mom banning me from seeing anyone in the Sons of Templar and leaving Zane.

"She can't stop me from seeing them, from seeing anyone," I

declared hotly. "She has no right to do that."

Kill's jaw was hard and he sat us back down, tucking me into his side. He kissed my head. "She's got every right, Freckles. She's your mom," he said quietly.

I snapped my head up to glare at him. "You agree with her?" I accused.

His jaw was hard as he shook his head. "No, babe, I don't agree with her removing herself from good people. People who care about her, about you." He squeezed me. "But I understand it. Babe, that shit that went down, that's heavy. It's crazy. You could have died," he declared, his eyes burning into mine.

"But I didn't," I began to argue.

"But you could have. The thought of that chills me to the bone, Freckles. Scares the absolute shit outta me. I can only imagine how your mom feels. You're all she's got now. She loves you more than anything. She'll do anything to protect you." He paused. "Even sacrifice her own happiness."

I blinked and cold realization settled over me, anger leaving me with Kill's words. "You're right," I whispered. "Oh my God, you're right." I gazed at him, fresh tears brewing in my eyes. "I was so horrible to her, Kill. I told her I hated her. How could I do that? I'm a terrible person."

Kill kissed my head. "You are not a terrible person," he told me firmly. "You're the best person I know. You love your mom. She knows that. Those words didn't mean anything."

"But I hurt her," I whispered, hating myself.

"Good thing it's easy to apologize then, isn't it, Freckles?" Killian said with a small smile. "I'll take you home."

I clutched his jacket, pulling him down. "Can we sit here for a bit?" I pleaded. "I just need some quiet."

Kill gave me a long look, then nodded, pulling me back to him. We sat there for a while, Kill holding me in his arms, not impatiently. Then, when I was ready, he took me home to give Mom a tearful apology. I didn't mention Zane or the club after that, realizing the pain she was in. That didn't mean I didn't think of them. Didn't worry about Zane. About Mom.

Chapter 23

TWO MONTHS LATER

"I don't like it," I declared, frowning at the house as Killian pulled away.

He grabbed my hand from my lap and brought it up to his mouth. "You don't have to like it, Freckles. But there's nothing you can do about it."

I snapped my head to him. "So you're saying you're okay with Mom going on a date, moving on from Zane, the love of her life, in a blink of an eye?" I asked sharply.

Kill glanced at me out of the corner of his eye. It was a guarded look like he knew he had potentially awakened the beast. "It's been two months. It's hardly a blink of an eye," he said carefully. There was a pause. "How are you so sure he was the love of your mom's life?"

I stared at him. "She's my mom. My best friend. I know."

I did. Anyone would. You just needed to take one look at them together. One peek at the way Zane's mask of indifference slipped when he was with us. See how my mom's smile was infinitely brighter when he was around.

I knew.

And I knew her smile had dimmed, her light had gone out, no matter how hard she was trying to hide it. She missed Zane. I missed Zane. He may have been part of our family for a short time, but he was our family. He wasn't meant to be gone.

Mom most certainly was not meant to be going on a date. I didn't care how handsome Clay might have been, or cool he was. Or the fact he may hold our future in his hands, considering he was in charge of whether we got gigs again and his club was the only place for miles worth playing in. He wasn't Zane. He wasn't right.

Kill sighed. "Yeah, that might be the problem," he muttered under his breath.

I narrowed my eyes at him. "What are you talking about?" I asked, instantly alert.

He glanced at me again. "It's just... I'm sure there's more to it than your mom told you." His tone was still careful.

I continued to stare his profile down. "You know something. Something about Zane," I accused.

Kill was silent a moment.

"Tell me, Killian."

"Freckles, it's not for me to tell. Let's just say, Bull's got some serious demons in his closet. If there's anyone to conquer them, it'd be your mom. She's about as stubborn and determined as her daughter." He gave me a small grin. "But even then, maybe they're just too big for her."

I blinked at him. He definitely knew something. Something about the reason why Zane didn't smile. About how sometimes I saw a glimpse of the pain behind his eyes and I wondered how someone could still walk around carrying that much sorrow. He knew and he hadn't told me. I wanted to be annoyed at this. But he was right; it wasn't up to him to tell me. I even respected him for respecting Zane enough not to tell me, even though Zane treated him with ill-concealed contempt the entire time we'd been together.

"They're not," I declared, looking out the window. "They can't be. He'll be back," I said with certainty. "He has to come back. 'Cause Mom has demons too. I might not know what they are, but I know

276

she needs him to fight hers just as much as he needs her to fight his."

Kill squeezed my hand. "He'll be back," he agreed. "No one can ever leave a Spencer woman once he realizes that they're one of a kind. Once he understands how special the thing he holds in his hands is. What a treasure it is," he murmured, pulling my attention back to him.

I smiled at him. Not for the first time, I thought about how lucky I was to have Kill. About how freaking ecstatic I was to have found the boy, the man for me at sixteen years old. I didn't care who said anything about it being impossible to find your soul mate so young, to recognize them, I was certain. I was looking into his ice blue at this very moment.

"I hope you don't ever leave me," I replied, my voice small. "I'm quite sure I'd be a Lexie-shaped shell if that ever happened," I admitted. I was also pretty sure girls weren't meant to say things like that to boys, structuring their entire sense of self around them like I had with Killian. I should have been able to be separate. Be someone without him. I guessed I could be me without him, but I found the prospect so terrifying I thought it wouldn't matter who "me" was without him.

Kill squeezed my hand again, his eyes moving to me once he'd pulled up at the curb.

"I've made a lot of bad decisions in my life, Lexie. I'm sure I'm going to make a lot more. One I know I'll never make is leaving you," he promised.

He leaned in and kissed me softly on the lips. "Ready to rock, Freckles?" he murmured against my mouth.

I grinned at him. "Always."

"Good." He knifed out of the car, and I dutifully waited for him to round it to open my door for me. I had argued over such a thing for a start, feeling stupid sitting there like a dork waiting for Kill.

"Freckles, not many chances in my life for me to be a gentleman. I can't afford to give you diamonds or fancy dinners. But I can damn sure open your door," he had declared roughly when I called him out on him.

I hadn't said a word since.

I grabbed his extended hand, and he kept it clasped in mine when he reached into the back to grab my guitar. That was another thing. When Kill was around, I never carried a thing. Not even my baby, my guitar my mom had scrimped and saved to buy for me. My extended limb. My sanity. Killian was the only person I trusted with it, which made sense because he was also the only one I trusted with my heart. He held both my sanity and soul in his large hands.

••••

"Beer?" a boy I didn't know asked, offering me a red cup, sloshing it slightly on my tan ankle boots.

I did my best to smile at him. "No thanks," I replied, scanning the pulsing crowd of people for Kill.

He shrugged, taking a sip from the cup himself. "You're a good singer," he declared. His eyes traveled my body. "And hot, too."

I glanced back to him. "Thanks," I muttered, starting to feel uncomfortable and out of my depth.

We had just played a house party. A birthday, or just a celebration of someone's parents being away, I wasn't sure. I didn't know who's house this even was. Sam had dealt with that. It seemed the last couple of months we'd been in high demand. Everyone heard about us playing at the clubhouse, and of course, everyone heard about the shooting. So it seemed we were the flavor of the moment, most likely because of our proximity to the event. But then people started liking us, our sound. It was strange.

Girls definitely liked Sam and Wyatt; they always had one hanging off them after a gig. Noah had the same effect, but he shrugged them off. Wyatt and Sam had seemed confused about this, but were too busy with their own "fans," as Sam called them, so they didn't give it much thought.

I knew the real reason. Noah hadn't told me yet, but I knew. I hoped he'd trust me enough to share with me, to take the weight off his muscled shoulders.

But I had never experienced guys picking me up after playing. That was because Kill was always right there as soon as I climbed off stage. He usually claimed my mouth right in front of everyone or made it very clear I was his. But this time I had gone to the bathroom. He'd walked me there and promised he would be waiting outside. Now, he was nowhere to be found.

"I'm Andy," the guy introduced himself, swaying slightly.

I smiled tightly. "Lexie. Sorry, I've really got to find my *boyfriend* now," I told him, focusing on the boyfriend part of that sentence.

A hand trailed my bare arm. "What your boyfriend doesn't know doesn't hurt him," he slurred.

I scrunched up my nose, before I could say anything or extract myself out of his touch, someone else did it for me. Hands at my hips yanked me into a hard torso.

"Yeah, but what he does know will hurt you," Killian said, his voice rough.

Even though this guy was seriously inebriated, he seemed to sense the danger he was in.

His eyes popped out and he held up his hands in surrender. "Sorry, bro," he said quickly before darting off.

I grinned, sinking back into Kill's embrace. "You should just put a sign around my neck, 'If touched, Killian Decesare will open a can of whoop-ass,'" I joked.

Kill's face disappeared in my neck. "Trust me, babe, even that wouldn't stop drunk assholes. Or sober ones for that matter," he murmured. "You're too damn pretty. Add that to you singing in that beautiful voice, a voice that attracts every boy in a hundred-mile radius, I'm screwed."

I giggled, turning in his embrace. "You have to admit, you're a little biased," I said, putting my hands around his waist and tipping my head up. "Which means you're bound to exaggerate."

Kill's gaze darkened. "I'm not exaggerating, Freckles. If anything, I'm understating it." He brushed my mouth with his thumb.

I raised my brow at him. "Well then, I'm not exaggerating when I say every single girl in this room is watching you with doe eyes."

I was right. As soon as Kill walked in, his arm slung around me; he was the subject of a lot of feminine gazes. Me being obviously attached to him didn't stop anything. I didn't blame them. Kill was hot. He seemed to have gotten taller in the time we'd been together, filled out more. He was always wearing all black, despite the weather. Most of the time he was wearing his black leather jacket. Because it was a balmy night, he was wearing a tight black tee, one that showcased his broad shoulders and muscled arms. He was a quintessential bad boy.

Kill's eyes didn't leave mine. "I don't see them, Freckles," he murmured, his face dipping to mine. "I've only got eyes for one beautiful, golden-haired girl. Everyone else is invisible. They don't exist to me."

My stomach fluttered at this. I had never felt insecure about other girls looking at Kill. I trusted him. Trusted what we had. But it still wasn't the greatest thing in the world watching girls salivate over the boy you loved.

His face changed. "You've still got an hour before curfew. I'm not keen on spending it here with drunk assholes leering at you. I'd much rather have you all to myself. Want to get out of here?" he asked.

I grinned. "Best offer I've had all night."

Kill touched his mouth to mine quickly. "Good. Let's get your shit. Then we're gone."

He released me but kept hold on my hand as he weaved through the crowd. The crowd actually separated for him. He held an air about him, a warning one. He may have only been seventeen, but seeing him among the boys around the same age, I saw it. He wasn't a boy. He was a *man*. It was painfully obvious right now. I watched the way his shoulders moved as he hoisted my guitar case over his shoulder and directed us to the exit. He gave a couple of chin lifts to boys in the crowd but largely ignored everyone.

"Lillian!" Sam's voice carried over the crowd. He appeared in front of us, his arm slung around a petite girl wearing next to nothing. I smiled at him and at the name he had taken to calling us.

"You're not leaving, are you?" he asked with a horrified face.

"'Fraid so," Kill answered, grinning slightly. Kill and Sam got on great, which was kind of funny considering they were the complete opposite of each other. Sam was loud, hardly ever serious about anything, carefree, and always had a grin on his attractive face. Kill was quite, definitely serious, most of the time he was downright broody, and his grins were reserved for me. Apart from the occasional one with the boys and mom. I liked it.

Sam looked crestfallen. "You cannot leave. We're doing keg stands. Lexie has to do one," he said, eyes cutting to me.

I laughed at the ridiculousness of such a statement. Of all the parties we played at, I never touched a drink. The drinks were flowing to be sure, but I wasn't interested. I was sure that made me boring and nerdy, but I didn't care. From what I'd seen, alcohol made people stupid and make bad decisions. Kill barely touched it either. He'd sip on one bottle of beer now and then, but no more.

He drove me to all of the gigs and had said, "Babe, I'm carrying precious cargo. Not doing anything to jeopardize my ability to get you home safely," when I casually mentioned it.

I may not have been interested in drinking, but the slight taste of beer on Kill when he kissed me afterward hadn't been half bad.

"That's not gonna happen in any universe," Kill told Sam seriously.

I held out the sides of my dress. "Not really wearing the right attire for keg stands either," I declared with a grin.

Sam's eyes went to my dress, then back to Kill. "Whatever. You can watch me kick Wyatt's ass then." His eyes went to the girl at his side. "Harriet's promised me a kiss if I win." He grinned stupidly.

"As riveting as that sounds, we're leaving," Kill drawled, his face blank.

Sam shrugged. "Go then, children, go! Be free," he called.

Kill shook his head at him. He gave a chin lift to someone further away into crowd. Wyatt held up a hand in farewell. I blew them a kiss as Kill dragged me off.

• • • •

"We gotta stop, Freckles," Kill declared in a husky voice.

He held his body taut above me, holding himself up on his forearms, his torso brushing mine.

"Yes, definitely," I breathed, fastening my hand to the back of his neck and pulling him back down to my mouth.

He made a sound at the back of his throat and kissed me with abandon as his hand moved to trail up my hip, resting at the bottom of my ribs, almost brushing my breast. A shiver went through me. A delightful shiver. One that made any proper thought impossible.

Suddenly the air seemed colder, and it enveloped me as Kill's body disappeared from atop mine. He sat up, breathing heavily. I watched his hand run through his hair like he did when he was frustrated.

I sat up, feeling intoxicated from his kiss. "I'm sorry," I whispered.

Kill's head snapped up, and he leaned over to cup my face in his hands. "Don't apologize," he ordered in a soft voice. "Never apologize for kissing me, Freckles. The taste of your mouth, kissing you, it's the best thing in the goddamn world. But, I want you so bad it hurts. Only thing that would hurt more is not waiting till you're ready. Till it's time."

I paused at his words. Kill and I burned hot and fast. With everything. I loved him more than anything. I was sure about that. I had never been surer about anything in my life. I wanted him. Every fiber of my being wanted... more than the kisses he treated me to every day. The kisses that got more intense by the day. The kisses that promised more. But I wasn't ready. I knew that. Everything that Kill and I already had consumed me. I wasn't ready for more. I wasn't sure I could take it.

"It doesn't make you... mad?" I asked softly. "That I'm not like... other girls," I alluded to the "other girls" being ones who hadn't waited.

Kill's hand tightened at my jaw. "Stop," he commanded. "Don't you dare try to measure yourself against anyone else. It's impossible. They're nothing, not compared to you. It's like the difference between a single flame and the sun. There's no comparison."

He sounded so sure, and salved my doubts completely. "Okay," I whispered.

"Okay," he repeated. He leaned forward, pressing a kiss to my mouth before standing. He grasped my hand and gently pulled me up. His hands rubbed my bare arms. They were covered with goose bumps, not because it was cold, but because of Kill. "Let's get my girl home," he murmured.

I was disappointed to be leaving Kill and what I came to think of as our spot—I overlook above town where we had our first date. We came up here all the time. To make out. To talk. To not talk, just sit side by side while Kill read and I either read or played my guitar.

I glanced over at the ocean, illuminated in the moonlight. The crashing of the waves was calming and comforting. "I wish we could stay here forever," I whispered. "Build a house here and live out our days."

Kill's body went tight at my words and he was silent for a long moment. "You're not meant to stay in one place, Freckles," he declared finally. "You're goin' places." His voice was strange, detached almost.

I grasped his hand. "*We're* going places," I corrected. "I don't go anywhere without you."

Kill didn't answer. He pressed a kiss to my head and bent to retrieve the blanket.

I followed him back to the car, not thinking much of that moment. I should have. Maybe it would have saved my heart later on.

Or maybe it wouldn't have done a damn thing.

Chapter 24

I dropped my bag in the living room the next day, depositing myself on the sofa. It was a rare day when the band wasn't practicing. I had Kill drop me and Gina off at the café to study together. She had been mute the entire time. I was pretty sure Kill scared the crap out of her. Not because he was rude, he went out of his way to be nice to her, but because she was like that around most boys. She had even less experience than I did. And she buried herself in books more than I did as well. She even walked the halls with her nose buried in them. I had tried to get her away from her books and to sit with us at lunch, but she'd blushed bright red the entire time and kept her eyes glued to her tray. I saw the way her gaze flickered to Sam when he wasn't looking, and I knew what that look had meant. She had a crush on him. Because he was a clueless, albeit loveable idiot, he didn't notice. And because he was a teenage boy, he didn't appreciate Gina's natural beauty.

I had asked her about it at the café earlier and she had flushed the same red.

"You should talk to him," I urged. "Or I can do it for you, give him a little push in the right direction." Sam may have been focusing on shallow girls, but I knew he was deeper than he seemed at first glance. Gina would be good for him.

She had gaped at me, horrified. "No, don't," she cried. "It's just... no. Someone like Sam would never give the time of day to someone like me," she muttered, glancing down. "I know that."

I reached across the table, squeezing her hand. "Someone like you? You mean pretty with a killer fashion sense and a kind heart?"

Gina looked up at me and smiled. "You're nice, Lexie. Nicer than I expected anyone that looks like... you with a boyfriend like Killian Decesare to be. Nothing like Stacy and those girls," she muttered, her eyes far away.

I swallowed the anger I felt at the unspoken meaning there. Stacy was exactly the kind of nasty person to be cruel to the kindest girl I'd met.

"So I know you're trying to be nice, inviting me to sit with you, trying to set me up with someone who's so far out of my league it's not even funny, but please don't," she requested kindly. "I don't want to sound ungrateful. I'm happy to have you as a friend... if that's what we are..."

I squeezed her hand. "Of course that's what we are."

She smiled again. "But I'm also happy with my books. On my own. Eating lunch with them. I feel uncomfortable when I'm around heaps of people and boys, especially ones that look like your friends. They're all so friendly too, but I just can't."

I nodded, feeling bad for pressuring the girl to do something that made her feel so uncomfortable. "That's totally fine," I replied. "I get it. Books are way better company than dorks like Sam anyway." I winked. "So we'll just stick to coffee dates with you and me?"

Gina relaxed as I let go of her hand. "Thanks."

I beamed, but I felt sad deep down, wondering what it was that pummeled her self-esteem down to nothing.

"The offer's always there though, you know that, right? You ever get sick of books, a terrifying prospect I know, but if that ever happens, you're always welcome at our table," I promised her.

She nodded again, and I didn't say anything more on the subject. I did plan on making sure I'd step in if I ever saw Stacy close to her again. She may have given Kill and me a wide berth lately, but she wouldn't screw with my friends.

I wandered home after coffee, which had turned into cake, which had turned into more coffee. It was later than I expected, but Kill had texted saying he had to stay late at the club, so I planned on losing myself in the *Bronze Horsemen*, rereading it for the millionth time.

"Hi, Doll," a voice chirped from above me.

I jumped high enough I was surprised I didn't hit the ceiling. My well-worn and tattered book went flying out of my hands.

"Jeez, mom. Are you trying to give me a heart attack?" I accused.

She grinned, rounding the sofa. "If you get a heart attack at sixteen, we're better to know the ticker isn't doing well sooner rather than later," she said, sitting on the sofa beside me.

I glared at her, picking up my book, making sure it hadn't succumbed to any damage. Once I was happy it would survive at least a few more rereads, I looked to Mom.

"What are you doing home this early?" I asked. Mom was busy at the hotel. She made sure of it, I thought. Now that Kill picked me up and took me to school, she was more than likely on her way out as I stumbled out of bed. She'd give me a quick kiss on the head and be gone. She would come home later than usual, to have dinner, watch a movie with Kill and me if we were home, and come to a gig every now and then. We still hung out on the weekends, but she made it her mission never to be idle. I knew why. Zane. She didn't want to stop because then she'd have to recognize his absence, notice her broken heart. It hurt my own seeing her like that.

Her face lost its false grin and she turned serious. "I've got something to tell you. Two somethings actually."

My heart sunk. Mom had been in bed when I got home last night. She had long stopped waiting up to make sure Kill made curfew; she trusted him. She trusted him with a lot ever since that horrible day at the club. I had wanted to wake her up and ask how her date went, but I also didn't want to know. I was terrified she'd say it went well. I wouldn't stand in the way of her happiness, not ever. But she belonged with Zane.

"Okay," I said carefully, bracing myself.

Mom clasped my hands, her eyes watering a little. "I talked to a lawyer today. Steve and Ava's lawyer."

It was so unexpected I flinched at the sharp stab of pain that ripped through me at the mention of their names. I never forgot them. Not one day, not one hour went past without thinking of them. Without missing them. Without feeling the absolute agony over the fact I'd never see them again, would never be able to pick up the phone and ask Ava for advice. But it had started to fade. The hurt. Only now and then did I feel the full force of it, when a memory hit me out of the blue, when I remembered the reality of what death meant.

Mom squeezed my hand, noticing my physical reaction. Pain painted her face. "Yeah, baby, it was the last thing I expected, too," she murmured. There was a long pause. "They left it all to us."

I screwed up my nose in confusion. "All of what?"

"What they left behind. The hotels, the house. The money," she explained, her tone flat. "You've got your own money too, which you get when you're twenty-one. Enough for any college you want to go to. Heck, you could go to college on the moon if you wanted," she attempted a joke.

I didn't say a thing. I was frozen. Steve and Ava had money; I'd always known that. They'd always give me exquisite gifts on birthdays and Christmas, and took us out to fancy dinners whenever they felt like it. They owned more than a couple of hotels. They had a really nice house in DC, plus one in Malibu. I'd known this in a kind of distant way, never thought much of it. Mom had never let them give us a dime, though I knew they'd offered a lot. Steve would always shove money in my pocket whenever I said good-bye, with a conspiratory wink. They hated that Mom struggled, but I knew they were as proud as real parents would be that she was determined to do it on her own. And she did. But it seemed they got the last laugh. They got to provide Mom with the financial support they'd always wanted her to have. Right when she didn't need it.

"Doll?" Mom said quietly, concern on her face. "You'll never have to worry about money as long as you live. Never have to feel helpless or lost. Steve and Ava made sure of that."

Her words made something in me snap and I stood up. "You think money is going to stop me from feeling helpless or lost?" I snapped. "I don't care about money, about *things*," I shouted. "I don't want it. Give it all away, burn it. I don't care. I don't want it," I choked out, tears streaming down my face. "I only want Steve and Ava to be back."

Mom stood up, her eyes shimmering. She pulled me into her arms. I went willingly.

She kissed my head. "I know, doll. Me too, me too," she whispered.

We stood there for a long while, long enough that my tears had dried, and I found the strength to pull out of Mom's arms.

"What's the other thing?" I asked, rubbing my eyes.

Mom blinked. "The other thing?" she repeated.

"Yeah, you said there were a couple of things. What's the other thing?"

Mom's face changed. The sadness was still there, but there was something else too. Maybe hope. And also despair. It was a strange combination to have on someone's face.

She took a deep breath. "Sit down, doll."

I frowned at her but complied, bracing for something horrible. That's what I did these days. Anytime the phone rang, it filled me with dread, with this utter sense of horror that it would be news set to ruin my life. Knowing it could happen once, I was certain it would happen again. It wasn't a question of if, it was a question of when.

"The lawyer wasn't the only person I ran into today," she began, her voice strange. "I—" She paused. "Zane's home."

I sat up a little straighter, and I felt a little flame of hope at that declaration. At the way she said him.

"Zane's home. And you talked to him," I clarified.

She nodded. "And, I found out some things. Some things that have made me understand a lot. Made me realize what I want."

I was fighting a smile. "Zane. You want Zane," I finished for her.

Mom smiled a small smile. It was real. Genuine.

I jumped up and down in my seat. "So you're back together?"

Mom nodded again.

I let out a little squeal, not caring I sounded juvenile and ridiculous. I pulled Mom in for a quick hug before letting her go. "This is awesome. Amazing. I knew, I knew he wouldn't be gone forever. Wouldn't let you go, let us go," I declared. I looked around the house. "Where is he?" I needed to see for myself.

Mom lost her smile, and something flickered in her eyes that made me lose my own. "He's at the club, filling in the men on some things, catching up on super-secret biker things," she told me, rolling her eyes.

I didn't say anything as I waited for her to tell me the thing that caused that sorrow tainting the happiness in her eyes.

"What I found out today, doll, I think you need to know it too," she said quietly. "Need to understand why Zane is the way he is."

"His demons," I muttered, almost to myself.

Mom leaned back a little, surprised at my observation. "Yeah, baby, his demons," she agreed when she recovered. She sighed. "I wish that growing up didn't mean having to understand that no matter how beautiful life can be, ugliness exists to make that beautiful possible." Her eyes locked on mine. "I wish you could live your beautiful life not knowing what lies on the other side of reality. The darker side." She paused. "But you can't. I want the absolute best for my baby, for you to be the best person you can be. To be the best person, you need to understand that darkness, experience it, as much as I hate that."

I felt an uncomfortable sensation at the back of my neck. I knew something bad had happened in Zane's life. I wanted to know what it was, but I found myself wishing I didn't have to. But Mom was right; I needed to know.

"It's okay, Mom. Tell me," I said, feigning confidence.

She gave me a long look. "Four years ago, Zane had a woman. A woman he loved very much. His person."

I sucked in a breath at this, but not just because there was someone before Mom. I wasn't stupid; Zane was old, he'd obviously been in love before. This was because I knew this didn't have a happy ending.

"From what I can understand, Zane four years ago was much different to present Zane," Mom continued. "He was different... before."

I knew it. The Zane we knew was 'after' Zane. Loss had split his world in two like it had mine. I had a sinking feeling it hadn't fractured his like mine had been. His had been destroyed.

"Her name was Laurie," Mom whispered, her eyes filling with tears. "Her name was Laurie, and she died. I'm not going to go into any specifics, honey. I don't want you to go looking for them either," she requested. "You may need to know the presence of darkness, but you don't need to wade into it. But it was bad. Worse than bad. And Zane blamed himself. For four years, he's lived convinced of the fact he was responsible for her death. For that long, he's lived in that darkness, honey. He became that darkness."

A single tear trailed down my cheek. "And then he found you," I whispered. "You were the person that took him out of that."

Mom squeezed my hand. "Us, Lexie. *Us.*"

"I hate that he had to go through that," I choked out, thinking of how hard it must have been for Zane. "I hate how cruel the world is."

Mom stroked my face. "The world can be cruel," she agreed. "But it can also be kind. Kind enough to give me the most beautiful daughter in the world. Kind enough to give Zane a chance to be happy. To give us a chance," she whispered. "Don't dismiss this world just yet, baby doll."

I blinked away my tears and smiled at her. "I won't," I promised, letting my happiness wash away the sadness.

I may feel things deep, to my soul, may be disheartened by the darkness of the world, but I'm glad I had a mom to show me the way back to the light.

•••

I wandered into Zane's garage, carrying my guitar. I watched him for a second, looking at him completely differently after what Mom told me, respecting him so much more, but feeling absolutely heartbroken for him. I couldn't imagine the hurt he carried around. Despite his huge muscles and his strength, he needed help with that. He needed Mom and me. I knew that. I didn't know what to say, how to help with something like that.

But I knew one thing that I could do. I could somehow reach his hurt, maybe numb it a little.

He was staring at his guitar, the one he played with me sometimes. I didn't understand the strange way he looked at it, moments before his face went blank and he picked it up to play with me. I didn't understand then. I did now. It reminded him of her. Held memories. Hurt him. And I'd begged him to play with me, to teach me, to pick up something that caused him pain.

I felt physical pain at that realization. I couldn't imagine the thing I loved more than anything causing my pain, being something different than a part of me.

"Zane," I called softly, not able to be alone with those thoughts much longer.

His head snapped up, and his entire face softened. His eyes flickered with a small glimmer of light.

I had already pounced on him earlier tonight. He'd held me in his arms a long time before he let me go and I went to the herculean task of filling him in on the past two months. I'd been so excited to see him I'd almost forgotten the reason why he left. I hadn't acknowledged his pain. I had to do that.

"Yeah, Lex," he answered, his voice soft, his eyes guarded. He obviously sensed the change in my demeanor, realized I knew.

I stepped forward slowly to stand in front of him. I craned my neck to meet his eyes.

"Can I play you a song?" I asked softly.

Zane nodded wordlessly.

I smiled at him and sat down in the chair I'd sat on many times before.

I started to strum and began singing the one song I hoped would be able to say everything I couldn't, "Unclouded Day" by Audra Mae.

Zane's body was frozen as I strummed the last few notes and my voice faded away. He stared at me for a long while. Then very slowly, and very purposefully, he pulled the guitar out of my hands and placed it against the chair. He pulled me up into his arms gently.

I knew what he was silently doing. He was saying everything I said in the song, the same things I didn't know how to say.

He let me go after kissing my head.

293

"You're not going anywhere now, are you?" I asked in a small voice.

Zane's jaw turned hard. "No, Lex. I'm here with you and your mom. I'm not going anywhere," he promised.

I smiled. "Good."

There was a long pause and I thought about what Zane had been through. About the loss he endured. I knew how it felt to lose someone who was your world. I only lost part of mine. A big chunk, that was for sure, and the pain was so great I reasoned I'd still feel the echoes of it for the rest of my life. But I had Mom, Killian, and Zane. I had all of these people to help.

"Four years ago, Zane had a woman. A woman he loved very much. His person."

His person. His world. Zane had lost it all. I hurt for him. Bled for him. But something else, some small, ugly part of me felt different. If this Laurie was his person, what was Mom? Was she still his person? Or was she his second.

Zane seemed to sense something because his large hand tilted my head up. "Lex?" he asked in a low boom.

I met his eyes. "As soon as I saw you, as soon as I saw the way you looked at my mom, I knew," I whispered. "I knew you were her person." His body jerked at my words. "I know it's silly, but I knew. At first, it was a dream built from books and songs, one I dreamt for my mom." I sucked in a breath to find the courage to say it all. "Then I met Kill and knew that this person thing, this soul mate thing, isn't a dream. And I was even more certain that's what it was for you and Mom. More complicated than what Kill and I have, but the same too, you know? The essence of it at least," I whispered, and Zane's stare was heavy on mine. "You're it for Mom. Her person. Her only person," I clarified.

There was a long silence as my words hung in the air, settled there. Zane's eyes never left mine and his body was tight.

"Jesus," he muttered. "Knew you saw a lot, kid, but didn't realize you saw *it all*." He paused. "You're right. It's complicated. It's also simple. I had love once. Four years ago. It was beautiful what I had then." His voice sounded tortured. "Life turned ugly after that. Won't elaborate, but it was dark. Then I met you and your mom. Found the light." He cupped my cheek. "What I got for your mom, it's love, but it's more than that. You're right. She's my person. My only person. Only one that was meant for me. My person," he declared, his meaning clear.

Despite the tears in my eyes at the torment in his voice, I grinned at him, beamed at him.

"Good," I whispered.

Chapter 25

ONE MONTH LATER

"**You don't talk about your Dad,**" I observed, twisting my hands in Kill's.

I felt his body stiffen beside me. "What's to talk about?" he responded in a flat voice.

I turned my head to regard his profile. "What he was like, what you used to do together. You're allowed to miss him," I told him quietly.

We were in our place. It was a beautiful day, and we had been gazing up at the cloudless sky in silence, letting the quiet seep in, the true quiet I only felt with Kill.

"He's pushin' daisies now, Lex. He's gone for good. There's no point in talkin' bout that. Dwelling on that."

I put my hand on his chest. "He's not gone for good. I bet he's somewhere, watching you. Proud of you," I whispered.

His icy eyes met mine. "There is no somewhere, Lexie," he said in a harsh voice. "There's life, then there's death. Nothing. Heaven doesn't exist for the dead. It exists for the people left behind, so they can fool themselves into thinking the people they love are something more than worm food."

I flinched at his words, at the certainty behind them. My hand left his chest, and I pushed off the blanket and onto my feet. I walked away from him, toward the edge of the cliff, looking at the sea. I knew he hadn't meant to cause the pain in my heart that his words had punctured. But he did. That belief of something more was something I clung to. Had to be certain about. I had to know there was a place where Steve and Ava were now. That they weren't just snuffed out of existence and buried in the earth. That Zane's Laurie was watching out for him, proud that he'd been pulled out of the darkness.

I hugged my stomach, eyes on the waves.

I felt his presence behind me. His hand came up to the center of my chest and he gently pulled me into his. "I'm so sorry, Freckles," he murmured into my hair. "That was an asshole thing to say, to hurt you with those words."

I kept staring at the waves. "You did hurt me," I agreed and his body stiffened. "It hurts me to think you believe that. I can't imagine how lonely you must feel being so certain your dad's not somewhere, he's not with you."

He squeezed me tight. "I'm never lonely, not since I met you."

I turned in his arms. "So what if something happened to me?" I asked. "Would you be able to think of me as just gone, as 'worm food'?"

Kill's entire body stilled at my question, and his jaw went hard. His hands came up to my cheeks. "Don't," he choked that word out. "Don't you ever say something like that, breathe life into the idea that the world could somehow keep spinning without you in it. You don't ever say this shit again," he commanded.

I put my hand on his wrist. "I was just—"

"I don't care what point you were trying to make, Freckles," he cut me off. "Make it some other way."

I nodded, slightly taken aback at his reaction. His hands left my cheeks, and he pulled me so I was tucked into his side, so we were both watching the waves. The only sound was the waves crashing for a long while. My mind was no longer silent. It was thundering with disquiet.

"I'm angry. I was angry." Kill broke the silence. "So angry, I didn't even know who I was without it. I was consumed with it." He kept his eyes on the waves. "It's easy to be angry, to embrace the fury instead of admitting anything else. I was so angry at him for leavin' me with her," he spat out, his hatred for his mother clear. "For turning her into... that. For leaving."

I turned my head to look up at him. "He didn't leave," I whispered. "I didn't know him, but I don't have to. Looking at your photos, at the way he looked at you, I can tell he would've fought, fought to his last breath to stay here for you," I said with certainty.

He squeezed me and kissed my head. "Yeah, I'm startin' to realize that now, Freckles."

I left it there, knowing it was enough sharing for Kill today. I had to be patient, had to let him go through this in his own time.

"You ever think about your dad?" he asked softly.

I laughed bitterly. "You mean the one who did actually choose to leave? To let me and Mom go? The one who Mom won't even talk about? That one?"

Kill looked down to meet my eyes. "Anyone who doesn't spend his every waking moment trying to find the beautiful girl he created, fighting to be in your life, he ain't worth being called a father," he declared hotly.

I gave him a small smile. "I guess. But I want to know him, you know? Give myself my own chance to decide that. So I don't wonder my whole life who he is," I said in a small voice.

"Can't speak for your mom, Freckles, but I'm thinkin' she's got a pretty good reason for keeping him outta your life," he replied, his voice tight.

I looked back at the waves. "I guess," I mused. "But I'm starting to realize that's not her decision to make any more."

"Mom, where's my dad?" I asked, sitting at the kitchen table.

It was after Kill had dropped me home. I decided to go straight to it. I needed to know. Kill was haunted by the ghost of a father long dead; I was haunted by an unknown father, very much alive, as far as I knew at least.

She froze, her coffee cup halfway to her mouth. She was leaning against the kitchen cupboards. Seconds ago, she had been smiling and engaging in idle chitchat as we often did.

She wasn't smiling now.

"What?" she choked out.

I sat up a little straighter. "My dad. You keep telling me you'll explain about him when I was older." I held out my hands. "Well, here I am, older and ready for an explanation."

Mom's face was pale as she placed her coffee down on the countertop and turned all of her attention to me.

"Doll face, I don't think you're ready to talk about him," Mom said quietly.

I met her eyes. "I disagree. I'm sixteen, Mom. I think I deserve to know why I've never had a father. Why I can't know him."

Mom blanched at that. "Lexie, you don't want to know him."

I let out a frustrated breath. "That's not your decision," I said, my voice raising with my anger.

Mom crossed her arms. "I'm your mother and you're my child, so it is my decision."

I rose from my chair so quickly it screeched against the floor. "I'm not a child!" I yelled.

She raised a brow. "Really? 'Cause you're doing a good job of throwing a tantrum like one."

"Really?" I hissed out. "A *tantrum* is what you're calling me wanting to know my father? It's my *right*!" I yelled. "I should get to

299

know what's so bad my own father doesn't even want me. Doesn't want to know me." I ended on a whisper this time. "You made that choice for me once, but now I'm old enough to question that choice, to know why you made it. Kill was destroyed by the death of his father. I know he'd do anything to get him back. And I've got one. I've got a dad that's alive and breathing. I owe it to myself to know who he is. You owe me that."

Mom stepped forward. Her eyes glimmered with hurt, with pain. I inwardly flinched at being the one who put that there, but I stayed firm. I needed this. I was getting this.

She clutched my hand. "You're right," she said finally. "You deserve to know. But I don't want to tell you. Not because I want to rob you of your father, but because I want to save you from him."

My heart dropped. "I-I don't understand."

Mom smiled a sad smile. "That, that right there is what I wish I could preserve. Blissful ignorance. It's another part of that darkness I never wanted you to see. To know." She sighed. "It was always a pipe dream. My girl's too smart to be ignorant to the darkness. Your dad, he's not a nice guy. Not in the way Wyatt's dad is up himself or Sam's dad drinks too much." She paused. "Even worse than Noah's dad, baby."

My stomach dropped. Mom knew more about Noah's dad than I'd imagined. I shouldn't be surprised, behind her sarcasm and humor she saw a lot. My stomach dropped because Noah's dad was bad news.

"I wish I could tell you different, honey. Tell you that he was just a stupid kid, not ready to be a father, and then you could go and find your dad. Maybe that stupid kid turned into a good man. You can't. He won't have. If anything, he's become worse. Worse than before." She squeezed my hand. "Before was pretty damn bad. You know how I said I'd protect you from anything and everything that could cause you harm?"

I nodded slowly.

"Breaks my heart to tell you this, doll face, your dad falls under that umbrella."

I stared at her, those words like acid, burning through my stomach.

"I'm so sorry, Lexie," she said, trying to bring me into her arms.

I stepped out of her embrace. I ignored the hurt look on her face.

"Does Zane know? Does he know anything about my father?" I asked.

She shook her head slowly. "No, Lexie. He'd—" She broke off.

I knew what she was going to say. I knew how protective Zane was over my mom, over both of us. I doubted my dad would be anonymous for long if he knew about him.

"Zane doesn't know. He doesn't need to know," she continued.

I stared at her in shock. "He doesn't need to know?" I repeated. "Mom, he's your boyfriend! He's your *person*. He told you about Laurie. He doesn't speak to anyone, but he speaks to you. To me. He needs to know," I informed her, my voice rising again.

She narrowed her eyes at me. "I disagree," she bit out. "He does not need to know something that might rip him back into the darkness."

I pursed my lips. I hated to admit it, but a little part of me understood her. Zane might have been protective over her, but she was protective of him. She loved him. She would die to protect anyone she loved.

She tried to step toward me again, to comfort me.

I stepped back, retreating toward my room. "I-I need to be alone right now," I told her, my voice flat.

She flinched but she nodded.

I turned on my heel to walk into my room.

"I'll be right here when you're ready, doll," Mom called to me.

I didn't turn around, just walked to my room and closed the door behind me. I wanted to slam it. I wanted to scream. To smash everything in my room. I understood what Kill meant. Anger was so much easier. A defensive mechanism. Something distracting you, obscuring the truth. Anger was easier than the reality. That my father was a monster. Mom didn't say it explicitly, but it was obvious. She wouldn't have gone to pains to get away from him if he wasn't. She wouldn't have had that haunted look on her face if it wasn't true.

I padded over to my desk and picked up my headphones and phone.

I had spent much of my childhood imaging my father to be some kind of hero too busy saving the world to be with his family. I'd dream he'd come and save us one day. Not once did I imagine him to be the villain.

•••

Hours later, I was in the same position, lying on my bed, staring at the ceiling, music blaring in my ears, thoughts on repeat in my brain. It was dark now; I'd missed dinner. I expected Mom to knock on my door and try to coax me out. I dreaded it. She didn't. She knew me. On the rare occasion I got in a mood, she left me to it. She knew I took my time to deal with things and respected that. Apart from the fight we'd had about Zane a month ago, we never fought. Not seriously. It killed me because I needed to talk to someone. I couldn't talk to Mom. And when I couldn't talk to Mom, I called Ava or Steve. I couldn't talk to them either.

I rolled over and looked at the time on my phone. It was late, really late. I yanked my headphones out of my ears. The house was quiet. Still, like a tomb. It was that loaded sort of quiet that a sleeping house had.

Zane and Mom must have gone to sleep. Zane lived with us now.

He technically lived across the street, but that was merely a place to park his bike. He spent all of his spare time at our place.

I had expected him to come in here, too. After he'd come back, we were closer than anything. It was like he was my... dad. I laughed on the inside. Apart from he wasn't. My dad was some kind of evil, someone my mom wouldn't even tell Zane about. The man who lived outside the law. The man who lived in darkness. Who I thought could fight anything.

My mom wouldn't tell that man about my father.

What did that say about him? About the blood that ran through my veins.

I sucked in a breath and made a decision. I grabbed a sweater and slipped out the door. I still had my shoes on. I hadn't bothered to undress when I lay on my bed. I did my best to be quiet. Much quieter than I was the times I'd snuck out to meet Killian in the backyard. Mom may not have been a light sleeper, but I didn't know about Zane. He was a big macho man. I expected he could sense movements of rebellious teenagers in his sleep from upstairs.

Somehow I escaped his macho man senses and slipped into the night, walking quickly to discourage the dark air from clinging to me. It was a futile effort considering how cold my blood had been since Mom told me what little she did about my father.

The night was quiet. Dead quiet. The suburbs in Amber were like a graveyard at this time of night. It wasn't like the city that always had the lights on. People were tucked in bed before the clock struck midnight most of the time. That was until I ventured closer to my destination. There were a few lights on and even a couple of groups of people congregated on porches. Luckily, I snuck past them unnoticed. I didn't think they were likely the people I wanted to meet up with alone in the middle of the night.

I was relieved when I reached my destination, more relieved when I saw both his car and bike in the dim light. I knew he spent as little time as he could at home, and he wasn't constrained by things like curfew, so he routinely was at the club until the small hours. My feet crunched across the dead grass as I rounded the house to the big window that opened off to the backyard. I rapped on the glass softly, shifting from foot to foot. I guessed I should have texted him first to make sure he knew it was me and not some intruder. My phone was halfway out of my pocket when I saw a dim light underneath the curtains, and then they were pulled back.

The window was yanked open the moment Kill's shocked face recognized me.

"Freckles?" he muttered, taking no time to put his hands under my arms and yank me into window. He did this effortlessly like I was as light as a feather. He set me gently on my feet and closed the window, pulling the curtains closed once more.

His concerned and frantic gaze settled on me as he clutched my arms. "What's going on? Are you okay?" He ran his eyes over me as if he were looking for injury.

I did the same, realizing he was shirtless and wearing low-slung sweatpants. His hand came under my chin, tilting it up to meet his eyes. "Lexie," he said firmly. "What's wrong, baby? Why are you here in the middle of the night?"

I looked at him for a moment then dived into his bare chest, suddenly bursting into tears.

His arms automatically went around me, his mouth to my hair. "You're okay, Freckles. You're okay. You're safe with me," he promised.

He very gently pulled me back to arm's length. "I need you to tell me what's going on," he commanded softly. His entire body was held taut, but his eyes were liquid.

I sucked in a breath and managed to get myself under control. "I just... needed you," I whispered.

Kill relaxed slightly. "You needed me," he repeated.

I nodded. "Mom, she... told me some things about my dad." I watched Kill's body stiffen once more. "I don't want to talk about it," I added quickly, desperately. I couldn't, not right now.

Kill looked frustrated and concerned, but he nodded. "Okay, Freckles," he murmured.

"Can I...?" I paused. "Can I stay here with you?" I asked in a small voice.

Kill's entire body jolted. There were questions in his eyes, a lot of them. And doubts, probably about the chances of Zane murdering him if he found out, but he must have seen something in my eyes because he nodded.

"I'll take the floor. You can have my bed."

"No," I said quickly. "I need to stay with you. I need you."

"Lex," he warned.

"Please."

He closed his eyes for a second then nodded.

I sank into his embrace once more. "Thanks," I whispered against his bare chest.

"You don't need to thank me for making one of the things I've wished for ever since I met you come true," he murmured against my hair. "Sleeping with you in my arms."

My belly dipped at this statement, regardless of the other things swirling in there. Kill released me again.

"Sit," he commanded, eyes going to the bed.

I complied and he kneeled at my feet, slipping my boots off.

I felt a flutter at this very intimate gesture.

He stood up, bending over me to slip my cardigan off. Goose bumps erupted the moment he did so, but not from the cold. I was burning hot. His eyes ran over me, something I couldn't place behind them. Then he shook himself a bit and is gaze moved to the top of the bed.

"In," he ordered softly.

I jolted slightly but then did as he ordered. I curled under blankets that smelled of clean linen and Killian. I instantly relaxed at the scent. The bed depressed as Kill entered it. He didn't hesitate before yanking me into his chest, arms going around me. We were silent for a long moment.

"Not gonna make you talk about whatever this is right now, Freckles," he murmured, "but I've gotta ask. You walk here?" His voice was tight.

I was confused at the question. "Yeah, it's not like I'm ready for the road just yet, despite your efforts," I replied, attempting a joke. Kill was very patient and I was better, almost ready to take the test, but I'd been putting it off. I liked those times when Kill taught me. His hand covering mine, teaching me how to change gears. I may have been deliberately prolonging the process.

His body went wired once more and the air turned thick. He rolled me over so I was half lying on him, my face looking into his. "Don't you ever do that again," he ordered, his voice hoarse. His eyes were hard. "Jesus Christ," he muttered to himself. "You walking through this part of town in the middle of the night." He shook his head, pulling me tight. "You're not going to make such careless decisions about your safety ever again."

I touched his cheek. "I was fine."

"You were lucky," he corrected. "You're so goddamn smart in some ways, baby. So damn innocent in others. I'd like you to remain that innocent, blind to that sort of shit. In order to do that, listen to me now. You need me in the middle of the night, you call me. No matter the time or day. I'm there. I'll always come for you," he promised.

I sensed me never being able to win this argument. "Okay," I agreed softly.

He seemed to relax a smidgeon, and he bent his head to press his lips to mine. I think he expected it to be a chaste kiss, but I had other ideas. I deepened the kiss immediately, yearning for him, needing him. He instantly complied, tightening me to him, hoisting my body up so I lay atop him, his hands trailing down my back, yanking me closer to him.

This was different. We were in a bed. Killian's bed. He was half naked, there was no curfew, and no one even knew I was here. There were possibilities here.

Suddenly I was flipped, Kill's body was hovering over mine. I knew he was holding some of his weight back. He merely brushed against my torso. I automatically wrapped my leg around his waist, needing him closer to me. He stilled with this movement. We were frozen a moment. Then Kill brought his head up. I watched him do this, guessing it was in great effort if the pulsing tendons in his neck were anything to go by.

"Not doin' this now," he rasped out. "Not when you're like this, Freckles. Not in this house."

I took a moment to move myself out of the fog. I was disappointed. I wanted him. I wanted to get lost in him, forget all of my problems in him so we were the only two people on Earth. But deep down, I knew that wasn't right, wasn't fair to use him in such a way. He meant more to me than that. I wanted it to mean more than that. I definitely didn't want it connected to the night I found out about my father.

Kill slowly moved off me, breathing heavily. He pulled me back into our previous position. "Sleep, Freckles. I've got you. Everything's gonna be all right," he whispered, kissing my head.

I was certain, curling up next to him, falling asleep in his arms, that he was right.

Oh how wrong we both could be.

Chapter 26

"No, Lexie, you cannot borrow that sweater," Mom declared as we walked into the house. "It's my favorite one, and I don't want the risk of it disappearing into the depths of your closet, never to be seen again," she proclaimed as we entered the living room.

"You're acting like I'd hold that sweater hostage," I shot back.

We had mended fences a few days ago, the morning after our fight.

I'd emerged from my room, feigning sleepiness. Even though I'd only just changed into my PJs and had been awake since Kill dropped me off an hour earlier.

Waking up to his mouth on my forehead, murmuring, "Time to get up, baby," was pretty much the best way to wake up ever. All of my problems didn't seem as big after a night in his arms. I had made him drop me down the street, slightly terrified I'd be caught hopping out of his car. Fate was feeling nice that day because I slipped in unnoticed.

I had padded over to my bleary-eyed mom and wrapped my hands around her waist. "I love you, Mom, and I'm sorry. I trust you."

She had patted my head. "Love you too, doll." She had let me go and gave me a long look. "I'm sorry too," she added quietly.

Zane was sitting at the table, dressed in his cut already, eyeing us warily. "Anything I need to know about?" he asked.

Mom gave him a smile. "Nothing to worry that pretty little head over," she declared. "Just a fight over a sweater," she lied.

Zane seemed to sense the untruth because he raised a disbelieving eyebrow.

"It was a very important sweater," she added. "Get back to brooding over your cup of joe, please. I slaved over that thing."

The side of Zane's mouth twitched. "You pressed a button on a machine, baby," he teased.

She put a hand on her hip. "And filled it with water and coffee. That constitutes cooking. It must mean I kind of like you. Count your blessings, buddy."

Zane's face turned serious. "Trust me, I do, every day."

Mom lost her smile and her eyes went all dreamy.

I had felt warm at that moment, at the little family we had. I understood Mom not wanting to ruin it.

Since then, things had been brilliant, amazing in fact. I had swallowed the bitterness of the conversation about my father and just let it go, let myself be happy Mom had Zane and she was happy, which brought me back to the current moment, days after our fight and reconciliation.

"It's happened before. Remember the time you wouldn't give me back my second favorite tee until I let you cook quinoa in the house?" she reminded me with her nose screwed up.

"One time," I argued.

She grinned triumphantly. "Remember—"

She was about to repeat a laundry list of offenses, I knew, so I decided to cut her off. "Okay, so I have a small"—I held my thumb and forefinger together—"history with clothing kidnapping, but I cross my heart it won't happen with this sweater." I made the gesture over my heart.

She rolled her eyes. I grinned. "Fine," she huffed out as she turned around to go upstairs.

"If you could get it for me, that would be great," I called.

She didn't respond, only muttered to herself about the pains she endured bringing me into the world.

I was still smiling when I wandered into the living room, aiming at quickly touching up my makeup before Kill picked me up. We were having one last driving lesson then hanging out at a café in town with the boys. I loved spending time with Kill just me and him, but I also loved it when everyone I cared about was with me.

My happiness turned into terror when I was faced with a masked figure in my kitchen. Pointing a gun at me.

I froze in place, staring down the barrel. I should have run. Should have screamed. I didn't do either. I was paralyzed.

The form stepped forward. "Make a sound and you die," a cold voice rasped. "Don't do as I say, you die. Try to run, you die." He leaned forward, enough so I could smell his rank breath on my face. My entire body shook and my vision swam.

"So I'd move that pretty little ass where I tell you, before I decide to disregard my orders and taste those quivering lips of yours," he drawled and I wanted to retch.

My blood ran cold as I heard my mom's terrified voice scream my name. I didn't think, didn't have any control over my actions. I ran in her direction.

I made it to the bottom of the stairs and saw my mom's face contorted in terror. "Run!" she screamed at me.

I was about to do that, run, right toward her. No way I was leaving her, but I felt cold steel on the back of my head.

Mom's eyes widened in horror and someone yanked her back.

"Remember what I promised?" the voice sneered.

I closed my eyes, everything going dangerously silent at the realization I was going to die. I thought of Mom. Of Zane. Of Kill.

Killian's was the last face I saw when the gun went off.

• • • •

It took me a second to realize I wasn't dead. That there had been a jolt in my body and grunting of flesh against flesh before the gunshot. My ears ringing, I turned, and in horror, I saw Kill wrestling with the man, red blossoming under his white tee.

Kill was shot. He was shot and he was still fighting the man with the gun. Then he wasn't. Then the man crumpled to the ground and Killian didn't hesitate to run toward me, grab me in his arms.

"Killian! Get her out of here!" Mom screamed from the top of the stairs.

Both of our gazes cut to where she was struggling with another man, one in a suit who had a gun he was lifting toward us.

Kill didn't hesitate. He grabbed hold of me and yanked me toward the door.

"No!" I screamed hysterically, fighting him. "I'm not leaving her. I'm not leaving Mom," I yelled as he lifted me and ran out the door. "Put me down."

"Freckles, stop," Kill ordered urgently, opening the car door and setting me in it. "We can't help your mom if we're both dead. I'm not lettin' you get hit. We need the club. Zane will get her," he promised.

Tears streamed down my cheeks. Kill must have noted this as agreement because he rushed around the car and screeched away from the curb before I even knew what was happening. He drove fast. Way fast. He sped through the streets like the devil himself was at our heels. I thought back to the man at the top of the stairs. He very well could be.

"Lexie, talk to me," Kill demanded. "Are you hurt anywhere?"

His urgent voice cut through my hysteria and I moved my gaze downward. Blood. There was blood all over my white dress. Mmy stomach lurched. My gaze snapped to Kill's tee. The previously white one. It was now almost completely red on one side.

"Oh my God," I whispered in horror. My voice was quiet when my mind was screaming. "You're shot! Kill, holy shit. Don't die," I pleaded.

He reached out his arm, the bleeding one, and gripped my own for a moment before his hands grasped the wheel. He needed both of them on it the way he was driving.

"I'm not going anywhere. I'm not leavin' you," he promised. "It's a flesh wound," he dismissed my horror.

"It's a bullet wound," I clarified in a thick voice. "From a gun. Oh my God. Mom," I whispered, starting to hyperventilate.

"Lexie." Kill's voice was urgent. "You need to tell me right now, are you hurt?"

I gaped at him. "You're bleeding from a bullet wound and Mom's...." I trailed off, feeling pain at the thought of Mom alone with that man. "And you're worried about me?"

Kill didn't move his gaze from the road. We were quickly approaching the road that led to the clubhouse. We'd be there in minutes. Minutes my mom may not have.

"Yes, I'm worried about you, Lexie."

"I-I'm... fine," I stuttered finally.

Kill's body relaxed a little and he screeched into the clubhouse, laying his hand on the horn as he did so. He nearly ran down a bike, parking inches away from it. He knifed out of the car as soon as it was stationary. I did the same.

"What the fuck are you doing, you crazy kid?" Steg yelled, coming out from a bay, glaring at Kill. His entire face changed as he registered the blood on Kill. His eyes flickered to me. He was instantly in badass mode.

"Prospect!" he screamed. "Get doc, now!" he ordered, striding purposefully toward Kill.

I let out a breath, knowing he was in good hands. I had to get to

Zane. I had to get him to save Mom, so I sprinted in the direction of the clubhouse.

"Lexie!" Kill bellowed from behind me but I didn't slow.

The entire room went silent the moment I ran in the room. I felt everyone's gaze on me. I only had eyes for one person.

"Zane," I nearly screamed in desperation.

He instantly turned to me, his eyes widening in horror, in fear as they flickered over me. In what felt like a second, he was in front of me, his hands at my shoulders.

"Where are you hurt, baby?" he asked, his voice thick, his eyes urgent.

I started shaking in his presence, unable to speak, to move now I was stopped. I thought of the gun at my head. At being prepared to die. At Mom. Oh my God. Mom.

Zane's large fingers grasped my chin so it tilted up. His eyes burned into mine. They were hard with concern. With panic.

"Lex, you need to tell me where you're hurt," he demanded.

I belatedly realized why he seemed to be barely holding himself together, why he was holding me like he expected me to collapse at any moment.

Blood.

I was covered in blood. "I-it's not mine. It's Killian's," I managed to choke out.

I prayed that Steg was getting him help. I prayed for Mom. I used every inch of my entire body to wish for both of them.

"Lexie," I heard a pained grunt from behind me.

I whipped my head around Zane still firmly gripping my arms. Kill only had eyes for me. He was shrugging off Steg, holding his shoulder.

Zane's body went tighter if that was possible and fury drowned the room. "What the fuck happened?"

I looked from Kill to Zane, registering what I hadn't said yet, what he needed to know. "They shot Kill. They've got Mom," I sobbed.

Zane's entire body flinched at that like he'd been shot. The absolute horror on his face was clear before he quickly masked it.

I clutched his arms. "You've got to save her. Find her," I pleaded. "Promise me."

Zane stared at me, his face dangerously blank. "I will. I promise."

●●●●

"You need to sleep, Freckles," Kill murmured, stroking my head.

"How can I? How can I sleep? I don't know where Mom is. If she's sleeping, if she's okay, if she's..." I choked the last of my words out.

Kill's arms tightened around me. "She's gonna be okay," he promised. "She's strong, just like you."

I pushed my head from where it was resting on his chest. "How can you know that?"

His eyes were searing into mine. "I know that 'cause Bull's not gonna accept anything less than finding her okay and sarcastic as ever. 'Cause I know what I'd do if that was you. I'd tear up this entire country if that's what it took," he said, his voice rough.

I blinked at him, a single tear trailing down my cheek. He kissed it away.

I glanced at the bandage covering half of his shoulder. He was shirtless. "Are you in any pain?" I asked softly, trailing my hand around the edge of the wrapping. He had barely let the "doc" stitch him up. He had been hell-bent on "briefing the men" on what had happened. Only when Steg had demanded he be stitched up did he comply. He did this without anesthetic while holding my hand loosely, his face blank. I think I'd flinched more than he did. Every time the needle threaded through his flesh, I felt it as if it was ripping through my own.

The young "doc" had barely snipped the thread when Killian had pushed up and strolled toward the "church" where most of the grim-faced men had disappeared into.

Zane had stayed with me for a while. I was tucked tightly into his side before he kissed my head. "Gotta get to finding your mom," he murmured.

I had nodded, my eyes on Kill. I had been focusing on that, on him. Because that meant my mind wouldn't wander.

Kill had kissed me quickly when I followed him to the door. "I'll be right back, Freckles," he promised.

I wasn't allowed in there. Of course. I felt a glimmer of anger at this. This was *my mom*. I deserved to know what was going on. But I wouldn't help her by throwing a temper tantrum right now.

Evie, Steg's old lady, had come up beside me at this point. "I've got your girl, Killian, off you go." She nodded to the door.

Kill gave me one more look and nodded briskly.

Evie turned me in her arms, directing us to the bar in the corner. I hadn't had much to do with her. She scared me, just a little. She was like the biker queen. Although Gwen was married to the president, it was clear Evie ruled this roost. Not in a mean way, just like she was the matriarch of this motley family. She was hard but in a beautiful sort of way. She had streaked, long auburn hair and wore heavy makeup. Despite being in her late fifties, she rocked it.

"Now I know this is a stupid-ass thing to say, considering it's your momma out there, but try not to worry too much, hon," she said, reaching over the bar for a bottle and two glasses. She turned to me. "Bull is gonna do everything humanly and inhumanly possible to get her back. The club too," she promised, pouring glasses.

"I know," I replied confidently.

She raised a brow in surprise and something that looked like approval.

She pushed a glass of clear liquid at me. "You've had a shock, honey, a big one. You need something to calm those nerves." She nodded to the glass.

I looked down at it. "I'm only sixteen," I pointed out.

"I look like a cop to you?" she said. "I ain't condoning you drinkin' the whole bottle. You just need something to take the edge off."

I stared at the liquid. Then I fastened my hand around the glass and tipped the entire lot down my throat in one go. I set it down on the bar with force. The bitter and fiery taste set my throat a light and I was sure I made some sort of face.

Evie looked at me in shock. "Well, shit," she declared. "You're perfect for Killian."

I let out a weird laugh-sob, my body not sure what to do. Evie poured another glass.

"Evie!" an accented voice called out in distaste. Gwen rushed up to me, pushing the glass out of my reach and squeezing my shoulders. "You're giving her booze? She's sixteen," she scolded.

Evie gave her a look. "We already established that. Look at her." She nodded to my bloodstained dress and my most likely tear-stained face. "That's someone who deserves a drink. Or five. She can surely handle it." She winked at me.

Gwen did look at me, her entire face softening. She pulled me into her perfumed embrace.

"I'm so sorry, sweetie," she murmured into my hair. "Your mom's going to be fine. Cade will make sure of it. Bull will make damn sure of it."

She let me go and my eyes watered slightly at Gwen's soft and sympathetic voice. I almost preferred the rougher concern of Evie. It was easier to face.

Gwen seemed to realize that because she wiped her eyes. "Right.

Let's get you into some new clothes. I keep some stuff in Cade's room," she said, grasping my hand.

So I had been dragged upstairs, given new clothes, and I scrubbed the blood off my skin. New clothes and clean skin couldn't do anything for the snakes coiled in my belly.

The entire rest of the day I'd stared at the door to 'church' that largely stayed shut, men striding purposefully in and out. Most of them came over, lifting their heads to Kill, making sure he was okay. Then hard, badass eyes had turned soft when they shifted to me. Some just gave me that look. Some reached in and gave my hand a squeeze. Lucky had leaned over and kissed my head, repeating the same sentiment that everyone had. That they'd find her. But hours passed and nothing. I had just stared into space, thinking of everything and nothing at once, trying to remember the last things I said to Mom. We were arguing about a sweater. A *sweater.*

Killian had sat beside me the entire time, tucking me into his good shoulder, murmuring to me every now and then, pressing his lips to my head. I didn't say much to him, but I clung to him like a life raft. Gwen was never far away either. She had Belle, her little daughter running around some of the time. I'd watch her, envious of the childlike innocence. Had I had that? I did. Until that day I lost Steve and Ava I'd had it. I'd never realized what a treasure that was.

She had seemed to sense something in me because she'd wordlessly crawled into my lap and watched the TV I had been staring blankly at moments before. I clutched the little body close to me, inhaling the baby scent. Kill had stroked her little head, and we silently watched until she fell asleep in my arms and Gwen carefully took her off me.

"You should try to sleep, honey," Gwen had instructed when the night got late, and I had given up on seeing my mom that day. I didn't think of the possibility of the sun setting on the last day I'd ever see her. That couldn't happen.

Kill sat up from beside me, stretching his shoulder slightly. "I've got a room here that I sometimes crash in, Freckles. Let's get you there," he offered.

Gwen scrunched up her nose but didn't say a thing.

When he was leading me by the hand, Zane had come out of the "church," his eyes narrowed at our hands, but he came over, pulling me out of Kill's arms. "You need to get some shut-eye, Lex," he ordered softly.

I nodded. "That's where Kill's taking me now."

Zane's gaze cut to Kill; it was hard. Kill stared him down, not wavering one bit. They seemed to have some wordless conversation before Zane nodded tightly.

"You'll wake up to a new day, sweetie. One where you'll see your mom again, and we'll be getting lectured on the viewing order of *Star Wars*," he promised, joking, which was unheard of.

I gave him a weak smile. He nodded and gave Kill a warning look before striding off.

And now we were here, me unable to welcome the oblivion, the quiet my disquiet mind craved.

Kill squeezed me. "I'm fine, Freckles."

"You took a bullet for me," I whispered. "I thought we'd talked about this."

"I'd take a hundred bullets for you."

I stared at him. "She has to be okay, Kill." My voice broke.

"She will be," he promised, tucking me back into his shoulder.

I didn't think I'd be able to sleep, but in Kill's arms, beautiful oblivion engulfed me.

Chapter 27

"Zane!" I called after someone had led me into the room called "church." It was filled with men in cuts, but I only had eyes for one. I ran into his arms, relaxing the moment his huge form engulfed me. I let myself settle there for a moment before pulling back to meet his eyes.

"You found Mom yet?" I asked on a vain home, though I knew the answer. If they'd found her, no way would Zane be standing here. He'd be right where she was, bringing her back.

"Not yet, darlin'," he said softly. I had expected it, but I still felt a stab when he said it. "We'll get her home soon," he promised, echoing what everyone had been telling me all along. It meant more coming from him because he was the one other person who had to get her back. There was no other option.

"I know you will."

His face changed, but I couldn't quite understand the expression. "Gotta ask you a few questions, Lex," he said, his voice soft.

He made the gesture for me to sit, so I did, feeling slightly uneasy. Cade, who sat at the head of the table, gave me a small grin. I grinned shyly back.

I felt uncomfortable knowing the attention of the room was on me, so I focused on Zane. "You holding up okay?" he asked first.

Was I okay? I was a hair away from falling apart. But I couldn't show him that. If he could be strong after what happened to Laurie and now facing losing my mom, I could be strong too.

I nodded. "Gwen's got me sorted. And Kill's going to be okay," I told him, not answering the actual question.

Zane looked at me with pride. "You're as strong as your mom is." Tears crawled up the back of my eyes at this. Luckily, he kept going before I could burst into tears in a room full of bikers. "Need to ask you about your dad," he continued, his voice even.

My blood ran cold. "My dad?" I repeated. "What does he have to do with this?"

Somewhere deep down I knew. Those eyes at the top of the stairs were familiar. I saw them in the mirror. I wanted to throw up.

"Not sure yet, maybe nothing," Zane continued, unknowing of the sickness crawling in my skin. "Just need to get hold of him in case he knows something that will help," he lied.

I knew he was lying. Trying to protect me. Mom had said my dad was bad, alluding to the fact we had to run from him. Now he'd found her.

I chewed my lip. "I don't know my dad," I explained, unsure of how much Mom had actually told Zane about him. Probably less than she told me, which was precious little. "Mom never told me much about him, apart from he was someone we didn't need in our lives," I choked out, my mind going back to the day when I'd fought with her about him and accused her of lying to me. She was protecting me. "We had a fight not that long ago about him. I wanted to know more, wanted to know why he didn't want to know me," I explained, my voice barely above a whisper.

My tear-filled eyes burned into Zane's. "We never fight, Zane, but we fought about him," I said, hating myself for that conversation. I took a deep breath. I couldn't change the past. I needed to tell these men what I knew. "She finally told me that we left for our own safety. That he isn't a good guy. That's all she said." I was so angry. Angry I didn't know more so I could help. "Do you think it was him?" I asked in a small voice. "Do you think my father would actually do something like this, try to shoot Killian, try to kidnap me?" I was asking because I was desperate for someone to tell me no, tell me that I didn't have the blood of evil running through my veins.

Zane leaned forward to cup my cheeks in his large hands. "Don't know, doll," he told me honestly. I restrained a flinch at him calling me what my mother called me for as long as I could remember. "But we'll find your mom. I'll find her, I promise."

I let that promise fill me up, let it chase away the ugly thoughts of a father I didn't know. He wasn't family I wanted. I had everyone I needed right in front of me and they would do anything to get my mom back. I nodded, blinking the tears from my eyes.

Zane's face was painted with that look of pride I'd seen before. He kissed my head. "How about you go and check on Kill," he suggested as his gaze flickered to the door.

I wasn't stupid. Zane couldn't care less about me checking on Kill, but he needed me out of the room. I wanted to stay, to be comforted by Zane's certainty, but I also needed them to find Mom. So I stood to leave.

"Lex," Zane's voice made me turn.

Then, right there, in a room full of badass, stern-faced bikers, his face softened.

"Love you," he said, his voice clear.

I didn't hesitate. "Love you to the moon," I replied with a sad smile. Then, before I could burst into tears, I left the room.

••••

"Lexie!" A voice jolted me out of my concentration on a spec of stained clubhouse carpet in front of me.

Kill and I glanced up at the same time to see Sam, Wyatt, and

321

Noah striding toward us. I instantly pushed off the sofa, letting go of Kill's hand to meet them halfway. I didn't hesitate. I dove into Sam's outstretched arms. They were tight around me immediately, and I let myself relax into his embrace. I felt more arms around me as Noah and Wyatt entered the fold.

After a long moment, they let me go.

"Came as soon as we heard," Sam said, no hint of a smile or joke on his face. It was unusual. His eyes bulged out at something behind me. I knew what it was the moment my body got pulled back into a hard chest. Kill never seemed to be able to be far away from me, to not touch me. Not that I minded. I needed to see him okay with my own two eyes. Every time he left me, all I could see was the blood blossoming on his shirt as he wrestled a man with a gun.

"Holy shit," Sam uttered. "It's true, you got fuckin' shot." His wide eyes were focused on the bandage clearly visible underneath Kill's black wifebeater.

Kill's body tensed. "It's a flesh wound," he dismissed.

"You are such a fuckin' badass," Sam muttered.

Wyatt gave him a sideways glance, and then his soft eyes focused on me. "We know anything new yet?" he asked softly.

I felt a lump in the bottom of my throat. Suddenly my mouth was dry and I didn't think I could speak without bursting into tears.

Kill saved me, as was his way.

"Boys just rode out with the five-oh," he answered for me, his voice tight. "They think they've got a lock on her."

All three boy's gaze turned hopeful.

"That's good," Sam said. He moved his eyes back to Kill. "That's good, right?" he asked like Kill was some kind of all-knowing oracle. I had to admit, I'd always felt like a kid next to him, but now the distinction between him and us was all the clearer. He had always held some kind of authority that came from his rejection of authority and in the way he held himself. Now it was impossible not to see. Being in the club where he belonged, standing here shrugging off a bullet wound he'd sustained fighting a man with a gun. Fighting for me.

Kill squeezed me again, kissing my hair. "It's good," he said firmly.

There was a long pause. "So what now?" Sam asked, his eyes flickering around the room. The place had all but emptied after the cops had left. That was after I'd given my statement to the deputy sheriff, Luke, who seemed annoyed we hadn't called the authorities straight away. He was gentle and kind with me, but I could see the frustration underneath that kindness. It did seem weird I didn't even think of the police, I guess. But the moment everything went down, all I could think of was Zane and how he'd die to get my mom back. Kill's words echoed in my head.

"But when you're a part of the club and someone screws with you, the club hits back. As one collective fist. And we pack a punch."

I guess I was becoming an outlaw without even knowing it, trusting my mom's fate with them.

There had been a busy atmosphere while they were here and then something changed and I knew they'd found her.

Zane had emerged from "church," his eyes scanning the crowded room until they landed on me sitting on the sofa, amidst the chaos, amidst it but away from it. I was trapped in my mind. The look in his eyes brought me out of my mind, and I surged off the sofa.

"You found her," I guessed when he made it to me.

He nodded. "Yeah, Lex."

I blinked away my tears. "Bring her back," I requested, my voice small.

He gave me a long look before he grasped the back of my head and pulled me into his body. "I'll bring her back."

And then he kissed my head and gave Kill a chin left and the club had all but emptied. Every one of the patched men plus the prospects had ridden out. I'd watched them from the window of the clubhouse.

"Courage, dear heart," Steve whispered in my ear when I felt like collapsing at the sight of those bikes leaving, going to find my mother. Hopefully, my living, breathing mother.

"Now we wait," I murmured, looking to the boys and leaving my memories behind.

"Now we wait," Kill repeated, kissing my hair.

Zane

"Can't believe we're fuckin' doing this," Lucky muttered, fingering his knife as he leaned against his bike.

"Workin' with fuckin' *pigs*," Asher spat out in disgust, saying it loud enough for the uniform in the cruiser to hear. He scowled at Asher but didn't move.

"Shut the fuck up, fuckwits," Cade barked, eyes on the same place Bull's were. "We're doing the only fuckin' thing we can do to get Mia back without getting ourselves locked up."

Bull hated it as much as his brothers did. Hated that he was standing behind fucking police tape while the brothers in blue charged into the fancy fucking house not two hours away from Amber. *Two hours.*

He had immediately given Crawford the details on where Mia was. Not because he wanted to; saying that shit went against everything inside him. But he had no other choice. He knew Crawford would put a tail on them, so there was no way they could storm the place themselves and murder every fucker inside like they originally planned. Well, not without disabling a cop, which each one of them would have loved to do, but that came with complications. And took time, which he didn't have. So he made a deal with the Devil. Or more likely, the one who thought they were the Devil. He'd given him not only Mia's location but the location of a major player in the heroin trade on the proviso the club was coming. Crawford's jaw had gone tight at this, but he agreed, as long as they kept their distance and let the police do their job. He had felt conflicted, giving information to the one man who had vowed to find a way to destroy his club, his family. Then he had caught a glimpse of Lexie, red-rimmed eyes but still looking strong, looking like she had hope. Then that conflict melted away.

Bull's entire frame tightened at the sounds of gunfire. They had better not fuck up their job. If they did, even their pissant uniforms wouldn't stop him from ending every last one of them. His hands itched to be in there, doing something, killing someone. Saving his woman. Instead, he was standing here like a loser. A quick glance at the tight faces of his brothers told him he wasn't alone. Then the gunfire stopped. Everything went silent. That was worse.

Bull stormed over to the uniform left watching them. "What the fuck is going on?" he growled.

The uniform paled, and he seriously looked like he was going to piss himself. Pussy. Bull was about to do something that may or may not get him arrested when the radio crackled.

"Got her. She's pretty banged up. Think her arm's broken—need a paramedic in here, stat," Crawford's voice clipped. "Also need bolt cutters. She's fuckin' chained to the wall."

Bull froze for a split second; then his monster roared to life. He did not give a fuck about uniforms or deals. He was going to his woman. As he strode toward the police tape, a uniform stood in his way.

"You can't go in there—"

He didn't even think; he just plowed his fist through the fucker's face and kept walking.

He heard the sounds of a struggle behind him and he was pretty sure his brothers were doing similar shit to what he'd done. If it had been any other day, he might've almost grinned. But Crawford's voice repeated in his head.

"Chained to the wall. Broken arm."

He broke into a run toward the house. He didn't take in the carnage or the uniforms cuffing various well-dressed scum. Nor did he move slow enough for any of the fuckers to act on the questioning looks that were sent his way. His eyes darted around the living room, aiming for where a basement would be. They fell on Bill, the sheriff, who upon making eye contact with Bull merely shook his head like a disapproving father. The old cop was a lot less high-strung than his piece of shit son and was the only reason they had some form of relationship with the local PD, which was necessary when the Sons needed them to look the other way. Not often, but on occasion. Bill was usually down with that, on the provision shit didn't hit his jurisdiction and they lined his pockets every now and then. Despite that, he was a good man. Bull didn't think too much of him though, more on the man who was in front of him, his hands cuffed behind his back.

Slightly younger than him he guessed, well dressed, in a white shirt and ridiculous fuckin' shoes. Hair all slicked back like a greasy piece of shit. The eyes. That's how Bull knew who he was. What lay behind them. The eyes of a killer. Empty. Devoid of anything that could be construed as human. Bull knew that look because it was what he used to see in the mirror after he went to work for the club. After he drained the life out of whatever fucker that deserved to be taken off this earth.

That look wasn't permanent. It was like the effects of a drug. A while after the killing, it drained away, back into the darkest recesses of his mind. After spending time with Mia, with Lexie, that look became a memory. The dark corner where it retreated to was bathed in light. The look in this man's eyes was permanent. Bull's entire frame tightened. This was the man responsible for taking Mia, shooting Killian, and trying to take Lexie. And sixteen years ago, almost killing her. Almost killing Mia. Thank fuck Lexie didn't look a thing like him. He found himself stepping toward the man who was staring at him. Involuntarily, he reached for his piece in order to put a bullet through his brain. He didn't give a shit he'd be killing an unarmed man in a room full of cops. Not in that moment.

Bill stepped forward, jerking the man behind him roughly.

"Not the time, son," he told him firmly, meeting his eyes.

Bull stared at him, struggling not to pummel the old man from getting in the way of justice. Of revenge.

"Go to your woman," he continued, not backing down at the no doubt murderous look on Bull's face.

That jolted Bull out of his haze. The monster took a backseat and Bull realized what was most important at that moment.

"Basement," he barked.

Bill nodded at him, a look of relief flooding the old man's face. He jerked his head to the hallway behind him. "In the kitchen, first door to your left." His voice held a note of something; couldn't be respect, but as sure as shit sounded like it.

A meaningful look was communicated between the two before Bull moved past them both in search of his woman. Bull didn't look at the maggot because if he did, he wouldn't have been able to control himself.

When he found the basement, he struggled not to take the stairs two at a time. He got to the bottom, not fully prepared for what he would see. His entire frame locked in place.

Mia on the ground, Crawford crouching beside her, gently moving her arm in his hands. Bull gritted his teeth at the fucker's hands on her. But he didn't focus on that, not for long. He focused on her face. Her beautiful peaches and cream face. It was now covered in purplish bruising. Both of her eyes were darkened with evidence of the brutality she withstood, one almost swollen shut. There were rings around her neck. Hand marks. Someone had tried to strangle her. Tried to squeeze the life out of her. Unbidden, the memories assaulted him. A surprise attack.

FOUR YEARS EARLIER

His eyes watched the monitor that measured the beats of her heart, that showed him she was still alive. Barely. Barely holding on, he knew that. His eyes moved to the bandage that covered half her face. He knew what was underneath it, what that tattoo meant. Meant he'd failed. Failed his most basic job. Protecting his girl. Shielding her from the horrors that came with being connected with him. Shielding her from the darkness. The evidence of his failure was everywhere. The burn marks decorating her delicate arms. The cuts and bruises covering almost her entire body. He couldn't even let himself think of what else they'd done to her. Not in this moment. But that was his failure too.

"Brother." He heard his best friend's voice, felt his hand on his shoulder. He didn't look up. Didn't move his eyes from that machine.

"Don't fuckin' touch me right now, Cade," he ordered quietly, his voice dead.

The hand left, but the presence didn't. There was silence for a moment, the beeping the only sound in the room.

"This isn't your fault," Cade began.

"The fuck it isn't," Bull snapped. "This shit—" he nodded to the bed, to his broken angel "—is *all* on me."

"Bull," Cade's voice was stronger, ready to fight him on this.

Bull whipped his head around to meet his friend's eyes. "They fucking *raped* her," he yelled, the ugly word seeming to echo in his brain, slicing him up inside. "Repeatedly," he continued quieter and he watched his friend flinch. "She's scared of mice," he told him. "Laurie's fuckin' terrified of the tiny things." His eyes moved back to the machine. "She's afraid of *mice*. How do you think she felt when they were doing, *that*," he spat the word, "to her?" He paused, choking on his breath. "Yeah, that's on me," he repeated. "Girl who lived her life in sunshine, losing it in the blackest, ugliest depths of hell." And as if she heard him, as if she couldn't keep it up any longer, the beeping stopped.

A single tear trickled down Bull's cheek.

••••

"Zane?" A small voice shocked him out of his own head. His own horrors.

He realized he had been locked on the spot, his eyes glued on Mia, but his mind straying to someone else entirely.

That voice, that very alive, very strong voice got him moving. He managed to make his feet move, and in a moment, he was in front of her, kneeling. He managed not to kick Crawford in the face, who merely released Mia and moved slightly away with a hard glare.

Bull cupped Mia's face with his hands gently, aware of the pain she must be in. But he had to touch her, to feel her warm skin under his. She met his eyes. He flinched, but not out of pain. Out of relief.

Her good hand stroked his jaw. "You're here," she said.

"I'm here," he repeated, his voice sounding rough, even to his own ears.

"Lexie?" she asked, her voice tight with worry.

He stroked her face. "She's good, baby," he assured her. "Killian too," he added when he saw her mouth open again.

Her entire body sagged. She searched his face. "I'm okay now," she promised him.

His eyes ran over every inch of her body. The clothes weren't hers but they weren't ripped. They weren't betraying signs of an unspeakable assault. That didn't mean it didn't happen. Bull swallowed the fire tickling at the base of his throat. His eyes worked their way back up to her face. It was covered in bruises. Bruises that made his fists clench and made him want to neuter the coward who thought he could lay hands on a woman. His woman. The eyes that met his once more made him calm. Because even though her face was battered, those bruises bringing the worst kind of déjà vu, the eyes were what held him together. They weren't broken, weren't empty. They were full, whole, strong.

"Marry me," he whispered.

Her entire frame jerked. "What?"

"Marry me," he clipped.

She regarded him. "You're asking me to marry you while I'm assuming I'm a delightful shade of purple?" she asked, half teasing.

Bull didn't react. Outwardly, at least. Only Mia. Only his Mia would find a way to make a joke at this moment.

She took his silence as affirmation of his seriousness. Her own face turned serious. "Of course, I'll marry you," she whispered with tears in her voice.

Bull didn't hesitate. As gently as he could, he claimed her mouth. He had needed to since the moment he laid eyes on her. Once he was done, he pulled back slightly. She was smiling. Almost laughing. Bull didn't know how the fuck this was possible. She had just agreed to become his forever. He was happy. Ecstatic. But she was still sitting in front of him injured, battered but not broken, and somehow smiling.

"What?" he clipped.

Her eyes twinkled and flickered to Crawford, who had been

watching the entire exchange with a blank expression. Bull had decided to ignore him.

"We totally have to make up a 'how did he propose' story," she informed him in a light tone. "The whole 'he did it in a basement where I was chained up after being kidnapped,' might not be appropriate for the grandchildren," she finished with a smile.

The tightening of his form went unnoticed at the mention of their grandchildren as paramedics, and more cops arrived. Bull was gently pushed to the side and he struggled to not punch the fucker that suggested he move further away. The look he gave the paramedic seemed to communicate something because no one uttered such a suggestion again.

"Zane, honey, can you do me a favor?" Mia asked in a raspy voice as paramedics readied to put her in the ambulance.

"Anything," he promised. He'd give this woman anything. She wanted the moon? He'd find a way to lasso the fucker and bring it back to Earth.

"You need to go and get Lexie, let her know I'm okay. Make sure she's okay. Bring her to the hospital," she ordered.

Bull's entire frame went solid, and he stepped forward so he was by Mia's side. He gave the man beside him a look that made him pause and step aside. Bull would do anything, lasso the moon for this woman, but leave her side? When she looked like this? When she'd been enduring horrors for over twenty-four hours? When he'd been enduring his own?

"I'll get one of the boys to get her. Call Kill, get the kid to meet us there," he told her.

He wanted his girl to be by her mom's side. He wanted to salve every bit of worry that had been tattooed on her pretty face, but that directly conflicted with the guttural need to not let the woman who possessed his soul out of his sight.

Mia reached out to grab his hand, to squeeze it. "I need you to get our girl," she insisted. "She needs you. I need her to have you. Please."

Bull gave her bruised face a long look. Etched it into his mind. Her bruised, battered but *alive* face.

Our girl. That's what she'd said.

"Lucky," he barked, not taking his eyes off Mia.

The men had stormed the area and had all been loosely gathered when Mia had been wheeled out, their faces tight with relief when they saw her. Then tight with fury when they *saw* her.

He felt Lucky's form beside him. "Ride with Mia," he ordered, every cell in his body resisting those words. "Make sure she gets taken care of. Don't let her outta your sight," he commanded, finally tearing away from his woman to face his brother's eyes. For once, they weren't twinkling with humor. "I'm going to get Lexie," he continued.

Lucky nodded tightly. "I got your woman. She's good. Get your girl, brother," he said, clapping him on the shoulder and giving it a squeeze.

Bull nodded and turned back to the stretcher that held half of his world. He bent down to lay his lips gently on Mia's.

"I'll be see you soon, baby," he promised.

"'Kay, fiancé," she murmured, grinning.

Only she could grin at that moment. Bull used every inch of his strength to straighten and give her a long look before he turned and went to his bike to get the other half of his world.

Lexie

We waited for what felt like an eternity, and then I heard the roar. That familiar roar of a Harley. Kill heard it too and his hand flexed in mine. His reflexes may have been quick, but he had nothing on me. I jumped off the sofa and was halfway across the room before he called after me. I didn't pause, didn't turn. I just ran out of the clubhouse into the parking lot. Various bikes were pulling back in, but I was searching for only one.

The one Zane was riding, the one that pulled up in front of me. I was afraid. I was terrified of looking at his face, at seeing the demons Mom had chased away return to destroy him, and destroy me too.

"Courage, dear heart."

I looked up at the same time he got off the motorcycle.

I would have collapsed right there if he hadn't been there to catch me. His arms circled around me.

"She's okay. We got her, Lex," he murmured against my hair.

I clung to his cut for a split second then found my feet.

"Take me to her," I commanded.

Zane grinned, properly, ear to ear. He reached over to his bike, retrieving a helmet that he fastened on my head. Once that was done, he nodded to the bike.

"Hop on."

I gaped at him. "Mom would kill me," I replied instantly. He knew Mom's rule.

He stroked my cheek. "I think she'll understand, just this once," he murmured.

He hopped on and I didn't hesitate. I got on behind him and fastened my hands around his waist. He didn't waste any time roaring out of the lot.

Kill stood watching me with my boys by his side. I blew him a kiss as we left. And in a gesture I didn't think any other person in the planet could execute while still holding onto his badass card, he caught the imaginary kiss and clutched it to his chest.

Then he was out of my sight and I buried my head into Zane's back, hoping upon hope that someone had answered my prayers, and everything would be okay.

I'd find out later that they had. Every single one.

Then even later, I'd find out they hadn't.

Chapter 28

Kill held my wrists above my head; they were clasped in one of his hands while the other spanned my ribcage, trailing down the side of my body, leaving a trail of fire in its wake.

His mouth moved against mine, devouring me, turning me into a mess of need and desire. His body was pressed against mine and my back was flush against the wall. I let out a sound at the back of my throat that would have been slightly embarrassing, but all I thought of nothing but Kill's mouth on mine and more.

I had wanted more, but I got less. A lot less. Kill was suddenly gone and halfway across the garage in what felt like the blink of an eye.

I stared at him, rubbing his mouth with the back of his hand.

"What—?" I began to protest but then my gaze moved to the door, which Zane had just stepped into.

His gaze was murderous on Kill. "It's eleven," he bit out. "You need to be at the club. Shit to do," he declared.

Kill returned his look and then nodded tightly.

Zane's gaze was on me and it softened immediately. "In the house in five, Lex," he said softly. "Also, your mom has instructed me to tell you, and I quote, 'If you don't get your butt inside before *The Walking Dead,* she'll feed you to the zombies the minute they start taking over the earth,'" he informed me, his eyes dancing slightly.

I wasn't fooled by the way he spoke. It was not a request. Zane took to enforcing Mom's loose curfew to something akin to how a drill sergeant enforced his soldiers. It may have disappointed me, saying good-bye to Kill, having to abide by rules when it came to my lawless boy, but Zane never annoyed me. It was something that I actually liked. It was how a father would enforce his daughter's curfew.

That's what he was to me. The moment he slipped the ring on Mom's finger, and even before that, he was my father. My second father. Steve was my first. The man who kidnapped and almost killed my mom and the love of my life was nothing. He wasn't dead to me because he never existed to me.

I didn't know where he was. I had a feeling he might not be in this world if Zane and Kill had anything to do with it. I knew that should affect me, screw me up in a multitude of ways, but somehow I didn't find myself haunted by my father's ghost. That was because ghosts existed in the darkest of places, and for the past six months, I'd only seen light. Apart from the day at the club, two weeks after everything. It had been hard to face the results of what happened after Mom was kidnapped, but we didn't have much time to focus on that, considering Zane proposed to her the moment he found her and declared he wanted a wedding as soon as possible. I'd gone into ultimate wedding planner mode, not letting Mom plan a thing. Hence me being at the club after a meeting with my fellow planners. Gwen, Amy, and Evie were amazing, helping out with anything and everything.

I was about to walk out of the common room and into the bays to where I knew Kill would be.

"Lexie," a raspy voice called, making me stop.

I turned with a smile on my face for the owner of the voice. Steg's wrinkled but attractive, albeit scary face was focused on me.

"Hey, Steg," I greeted warmly. What Kill had said about him not being nice just simply wasn't true. I felt a connection with the older, ex-president of the Sons of Templar MC. I guessed he could be scary to anyone who threatened his family, but to me, he was always a bristly kind of soft. He didn't treat me with kid gloves; I liked that. Kill and I had been over there for dinner a few times in the past few weeks and a lot while Mom was still in hospital. Their big ranch out in the middle of nowhere was like a fortress and a second home. I liked how they treated Kill, with the same kind of bristly softness they treated me. Granted, Steg was a lot bristlier, but it was apparent he cared for Kill. He deserved that, people who loved him.

"You got a second, sweetheart?" Steg asked, his face strangely blank.

I furrowed my brows slightly at the look but nodded. "Sure," I said, stepping toward him. "I was only going to hang out with Kill while he worked anyway."

Steg gave me a half grin. "Well, let's give the kid a few more minutes of concentration," he teased. He nodded toward the door marked "Church." I bugged my eyes out slightly at this invitation but followed him into the room. I immediately knew something was wrong. This room didn't hold happy memories for me. The last time I was in here was when Mom was kidnapped, when I didn't know if I'd see her again. I wasn't supposed to be in here.

"Sit down, sweetheart," Steg invited, nodding to a chair.

I swallowed and did as he bid. He sat on the one beside me, moving it slightly so he faced me.

His silvery gray eyes regarded me for a long moment before he spoke.

"Well aware that Bull, your mom, and Kill aren't gonna be the ones to tell you this. They're hell-bent on protecting you from everything the world throws at you. Know for a fact Kill would damn near shoot me for having this conversation, despite the fact

I'm the man who brought him up." He paused. "That's a testament to how much you mean to him, but the kid means something to me, to the club. The club's in his blood and always will be. Looks like club may be in his blood, but you're under his skin in a way it looks like you're gonna stay there. He's gonna patch in, which means you're gonna be an old lady. We protect old ladies. Die for them if need be. But you ain't gonna make it in this world without knowing what it is. So I'm gonna tell you. I'm doin' this 'cause I like you, sweetheart. 'Cause I know you're strong enough to handle it," he said, his voice rough and no-nonsense.

I sucked in a breath at all of this. It was a lot to take in unprepared, and Steg wasn't giving me much time to let it process. He didn't seem to give me any time before he started talking again.

"Your mom hasn't told you much about your dad, about how he was connected to the murder of your grandparents?" he asked, though it wasn't exactly structured as a question.

My heart sank and I shook my head slowly, tasting bile. Mom barely spoke about Steve and Ava's death since it happened. She talked about them all the time. She didn't let the memory of them dim, didn't let sorrow bury their spirits. They were always with us. But this, the darkest black of reality didn't come into our lives. I tried not to think of it, of the ugliness. Tried not to wonder about the faceless person walking this earth, breathing free after doing this. I tried to swallow the fury I felt when I thought of this. I was successful most of the time. There was enough light in my life to chase away those dark thoughts, but sometimes in the middle of the night, when I couldn't escape them, when the light wasn't there to chase them away, those thoughts came back.

Steg nodded briskly. "Didn't think so. Man was a piece of shit. Lowest of the low." He paused. "Know this 'cause the way this club used to run, it put me right down there with those people. The low people. Your dad, he was further. So low that when he was Kill's age, he didn't turn into the man your man is. He was evil. A coward. Even then. He was involved in shit that made him powerful. And powerful men with evil blood are fuckin' dangerous, which is why your mom left. She knew he'd kill you, both of you otherwise. Strong woman your mom," he said with respect, with pride. "Strong woman brought up a strong daughter," he added, laying his large hand over mine.

I looked down at it with detachment, still digesting his words. He wasn't finished.

"Your father didn't feel love, but he did have a sick infatuation with your mom. Sick enough he spent almost sixteen years lookin' for her. Those sixteen years he became more powerful, more evil, his soul rotted and twisted," Steg spat, his voice moving toward fury. He squeezed my hand. "It was his rotten and twisted soul that took Ava and Steve from you," he said the words quickly, like ripping a Band-Aid off quickly. I guessed he hoped the initial sting would subside as quickly as he said the words.

If only. Agony settled into my soul at these words. Into my blood. The blood that was half his. My father. My father was the one who killed my family.

"Stay with me, sweetheart. We're not done yet," Steg said softly.

I blinked up at him. "Not done?" I choked out. "What else is there?'

I asked, but I knew. Somehow I knew.

"Evil men like him, they see beauty, pure beauty, like what you've got, what your mom's got, and they have to possess it. When it gets away from them, they will dedicate their life to get it back. Not to nurture it like Bull does, like Kill does, but to destroy it," Steg explained. "He spent sixteen years lookin' for it. He found it. Not because Steve and Ava told him. They died protectin' you and your mom. 'Cause somehow coincidence favors those evil souls in some sick joke." He paused, musing for a second. "Maybe coincidence favored you 'cause he found you just when you found yourself a family that would die before they let anything destroy you. That would never let that happen," he corrected. There was a long pause. "So that's it. What the people you love would die to protect you from, but what you need to know, just the same."

I was silent for a long while. Steve and Ava dead because of him. My mom endured twenty-four hours of hurt because of him. Zane went through the nightmare similar to what happened four years ago because of him. I feeling complete and utter terror at the thought of losing my mom like I lost Ava and Steve *because of him.*

I lifted my head to give Steg an even stare. "Did he pay?" I asked flatly. "Did you make him pay?"

Steg jolted, and I saw the surprise in his eyes before they turned hard. He nodded. "Yeah, darlin', Bull made him pay."

I nodded. The fury that had pulsed through me like some kind of monster seemed to quiet slightly.

There must be something wrong with me for thinking this, for feeling this, about my own father.

"Proud of you, Lexie," Steg declared. "Consider Kill to be a son to me, family. You're my family too. I know a lot of strong women. Heck, I'm married to a warrior in fuckin' heels. They're the only kind of women that survive this life. You're growin' up to be one of them. You are one. Couple more years, you might give my warrior in heels a run for her money." He winked. "You tell her I said that, I'll deny it," he joked, his tone lighter than it had been before.

I smiled at him weakly, the weight of his previous words heavy on my soul.

"I'll let you get to your man," he said, standing. "I'm gonna go put some Kevlar on in preparation for him findin' out what I told you," he declared, half joking.

I did the same. "You don't need to worry about that. I won't be telling him."

Steg frowned at me. "Didn't tell you this to keep it a secret, darlin'."

"I know," I replied. "But he doesn't need to steal anything else from me. He took Steve and Ava. He tried to take my mom, my happiness, my future. He isn't taking a second more," I said.

Steg regarded me. He shook his head and bent in to kiss my forehead. "Perfect for him," he murmured.

Steg moved to open the door.

"Thank you," I said to his back. "Thank you for telling me."

He stopped and turned. "You're welcome, darlin'," he replied before giving me one more look and leaving the room.

I followed him after a beat and walked on lead-filled legs to the bays in a sort of dream. It almost felt like I was walking underwater, wading through the thick air as the words and thoughts surrounded me.

"Lexie?" Killian's alert and concerned voice jerked me out of my mind.

My head lifted to see him in front of me, his face a mask of worry. I'd made it out to the garage where he was working without even noticing.

"What is it?" he demanded, clutching my arms.

It was safe to say Killian was uber protective over me lately, as if he hadn't been before. He seemed to make it his life's mission to make sure nothing else ugly touched me, which was precisely why I wasn't telling him anything. We were just getting back to beautiful. I wouldn't pollute that. I could deal with this darkness on my own; somehow I knew I had to.

"Nothing," I reassured him, giving him a smile. "Just a million and one wedding tasks to get through."

Kill frowned at me, seeming to see through my lie before he shook his head and kissed me softly. "Don't stress out too much, Freckles. You got a bride, a groom, someone to marry them, and your family. You don't need much else," he said with a twinkle in his eyes. "And music. Your beautiful voice needs to be the soundtrack to this particular event."

I grinned back and this time it was genuine. I grasped his hand and directed us to the inside of the bay where I'd dumped my school stuff and guitar earlier. Or where Killian dumped it. I never carried much when Killian was around. His strong arms carried everything for me. Even my heart.

"Okay, well, I better rehearse then," I said, glad to move the subject away to happier things. "You've still got work to do, right?" I asked, nodding to the car.

"Yeah, Freckles, but I won't be too long," he promised.

"No problem. I like being here. I'll play, you work."

Killian moved me so his hands rested on my hips, his forehead resting against mine. "Could think of nothing better, baby," he murmured. His eyes touched my lips. "Well, maybe one thing," he said softly and then his lips were on mine. He kissed me until all of my ugly thoughts were just a memory, and there was only me and him in the entire world.

I knew everything would be okay. As long as I had Kill, darkness could never take me over.

●●●●

My stressful and slightly frantic wedding was worth it when the day came along. We had it at the club and Steg officiated it. I walked Mom down the aisle. Zane's eyes were clear of demons, only light remained. We were surrounded by family, and it was beautiful.

Of course the band played at the reception, and even Sam hadn't complained about the "sappy love songs" we played the entire time. Kill had sat with a beer in his hand, watching me the entire time. I'd sang every word of my songs to him. That was until Wyatt kicked me off the stage to dance with Kill. He surprised everyone by singing an acoustic version of "Sweet Child O' Mine." I knew he could sing, we did duets all the time, but I didn't realize he could carry the song with so much emotion.

Not that I had much focus on him singing. All my focus was on my boyfriend, my big, badass and broody boyfriend dancing with me.

The big, badass, now prospect of the Sons of Templar MC was going to get in trouble with my now stepfather and member of the Sons of Templar MC if I wasn't careful.

"Okay, Zane," I replied, with a smile.

He gave Kill one more look, and then he was gone.

I turned my full attention to Kill, who watched the doorway for a second then strode back to me.

I clutched the sides of his cut. "Do you have super senses or something?" I asked against his mouth.

He rubbed his nose against mine. "No, just good modes of self-preservation," he murmured. "I like my head attached to my neck."

I giggled against his mouth, trailing my hands up and down the leather of his vest. He'd just began prospecting for the Sons. He turned eighteen a few weeks ago and had dropped out of school that very day. I missed him in the halls, more than anything. But he still dropped me off and picked me up, if his "duties" allowed. "Duties" I was allowed to know precious little about. He was happy, finally where he felt he belonged. That was enough, for now.

"I'll pick you up tomorrow," he promised.

"You don't have to. I know you're busy with... club stuff," I told him. "It's just another gig. You've been to a million," I said, feeling bad he spent basically every weekend in the crowd or lugging my guitar around now that things had started to get serious for the band.

And I meant serious.

We had played more gigs around town, and out of town on the odd occasion. Word got around. It was good. Then Sam decided to upload one of our covers of Macklemore's "Can't Hold Us" on YouTube. It was meant to be a bit of a joke more than anything, a barb at that moment with Mr. Hazelton last year. We changed it around, slowed it down, made it ours. We hadn't expected much more than a few views from Mom, who had promised to go around every computer in the hotel and view it.

We were up to two hundred thousand.

Two hundred thousand people had viewed it. I was pretty sure that wasn't Mom clicking and re-clicking. Though I wouldn't put it past her. We were getting a response. Noah, Wyatt, and Sam got messages from girls daily. I got messages from boys too. Mostly gross ones, ones that Kill had read with a tight jaw. So things were going well. Better than we could have ever dreamed. It wasn't a dream, though. It was work. Hard work. When I wasn't at school or studying, we practiced. When we weren't practicing, we were writing songs. We had a few good ones, and Wyatt was trying to persuade me to let us perform a song I wrote at the gig tomorrow night.

Kill fastened his hands at my neck and touched our foreheads together. "Freckles, I'm never gonna miss a single one of your gigs. Never gonna miss my girl owning the stage, owning my soul," he murmured. "It's not just another gig to me. 'Cause it's not that to you. I'm coming."

My stomach swirled at his words. "Okay."

He nodded. "Now we've got approximately two minutes. I wanna spend them kissin' you."

Then his mouth descended on mine, and we spend the next two minutes in the beautiful limbo that was ours and ours alone.

"Oh, Zane totally caught you making out," Mom teased when I floated back into the house two and a half minutes later.

My gaze shot to her. "He did not," I protested, red creeping up my cheeks.

Mom licked her spoon then put it back in the tub of peanut butter. "Did so," she argued. "He came in here with his 'I'm gonna get my buckshot' glare and was muttering something about how he was going to make sure Kill was on clean up duty for the rest of his life, whatever that means," she said, spooning more peanut butter into my mouth.

I scowled at her. "Whatever," I snapped, stealing the tub from her.

"Hey!" she protested with her mouth full.

I grinned at her, sinking beside her on the sofa. She lost her anger and slung an arm around me.

We sat in harmony watching the TV.

"I'd like to see Glen and Daryl in a fight," she mused, eyes locked on the TV.

"Glenn, hands down," I replied.

She fumbled for the remote, pausing the show so she could give me her full attention.

"Dude, seriously?" she asked. "What are you? I was sure I didn't drop you on your head as a child, but now I'm rethinking it."

"What are you fighting about now?" Zane asked, yanking Mom into his arms as he sat down.

"Hubby, please inform my delusional daughter that Daryl Dixon would own Glenn in a fight to the death," she requested.

Zane gave her a look. "We're talking about fictional characters here?" he clarified.

Mom nodded.

He chuckled, shaking his head. "Babe," was all he said.

She sat back a little. "Babe is not an answer," she snapped.

"It is when they're not real," he replied.

Mom held her hand to her chest. "You did not just say that."

He shook his head and pulled her in for a quick kiss. Her eyes were dreamy when he let her go.

She cut her eyes to me. "Game changer, Zane Williams would own them both," she told me with certainty.

I glanced at him. His huge tattooed arms fastened firmly around my mother in a way that made me think he would never let her go if he had anything to do with it.

He hadn't let her out of his sight after he got her back from... *him*, the man I refused to think of as my father. The man that put her in the hospital. Broke her arm and made me face my beautiful and bubbly mom battered and bruised in a hospital bed.

"Tell me the truth, did I go overboard on my eye shadow?" she rasped the first time I laid eyes on her bruised face.

I'd let out a choked laugh, which turned into a sob, and I'd dove into her outstretched arms. We'd laid there for a long time, Zane standing on Mom's other side, his hand on her head.

Somehow we'd got through it. The nightmares, the flashbacks, the reality of what happened. We got through it because of what we hadn't lost. What he hadn't taken from us. Kill got better, Mom's bruises faded, her arm healed. Zane and Mom got married. Happiness sprang from the darkest of places.

SIX MONTHS LATER

"Thank you, thank you, everyone, you've been amazing," I shouted into my mic after we'd finished "Me & Bobby McGee" by Janice Joplin.

I was almost deafened by the screaming that came after my words. I was pretty sure most of it was coming from the crowd of women right up front. Mom, Gwen, Amy, Rosie, and Lucy. They were at almost every gig—well, not Gwen as much considering she had two kids, but she was at this one. Everyone was at this one. The entire bar was lined with huge men in Sons of Templar cuts. I only had eyes for one at that moment. Icy blue eyes had been locked on me the entire time. Eyes that I sang to, even when I wasn't looking into them.

"I wanna do something a little different to finish off our set," I murmured into my mic, looking to Wyatt at my side, who was grinning. "This isn't a cover. This is one of our own. I hope you like it," I said, starting to strum.

I wanted to close my eyes. Wanted to escape somewhere different while I laid my soul bare to a room full of strangers. I didn't. I kept my eyes on the one person who I wrote the song for. The person who owned the soul I was exposing with the words I was singing.

As deep as the ocean
As unyielding as the wind
Stronger than diamonds
I'm going crazy and becoming sane
My world is filled with the echoes of silence

Ride along, ride free
Ride down that lonely highway with me
Sometimes lost, but never found
I'm only me when you're around

Freedom from chains is being chained to you
I'll ride to the edges of the earth if that's where you'll take me to
Or I'll stay rooted to this ground
It doesn't matter where I am, as long as you're around

Ride along, ride free
Ride down that lonely highway with me
Sometimes lost, but never found

I'm only me when you're around

I'm crazy, I'm sane
I'm loud, I'm quiet
My soul's melody is free
These echoes of silence are a part of me

• • • •

"Holy fuck!" Sam screamed over the top of the cheers that followed us backstage.

He turned to me and started shaking my shoulders. "They fuckin' loved it!"

"Dude, don't give her whiplash," Noah instructed, but even he was grinning.

Sam didn't let me go. Instead, he yanked me into his arms for a quick squeeze before letting me go. Then he turned to Noah, clutched the sides of his shoulders and kissed his head before jumping around like an idiot.

"Grammys here we come," he chanted.

Wyatt rolled his eyes, following him. "Hold it together, you dick. We've got a record exec coming back here," he demanded, following him.

Noah slung an arm around my shoulders. "You okay, Lex?" he asked quietly.

The boys were grinning, but I wasn't. At least I didn't think I was. I felt almost out of my own body.

I'd sang my own song to a crowd full of people, and they'd liked it. Loved it. There was only one person who I didn't know about. Only one person's opinion that matter. And it wasn't the record exec that Clay had invited here. It was the owner of the icy eyes that had hardened the moment I started singing that song. The face

348

that had turned blank through the rest of it.

"Yeah, I think so."

He squeezed me. "You were amazing. That song, it's beautiful," he reassured me. "Record exec has to be tone deaf or an idiot not to like it."

I nodded. "Yeah," was all I said.

Noah turned me in his arms. "That's not who you're worried about though, is it?" he asked, seeing more than the other boys.

I shook my head.

"He'd also have to be an idiot not to like it," he declared softly. "But considering Killian is far from an idiot, and he is honestly convinced you are solely responsible for producing the oxygen he breathes, you've got nothing to worry about," he said, his voice firm.

I gave him a shaky smile. "Thanks, Noe."

We didn't have time to talk more because we were just about to meet the record exec that might change our lives forever.

Chapter 29

"Okay, so that went well. Like really well," Mom exclaimed in excitement as we walked around the club.

She squeezed her arms around my shoulders. "You're going to be rich and famous," she half squealed.

"Eardrums, Mom," I replied.

She squeezed me tighter. "You don't need eardrums to sing," she decided.

I rolled my eyes. She was right. The meeting went well. So well, that he promised to call us and it sounded like he actually would call us. Sam and Wyatt had tried to keep serious, broody rocker expressions the entire time and started shouting and jumping around as soon as he left the room. Noah had even full-on grinned. So had Zane, who of course had been there. He was uber protective of not only Mom but me too. Mom was there because she had demanded to be and had taken her "Momager" role very seriously. Not that seriously if the way she met Will, the exec, was anything to go by.

I shook his hand. "I'm Alexis, but everyone calls me Lexie," I said with a nervous smile.

Will smiled back. "Nice to meet you, Lexie. You've got one heck of a voice," he stated. He nodded to Mom. "This your sister?" he joked.

Mom stepped forward and grinned, though Zane was scowling at him from behind her. "I'm Mia, but everyone calls me awesome," she said, oblivious to her husband's death glare or serious forms of introduction.

It hadn't been serious though. It had been informal. Will was a nice man and seemed to really understand our sound. Things were looking good. Looking great, in fact. But I couldn't properly focus on that. All I could see was Kill's blank face as I sang my song, his song to him. I chewed my lip as we walked, oblivious to Mom's chattering and Zane's clipped but amused replies.

That was until we saw Kill's car parked beside ours and his tall body leaning against it.

I wanted to run over to him, into his arms, but I was unsure. I felt strange now after singing to him, after not being able to read his face. He pushed off the car and walked toward us.

"Hey, Kill," Mom greeted with a grin. "I had a feeling you'd be waiting for our little rock star. Get a lock of her hair now. It'll sell for thousands on eBay in the future," she instructed.

I rolled my eyes but couldn't see Kill's expression properly in the dim street light. He nodded his head to Zane. "You guys mind if I take Lexie home?" he asked, his voice rough.

I held my breath. It was after midnight; my curfew was one on weekends, which it wasn't.

"Of course," Mom said and I relaxed. "I can make an exception this once... don't you try and silence me with broody looks, Zane," she snapped, turning her head to him. "If I want a villa in Tuscany, I have to stay on her good side," she informed him.

"You want a villa in Tuscany, I'll buy you one," he declared, yanking her into his body.

"It's not the same," she replied.

We both looked at him expectantly. He sighed and shook his head. "Jesus Christ," he muttered. That was approval in Zane world.

"Thanks," I chirped and grabbed Kill's hand before Zane could bark out any commands.

Kill took me to the passenger side of the car silently, opening the door for me. He rounded the car and backed out in silence too. I played with my hands, not comfortable in this kind of silence, especially after the song.

"So the meeting went good, I think," I said finally, having to fill the loaded silence.

Kill's hand came to engulf mine, which relaxed me a little. "Not a surprise, Freckles," he murmured.

There was another pause.

I took a deep breath. "The song," I started, needing to explain somehow.

"Stop," he commanded, interrupting me.

My heart fell at his harsh tone.

"We aren't talking about that now," he declared. "Not when I'm driving and I can't give you my complete attention. Can't hold you in my arms. Can't kiss you."

My heart soared again. Okay, so he didn't hate it.

"So we're not going to my place," I deduced after his words had filled up the car.

"No," he clipped.

"You're willing to risk Zane's wrath then?" I asked, knowing he'd probably be timing us.

Kill brought my hand to his mouth. "Willin' to risk anything for you, Freckles. Don't forget that."

His words filled me up even more, and I didn't need any more the entire drive to the spot. Our spot.

The moment he turned the car off, my seatbelt was off and I was yanked across the car to straddle him. I didn't even get the chance to say anything. Kill's mouth on mine silenced me. Silenced everything. Silenced my soul. It was nothing but his mouth on mine for what felt like an eternity and a moment all at once.

"There's nothin' I can do, can say to you after that song, baby," he murmured against my mouth. "I've never heard anything more beautiful than you singing those words, knowing that was mine. You are mine," he said, squeezing me. "Also, I'm pretty pissed that that's the first time I've got to hear one of your songs, in front of a crowd where I couldn't drag you off to do that. Almost went crazy waiting for you to be in my arms," he declared roughly. His hands framed my face. "Why haven't I heard that sooner?"

I gave myself a moment to get my thundering heart under control.

"Music is my soul. My heart beats to a melody. *I'm music.* It's me. Playing one of my songs out loud, to a human person, that's laying out my soul right there in front of them, exposed and vulnerable. Do you know how that feels?"

I felt Kill's gaze on me and his hands flexed. "Yeah, Freckles, I've got some idea. A part of you, your soul, couldn't be anything but beautiful. I'm quite happy to have us on even ground, for you to lay it bare to me, considering mine already lays at your feet."

His mouth touched mine again.

"Music is my soul," I whispered against his mouth. "Which means my soul is never quiet, my mind is never quiet." I stroked his hand. "Except when I'm with you. You're the quiet to my melody. You're part of my soul too, you know that, right?"

Kill rested his head against mine. "Yeah, I know that," he replied, his voice rough, flat almost.

We stayed like that for a long while until it was obvious we needed to leave if Kill valued his life. I valued it.

I thought I'd be floating on cloud nine after tonight. After his words, after his reaction to my song, but something had changed, been lost after Kill deposited me back on my seat and began to drive me home. I couldn't put my finger on it. He still held my hand in his, rested it on his thigh, bringing it to his mouth every now and then. But there was something that changed. I told myself I was just

353

being stupid, convinced myself I was making something out of nothing.

It would haunt my dreams that I hadn't trusted my instincts that night.

••••

"How do you guys feel about missing prom?" I asked once we had taken a practice break.

Sam gave me a horrified look. "Prom? You do know that's a guaranteed night to get laid, right?"

Wyatt punched his shoulder. "Dude," he warned.

Sam rubbed his shoulder. "What? Lexie knows this. The entire universe knows this fact. What could be so important to miss that?" he asked me in genuine shock.

"Kill's patch party," I answered.

All the boys were still.

"In," Sam said after a moment. "Totally. Screw prom," he decided like he hadn't been attached to it a moment ago.

Wyatt grinned. "Serious? Kill's getting his patch?"

I nodded. "Lucky called earlier today asking if we'd want to play at the party. After he managed to clear it with Zane, of course," I told them. I didn't tell them it was Lucky who told me and not Kill. Didn't add that Kill hadn't said a thing to me. That I hadn't heard from him since that night I told him about our record deal. It made me feel slightly uneasy, but I remembered what a big deal the patch was to Kill, how much they expected of him. He was busy. That was no reason to doubt us. Nothing could make me doubt us.

"That is fuckin' badass," Sam exclaimed. "Lexie, you're gonna officially be an Old Lady."

I screwed up my nose. "I'm not even eighteen. I'm not fond of being called old."

It was a joke. I knew what kind of respect came with that title. What it meant. Mom had explained it to me when Kill started prospecting.

"These guys, these bikers, they're different than normal men," Mom explained. "Kill's never really been a normal boy, never really been a boy. He's always been one of them," she continued, knitting her brows together. "When he's patched in, hon, it's all going to change." She squeezed my hand. "You two are intense. Always have been, since day one, it seems. It worried me, still does, but not when I know Kill would do anything for my baby girl, jump in front of bullets if need be." She paused, giving me a long look. "I love it for you and it also unnerves me, I won't lie, baby doll. But I'll never stand in the way of your happiness," she promised. "You just need to know things are gonna change with Kill being in the Sons now."

I gave her a smile. "Some stuff might change," I agreed. "But the important stuff will stay the same. How I feel about Kill's never going to change, not for as long as l live."

I guessed a lot of moms might have dismissed such a declaration. But not my mom. She knew. She knew because she knew me and she saw us. She also knew because she had what I had. She had it with Zane.

She brought the hand she was holding up to kiss it. "I hope not, doll."

She was right, things did change. It started that night when Kill and I were at our spot, and I put my arms around him as we stood watching the sunset. I slipped my hands under his prospect cut to find something hard, metal, and foreign. Kill flinched away at the same time as I did. I stepped two steps back, gaping at him.

His eyes registered something and he stepped forward. "Freckles," he began softly.

I held my hand up to stop him at the same time I retreated. "No, Kill," I said firmly. His jaw hardened but he stopped.

"That's a gun," I stated, nodding to the place it was tucked into his jeans.

"Freckles—" he began again, his voice soft.

"A *gun*, Kill," I repeated, cutting him off.

His face went blank. "Yeah, Lexie. It's a gun," he agreed in a hard voice. "I'm part of the Sons now. It comes with the territory."

I blinked at him. "A gun, one that shoots people, kills people, comes with the territory?" I clarified. I didn't know why I was acting so shocked. I should have known. Zane carried a gun. I'd seen it many times. The club was into... things, things I didn't know about, but things that required firepower. But they were men. This was Kill. He was one of them now.

"Yeah, Lexie. You knew this," he said, crossing his arms. "This is the life."

What was unsaid was, *"Get used to it. There's nothing that you can do to change it."*

I stared at him for a long time. "If you carry a gun, then it means you might be in situations where you need to use it," I whispered, hugging my arms around myself.

Kill was obviously done letting me keep him away. He stepped forward to bring me into his arms.

"I can't bear the thought of anything happening to you," I croaked into his chest. "At you getting hurt."

Kill stroked my hair. "Nothing's gonna happen to me, baby, I promise."

Sam stepped forward, peering into my face, jolting me out of my memories.

I leaned back. "What are you doing, weirdo?"

"No, I'm pretty sure I can see wrinkles," he decided.

I punched him in the shoulder. "No, you can't," I argued.

He reared back, rubbing the spot. "Why does everyone think they can punch me?" he complained. "You've got more strength

356

than you should being that small," he added, regarding me skeptically.

Noah pulled him into a headlock. "People keep punching you because you keep opening your mouth and letting every thought pour out without using that thing between your ears." He paused. "Maybe there's nothing there."

Sam pushed him back. "Whatever, you're all just jealous I'm the most attractive and talented of the band. I'll obviously get the most stalker fans," he said modestly.

I laughed. "You can have all the stalker fans you want. I'm quite happy staying out of that."

Wyatt raised a brow. "Dude, look at you. No way you're staying out of anything if we hit the big time. We'll have to hire an army of bodyguards," he declared.

I poked my tongue at him.

"An army?" Noah repeated. "Who needs an army when you've got a newly patched boyfriend who can shoot laser beams out his eyes?" he joked.

Sam laughed but for some reason, Wyatt didn't. His face turned serious.

I didn't have time to think on that because Sam's face turned serious. "Wait, what do you mean 'if' we hit the big time. It's when. We've got a fricking record meeting in a couple of days. Not to mention"—he held up his finger in a hold on gesture, pulling out his phone—"Eight hundred thousand views on our latest video. Dudes, that's almost a million. We're already famous."

"Internet famous," I corrected. "Not the same thing."

Sam narrowed his eyes. "Why do you insist on hurting me so?"

I laughed. "Because it's so easy."

Sam looked affronted. "I resent that. I'm tough. Just because your boyfriend may or may not be the terminator, you're not a good judge," he decided.

"The terminator?" a deep and amused voice repeated.

I moved my gaze to the owner of that voice, and my belly did the dip that it always did when I saw Killian. He was giving Sam a half grin, his arms crossed casually. They were crossed in such a way I could see the veins protruded from his forearms. He was wearing all black, like always, along with the prospect cut he'd been wearing for the last six months. His inky hair was messy and getting longer, brushing the collar of his cut. The stubble on his face was rough and made him look even more like a man and less like the boy I'd met almost two years ago. He'd always be that boy to me. The boy I loved was turning into the man I loved.

"Bro, you jump in front of bullets and refer to bullet wounds as 'flesh wounds.' You're obviously not human," Sam declared. "Plus, you've managed not to be murdered by Bull, so that's terminator in my books."

I laughed again; I couldn't help it. I felt Kill's dark gaze on me as I did so. He didn't move toward me, which was strange. He always gave me some sort of physical gesture when he saw me, regardless of the audience.

"Congrats, bro," Wyatt said, moving forward to shake his hand. "On getting the patch, it's awesome."

Kill's face went blank, but he nodded and shook Wyatt's hand back. "Thanks."

Noah and Sam followed suit, but Sam gave him the man hug, clapping him on the back with one hand while the other was clasped at his chest.

No one else noticed because they didn't watch Kill like I did, but he flinched slightly when Sam's hand came down on his back.

Once they had given their congrats, they all packed up.

"We'll let the lovebirds celebrate," Sam declared with a wink. "Remember, practice tomorrow," he said seriously.

Wyatt rolled his eyes. "Like we could forget. You've written out a goddamn timetable for the entire day, including bathroom breaks."

Sam put his hands on his hips, looking comically like some kind of angry housewife. "Well *excuse me* for being serious about the record company meeting we have in two days," he exclaimed.

"No one could ever accuse you of being serious, bro," Noah said, clapping him on the back. "Bye, babe," he said, giving me a chin lift.

Sam scowled at his back. "Just remember, a keyboardist is much more replaceable than a sex symbol drummer," he yelled at his back, giving me a distracted wave.

"I'll sort him before he combusts, don't worry, Lex," Wyatt reassure me, hoisting his guitar over his shoulder and kissing my cheek. "Catch you tomorrow, 0900," he joked, lifting his head in farewell to Kill.

"Bye," I called.

Kill and I both watched the boys leave in silence.

I narrowed my eyes at him once they pulled away.

"Freckles—" he began in a strange voice.

I stormed forward. "Turn around," I commanded in a quiet voice.

He jolted slightly. "Lexie—" he tried again.

"Turn around," I demanded, eyeing him sharply.

He sighed but did as I asked.

First, I grasped the top of his cut, pulling it off and laying it carefully on the sofa beside us. Then I put my hands on the bottom of his tee and very gently pulled it up. I gasped when I uncovered his back. His back covered in plastic covering, a very red, very fresh tattoo covering the entirety of it.

I knew what it was. It was the same insignia on the Sons of Templar patch. A grim reaper brandishing a sword and riding a Harley through a road of skulls. And Kill had the thing tattooed on his entire back. I visibly flinched at the pain I knew he'd been in. Without me there. Without telling me. I carefully traced my finger along the edges of the plastic covering.

"Why didn't you tell me?" I questioned in a hurt voice.

Kill turned and I lost purchase on the shirt. He grasped my neck. "I couldn't, Freckles. I wanted to. Fuck it's the best news I've had my entire life, apart from hearing your mom was okay that day, and apart from the day you agreed to be my girl." He paused. "Every good thing that happens to me is usually connected to you. If it's not, it doesn't become real until I share it with you." He stroked my cheek. "But it's the way the club works, babe. Stays within the club."

I brought my brows together. "Why didn't you tell me today?" I asked, hating that I sounded like a whining girlfriend. "About the party? Lucky was the one who told me."

Kill's face was hard. "I didn't tell you 'cause I've been trying to get it canceled," he bit out.

I reared back. "Cancelled?" I repeated. "Why the devil would you want to do that?"

"'Cause it's on Friday night," he elaborated like that was meant to mean something.

I waited for more. "And?" I asked when more didn't come.

"And that's the night I'm meant to take my girl to prom," he murmured.

I jolted. "You think I care about prom?" I asked him in disbelief.

He was the one who looked shocked now. "Babe, you're a girl. Every girl cares about prom."

I grinned at him. "I thought we'd established that I'm not your normal girl," I teased.

Kill's face went serious. "I knew that already, Freckles. I know that," he said, something moving in his eyes, something I couldn't recognize but something I didn't like.

"I don't want you missing out on your prom, not for me," he continued.

I put my hand over his wrist. "Prom is nothing to me, silly. Nothing could be more important than the boy I love getting the one thing he's always dreamed of."

His eyes blazed. "No, Freckles. I've already got the one thing I've always dreamed of," he murmured. Then his mouth descended on mine. It wasn't hungry and desperate like our kisses of late had been. It was slow, gentle, full of feeling and something else that mirrored the look in his eyes.

It took a few moments for me to get my heart back to its normal rhythm after that.

"Can I play you something?" I asked when I got my breath back.

"One of yours?" he asked softly. Ever since the night I sang "Echoes of Silence," Kill had damn near demanded I play him every song I'd ever written to him. He'd sit for an entire afternoon, watching me, listening to me sing. He'd done it at the beach one day until I decided enough was enough and put my guitar to the side. Kill immediately brought me into his arms, kissing me softly.

"Makes me so proud hearin' you, Freckles," he murmured.

I snuggled into him, not saying anything, just watching people around us, happy to watch the world go by in Killian's arms.

"I want that." I nodded to the old couple, holding hands and smiling to grandchildren squealing with laughter around them.

"What? Wrinkles?" Kill teased.

I sat up and punched him in the shoulder. It was like punching a rock. I rubbed my hand absently. Kill saw my movement and brought it up to his lips. The moment they touched the knuckle, the pain disappeared.

"No," I said finally, gazing into his eyes. "I want roots. I want them curling into the ground beneath my feet and giving me somewhere to belong."

Kill stiffened. His eyes flickered over to the couple once more. "You don't want roots, Freckles," he disagreed. "You don't want roots when you've already got wings. When you're poised to take flight."

"Who says I can't have both?" I asked with a grin.

"Physics."

I shrugged, letting him pull me back into his arms. "Who says physics has to dictate anything?" I said into his chest. "I'm making my own destiny."

Kill didn't say anything. His body stiffened and he squeezed me a little tighter.

I shook my head, both to get myself out of my daydream and to answer Kill. "Not this time."

Kill kissed me again. "Couldn't think of better than hearing my girl sing at the end of the day."

I stepped out of his arms, and he went to sit on the sofa, slipping his cut back on with a slight flinch.

I hated to see that but put my guitar on and sat on a stool in front of him. Without breaking eye contact, I sang "Lost Boy" by Ruth B to him.

When I finished, he stood immediately. The guitar was gone from me before I even knew what was going on. His mouth was on mine once more and it wasn't gentle. It was hungry. It had an edge, one that all of our kisses had these days.

For a year it had been the desperate kisses that we tried to drain as much out of as we could. It was the prolonged make out sessions stolen in the back of his car or on top of a blanket at our spot on the cliffs. But it never progressed past those feverish moments. Sometimes it got close. Sometimes all I wanted was everything the kiss promised. But Kill always pulled back. Said it wasn't time. Somehow sensed I wasn't ready when I had lost all thought.

But I was now. I'd made the decision. I just hadn't known when. Now I did. The night when he finally got everything he wanted was when I'd finally give him all of me.

Unaware of my decision, Kill pulled back. "You think I'm lost, baby?"

I shook my head. "No. You're free," I clarified. "I was lost until I found you. You're my Neverland, Kill," I whispered.

Kill's eyes darkened. "I'm only free 'cause I've got you," he replied. Then he claimed my mouth once more.

Chapter 30

I stood in front of the mirror, regarding myself skeptically. I had spent the better part of the day on this outfit. My entire wardrobe was scattered on the floor, every piece of makeup my mom and I owned was scattered on my desk. It was reminiscent of the day I had been freaking out over my first gig. Apart from that, the nerves at the bottom of my stomach were much more intense. It wasn't just a gig. This was it. The day. The day I'd give Kill everything. He already had my heart. My soul. The one thing I'd been holding back was finally going to be his.

"Wow. Excuse me, young woman, can you please tell me where my teenage daughter has gone? About yay tall and answers to the name of Lexie," Mom said from the doorway, holding her hand up to her shoulder.

I turned fully to her. She was looking amazing as usual. She was invited to Kill's party, obviously. She'd gone all out like usual. Her hair was straightened so it was long down her back and she was wearing a clingy black dress with a high neck and long sleeves. She had multiple strings of necklaces dangling on top of it. She didn't look like she was going to a biker party. She looked like she was going to a cocktail party, but if Gwen and Amy were there, which they would be, she'd be in good company. They were always dripping in designer duds.

"Is that your way of telling me I look okay?" I asked, tugging at the bottom of my dress.

I could not be mistaken for going to a cocktail party. Unlike my mom, I hadn't tamed my white blonde ringlets. I had piled half of them on top of my head in a messy bun while the other half tumbled down my back.

My rainbow crochet dress was a vintage store find I'd never thought I'd find the occasion to wear. That was because it was very short and pretty skimpy. It was a halter neck that tied in the back. The multicolored fabric was stripped down and swirled into a circle at the scalloped hem. It was like tie-dye in crochet. The hem finished well above my knees. Well above. I compensated with the amount of leg I was showing by wearing over-the-knee, suede-heeled, black boots. Multiple silver bracelets jangled on my wrists and I'd gone for a dark brown smoky eye.

Mom walked forward, her eye running over every inch of me. When she made it to me, those eyes were watering.

"I think you look more than okay, doll. You look like a woman that I always knew you'd turn into but I didn't realize it would happen this soon." She continued in a shaky voice. "I'm not ready for you to grow up. Not yet. Can't you stay my little girl forever?"

I felt my own eyes glisten. "I'll always be your little girl," I promised.

She searched my eyes, and I felt uneasy like she could see my plans for tonight. I'd always told her I'd come to her when I was ready to go further with a guy, but I didn't want to. I didn't want to turn it into anything but mine and Kill's. For now, at least.

I took a deep breath. I might not be able to tell Mom about what tonight had planned, but I had to make it possible.

"Since tonight's... special, and I'm almost eighteen...." I started.

Mom leaned back. "Oh, I know this tone. This 'almost eighteen' talk," she interrupted.

I grinned. "Well, I am almost eighteen. Almost a grown adult. One with a meeting with a record exec tomorrow morning," I reminded her as if she'd forget.

Yes, tomorrow. The meeting after the gig had gone well, more than well considering the exec was actually traveling to Amber to meet with us on a Saturday. I was beyond excited. I knew what this meant. My dreams might just be coming true. Somehow, the prospect of a recording contract tomorrow paled in comparison to what I was going to give Killian tonight. What we'd have.

"So such circumstances require a renegotiation of curfew," I explained.

Mom raised a brow. "Is that so?"

I nodded. "I think so, especially if you want me to recognize you in my Grammy speech."

"You know blackmail's illegal, right? I could have you prosecuted for this," she threatened.

"Then you'd never get to meet Adam Levine," I countered.

Mom dismissed him with a wave of her hand. "Adam who? Have you seen my husband?" She paused. "The husband I'm going to have to distract from watching the clock so he doesn't go postal when you don't arrive home at your previously agreed upon curfew," she added.

I grinned wide. "Thank you, thank you," I chanted, throwing my arms around her.

"Don't thank me now. Do it when the cameras are rollin', babe," she replied when I released her.

"Done," I agreed.

Her face turned serious. "I trust you, kid. You've been an adult for longer than I have, it seems. You've never been a normal teenager. Always been special. Mature. But that doesn't mean you still aren't seventeen years old. I trust you, so just make good decisions, okay, doll face?"

I nodded again. "Always, Mom," I promised.

I had never been more certain about any decision in my life.

How could *this* with Kill and me be anything but good?

••••

"Holy crapballs, I'm nervous," I exclaimed, jiggling my knee.

Noah put his hand on it, stilling my jerky motions. He gave me a smile. He didn't say anything, just gave me quiet support, as was his way.

Sam turned around. "Dude, why are you nervous? You never get nervous. This is your boyfriend's—no wait, old man's party."

"Which is exactly *why* I'm nervous," I replied. "It's a big night for Kill, the biggest. I don't want to screw it up."

Sam's eyes popped out. "As if us playing could screw it up. That biker club isn't going to know what's hit it," he said confidently.

That wasn't what I was nervous about. Playing in front of a crowd, singing in front of one, it didn't worry me. It came naturally now. It was the *after*. It wasn't the crowd. It was the lack of one. Just me and Kill. I hadn't seen him all day. We'd been practicing for the meeting and he'd been busy with "club stuff" so he couldn't pick me up. Not that Sam would have let him. He was a force to be reckoned with at the moment. We'd practiced within an inch of our lives. I thought we were going to be okay.

We pulled up outside the party. It was already spilling out with people and we could hear the base from inside the car.

I took a deep breath and exited with the boys, my guitar over my shoulder, my heart in my throat. It dropped right to my stomach when we waded through the people who greeted us fondly and my eyes landed on Kill. Kill with a new patch on his back. A full patch. All he ever dreamed of. It was not the patch I was looking at, but the bright red nail attached to a very female hand trailing down that leather.

She was wearing a red dress. Much shorter and much tighter

than mine. I couldn't see her face, but I could tell she was older than me, a woman. Experienced. One of the women who hung around the club. Mom, Zane, and Kill had all tried to protect me from finding out the role of such women, but I wasn't an idiot. I wasn't blind. I knew what they were. Women who hung around the club but didn't belong to anyone; they belonged to *everyone*. In the biblical sense. I hadn't judged them as I knew many people already did. Everyone was fighting their own battles, had their own stories. I couldn't judge them based on the cover.

I fought very fricking hard not to judge that cover. I realized I had stopped in place when Sam collided into my back.

"Dude, what gives...?" he started to say, but then his eyes followed mine.

"Oh shit," he mumbled under his breath, all lightness gone from his voice.

Kill shrugged the hand off, while he turned, a beer in his hand. His eyes met mine the moment he turned. He froze for a second. Then he moved, pushing through the crowd and ignoring the shouts and claps on the back.

The guitar was gone from my hands and over Kill's shoulder the moment he got in front of me, his hand in mine and he dragged me through the crowd, ignoring everyone as he took us up the stairs into the clubhouse. He didn't stop in the common room, just lead us into a hallway and into the room I'd slept in one horrible night.

It was a lot more decorated now. The moment he started prospecting was the moment he moved out of his mom's. He hadn't spoken to her as far as I knew. I did know he got groceries delivered there once a week and paid the electricity bill.

The room was small and only had an unmade double bed and set of drawers. His photos were scattered everywhere, the one of me and him on the table beside the bed. There were a lot more scattered around it now. Ones of him carrying me into the surf at the beach, a photo both him and Zane had grumbled about being in, with Mom and me at Valentines. Kill leaning against his bike in his prospect cut, his arm slung around me. Me and Kill dancing at Mom's wedding, his forehead touching mine and him gazing at me like no one else existed in the world.

Memories. Beautiful memories of a beautiful year that had been the happiest of my life. We didn't have drama like other couples our age did. There were no misunderstandings that separated us or passionate fights. Only passion. Only love. Love that made me crazy and sane at the same time. Love that spread to every part of me.

He threw my guitar down on the bed and his eyes landed on me. They were dark.

"What are you wearing?" he clipped.

I looked down self-consciously, my stomach dropping. Then I remembered that painted nail. My head snapped up. "You don't like it? Obviously, you prefer red dresses," I shot at him.

We may not have had a proper fight yet, but it looked like it was going that way.

His eyes flickered with confusion. "Come again?"

I stepped forward. "Don't play dumb. The woman all over you." I hated that my voice turned into a whisper in the end.

Kill's entire face softened and he ran his hands through his hair. "Jesus, babe. She's nothing. I don't see them. Not when all I think of is you."

I rolled my eyes. "Yeah, you looked like you were dreaming of me when she was touching your cut," I stated with sarcasm.

Kill stepped forward. His hands came to my hips. "Of all the things you have to worry about, Freckles, girls like that don't even factor in. You're the only girl I care about. That there will ever be," he promised. "No matter what."

I relaxed slightly, my hands trailing over his back. "She touched your cut," I whispered. "Before I got to. It's the most precious thing

369

to you, and she touched it before me."

Kill's body stilled. "That's not the most precious thing to me, Freckles. I'm holding the most precious thing right now, in my hands. In a rainbow dress that might just make me go crazy. Might be the first man in history to murder his brothers first night he's patched in." He paused. "That's what I'll do if they even *look* at you too long," he declared fiercely.

I smiled and stroked his cheek. "I don't see anyone but you. I'm yours. Only yours," I promised. "Forever."

Killian pressed his mouth against mine and he kissed me deep and long.

"I want to be yours," I murmured against his mouth.

"You are, babe, you always will be."

"No," I whispered. "I want it all to be *yours*. I want you to be mine. Tonight. I'm ready," I clarified in a shaking voice.

Kill froze. His entire body was taut, and he pulled back so he could gaze into my eyes. There was a long, loaded silence between us. "Freckles," he choked out.

We both jumped when a pounding sounded at the door. "Killian, you are not allowed to hide out in that room with your girl, no matter how pretty she is," Lucky's voice shouted through the door. "Not if you want Bull to *not* murder you the first night as a patched Son," he added and I heard a smile in his voice.

I smiled shyly against his mouth. "I better go get set up." I went to pull out of his arms, but they flexed around me. Kill's eyes burned with a lot of things I didn't recognize. One thing I did. Pure hunger.

"You sure, Freckles?" he rasped.

I kissed him lightly. "I've never been more sure of anything in my life," I murmured.

His hands flexed around me. "Neither have I."

• • • •

The cheers from the rambunctious crowd were all but deafening. I barely noticed it. My eyes had been glued to Kill, sitting amidst the chaos, his hand clenched around a beer, and his eyes never leaving mine. Before I had gone up on stage, he had glued me to his side while many of the men tried to get him drinking various spirits and laughing when he didn't let me go to do so. They all knew me, knew us, so they respected it. They also respected the fact that Zane was staring daggers at anyone who even offered me a beer. Hence why I was sipping on soda.

Mom and Zane looked happy. Ecstatic. He had her in a hold that was similar to Kill and she was never far from his side. It filled me with utter joy. Though I did notice she was also on soda. My mom didn't drink much, not compared to the Sons of Templar family, but she did partake at events like this. I knew why. My heart soared at the reason why. I'd been running around the house looking for my guitar, thinking about tonight, about tomorrow. Then I was thinking about neither of those things. I was thinking about the positive pregnancy test in Mom's hands and the utter joy at the prospect of having a brother or sister.

Right now, my mind was quiet. Silent. Despite the yells and the cheers. Everything fell away when I gazed into Kill's eyes.

"This is our last song," I rasped, leaning into my mic and jostling my guitar. "You all might know a certain man who was patched in tonight," I continued, my eyes never leaving Kill.

The crowd erupted into chaotic cheers at this. I waited for it to die down. My eyes cut to Sam for a second, who grinned and shook his head. He had declared I was "batshit crazy" for singing a love song to my "Old Man" on the night of his patch party. I may have been crazy, but I was also sane.

"This one's for you, Kill," I whispered and began to strum the chords of "No Matter What" by Papa Roach.

I didn't look anywhere but Kill the entire song. Every word I sang to him. Every strum of my guitar was for him.

Sam was wrong. Apparently, I wasn't batshit crazy for singing a song in front of badass bikers. They loved it. I might have been happy about this if they'd existed at that moment. If anyone but Kill and I existed.

So when Kill walked up to the stage and yanked me off it, I ignored all of the boos and shouts as he dragged us through the crowd.

He wouldn't have been able to do so had Zane been there, but he and Mom had left after our first set.

"Call me, you need to be picked up," he had commanded, his eyes cutting to Kill.

I nodded. "I'll be fine, Zane."

He gave me a long and skeptical look before nodding.

Mom kissed my head. "Have fun, doll," she murmured. "Not too much," she added quickly.

So that's how I found myself out of the party and in Kill's room as he slammed the door behind him. We stared at each other for a long moment, and then we weren't apart. He was on me in two strides, pushing me against the wall. I let out a sound in the back of my throat as he hitched my leg up and ran his callused hand along my bare thigh.

He had never touched me like this before. Been this rough. Rough in a good way. His fingers tore through my hair, ripping my ponytail holder out, brushing through the newly free curls. His mouth left mine to travel down my neck.

It was then I realized he'd been holding back. For almost two years, he'd been holding back, respecting me, waiting. There was no waiting now.

He yanked me to him, so I was pressed against his hard body. I sucked in a breath.

"Freckles," he muttered, his voice hoarse, "you've gotta tell me now if this is what you want. If you're ready." He rested his head against mine, breathing heavily. His hand was on my upper thigh. "I'll wait for you if you're not. Forever. If need be. But I need to know before this goes further, before I lose complete control, if this is what you want."

"I've never wanted anything more, Kill. I've never wanted anything but you." My hands went to his cut and pushed it off his shoulders. They were shaking as they pulled at his tee and it went completely over his head, dropping to the floor. My eyes ran hungrily across his chest, my fingers trailing after.

Kill's hand went to my chin, and he tilted it up so our eyes met. "Any time this gets too much, you tell me, Freckles," he ordered.

"It's already too much," I admitted. "I already want you so much I feel I might burst."

His eyes darkened as I lifted my arms to the tie at my neck and untied it, my nerves fluttering in my stomach. The front of my dress fell to my hips, and it took every inch of willpower not to cover myself with my arms.

Kill's eyes turned to liquid and he hissed out a breath. My nervousness melted away with his gaze, the utter love, reverence, and amazement in it. He rubbed the back of his hand against his mouth.

His eyes met mine. "You're so fucking beautiful," he murmured, and his hands went to the edge of the dress and gently pulled it fully off. His hands tickled over my bare hips, skirting up my rib cage to either side of my face. "Need to tell you this now, baby, before you give me the most precious gift a man could ever get," he said. "I love you. Know I haven't said it in so many words, but I love you so fuckin' much, Freckles. So much it scares the shit outta me," he rasped. "Those three words used to terrify me. They were the last things I said to my old man last time I saw him. I was convinced those words were the kiss of death. Good-bye somehow. I never want to say good-bye to you, never want to let you go. That's why I haven't said them," he explained. He paused. "But now I understand, no matter what, I'll never let you go. No one else on this planet's gonna hold my heart in their hands. Only you," he promised. His hands tightened, and his eyes danced with emotion my thundering heart didn't understand. "Promise me you'll remember that. No matter what. How much you mean to me. How you mean everything to me."

"I promise," I whispered through my tears.

Kill wiped them away. There were no more words that night. Words were not needed. He gave me the most beautiful night of my life.

Chapter 31

I ran down the dock, my heels seeming to echo louder than the waves at that moment. I only had eyes for one thing. One person. The cut that had the familiar patch on the back. The patch I had come to love. The boy wearing it I loved more than anything.

"We got it," I half shouted when I made it to his side, breathless. "The contract. They offered us a freaking *record contract*," I squealed, my grin threatening to split my face.

Not only did we get a record contract, but we were also getting money. A lot of it. Enough that Wyatt had choked on his water the moment Will, the record exec, uttered the sum.

Sam had patted his back absently, his eyes on Will. "Don't die, bro," he hissed. "Record contract's void if our bass guitarist drops dead before he can sign on the dotted line."

I had let out a choked giggle at this, in a kind of shock. We had all been willing to sign anything thrust in front of us at that moment, but Zane had spoken up and demanded all sorts of things to be in our contract, things I wouldn't have thought about.

Will had relented to everything immediately. I didn't know if it was because he wanted us so bad or it was because my biker stepdad was glowering at him and promising violence if he didn't get what he wanted. Whatever it was, I didn't care.

I had been itching to sign when Zane's huge hand had squeezed mine. "You sure about all this, Lex?" he asked, his voice totally different with me than it had been with Will. "Your entire life's gonna change the moment you sign that," he declared, nodding his head toward the table.

I grinned at him. "You're wrong. My life changed the moment Mom and I came to Amber. When we met you. When I met Kill." My eyes flickered over to the sofa. "My boys. The moment I found out I'm going to have a little brother or sister," I whispered and Zane's mouth turned up. I squeezed his hand. "This will change a lot of things, but the most important things will stay the same," I added.

He gave me a long look before kissing my head and nodding.

Sam let out a dramatic breath. "Thank the lord," he exclaimed. "I thought I might have to take on Bull in order to get my dreams of the cover of Rolling Stone to come true," he uttered, giving Zane a look. "I'd do it too," he added.

Zane shook his head, the corner of his mouth turning up slightly.

I looked at my boys. "Should we do this?"

They nodded.

So we signed on the dotted line. Unquiet Mind was officially a band with a record contract with one of the biggest companies in the world.

Killian stayed staring at the waves. As if I hadn't spoken. As if the thrashing of the tide had deafened him, hypnotized him.

I shook his shoulder. "Earth to Kill, did you hear that?" I asked, still floating on cloud nine. "Your girlfriend is going to be a rich and famous rock star. Of course, you'll need to be my valiant body-guard, protecting me from rabid fans," I teased. Despite my tone, something stirred deep in my belly, an intuition, a sick feeling that started to curl up my throat like a snake.

Killian slowly turned, and the feeling completely replaced any elation that I had been feeling moments ago. I failed to believe, to remember any happiness I had been feeling moments ago. Not with Killian's face regarding me in a cold, impersonal way that made me visibly flinch.

"Kill," I whispered, my hand clutching his shoulder.

His gaze flickered down to where I was touching him, clinging to him it seemed. Very slowly and very purposefully, he moved his hand to cover mine. For one glorious moment, I thought the touch would turn into a caress; his face would clear and the boy I loved would return. This moment in time would become a fleeting memory. That was all that thought was though, a wish.

His hand tightened around mine then lifted it off his shoulder, letting me go the moment his intention was clear.

I let it hang numbly at my side, a prickling sensation originating from where he had touched me. It traveled up my arm. I feared it would settle in my heart if something didn't happen soon.

"Kill," I repeated, my voice was barely above a croak, tears settling behind my eyes.

His cold eyes regarded me for a moment. "This is over," he said finally.

I never thought three words could be so powerful. I knew the three words he had uttered to me only last night had the power to elate me, make me feel safe, warm, protected, ecstatic. I had no idea three more words could utterly destroy me. Leave me in tatters.

"W-what are you talking about?" I stuttered.

Killian glanced at the sea, then back to me. "Look, this, us? It was never gonna last. Be real. We're not meant to be. You're not right for me, Lexie," he said, his voice robotic, devoid of emotion.

I was surprised I was still standing, not screaming, the pain was that great. I shook my head quickly, frantically, so my curls whirled across my face with the movement.

"You don't call me that," I said. "I'm not Lexie to you. Everyone else, maybe. But I'm yours. Only yours," I babbled, I begged.

His eyes turned cruel, and I could scarcely believe the words the came out of his mouth next. "Yeah, Lexie. You were mine. Last night you were all mine. I got what I wanted, the *only* thing I wanted.

Now, I'm done," he declared.

I half expected him to brush his hands together in a gesture that he was wiping his hands of me, casting me aside like some... object. Trash. Not the treasure he had falsely led me to believe he thought of me as.

Tears were running freely down my cheeks now. The wind picked up and salt water sprayed my face. I could scarily realize where my tears ended and the ocean began. My hurt was so deep, I mused I could fill the ocean, rival its depth with the chasm of my sorrow.

"You don't mean that. You're lying. I don't know why. But you need to stop. Stop right now," I demanded hysterically. "Stop," I pleaded.

"I've told you this, babe, about the club, what it means. I need to be free. I don't need chains," he continued in an emptiness, oblivious to me bleeding to death before his ice cold eyes.

I blinked rapidly, forcing the tears from my eyes. I was his chains. That's what he meant. "No one is free, even the birds are chained to the sky," I whispered in a broken voice, aching to get through to him, not beneath using Bob Dylan, *our* Bob Dylan to shake him awake, to somehow wake up from this nightmare.

Killian didn't flinch. Didn't say a word, merely stared at me with those empty eyes.

Empty eyes that I would see in my dreams every night for five years to come.

I couldn't stand it. I couldn't stand the person who held my heart, my entire soul, to stare at me like I was nothing. Reduce me down to nothing. So I turned on my heel and ran, sprinting down the dock like my life depended on it. Like I could somehow outrun the pain of heartbreak.

Stupid girl I was, I should've known it was impossible to outrun. It would follow me everywhere. It would become a part of me.

378

Killian

He watched her sprint away from him, and he was surprised he didn't sink to his knees. He wanted to. The power of his agony, his hatred of himself was that strong. He was tempted to fling himself into the ocean.

He hurt her. He saw that the moment he spoke those ugly words. He watched as he destroyed the only thing on this earth he loved. The only thing on this earth he would gladly give his life to protect.

He wanted to go after her. That superseded the urge to sink to his knees and howl at the waves. It superseded his urge to breathe.

He couldn't do that. He clenched his fists to his sides, so tight that he felt he might snap his knuckles. Going after her was not an option.

She'd recover from what he just put her through. He was certain. He had to be certain. It was for her own good.

It was the right decision. The only decision. His girl, his Freckles.

"You don't call me that. I'm not Lexie to you. Everyone else, maybe. But I'm yours. Only yours."

He flinched at the memory of those tortured words. She would be. Only his. Forever. He would die for her, which is what he did, right at that moment. The piece, the only tiny piece of him that could be classified as good was what she created. That piece died the moment he spoke those words, the moment he broke the heart that she had given him freely. He thrust a dagger in his own.

But it was for her. That horribly exquisite pain seeing her like that, it was ultimately to give her a life that wouldn't be possible if he stayed with her. As an anchor. Dragging her down. Keeping her rooted to the ground when she deserved to fly.

So he watched her curls flying wildly in the wind as she sprinted down the dock. He watched with the pain shredding his insides, his eyes glued to her until she was out of sight.

His hand moved up to touch the wetness at his cheek; he tasted the salty liquid on his lips. It wasn't the sea that caused this, the waves crashing on the dock. It was the last of him dying a death. A part that would stay on that dock for the rest of his life.

Epilogue

Killian

SEVEN MONTHS LATER

Killian sat with his elbows resting on his knees, his gaze glued to the white linoleum floor beneath him. Razor blades chewed at his stomach when he heard the doors to the hospital open. His head snapped up.

Not her.

He sighed in relief and tightened up with tension at the same time, as he had every time someone had walked through those doors. His gaze flickered to Bull, standing away from everyone else, his face blank, devoid of anything. It was reminiscent of the before Bull, the one who had almost lost his humanity. Killian knew he was preparing, bracing for the demons Mia and Lexie fought back to destroy him once more. The entire club was waiting for it, taking up the hospital room. Waiting to hear news on Mia and the baby. There were no smiles, no excitement, no happy chatter that he guessed was normal when waiting for a baby to be born. Not when Bull had found Mia bleeding and unconscious a couple of hours ago.

No. There were no smiles.

Killian felt anger bubble up within him. It was new. For the past year, he had been numb. Unfeeling. Apart from the times he unwittingly turned on the radio and heard *her*. Turned on a TV and saw *her*. Opened a fuckin' magazine. She was everywhere. His girl was taking over the world, just like he knew she would.

Apart from the fact she wasn't his girl anymore, he saw to that. That was why it felt like a thousand bullets passed through his body when he heard her throaty voice singing tortured songs. When he saw her on stage with thousands of people screaming at her.

That was why he made a conscious effort to not turn on the radio, not look at a magazine, not watch TV. The pain would kill him if he didn't turn it off. So that's what he did. He became a version of what Bull used to be. Didn't smile. Didn't laugh. Lived for the club. Took pleasure in doing the darker deeds, which helped numb him even more.

Then he was a fuckin' glutton for punishment. 'Cause every show she played, every one that got bigger and bigger as the band got bigger, he went to. He made a promise.

"Freckles, I'm never gonna miss a single one of your gigs. Never gonna miss my girl owning the stage, owning my soul."

It didn't matter he'd broken every other promise he made to her, that he'd never leave her, never hurt her. He wouldn't break that one. So he went. Struggled through the gut-wrenching pain at seeing her on stage, loving her and hating himself more than he thought possible.

The hours after he broke it off, he actually didn't know how it'd be possible to live with that self-loathing. That was until he parked himself at the club bar and commenced in drinking himself into oblivion.

Bull had stormed in about midway through. The way he glared at him told Kill he knew. Knew what he did to her. His stomach clenched.

"You gonna kill me, at least let me finish my beer," Killian said, his voice flat.

Bull stared at him for a long moment; then he stepped forward. Killian didn't even flinch. He'd welcome any other pain to distract him from what was killing him right now.

Bull surprised him by reaching over the bar and grabbing a bottle of whiskey and two glasses. He poured the liquid into them and pushed one Killian's way.

Killian raised a brow but took the glass and downed it, savoring the burn as it made its way down his throat.

Bull did the same. He regarded the glass for a moment then his dark gaze moved to Killian.

This is it. He's going to kill me now, Killian thought.

Instead, he clapped him on the shoulder in an almost comforting gesture. "Know why you did it," he grunted. "Why you're lettin' her go," he clarified. He looked around. "She's better than this place. Destined for more. She wouldn't have left it."

Killian nodded in agreement.

"So I'm not gonna kill you for destroying her," Bull growled and Killian flinched. "I'm not gonna do it 'cause I know you did it so she could do what she was meant to."

There was a long silence after Bull's words and he gave his shoulder another squeeze before leaving Killian with his thoughts and, more importantly, the bottle.

Kill stared at the man's back, at the hard cut of his jaw, seven months on from that day. He respected the hell out of Bull. Even *liked* him. He was his brother. His family. Lexie's family.

He was so fuckin' angry at the fact that both he and, more importantly, Lexie were getting faced with this shit. That life was shittin' all over what they'd built from the ashes of their old lives.

The doors opened again, and Killian froze the moment his eyes cut to it, locking with the eyes he saw in his dreams. He flinched at the utter sorrow and despair in them and the way they hardened looking at him. She quickly moved her gaze away, running to embrace Bull.

Sam, Wyatt, and Noah trailed after her. They all gave him murderous glares the moment they realized he was there.

He didn't care about them. His gaze was locked on the blonde head that was bent close to Bull. At the little body encased in some beautiful hippy getup that was her. Completely her. Heartbreakingly beautiful.

He clenched his fists on his knees. She was there. Right *there*. Beautiful. Fucking stunning. Hurting. And he couldn't fuckin' touch her.

He didn't know if he would be able to swallow his anger, his hatred for himself, but he somehow managed it.

"Mia Williams?" a brisk voice asked.

Killian shot off his chair before he even realized he'd done it. A doctor was speaking to Lexie and Bull. His heart stopped, literally stopped. He hoped, he fuckin' *prayed,* that doctor wasn't breaking what was left of his girl's heart.

Not my girl, he reminded himself. No, she'd always be his. No matter what. And he'd always be hers.

He sank back into his chair when he saw the smile on her beautiful face, the moment she embraced Bull.

It was one fleeting moment, he almost missed it, no way he could hold onto it, but he could taste it. Happiness. For the first time in seven months, a little of the sweet he'd become accustomed to in the two years he was with her.

Then it was gone. As soon as she and Bull followed the doctor behind some doors, it was gone.

"Thank the fuckin' lord," Lucky exclaimed from beside him, grinning and slapping him on the back. "We've got a kid! Time to party," he declared with a glint in his eyes.

Everyone else quickly lost their somber moods and smiles

spread through the group. Apart from Killian. He didn't smile. His eyes were locked on those doors, and they stayed lock for he didn't know how long. Long enough for people to leave, for him to reply that moment seven months ago hundreds of times.

He couldn't do it. He couldn't have her so fuckin' close and not see her. Touch her. Say fuckin' sorry. Beg for her forgiveness. Every reason for letting go melted away and all that mattered was Lexie.

He pushed off his chair, one destination in mind.

Lexie.

He didn't get far before a large form blocked his way. His eyes met familiar ones. Ones that weren't light and smiling like they usually were. They were hard and full of fury.

Being a rock star hadn't changed him much. He'd filled out a bit more, his hair a bit more "done," clothes noticeably more expensive, still all black. Silver round his neck and knuckles a fuck of a lot more expensive.

"Get out of my way, Sam," Killian gritted out.

"No fuckin' way," Sam answered, stepping forward slightly. "No fuckin' way are you going anywhere near her after what you did," he spat. "You broke her. Fuckin' *shattered* her. You wouldn't even recognize her if you spoke to her," he continued, and Killian flinched with his words.

Sam's eyes hardened. "You are not destroying what's left of my best friend," he declared.

Killian stared at him a long time, then at Noah and Wyatt, who flanked him, both glaring at him in hatred.

"I'm not keen on causing Lexie pain, especially on the one fuckin' day in seven months she's had to be happy," Wyatt gritted out. "But I will if you try to talk to her. Swear to God, I'll fuckin' kill you if you try to do that. Motorcycle cut or not," he promised.

Killian clenched his fists to his sides, breathing rapidly. He realized on their faces the bitter truth of what he'd done. He felt fresh hatred for himself and he swallowed it. He knew what he'd done.

He'd lost his girl forever.

"Take care of her," he choked out to the boys. Then he turned on his boot and walked out. Walked away from them. From her.

That fleeting glimpse of her, that taste of happiness would be what kept him going for three more years. Three years until he saw her again. Until he realized what a huge fuckin' mistake he made. Until he vowed to do whatever he could, die if need be, to get her back.

To get her safe.

Lexie and Killian's story concludes in

Skeletons of Us

book two in the Unquiet Mind series

"None of me is left for you because you took it all away. There's just an empty body. A skeleton. That's all we are now, weathered bones of a long dead love that died that day on the dock. That you killed that day on the dock."

Playlist

"Breathe" Pearl Jam

"The Greatest" Cat Power

"Lost Boy" Ruth B

"Knockin' on Heaven's Door" Bob Dylan

"We Don't Eat" Alice Kristiansen
(Cover of James Vincent McMorrow)

"Monsters" Katie Sky

"No Matter What" Papa Roach

"Church" Hozier

"Scar Tissue" The Red Hot Chili Peppers

"The Unclouded Day" Audra Mae

Acknowledgments

With every book I write it seems the list of people to thank gets longer. This is in no way a bad thing. My writing journey has been full of ups and downs (mainly ups) and I'm lucky to have met some wonderful people along the way. I've also been reminded how many amazing people I already have in my life.

Mum, how lucky I am to have you. You've always been my biggest cheerleader and have believed in me even when I couldn't believe in myself. None of this would have been possible without you. You're my hero.

This book wouldn't be what it is without my wonderful team of betas. These special ladies helped to make this book what it is. Ginny, Caro, Amy, Sarah, and Judy... you are amazing. Thank you.

Andrea, Momma Bear and beta extraordinaire, you are such a positive force and I'm so thankful I've got you.

Amo Jones. What would I do without you? You're a wonderful writer, an irreplaceable friend, and a spectacular person. Love you always.

And to you, the reader. Thank you. Thank you for reading my books. Thanks for every e-mail, comment, and review you give me. None of this would be possible without you.

xxxx

also by
Anne Malcom

the Sons of Templar series

follow

website
www.annemalcomauthor.com

email
annemalcomauthor@hotmail.com

facebook
www.facebook.com/anne.malcom.14

About The Author

ANNE MALCOM has been an avid reader since before she can remember, her mother responsible for her love of reading. It started with magical journeys into the world of Hogwarts and Middle Earth, then as she grew up her reading tastes grew with her. Her love of reading doesn't discriminate, she reads across many genres, although classics like Little Women and Gone with the Wind will hold special places in her heart. She also can't get enough romance, especially when some possessive alpha males throw their weight around.

One day, in a reading slump, Cade and Gwen's story came to her and started taking up space in her head until she put their story into words. Now that she has started, it doesn't look like she's going to stop anytime soon, with many more characters demanding their story be told as well.

Raised in small town New Zealand, Anne had a truly special childhood, growing up in one of the most beautiful countries in the world. She has backpacked across Europe, ridden camels in the Sahara and eaten her way through Italy, loving every moment. For now, she's back at home in New Zealand and quite happy. But who knows when the travel bug will bite her again.

41226284R00226

Printed in Poland
by Amazon Fulfillment
Poland Sp. z o.o., Wrocław